THE

SWORD'S

REVENGE

---- BY ----
DUTCH D. BIRD

Dutch D. Bird
#21 of 2200

β
Presage Publishing

PUBLISHER'S NOTE

This novel is a work of fiction. Names, characters, places, and incidents either are the product of the author's imagination or are used fictitiously, and any resemblance to actual persons, living or dead, events or locales is entirely coincidental.

Presage Publishing
830 S. Boulder Highway
Box 136
Henderson, NV 89015
e-mail: presagepub@aol.com

Cover Design by Dutch D. Bird
Cover Layout by Freshwater Art

First Presage Publishing Printing, October, 1998

An obscure figure ran blindly down the dark city street. The man's breath was heavy and sporadic, but he had no intention of slowing his sprint. From behind came the frightening sound of a siren, blaring through the dense night air. A bright beam of light emerged from the top of a flying sphere, which effortlessly chased the figure. The beam instinctively scanned the street for its objective, quickly bypassing the usual city landscape. The roaming beam spotted the fleeing man, locking in on him.

Once in the sphere's sights, the man dove to the ground, cowering against the wall of an abandoned building, knowing that he had only a few moments left to live. The sphere fired a concentrated barrage of bullets, killing its victim instantly. Without varying speed, the emotionless assassin continued on its flight.

Several moments later, another sphere floated lazily down the street, stopping directly over the corpse. Two metallic arms emerged from the front of the machine, lifting the lifeless body into a hole in its top. A grotesque grinding sound could be heard, as the robot shredded the body for disposal. Upon completion of the task, the second sphere resumed its flight down the dismal city street.

A full two minutes passed, before a second figure fled from his hiding place in the shadows of a nearby building. The man, clad only in black clothing, knew that if he had been spotted by either sphere he would have also been killed.

A heavy breath escaped from the man's lips, as he hurried along the familiar run down sidewalks of New York City. For the third straight day the city had been drenched by rain and more of the same was forecast for the next week. The short heavy man turned a corner and entered his basement apartment, just as a squad of police cars sped by along the slick asphalt, leaving the sounds of their sirens to echo interminably through the barren street.

The obviously relieved man was greeted immediately upon entering the apartment by another, clad in a white cloak. The greeter's long beard and unkempt hair gave him an evil appearance.

"Bill, it's about time you arrived," the man said, fishing his hand inside the pocket of his cloak. A moment later he pulled out a scrap of yellow paper, where he had written several notes. "Andy has called you three times already today. He says he can buy the part you need on the black market for two thousand."

"Hello, Jim," Bill replied a bit startled. His heart was still racing, from the excitement on the street. He took a moment to wipe the moisture away from his round face with the palm of his hand, before removing his jacket and hanging it over a hook on the wall. "I didn't expect to see you here tonight. Did he try to talk them down?"

"I suppose. I didn't really ask any questions. He wants to know if he should buy it, or haggle for a lower price."

"Tell him to buy it," Bill said with a sigh. He kicked off his wet shoes and stepped into the main room of the apartment. "The officials will find out our plans if we let too many black market people know what we are doing. I wouldn't doubt if the officials actually controlled the black market."

Jim nodded, before his tall thin figure vanished through the same door he used to enter the room. Bill slumped into a chair, facing a screen that resembled a television. A green couch in the center of the room gave the place its only home-like feature. A multitude of papers, all covered with endless notes and calculations, were scattered over the worn piece of furniture. Various pictures hung from the walls, most faded to the point were the picture depicted was barely recognizable. Several aging chairs, a couple tables, and a stained blue carpet finished the decor of the room.

Bill and his assistant, Jim Gray, worked for the Protectors. Both were top rated scientists. The Protectors was the name the government leaders had bestowed upon themselves after gaining control, although everyone knew the name to be a farce. If the Protectors were protecting anything, it was their own interests. The scientists were instrumental in carrying out the agenda dictated by the government, but more likely than not they were opposed to the underlying philosophy. For the time being, they were powerless to voice their dissent. The hate they felt toward the Protectors had to stay locked up inside, for they knew if the slightest hint of revolt showed they would be killed. Even their privileged position within the government, would not save them if they were accused of treason.

The part Bill was waiting for would complete his dream. Except for the few people entrusted to help him, his dream had been kept secret. He could hardly believe that after years of work, his life's project would be complete in a matter of hours. The masterpiece of his own creation, a time machine, would help in his quest to overthrow the Protectors. At least, that is what he hoped.

A beeping from the terminal awakened him from his daydream. Displayed on the screen were the headlines of the evening news. '500 murders in one week. A new all time high for the city.'

Bill had grown accustomed to literature of that nature. Since the Protectors came into power, the city of New York and all surrounding areas were in a constant state of rioting. Although he knew the figures in the news were highly inflated, in order to scare the population into submission, death in the city had been rising at an alarming rate. The murder he witnessed earlier, at the hands of the government's electronic watchdogs, would surely find its way into the murder tally. The news never separated the murder count into government sponsored versus non-government sponsored, but Bill suspected the later was dwarfed by the former.

Twenty years had passed since the war ended in 2166. The five year battle was fierce and bloody. The Protectors had grown from a small localized crime group to a massive and vicious organization. They quickly overcame the existing governmental structure, but struggled for several years to eliminate all opposition. Even with their rule firmly established, the heartless leaders continued with their inhumane massacres. The population, as a whole, was forced into a near slavery situation; little pay in exchange for lengthy work hours. All trouble makers were quickly silenced.

For the past ten years, the city had been run under a curfew. Anyone found in the streets after dark would be killed on sight. The Protectors were so secretive that the citizens weren't even sure if life existed west of New York state. In fact, even though the Protectors controlled the entire area between New York and Boston, the citizens had no contact with others outside their immediate surroundings. All private communication devices had been banned shortly after the war began, and only officials within the organization, the scientists among them, had access to the technology that still existed. Bill's dream was to change the situation, but he knew the fight ahead would be a long one.

Jim reentered the room, stopping to stare over Bill's shoulder at the screen. After reading the headlines, he just shook his head in disappointment. "Typical lies," he said. "We both know that the population would dwindle to nothing in no time, if the murder rate was that high. Oh, Andy said he will pick up the part and be here within the hour."

"Good, that will give us enough time to get the machine ready for a test run." Bill pushed a button on the terminal and the screen went blank.

Both scientists left the impersonal living room. disappearing into the back room. The room, formerly a bedroom, had long ago been converted into a small laboratory. Various pieces of scientific equipment filled every available space. Chemical odors rose from the multitude of beakers and test tubes that covered several rows of tables. Piles of electrical equipment and circuit boards covered the remaining work stations. Many of the experiments were useless fronts to fool the inspectors, who made twice weekly visits to all of the Protectors' laboratories. Bill walked by without giving notice to any of them. He pushed a small button, hidden behind a storage cabinet, which in turn released the cabinet from the wall. As the sheet metal object swung aside, the entrance to a secret room was revealed.

With the flick of a switch, incandescent bulbs filled the room with a bright light. Several shelves of aged books were placed along the otherwise barren walls of the alcove. Bill had purchased most of the books from various black market organizations, paying as much as a thousand dollars for a single volume. In recent months the prices for goods purchased on the black market had skyrocketed, as the Protectors slowly eroded one of the last two threats to their rule.

In the center of the room stood Bill's prize, the white light shimmering off its highly polished metal frame and glass body. The top of the pyramid shaped object had only a few inch clearance from the ceiling. The four sides were composed of a special thick glass, which took the scientists nearly two years to formulate. Early into the design of the machine, Bill decided that lead would be best for the floor, but creating a single piece of the heavy metal was impossible given the circumstances. Instead, he created hundreds of interlocking shapes, which when assembled correctly formed a sturdy, structurally sound slab. Realizing that the time machine would weigh an enormous amount, Bill had requested a basement apartment to ensure that the floor would support the massive weight of his creation.

Computers lined each wall inside the fifteen foot square pyramid, except for the one which housed the door. Hanging from the angled walls were various pieces of equipment. Every available cubic foot of space inside the vehicle had been utilized. Bill walked over to the machine, placing his hand on the glass. His heart told him that his dream was about to come true.

"I still can't believe we actually built this machine," Bill said, marveling at his work. "This time machine will help us defeat the Protectors and put the people back in control of the government."

"Don't get too excited," warned Jim. The persistent twitching of his right hand caused him to instinctively hide it in his pocket. "We still need the coordination control, and even then we don't know if it will work."

"Of course it will work!" yelled Bill defensively. His heavy face turned a dark shade of red. "I have studied these plans for over five years, and this machine will most definitely work. All I need now is the last piece, then we will be able to start our revolt."

From the street outside, they could hear the sirens of a sphere tracking down its prey. The inevitable sound of bullets striking the brick wall of Bill's laboratory followed. The victim, probably a member of the rebel force, had surely died instantly. The rebel force, despite all attempts by the officials, still existed as a formidable resistance. Besides the several black market groups, the rebel organization was the last viable enemy within the Protector's realm of power. The scientists stood in silence, waiting for the next gruesome event.

The sound of the sphere shredding the body made Bill shudder. It reminded him of what he had witnessed earlier. He hadn't recognized the previous victim as being in the rebel organization, but then again secrecy was essential to the survival of the group. Bill knew it was not necessary for the spheres to grind its victims in such a manner, but it was just another psychological scare tactic used by the Protectors to keep the citizens in line. Spheres monitored his part of the city constantly, more than any other part of the Protectors domain, as most of the government's top people resided nearby. Bill was fortunate enough to have access to the flying schedules of the spheres, which allowed him and his assistants to travel the streets at night with relative safety.

"You see what those Protectors have done to our country. Constant fighting and murder," Bill yelled angrily, his face still red from his earlier outburst. Less than half the population was old enough to remember any significant aspects of life before the war. He and Jim were both young teenagers when the first Protector offensives took place. Bill waved a twentieth century history book at Jim, who had grown accustomed to Bill's frequent eruptions of this nature. "And we are going to change that. We are going to set up a government like that of the twentieth century. Granted, the government before the Protectors was something special, but the structure of the twentieth century is something even more enviable. We are..." A loud pounding at the front door interrupted him.

Hurriedly, the scientists turned off the light, vacating the secret room. Bill stood inside the darkened laboratory, watching as Jim answered the door. Outside stood the small scrawny body of Andy Marshall, dressed from head to toe in black. Andy, an unofficial member of the rebel cause, helped Bill with his projects. Andy's job was to deal with the black market and procure the necessary monies to purchase equipment. In his arms he held a box wrapped in plain brown paper. Several wet spots were visible on the package, signifying that the rain had resumed.

"Here it is," he said with a large toothy grin, which stretched clear across his skinny face. He plucked the black knit cap from his head, tossing it onto the coat rack. His jacket was just as quickly removed and discarded over a chair. "They gave me no problems. I gave them the money, picked up the box, and left. I think they are beginning to trust me now. They didn't even search me to check for weapons or bugs."

Bill quickly emerged from the shadows. He scurried across the living room, snatching the package from Andy. Without bothering to say hello, he promptly vanished into the laboratory, reentering the secret room. By the time Jim and Andy caught up to him, he had already removed the contents of the package and was carefully examining the part.

"It looks perfect. Everything seems to be intact," he mumbled to himself. Without paying any attention to the others, he stepped into the time machine and placed the mechanism into position.

"I sure hope it works," Andy said, watching with excitement. Jim and Bill had long ago grown accustomed to his high pitched crackling voice.

"It had better work," Jim added. "After all the time we put into making it, it had better work. I would hate to be around Bill if it didn't. He would go on a rampage that would last a week."

Another knock came from the front door interrupting the trio. Realizing that Bill had no intention of leaving his creation at the present, Jim left the secret room to answer the door. Ken Gidlock, another of Bill's assistants, entered the apartment. Behind him in the dimly lit corridor, stood a tall dark figure dressed in a black leather jacket. The stranger made no attempt to hide the long bladed knife he held in his hand.

"Hi, Ken, who did you bring with you?" Jim asked in a loud voice, as a warning to the others.

"I don't know who he is. He was hiding in the alley. As soon as I entered the building, he came running after me. He says, he is Andy's brother."

"Where is he?" yelled the man. He shoved Ken in the back, causing him to stumble down the steps leading into the living room. The man then stepped through the door, waving the knife threateningly. "I know he is in here because I followed him. Now where is he?"

At first Jim had thoughts of overpowering the intruder. He matched the man in height, but not in bulk. With Ken's help they could surely overwhelm the man, but the fact that the intruder had a weapon quickly killed the idea. At this point he felt it too risky. After hearing the commotion, Andy walked out of the back room to discover its cause.

"There you are you little delinquent. What are you doing here? And I want an answer now," ordered the man in a harsh tone. He slammed the apartment door closed behind him.

"What is the meaning of this intrusion?" Bill yelled, rushing into the living room. He had donned his white smock, in an attempt to act as if the situation were normal.

"I'm Andy's brother. I also work for the police. My job is to find rebels and have them purged from society," the man said, directly quoting propaganda. "I have been keeping an eye on Andy for some time now. I know all about his dealings with the black market, and suspect him and the rest of you of treason against the Protectors."

"Joe, we aren't rebels," Andy protested.

"I should say we aren't rebels," Bill said stepping forward. The situation started to worry him. If the Protectors were to find out about his operation, or even suspect that there was a potential problem with one of their top scientists, all of his work would have been for nothing. "My name is Bill Shmatz, lead scientist at this laboratory. We only deal with the black market for supplies I need for my experiments. Everything we do here is for the Protectors, I can assure you that," he said lying through his teeth.

"I already know who you are, Mr. Shmatz, and I don't believe a word you just said. If you were doing something for the Protectors, they would supply you with all the equipment you need," Joe said. He put his knife away and pulled out a gun, suddenly realizing that he was grossly outnumbered.

"But we aren't rebels," protested Andy, once again.

"You must know that the Protectors can't get their hands on everything," Bill said in a calm tone. "The black market would never sell anything if they knew it was going to be used by the government. It is essential that we deal with them in total secrecy."

Jim, who had moved to the back of the room during the conversation, tried to slip into the laboratory, but Joe spotted him.

"Hey, you, get back in here before I shoot you where you stand."

Jim slowly turned around, finding himself faced by the barrel of the gun. He raised his hands in mock surrender and walked back toward the living room. Knowing the brutal reputation of the Protector's police force, he silently sat down on the sofa.

"If you aren't rebels, prove it."

"Take a look around. If you see anything out of the ordinary, you can turn us in. I can assure you, however, that we aren't rebels. The Protectors have sanctioned all of our experiments. I can show you all of the paper work," Bill offered. He had a gut feeling that they were going to end up in trouble. Joe would certainly find some reason to charge them with treason. The only thing he could do was to stall for time, until a solution could formulate itself in his brain.

Bill led the way into the back room. Joe wasted no time beginning his search. He scrutinized all the equipment in the laboratory, asking questions about each piece. He practically ignored the beakers and test tubes, instead taking a keen interest in the electronics. It was then, pausing for a moment after picking up a circuit board, that he noticed a crack in the wall behind the cabinet, which had been left ajar when Bill came running into the front room.

"What is that?" mumbled Joe, replacing the circuit board and moving toward the cabinet. He eyed the scientists and his brother with suspicion, trying to read their expressions. He saw nothing in their faces that seemed out of the ordinary. With a mighty shove, clearly more force than was needed, he pushed the object aside, revealing the secret room. "What's in there?" he asked, looking into the darkness.

Bill felt his heart skip a beat. He strained his mind, trying to come up with an answer. "It's only a storage room," he finally blurted out. He stepped forward, but was stopped from progressing further by Joe. "There is nothing of importance in there," he said, trying to sound calm, but knowing that he didn't.

"We'll see about that," Joe said, with a sinister laugh. Keeping an eye on his four suspects, he fished his hand into the room, quickly finding the light switch on the wall. His attention immediately focused on the time machine. "Just storage? What is that thing in the middle of the room?"

"It's nothing. Just an old experiment I worked on about a year ago. It never did work right. In fact, it never worked at all," Bill said, with a embarrassed laugh. He looked over at Jim, who was wearing a sarcastic grin caused by the derogatory statement he had just made about his prize invention.

"Old? It doesn't look too old to me. In fact, it looks as if you just finished polishing it," Joe said, as his grin grew larger. "What was it supposed to do?"

Bill's mind went blank.

"It was supposed to make people younger," Andy quickly replied. Bill gave a satisfied glance in his direction.

"Yes, the Protectors asked me to invent something that would make them younger, or keep them alive longer, so they could stay in power indefinitely," Bill explained. He hoped that Joe's curiosity would be quelled by his response.

"For some reason, I don't believe you," Joe replied. "You know, you won't be the first scientists that I turn in for treason. Just two weeks ago I found a chemist plotting to poison one of the council members. Strangely enough, he died by his own invention."

Just then the sound of sirens filled the air. The sirens weren't from the spheres, which never patrolled in groups. The sirens were from police cars. Clearly a half dozen had flooded the street outside Bill's apartment. Yells of terror could be heard, echoing off the brick buildings. The noise level indicated that many people were involved. A rapid pounding soon followed, coming from the front door of the apartment. Joe casually motioned Jim to answer it. He had no fear that the scientist might try to flee, with all of his coworkers just outside.

As soon as the bolt cleared its housing in the door frame, a dark figure burst into the apartment, knocking Jim to the floor. The man didn't stop to check on the scientist's condition. In fact, he continued his sprint through the living room, not even realizing that another person was present. The figure ran straight into the secret room, diving into the time machine, just as Bill opened the door to show Joe inside. Bill and Ken alertly ran in after him.

A swarm of police quickly flooded the apartment in search of the intruder. In a strange twist of fate, their orders were to protect the occupants of the building from the intruder. This was of no consequence to Andy, who quickly realized what was happening. He used his limited strength to pull his brother into the time machine, just as the door closed. Three policemen entered the secret room, quickly spotting the man they were chasing. Without hesitation, they opened fire on the machine. The bullets entered the glass and stopped dead.

"Stop!" Joe yelled, ripping his identification from his jacket pocket. Since the time machine was sound proof, the police could not hear the warning, but he held the badge up against the glass for them to see.

The momentary lapse was all that Bill needed. Frantically fidgeting with the controls, the scientist was able to hit the required sequence of buttons, and the time machine began to disappear. Just as it did, Bill noticed that the police had opened fire once again. Several more bullets entered the glass walls of the vehicle, before everything went white.

CHAPTER II "THE PAST"

A continuous barrage of sparks struck the outside of the time machine, practically blinding the occupants. Joe shielded his eyes with his arms, wondering what kind of weapon had been fired by the police. The scientists knew what was happening, but were as much in shock as Joe, seeing that they had no inclination of what to expect during time travel. The phenomenon lasted for just a few seconds, then all turned quiet. The sparks were gone, but the brightness caused by them, had temporarily blurred the vision of the time machine's occupants.

The stranger, who moments before had been the subject of a massive police chase, was the first to make a move. He quickly rose to his feet, pointing a machine gun at the others. His face and hands were covered with a black substance, frequently used by the rebel forces to camouflage themselves at night.

"Open the door," he demanded in a loud voice.

"There is nothing to fear here," Bill replied in a comforting voice. "We are away from the police."

"I don't care. Just open the door, or I'll kill you and open it myself," the man countered, in a tone that made it obvious that he was used to getting what he wanted.

Reluctantly Bill pushed a button and the door slid open. The stranger made a sweeping scan of the time machine, searching for anything of value. Finding nothing of interest, the man fled, disappearing into the forest surrounding the field in which they had landed. Bill stood in silence, as the man vanished from sight.

"It's too bad he didn't listen to me," Bill said in a sorrowful voice, looking down at the controls. "He is going to be surprised out there."

"Why do you say that?" Joe asked. The fact that they were no longer in the laboratory had not completely sunken in yet.

"In the confusion of the police raiding the apartment, I had no time to set the controls for which time we were to go. As a result, we've ended up a million years in our past," Bill explained matter-of-factly.

Joe stared through the glass of the time machine. His eyes followed the grass from the edge of the forest right up to the open door of the vehicle. "You mean we are actually one million years in the past?" murmured Joe. As he glanced at the surrounding jungle, a nervous look spread over his normally stern face.

"That's exactly what I mean," Bill replied.

"We were lucky that the part I bought today worked," Andy said with a smile of accomplishment. "Otherwise we would still be in the lab surrounded by the police."

"Then you are rebels," Joe said, suddenly finding his composure. He grasped his weapon tightly, aiming it at Bill. "I knew you were lying to me.

You were using this machine against the Protectors. I should kill you all right now."

"I don't think you want to do anything rash, Joe. Under the circumstances, I have no problem admitting our alliance with the rebel cause. Although, you knew that already," Bill said calmly, feeling that he now had the upper hand in the situation. "But killing us would serve no purpose. The Protectors aren't here."

Joe looked outside at the forest again. He had no idea if what Bill was telling him was the truth, but obviously they weren't in New York City. The thought of being stranded in the past, or wherever they were, did not appeal to him. Slowly he lowered his gun and put it away.

"Why don't we go outside and look around," Ken suggested, breaking his silence. He did not wait for any acknowledgment, before stepping through the open door into the field. The foot tall blades of grass completely hid his feet. The moisture in the thick undergrowth instantly soaked his pant legs, sending a chill through his body. Everyone followed Ken outside, except for Joe. He stood just inside the door, staring out into the forest.

"Why aren't you coming out?" Andy asked, not caring to miss a chance to prod his brother. "What! Are you afraid?"

"Not exactly. It's just that we don't know what is out there," Joe replied. To his disappointment no one paid the slightest attention to his protests. Reluctantly, once again removing his weapon, he stepped from the perceived safety of the time machine to join the others.

The four cautiously walked toward the edge of the field, where the stranger had fled into the jungle. It was a small clearing about a hundred yards across. The time machine had landed off in a corner just several yards from the surrounding forest. The jungle, comprised of various towering trees, looked ominous and colorful.

The coolness of the moisture in the grass, actually offered the travelers some comfort from the warm temperature. The air, thick and humid, contained a noticeable tint of yellow; but the discoloration wasn't enough to hamper their vision. A mixture of loud animal noises filtered in from the depths of the forest, raising some alarm.

Joe, still leery of the strange surroundings, lagged behind the group, staying as close as possible to the time machine, in case shelter was needed in a hurry. Not being in the comforts of his own environment had taken away some of the forcefulness of his personality. As he walked around the machine, he noticed that the bullets were not only stuck in the glass, but they had been melted into unidentifiable blobs of metal.

"Hey, look at these bullets," he yelled to the others. He rubbed his hand over the glass, which felt completely smooth, just as if nothing had happened to it. When the others arrived, he questioned Bill as to why the bullets had melted.

"It is because of the friction encountered when traveling through time. That is why I used this particular glass. Of course, I had no way of knowing exactly what would happen on the journey through time. Although, my hypothesis turned out to be correct. You have seen first hand how the glass resists breaking, when it was struck by the bullets. It also resists melting up to remarkable temperatures. I had to use a special chemical process to form the panes. A process I invented, by the way. The chemicals modified the composition of the glass so I could form it using conventional heating methods. After forming the panes I removed the chemical with an additional procedure. A cooling system inside kept us from feeling the heat."

"Who was that person the police were chasing?" Andy asked. It was the first time any of them gave the stranger a serious thought.

"Because of him we were almost killed by the police," Ken said angrily.

"I can answer the question of who he is," Joe said. "I could tell by the clothes he wore that he was a rebel. He also reminds me of one of the rebel leaders, but I'm not sure. I only saw him for a moment."

"Hey," Andy interrupted. "Look over there. It looks like a path." He broke out into a jog toward the area of the forest that he spoke about. Bill yelled for him to stop, but Andy didn't hear.

"It is a path," Andy yelled, jumping up and down waving his hands. To the others it looked as if his thin arms were blowing uncontrollably in the wind.

The three caught up to him, finding the path to be about five feet wide and well traveled. Several small plants poked up randomly through the packed dirt floor. The long limbs of the trees drooped over the path allowing very little light to penetrate.

"Do you think we should follow it?" Ken asked in an aroused tone. He had always been interested in adventure stories. All of a sudden he found himself in the middle of one.

Joe, however, didn't quite carry the same enthusiasm. "I don't think it is a good idea. We don't know what made this."

"Yes, it could be dangerous," Bill agreed. "But just think of it. We will be the only people to know what kind of animals lived in this time. I say we explore the area for a while." He paused for a moment. "We can't return to our time. The police will kill us as soon as we appear. They are probably still in the laboratory."

"I think we should go back and take our chances," Joe pleaded. After all, being a member of the police he had relatively little to fear from them, especially if he could return with three prisoners. "And since I have the gun, I think I should be the one to make the decisions."

"Joe, it is time you realize that you can not go back to the life you had. The officials will undoubtedly accuse you of being a member of the rebel force, just by the simple fact that you were associating with us when they entered the apartment. You have probably already been listed as an enemy to the Protectors."

Joe gave the matter some thought. "You might have a point there," he said at last. "But I think we should have more protection than just a gun and a knife. We really have no idea what we might find out here."

"I have a gun in the time machine," Bill said. Weapons of any kind were forbidden by the Protectors, but Bill had purchased one on the black market anyhow. "It only has a couple of rounds in it, but it will have to do."

He ran back to the time machine, returning with the gun in hand. After several moments of persuasion, Joe relinquished his knife to Ken, in order to spread the protection among the group.

"What about me?" Andy asked in a whiny voice. "Don't I get anything?"

"Not unless you can make something appear," Ken joked, studying the handle of the knife. It was the standard model issued to everyone on the police force.

"Just stay close to us. I doubt we will run into any trouble," Bill added.

The time travelers walked slowly through the dimly lit path. The rich red soil had over time been trampled flat and hard. Andy, Bill, and Ken took their time studying the strange trees and plants that surrounded them, while Joe nervously jumped at every sound, ready to fire his weapon. The vegetation seemed to be mysteriously disturbed by the intrusion of the humans. Several times Joe thought he heard incoherent whispering sounds, only to be convinced by the others that his own paranoia caused the phenomenon.

The howls of distant animals echoed loudly through the jungle, reminding Bill of the sirens back in his time. The sirens were always shrill and loud, while the howls were varying and somewhat pleasing. Although many different types of animals could be heard, none could be seen by the travelers. The air in the forest felt cool, aided by the setting sun. The numerous overhanging tree limbs filled a dual role, offering protection from the sun and forming a natural wind tunnel. As a result, a steady breeze blew directly into the faces of the adventurers.

The tremendous variety of vegetation sent Bill into a frenzied state. His scientific expertise was as far removed from plant life as possible, which probably explained his excitement. A small multicolored plant soon caught the scientist's eye. Like a child seeing its first flower, he bent down to examine it. The unique leaves of the plant were perfectly square, covered by bands of color representing every shade of the rainbow.

"Bill, what are you looking at?" Ken asked, after noticing that his partner had remained crouched in the same position for several moments. Bill didn't reply, he just sat motionless looking at the plant. "Come on. Whatever it is, it can't be that interesting."

Once again, Bill offered no reply. Frustrated, Ken left the plant he had been examining and walked up behind his partner. Bill gave no indication that anyone was standing directly behind him, as Ken tapped him on the shoulder. Now completely irritated, Ken shoved Bill. The hefty scientist rolled over sideways, sprawling out on the ground.

"What happened?" Bill asked quizzically. He rose to his feet, looking nervously at the others. "While I was looking at that leaf, I suddenly felt hypnotized. In the back of my mind I could hear you talking, but I couldn't take my eyes off of it." Using his peripheral vision to locate the plant, he carefully plucked off a leaf. "Look," he said, holding the object up to Ken, whose eyes instantly glazed over in a hypnotic state.

"I think he looks good that way. Maybe we should leave him like that," Andy joked.

Joe gave only a slight smirk. Clearly he did not find the scene amusing.

Bill removed the leaf, breaking Ken from his trance. "This leaf is remarkable. I think I will save it and examine it further when I get back to the laboratory. He carefully placed the leaf in his pocket. Again, the realization that he couldn't simply go back to his laboratory rushed through his brain. Everything he had accumulated, both personal and professional, had been forfeited to the Protectors. While he knew that such a day was imminent, he had not been able to prepare. Yes, he had the time machine, but other valuable equipment had been lost. He would have to start over.

"Bill, what do you make of this yellow air?" Ken asked. The distinctive tint was less obvious in the dim light of the jungle than in the openness of the field. "Surely there can't be pollution this far back in time."

"No, I don't think it is pollution. At least not the type of pollution that we would expect in our time. I'm guessing that it could be extra amounts of sulphur in the air, but I wouldn't worry about it. If it were poisonous, we would probably be dead by now."

"Don't you think we should leave?" Joe asked, becoming edgy. "I don't like standing around in one place. Those animals sound as if they are getting closer."

"No, not yet. I have to know more about the animal life in this time. After all, I might never again have the opportunity," Bill explained, studying a bright red plant.

"I agree with Bill," Ken added. His sense of adventure grew with every breath. "If these animals were dangerous, they would have attacked us by now."

"Like you are some kind of an expert on wild animals," Joe said sarcastically. He knew that the scientists exposure to animals was probably zero.

"Be careful not to get hypnotized by that plant," Andy said with a grin, ignoring the complaints tossed about by his brother.

"Don't worry about it," Bill said rising from the ground. He held a few leaves in his hand. "It's just an ordinary plant."

Joe's complaining soon began to take its toll on the scientists, as they quickened the pace of their examinations. Soon they were not even bothering to stop, as a casual glance in the general direction of an interesting plant was sufficient to satisfy their curiosity. The few patches of dimming light that were able to filter down were just enough to keep them traveling on the path. After ten minutes of brisk walking, they were met by a blast of warm air as they emerged into a small field similar in size to the one they just left. The only difference, a huge towering mountain range stood before them.

The mountains stretched out of view in both directions. The humans were dumbfounded as they stared at the sheer cliff, rising hundreds of feet into the air, facing them. None of the time travelers had ever seen anything so massive. Even the tallest buildings in New York were dwarfed by the towering cliffs. The setting sun reflected brightly off the smooth surface of the rocks, while a sudden gust of cold wind blew down the cliff making Andy shiver. At the base of the bluff a small hole, which they assumed to be a cave, could be seen. With a renewed energy, Bill hurried over to the location. Ken and Andy quickly followed, while Joe cautiously made his way across the clearing.

"A cave," Bill yelled acknowledging the obvious. Never in all his dreams had he imagined that so many wonders of nature existed. The life he led under the Protectors regime left much to be desired. "And footprints!" he exclaimed, dropping to his knees to examine the prints more closely. The soft soil around the cave entrance left perfect images for him to study. "By the size of these prints, I would surmise that these animals are about four feet tall." He crawled over to another print. Four long toes grew out of the circular foot. "It seems strange, but it appears that these animals walk on two feet."

"Your description is closer than you think," Joe said matter-of-factly.

"What makes you say that?" Bill questioned, rising from the ground. It was then he realized what Joe meant by the remark.

Numerous small human-like figures, armed with primitive spears, had left their hiding place in the jungle and slowly moved in on the startled group. The large number of the creatures made escape impossible. A moment later, the time travelers found themselves in the center of a thirty foot circle.

Four more creatures exited from the cave entrance. The circle of creatures broke, allowing the four newcomers to enter. Bill assumed the leader to be among them. Since he meant no harm, he slowly moved closer to the group with his arm extended, as if to shake hands.

The creatures, however, did not take his act as one of friendship. No sooner had he started to move, one of the four let out a mumbled yell. The circle instantly began to collapse around the humans. The creatures charged at the helpless travelers, with spears raised and hatred in their eyes.

Joe's instinctive military training took over. He quickly moved into a defensive stance, shooting each of the four greeters in the head. All fell to the ground, without so much as a cry of pain. Joe then emptied his gun into the mass of creatures. Several fell to the ground. The loud popping that filled the air after each shot did nothing to deter the rush. Before Joe could set himself for hand to hand combat, a wet hand slipped over his mouth. A cloud of blue gas secreted from its fingertips, and the former policeman for the Protectors slumped quietly to the ground. Each of the other travelers met the same fate. In a matter of seconds, all four humans lay pale and lifeless on the red soil.

CHAPTER III "ESCAPE"

Bill woke and found himself in darkness. An initial claustrophobic panic quickly subsided, upon finding that he was in no imminent danger. A few scattered torches, lit along the walls, feebly illuminated the chamber with an eerie glow. Trying to move, he found that wet slimy ropes bound him at the wrists and ankles. A thick condensation on the rock slab he was lying on had thoroughly soaked his clothing. His muscles screamed out with painful cramps, protesting the damp environment they were forced to reside in. To make matters worse, the air had a dank mouldy odor to it forcing him to breathe in short awkward breaths.

Several minutes passed, before his eyes were able to adjust to the darkness of the room. The only sound, in addition to the pounding of his heart, was the constant dripping of water, from some far reaching corner of his surroundings. Slowly the dark outline of a doorway became apparent at his left. To the right, the pale and motionless body of his assistant could be seen.

"Ken, are you all right?" Bill whispered, not wanting any of the creatures to hear. He was thankful that none were in sight. Speaking caused him to taste the unpleasant remnants of the knockout gas. After clearing his sinuses, he spat a glob of phlegm onto the floor. Even so, the sharp bitter flavor burnt his throat every time he swallowed. "Ken, are you all right?" he repeated a little louder. No response came from his partner.

Bill squinted to verify that the person next to him was actually Ken. He could see large drops of moisture forming on his partner's hair and face. By Ken's morbid appearance, Bill thought the worst. Before he could call for a third time, Ken gave off a low groan.

"Bill, is that you?" came the scratchy voice. He tried to move, but met the resistance of the ropes that bound him. Several coughs followed, before he could roll onto his side and gasp for fresh air. "What happened? Where are we?" His head ached badly and his blurred vision didn't help the matter.

"Those creatures knocked us out with some sort of gas that secreted from their hands. As for the second part of your question, I don't know where we are," Bill answered solemnly.

"Where is Andy and that idiot of a brother of his? Are they in here, too?" Ken asked, straining his eyes to see in the dark. The pain in his head intensified causing him to slam his eyes closed to shut out the discomfort.

"No, they're not in here. Either they're dead, or they were brought to another part of the cave," replied Bill, struggling to free himself from his bonds. A drop of condensation fell from the ceiling striking him on the forehead, but he paid it no attention.

Ken moved his legs, feeling the uncomfortable squish of water next to his skin. The cold rock slab he lay upon sent a chill through his body. "How long have we been in here? My clothes are soaking wet." "So are mine. The gas they used on us could have lasted a few minutes or a few days. I have no way of knowing."

A creature passing outside the cell, heard the humans talking, and entered the room to observe. Bill found it difficult to see the details of the creature in the darkness, but he managed to get a decent look none the less.

The creature stood about four feet tall, just as he had earlier surmised. Its nose protruded out like a dog, but the end looked flat like that of a pig. Two drooling fangs hung from its mouth, while two similar ivory horns stuck out of its head. A thin ridge of scales ran from the creature's skull to midway down its back. Four long fingers, each with a suction cup like formation at the tip, grew from the thin bony hands. All in all, Bill found the creature quite repulsive to look at.

The creature yelled some orders in a strange language. Within seconds, two armed guards entered the room. A foul earthy odor rose from their bodies. Bill could almost see the dirt caked onto their skin. In the dark it didn't appear as if the creatures wore any form of clothing.

One of the guards looked over Ken curiously. The creature positioned its head only inches above Ken, breathing heavily into the prisoner's face. Ken grimaced at the gruesome odor, actually gagging several times before managing a satisfactory breath of air. The creature gave a puzzled expression, causing a drop of saliva to fall from one of its fangs onto Ken's cheek. The scientist squirmed, trying to brush the foul smelling liquid from his skin. The creature took the movement as an act of hostility. It quickly raised its spear in a manner to kill, but was refrained from taking action by the first creature. The two guards spent a few more minutes examining the prisoners, careful not to get too close. They talked to each other in a tone that seemed to the humans as if they were being laughed at. The first creature then ordered the two guards to leave, before leaving itself a few moments later.

"Do you believe that? That stupid thing drooled on me. If I could have, I would have spat right back in its face," Ken said, still trying to wipe away the saliva with his shoulder.

"Then it would have killed you for sure," Bill remarked.

Ken gave a sarcastic laugh and said, "What do you suppose that was all about anyway?"

"I have no idea. I suppose they are just curious. We must seem rather strange to them. I just hope they don't come back for a while. I think I can loosen my binds enough to slip free."

Bill struggled for a few minutes with the rubber-like ropes. Whenever he pulled, the material stretched, but when he relieved the pressure the elastic ropes collapsed even tighter. After a few minutes of persistent struggling, his binds finally began to lose some of their elasticity, but not nearly enough for him to escape.

"These creatures don't believe in light do they? This place is almost pitch dark," Ken said, eyeing the chamber. Even though he was tied up and being held prisoner, his sense of adventure had returned. Oblivious to his current situation, he noted the contents of the room.

The chamber contained four large slabs of rock, two of which the scientists were lying on. Thick pools of moisture could be seen on the two vacant slabs. A three foot tall primitive clay urn, decorated with a faded geometric design, stood in the far corner. Pushed up against one of the walls he saw half a rotted out tree trunk. Apparently the creatures were not ones to worry about keeping a clean cave, as countless dew covered cobwebs hung from the ceiling and walls. Ken couldn't find a single item that made him like the place. While viewing the room, he simultaneously tried to free himself; but to no avail.

"I guess they have been living in this place so long that their eyes have adapted to the dark. That is probably why they don't need much light. You know, I once read about a type of fish, who lived so far under the ocean, that they had absolutely no light to see by. As a result, they eventually lost their eyes. Skin grew right over them," Bill ended abruptly, as a creature passed outside the room. He waited for a few seconds, allowing the creature to move a safe distance away, then resumed. "I think I can get my hands free now."

The elastic fiber in the ropes had finally degraded to the point where Bill could pull his right hand loose. "There, free!" he exclaimed loudly, quickly closing his mouth and looking toward the empty doorway. After unraveling the rope from his left hand, he instinctively placed it inside his pocket. When he found the time, he would examine it in detail. "Do you still have the knife Joe gave you?"

"I think so. It should be inside my jacket pocket, if the creatures didn't take it."

Bill tried to stand, but was quickly reminded of the binds around his ankles. He slid off the slab, hopping the short distance to Ken. Luckily the creatures hadn't bothered to search the prisoners, as Bill found the knife still in Ken's possession. Hastily, he cut at the ropes around his ankles. The binds stretched, but the blade easily sliced through the vegetation. He took a moment to rub the soreness out of his muscles, relieved that the spasms in his legs had begun to lessen in intensity. Deftly he attacked the binds confining Ken. Moments later both were free.

"Now what do we do?" Ken asked, massaging his tender muscles, but not after wiping the saliva off his face. His neck ached, causing him to stretch it in peculiar angles. "If we stay here too much longer, one of them will certainly find out that we are free."

Just as he finished, the footsteps of a creature could be heard walking toward their chamber. As if reading each others mind, the scientists quickly jumped back onto their slabs, resuming their pre-escape positions. The creature stopped momentarily and peered into the room. It eagerly looked around the hallway, as if checking to see if anyone was watching, then stepped into the chamber. Just as it reached the foot of Ken's slab, several muffled voices echoed from the corridor. The creature quickly fled from the room, hurrying on its way.

Bill gave a sigh of relief, as he waited for the second group of creatures to pass by. These creatures passed without even the slightest glance into the prison cell. Bill then quickly jumped to his feet, looking around the room in search of weapons. Unfortunately, there were none. Then he remembered the leaf in his pocket.

"I've got it!" he exclaimed. "I'll hypnotize the next creature that walks by. After I do, you can use your knife to kill it."

Ken nodded in agreement, moving over to the doorway as ordered. His heart beat quickened, as he stared out into the passage. The features of the corridor were rough, making it look as if the cave were a natural formation not constructed by the creatures. To his disappointment he could find no torches in the passageway. His hopes of taking one from the chamber were quickly shattered, as they were secured to the wall with an intricate structure of vines. "Which way should we go? We don't know the way out."

"We'll just have to guess. Quiet. Here comes one now," Bill whispered, hearing the unmistakable sloshing of a creature's footsteps.

Bill waited just inside the chamber, flattening his rotund body the best he could against the wall. Ken stood on the opposite side of the doorway, knife ready to strike. Bill kept one finger up against his lips, signaling unnecessarily to Ken to keep quiet, until the creature had moved to within a few feet of the chamber entrance. Using a quickness one would not attribute to a man of his size, Bill jumped out into the tunnel holding the leaf up to the creature's eyes. The unsuspecting creature instantly stopped, its eyes black and glassy.

An instinct Ken never knew he had took over his actions. The scientist who had never killed anything besides insects during his life wasted no time in plunging his knife into the creature's chest. Ken had no idea the most effective location to stab the creature, so he took aim for the area where he thought the heart would be, assuming that the creature had such an organ. A single stream of yellow-brown liquid spurted into the air, as the knife was removed from the creature's rough skin. Since it had been hypnotized, the creature didn't let out any cries of pain. It just fell silently to the floor.

"That was easy enough," laughed Ken, grabbing the creature's spear. He quickly handed the weapon to Bill, before dragging the limp body into the chamber.

Bill could not resist the temptation to make at least one professional observation of the strange little creatures. After taking the weapon. he reached down to feel the blood that oozed out of the creature's wound. The thick slippery texture almost made him sick to his stomach.

Before they had a chance to leave the murder site, another creature made its way down the passage. The scientists once again took their position inside the chamber. This time, however, Ken didn't wait for Bill to hypnotize the victim. Using the same agility he displayed earlier, he swiftly jumped out in front of the stunned creature, slitting its throat with the knife. The blade slipped easily through its rubber-like flesh, finding little resistance. The wound caused the creature's head to fall backwards, exposing the gruesome innards. Ken quickly jumped back, but not in time. The sickening blood spilled onto his clothing, before the body fell to the ground. For a moment Ken stood motionless, frowning as he looked down at his soiled clothing.

Ken's pouting didn't last long, as both escapees realized that time was of the essence. The scientists raced blindly down the dark tunnel, dodging the occasional outcropping of rock with remarkable dexterity. Many side passages were passed by, with Bill randomly selecting the direction of travel. The floor of the tunnel, submerged under a couple inches of water, hampered their sprint, but even under ideal conditions the tight turns of the cave didn't lead to high speeds. The water also served to hide irregularities on the floor. At one point Ken tripped over a submerged rock. The scientist slid head first down the tunnel, splashing in the near stagnant water. Ken quickly picked himself up, ignoring a small gash in his palm.

After traveling down a relatively straight stretch of tunnel, the duo reached a corner and stopped. Bill, huffing and puffing almost uncontrollably, cautiously peeked around into the passage that lay beyond. He saw the dark outlines of two creatures walking toward them, unaware that the humans had escaped.

"Here comes two of them," he whispered between breaths, holding up two fingers. His scientific work for the Protectors had not prepared him for physical exertion such as this. "I'll get the one on the right. You take care of the other."

The two creatures, talking softly amongst themselves, turned the corner only to meet their death. Bill rushed forward, just as the creatures approached. The creature closest to him stopped, its eyes wide with terror. Bill paid no attention to the creatures obvious motion for surrender, before driving his spear through its neck. The creature let out a screeching yell that quickly diminished to a low gurgle. But the warning was sufficient to notify all that were nearby. Meanwhile, Ken rammed the blade of the knife into the skull of the other. The creature stumbled forward making a grab for the head of its attacker. Ken felt the scaly hand brush the back of his neck, before the creature fell limply to the ground.

"If they didn't know we had escaped, they will now," Ken said, referring to the scream let out by Bill's victim.

"I think you are right," Bill answered. He tugged at his spear, but it stuck firm in the creature's neck.

"Don't bother with that. Just take this one," Ken said, picking up the weapon from the creature he had just slain.

The scream did indeed warn the others of the escape. From behind, angry yells could be heard, as the creatures searched for the escaped prisoners. The small creatures were quick on their feet, and infinitely more comfortable navigating the twisty maze-like passages. The sound of splashing footsteps rapidly closed in on the escapees.

"Just keep running and don't look back," Bill yelled, pushing his over weight body to its limit.

Against seemingly astronomical odds, they had picked the correct direction to flee. Up ahead they could see the outline of a cave entrance. Many yells could be heard from behind, but the path ahead was clear of any obstacles. As the duo stepped from the cave, they were greeted by the last rays of sunlight for the day. A cool breeze chilled their wet clothing, sending a passing shiver up their spines. No creatures were visible outside. Picking up speed, now free from the cramped confines, they fled into the jungle. The path they followed proved to be very dark, but they ran on unheeded.

"We'd better hide in the jungle," Bill suggested. He stopped for a moment, hands on his knees, trying to regain some energy. He could feel his heart pounding wildly in his chest. A quick glance back down the path revealed no pursuers. "I bet those creatures know their way along these paths better than we could ever hope to."

Ken agreed, quickly making his way into the camouflage of the thick foliage. The vegetation slowed their progress somewhat, but the vines and plants had little substance and were easily pushed out of the way. The two stumbled upon a large rock, taking refuge behind it. Within seconds, a group of creatures passed by on the path in a rage of fury.

"There they go," Ken whispered with a sigh of relief. His breath was short, as he also had little need to run in his time. "Do you think we should go now?"

"No, there must be more of them around. I think we should wait until morning. If the creatures can't see well in the light, as we suspect, we should be fairly safe then."

A few minutes later, the same group of creatures ran back down the path toward their caves. They were yelling what Bill presumed to be curses of not finding the escaped prisoners. As the creatures moved further away, the yells and screams faded, finally ceasing altogether.

Feeling safe, Ken relaxed, finding a comfortable position next to the moss covered rock. He stared up at the sky through a small hole in the thick foliage. The lack of cloud cover allowed several stars to look down upon him. Some of the stars even seemed to dance from one side of the sky to the other, as if teasing the human. The steady wind made a whispering sound through the trees. To the weary human it sounded as if it was saying 'caves' over and over.

"Do you think they have stopped looking for us?" Ken said, after a long stretch of silence.

"I hope so. I still think that we should wait here until morning though," Bill replied. He stared out at the path, but could see nothing in the darkness. "We have no idea where we are." Leaning back against the rock, he tried to sleep, but his mind wouldn't let him. It kept reminding him of the unknown fates of Andy and Jim.

The scientists decided to take turns sleeping, in case a group of wild animals should stumble upon them, but soon both were snoring in rhythm with the wind. Fortunately, the night passed quickly and quietly. When morning arrived, the sky rapidly lit up with the same yellow tint that was present the day before. As the sun rose into the clear sky, the temperature increased as well.

"Let's get moving," Bill offered in a refreshed voice. His hair had been mussed by the activities that followed their landing in the ancient time, but its relatively short length kept it from becoming unruly. "I think the best thing to do is to get back to the time machine as quick as possible. There we can decide how to get Andy and his brother out of the caves." He paused and added under his breath, "Assuming that is where they are."

"I think we should look for food. I'm hungry," Ken said. His growling stomach reminded him that he had not eaten since early the previous day.

Bill didn't reply right away. He also felt hungry. In fact, he felt that he could eat three times his normal breakfast. But his main concern was Andy. "We can look for food on the way to the time machine."

The rested scientists easily found their way back to the path. They studied the area for several minutes, before accepting the fact that the creatures were not waiting in ambush. Keeping a quick pace, the two headed away from the mountain range. Though the trees provided significant protection from the blistering sun, the heat and humidity were quickly becoming unbearable.

The growl in Ken's stomach kept his eyes wandering through the jungle for something edible. Not long into their hike, he spotted something promising out of the corner of his eye. A few yards off the path stood a large tree with dark green foliage. Mixed in with the green leaves were a multitude of yellow spheres, hanging from thin brown stems.

Realizing that hunger had started to dominate his thoughts, Bill was equally interested in the tree. "Let's check it out. The fruit could be edible."

Several small thorn bushes separated the scientists from the tree, but Ken's hunger overrode the annoying pricks he received, as he trampled through the underbrush. Using the knife, Ken cut a yellow ball from a low lying branch. The firm grid like surface of the sphere felt unusually warm. Of course, he had never even seen a fruit tree, never mind actually picking a fresh piece. He tossed the ball around in his hands for a few moments, marveling at its surprisingly light weight. Finding a seam in the grid surface, he used the knife to cut the fruit in half. Just as he pulled the two pieces apart, a mass of black larvae fell to the ground from inside the sphere.

"What!" Ken yelled, dropping his knife and jumping back from the larvae. Within seconds, hundreds of small insects emerged from the jungle and began to feast on the prematurely hatched larvae.

"I'm glad we didn't just bite into it," Bill said, watching the episode from the path. A sickly feeling spread through his stomach, as he imagined the vulgar feeling of larvae sliding down his throat.

"Maybe we should wait until we get back to the time machine, before looking for food again," Ken said, looking down at the glob of insects. Suddenly his desire to eat had disappeared. Locating knife in the underbrush, he frantically wiped the blade in the grass, trying to get the larvae remnants off.

The disturbing experience placed a damper on an otherwise pleasant morning. The two talked very little, as they hurried along the path toward the time machine. Bill ignored the numerous strange plants that he was so eager to examine upon arriving in the strange jungle. His only thoughts were on finding Andy.

The thick foliage soon thinned, revealing a patch of light in the distance, indicating that they had reached the end of the path. Before reaching the clearing, however, they were interrupted by a deafening roar. The two whirled around, Bill raising his spear and Ken taking guard with the knife.

A huge animal stood before them growling in a low tone. The beast stood over five feet tall on all fours, stretching over seven feet from head to tail. The latter branched out into three sharp prongs, which could easily tear through human flesh.

The creature featured an ivory colored circular horn growing from the middle of its forehead. As the animal lowered its head and scratched the ground with its front foot, it became apparent that the horn could be used as a deadly weapon. The long flat ears of the beast pointed straight into the air, not even wavering as its moved its head from side to side. Six short clawed toes could be seen equally spaced around its circular feet. For the moment the animal just grunted at the humans, eyeing them suspiciously.

The scientists stared in awe, not sure what action to take. Attacking such a large animal could very well be suicidal. Then without warning, the beast let out an ear piercing roar revealing several rows of razor sharp teeth. The roar was so loud that it almost made Ken drop his weapon to cover his ears. All of the distant animal sounds in the jungle were silenced, even the wind stopped after the hideous roar.

"Back away slowly," Bill ordered, gradually moving toward the exit of the path.

Strangely, the creature had absolutely no hair on its body. This odd trait only acted to blind its prey, as the powerful rays of sunlight filtered in through the trees, reflecting off its shiny shin. The creature followed the scientists toward the exit, matching their movement step for step. The closer the humans moved toward the open field, the more blurred their vision became. Eventually, all they could see was an undefined mass of light.

As the time travelers stepped out into the brightness of the field, the beast raised its head, jumping up onto its hind legs. Towering over the humans, it gave off an excited whine. It then lowered its front legs to the ground, promptly dashing forward. The creature leapt at Bill, all four feet leaving the ground. Bill turned to run, but he was tripped up by a rock. The rotund scientist fell backward, with a terrified yell. Flat on his back, he looked up in horror, seeing the claws of the beast turn into small deadly knives aimed for his face. Luckily, he had not dropped the spear during his tumble. Though he was not conscious of the spear, he had fallen with the tip of the weapon pointing up. The animal landed square on the point, causing it to release another ear piercing screech. The momentum of the animal carried it and the spear over Bill's head. A cloud of dust billowed into the air, as the beast struck the ground. The creature stirred for a moment, taking one final glance at the humans, before rising to its feet. It shook the spear from its body and fled into the jungle.

"Are you all right?" Ken yelled, rushing to the shaken body of his partner.

"I'm fine," groaned Bill. He rose slowly, brushing the red soil from his clothing. "I thought for sure that it was going to land on me. I could practically feel those claws tearing into my skin." He paused to catch his breath.

"I thought you were a goner," Ken said.

"Thanks for the vote of confidence," Bill replied, clearly shaken by his near death experience. He cautiously stepped over to the spear to pick it up. "I don't want to leave this behind."

The humans were too busy recovering from the attack to notice that the jungle had returned to normal. The distant cries of animals and birds once again mingled with the musical wind.

"What do you think of that?" Ken asked quizzically, pointing to the splotches of yellow blood covering the spear. "That thing has yellow blood, just like the creatures in the cave."

"I don't understand it," answered Bill, touching the quickly drying liquid. "I have no knowledge of any animals on earth ever having anything but red blood. Some major disaster must have occurred between now and our time to change yellow blood into red."

"Interesting indeed," Ken mumbled, his mind had become lost in some far away thought.

"We had better get moving, before some other animals come along that we can't handle," Bill said, finally regaining his composure. He looked into the forest, making sure that the beast had not returned. For some reason he felt sure that he would meet up again with the animal. "I sure wish I had a test tube with me. I'd love to bring some of this blood back to the laboratory. That is, if I had a laboratory to bring it back to."

The excitement of the encounter had caused the scientists to loose track of their mission. They had failed to notice that the air temperature was remarkably warmer outside the protection of the thick foliage. They also failed to immediately notice what stood directly in front of them.

"I don't believe it," yelled Bill, staring angrily into the field.

CHAPTER IV "THE SEARCH"

"We followed the wrong path," Ken said, breaking the momentary silence. His face, sweaty and dirty, wore an absolutely blank expression. The object they had totally overlooked during their scuffle with the shiny beast, a large towering rock, stood in the middle of the field that lay before them. The structure reached into the sky taller than any nearby tree. Perfect in every detail, the pure white stone was in the form of a cylinder. A mysterious glow emitting from the rock went unnoticed by both humans in the bright sunlight. Sensing no danger, the scientists quickly walked up to the monstrous rock, taking refuge in the ample shade it provided.

"I was positive that we were following the same path we walked on yesterday. We have wasted the whole morning," Bill said in disgust. He tossed his spear up against the base of the cylinder in anger and promptly sat down next to it.

"Don't worry about it," Ken said, trying to calm Bill. He placed his hand on the surface of the cool white rock and looked skyward. The structure was both mystical and soothing. "We have plenty of daylight left to find the right field." Silence followed, as Ken removed his jacket, using it's relatively clean inside lining to wipe his face. He was shocked to see how much dirt transferred from his face to the garment. Leaving Bill to fume to himself, he just sat quietly, staring out into the jungle. Several minutes passed before he broke the silence. "I know this is a bad time, but I'm still hungry. My stomach won't let me forget that I haven't fed it for a while."

Bill remained quiet, slowly getting over his frustration. "Yes, I'm also hungry," he finally said. "If we don't find the time machine soon, we are going to have to concentrate on finding something edible. I wouldn't touch any of the animals though. That yellow blood is probably poisonous to us."

Knowing that they should be moving, but too tired and frustrated to rise to their feet, the scientists remained sitting next to the gigantic rock. In the shade the air temperature proved to be very appealing. The rock itself seemed to be much cooler than the air, causing them to press their backs right up against smooth surface to gain as much comfort as possible. The fiery sun gradually rose over the tree line, reducing the amount of shade available for the weary humans. As the sun rose to a position almost directly overhead, the temperature steadily increased. No clouds were visible in the yellow-blue sky, just the snow capped mountain peaks, which loomed formidably over the treetops.

"Ken, how high would you say this thing is? A hundred forty or fifty?" Bill asked, staring intently up the side of the rock.

Ken studied the rock for a few seconds. "Yes, that sounds like a good guess. Why do you ask?"

"I figure that if we could climb to the top of it, we should be able to spot the time machine."

"Are you crazy?" Ken laughed. He lowered his squinting eyes from the top of the cylinder to the lush green grass that they sat upon. "I think the heat is roasting your brain. The side of this thing is as smooth as glass. You couldn't climb it in a million years." Ken laughed again, then stared out into the jungle. "And that's just what we have. A million years."

"As it stands now, we really have no idea where we are. Although we're not totally lost. From where the sun rose this morning, I'm fairly sure we are on the correct side of the mountain range. The only question I have is whether the time machine is north or south of our present position."

"For all we know, we are miles from the time machine. Those creatures could have dragged us through their tunnels for hours," Ken said.

"I doubt it," Bill replied, staring into the forest, still too tired to rise. "I don't think we are too far away. Those creatures don't appear to have the strength or stamina to drag two full grown humans too far."

"Especially since one of those humans is a bit more fully grown than the other," Ken joked, laughing out loud.

"Don't crack a rib," Bill replied, as Ken rolled over on his side, still laughing.

The surrounding jungle contained many types of trees, most of which were unknown to the scientists. Personally they had only seen a handful of trees in their time, mostly oaks, maples, and pines. During the war the Protectors had destroyed most of the forests, using the wood to aid with their war effort. Even after the war, the forests were systematically cut down, with no plans of reseeding even contemplated.

"How about walking around the thing anyway?" Bill suggested, watching the shadow they were resting in shrink to fifteen feet wide. "I'm curious to find out how big it is. We can't stay here much longer. Remember, we have to find Andy and his brother."

"I suppose we should keep an eye out for the rebel also," Ken added. "Yes."

They rested for a few more minutes, until the sun reached their extended feet. With the shadow of the rock all but gone, balls of sweat began to form on their foreheads. If the scientists had a thermometer, they would not have been surprised to learn that the temperature had breached the one hundred degree mark. Bill picked up his weapon and offered Ken a hand in rising to his feet.

"This is very strange," Bill commented, as they finished the first quarter of the trip around the structure. "This rock seems to have been constructed by some intelligent beings. The sides are flawless and the base appears to be the shape of a perfect circle. This couldn't have happened by itself in nature. I doubt the little creatures made it. Just looking at the primitive caves they live in should rule them out." He looked up at the cylinder, still trying to figure out a way to climb it, even though he knew it to be impossible. They walked a few more steps, then he spoke again. "What would you guess the circumference of this thing is?"

"What difference does it make?" Ken said sarcastically. Bill's persistent conversation about the cylinder, paired with the uncomfortable heat, strained his patience. "Knowing the circumference isn't going to help you climb it."

"I know that. I'm just curious," Bill snapped back. "Just give a guess."

"Oh, it's hard to say," Ken replied, stopping to study the base of the rock. "By the degree of arc, I would guess that it is about four hundred feet or so." Bill gave a satisfied mumble, and the two continued walking in silence.

As they reached the halfway mark of their journey around the structure, exactly opposite to the path they had used to enter the field, they stopped. Childish smiles instantly appeared on their faces. To their surprise, they found a ten foot tall entrance leading straight into the heart of the rock. The end of the passage, which was barely visible from the outside, looked as if it ended in the exact center of the cylinder.

"Didn't I tell you this wasn't a natural formation?" Bill said, entering the passage.

"You're going in there?" Ken asked, still standing in the blistering sun.

"Sure," Bill replied. "We might find something to help us. Besides it's much cooler in here."

Thoughts of a cooler temperature was all that was needed to convince Ken to enter the cylinder. Bill took the lead, keeping his spear raised and pointing straight ahead, just in case an animal decided to have human for lunch.

The temperature inside the rock proved to be dramatically cooler than the outside air. In fact, it almost felt too cold. The brisk air greeted their sweat drenched clothing, sending chills through their bodies. The five foot wide passage provided plenty of room for them to walk. Ken had drawn his knife, keeping it ready in his right hand, while carrying his soiled jacket in his left. After traveling about sixty feet, they came to a small chamber in the center of the structure. The walls inside were as white and smooth as the exterior. The chamber, a seven foot circular room, housed a spiral staircase, which circled up into the rock. A light sweet odor blew down the stairs, luring the travelers upward.

"I think you have found your way to the top," Ken said with a grin, but Bill had already moved to the base of the stairs.

Ken quickly followed, not wanting to be left behind. There were no visible seams in the flawless rock, leading the scientists to believe that the hollow staircase had been painstakingly chiseled from a once solid cylinder. The white polished stairs acted like magnets, attracting the human's feet to their smooth surface. It was as if the scientists had suddenly been transported to a different planet, featuring a much greater gravitational pull. A significant force was needed to release their feet from the two foot wide steps, but the duo trudged onward regardless.

After climbing about a third of the way up, Bill stuck his head into the emptiness of the spiral and looked skyward. Ken followed in the same manner. A swift breeze blew up the column of air, mussing their already tangled hair. A tiny spot of light indicated that the stairwell did indeed reach the top of the strange structure.

As they passed what they guessed to be the halfway point of their climb, a quick glance down revealed how high they had ascended. The floor looked distant and tiny. It was at this point that small parallel grooves appeared in the steps. The scientists could only guess that they were included to give extra traction, not that traction was needed with the magnetic-like force present in the strange rock. The staircase offered no railing or barrier, forcing the climbers to stay as close as possible to the wall.

Suddenly, a small brownish-gold animal ran down the stairs, stopping several steps above the humans. It stood frightened for a moment, as both parties were clearly startled. The animal briefly observed the humans, before quickly turning and fleeing back up the stairs.

"What was that?" Ken asked in astonishment. "It looked like a dog."

"It sure did. It looked too much like a dog to be anything else."

"I didn't know that dogs were around in this time," Ken said. "Of course, our knowledge of history is not very complete."

"No, I can't say that I'm too familiar with the course of evolution. But that dog looked very domesticated."

"Just keep your spear ready," Ken added, as they continued their climb.

The velocity of the wind inside the spiral picked up sharply, as the duo reached the three quarters mark of their journey. Not only did the wind continue to blow straight up the hollow between the steps, it also began to swirl around in the staircase as well. Another quick glance down showed that the floor had become all but invisible to the humans.

The scientists struggled to climb a few more steps, as the magnetic force present grew stronger. The effort needed just to remove one foot practically exhausted them.

"Do you think we should turn back?" Ken asked.

"No, we are almost there," Bill replied, raising his voice to battle the howling of the wind. "We need to find the time machine and this might be the easiest way."

Bill plucked his left foot from a step, using his arms to help in the effort, then placed it down on the next. To his surprise it felt as if the new step had less of a gravitational pull than the previous. After straining to climb a few more steps, he was sure that the effect was diminishing. But the velocity of the wind showed no signs of subsiding. The ferocious swirling gusts effectively blinded the humans, causing them to squint or suffer a stinging pain on their eyeballs.

"I think we had better go back," Bill yelled over the howling wind.

Ken turned to retreat down the staircase, but lost his balance, falling on his rear. It was then that the full power of the wind hit him. The vacuum effects of the spiraling wind pulled him towards the center of the spiral. Bill tried in vain to grab his partner, only succeeding in losing his own balance. With nothing to grab on to, both scientists were sucked into the hollow separating the stairs. A force like they had never felt before propelled them upward. Their eyes were tightly clenched, mostly out of fright, else they would have seen the powder yellow-blue sky rush toward them. A moment later the wind stopped, causing the scientists to reverse their direction of travel. With their eyes still closed, bracing for the inevitable landing, they crashed with a thud on top of the cylinder.

"Wow, what a ride!" exclaimed Ken, realizing that he was none the worse for the experience. He rose wobbly to his feet, wearing a boyish grin. The wind had dropped the time travelers approximately five feet from the stairwell. "At least your wish came true. We are at the top of the rock."

"Yes, but I think I could have made it up here on my own," Bill grimaced.

"Look over there," Ken yelled. "The dog is walking toward the edge."

Bill struggled to stand, before turning to watch the dog. The animal's golden fur shone brightly in the sun, as it walked slowly along the edge of the circular platform. Every several steps the animal would stop, sniffing the rock intensely. Noticing the humans, it glanced up for a moment, apparently satisfied that two had reached the top of the cylinder, then resumed sniffing. Though it was startled by the humans presence inside the rock, it did not seem bothered by their company out in the open.

"We should be able to see the time machine from up here," Ken said, focusing his attention on the surrounding area. A strange sensation filled his body from being in the open so high above the ground. As he looked out onto the surrounding treetops, his knees began to buckle slightly. Only by sitting, did he feel secure.

"Take it easy," Bill said, apparently unaffected by the high altitude. He placed his hand on Ken's shoulder in an offer of support, but Ken waved him away.

"I'm okay," Ken replied. "Just a little dizzy."

Their vantage point offered a magnificent view of the surrounding area. To the east, they could see the small creature's mountain range, which ran endlessly out of sight in both directions. On the western horizon they could see another mountain range, which appeared to run parallel to the one from which they escaped. They had no way to tell the size of the new mountain range, as it seemed to be quite some distance away and only the very top of the peaks were visible over the trees. Many small fields and strange land formations filled in the terrain between the two mountain ranges.

"There it is," Bill shouted, pointing his finger to a small field not far from where they stood. "The time machine is there. Do you see it?" The polished body of the time machine glittered unmistakably in the bright sun light.

"Yes, and there seems to be a path leading directly to it," Ken added, fighting off his fear of heights to successfully rise to his feet.

"See, those are the cliffs where we were attacked," Bill continued, pointing to the unmistakable broken rock cliff face. He found the entrance to the path they just traveled upon and traced the route back toward the mountains. "We must have exited the caves just to the north of the cliffs."

"It looks like the path to the time machine is not covered by tree branches, like the other paths have been. It's probably going to be quite hot," Ken said.

"Yes," Bill replied, before a puzzled expression crept over his face. "It should be hot up here, but I feel comfortable."

"It's probably just an effect of the rock," Ken replied, now clearly at ease moving around on the surface of the cylinder. "I'm not sure..."

"Hey, the dog just walked over the edge," interrupted Bill, rushing to the spot where the dog had been standing. His comfort with heights had found its limit, as the view of the distant ground caused him to drop to his stomach. Determined to discover the dog's fate, he crept slowly to the edge and peered over. Allowing only his head to hang over the side, he stared down in disbelief. "I don't believe it. The dog is walking down the side of the rock, just as if he were walking on the ground."

Ken fought back his new found fear of heights and crawled over next to Bill. The height clearly made him dizzy, causing him to stretch his feet as far back from the edge as possible. Even though the thought of falling raced through his mind, it did not stop him from enjoying such an impossible feat. His stunned eyes watched, as the dog actually walked down the side of the cylinder. As the animal neared the ground, it casually jumped to the thick green grass, then raced off toward the jungle. Before disappearing into the foliage, the dog stopped and turned toward the humans. It offered a couple of friendly barks, wagging its tail as it did so. A moment later it was gone.

"Amazing," Ken said, too dumbfounded to move.

Bill stuck his hand over the edge, touching it to the side of the cylinder. A strong gravitational force held it in place. It seemed that the same force present inside the stairwell acted on the outside surface as well.

"This rock is very strange," Bill said rising to his feet. "It seems to have its own gravity. That is how the dog could walk down."

"I've just thought of something else," Ken said, inching away from the edge. Once a safe distance away, he stood upright. "Did you notice how we could see inside the rock, when there was no light source present? The light entering through the hole up here and the door on the ground would not be bright enough to allow us to see as well as we did."

"I wish I knew who built this. There is no way this rock is a natural formation," Bill said, staring down at the structure. He made one last mental note of the location of the time machine, before moving to the stairs.

As soon as the rotund scientist descended to the second step of the spiral staircase, he found himself sailing backwards through the air. A moment later he was sprawled out on the surface of the rock, in quite the same manner as his arrival.

"Whoa!" Ken yelled, rushing over to help Bill to his feet. "I forgot about the wind. How are we going to get down?"

Bill slowly shifted his vision from his partner's face to the edge of the cylinder. "I suppose the same way the dog did. We'll just walk down the side."

"I don't like the sound of that," Ken replied quickly. His heart began to race, as he watched Bill approach the edge.

Ken reluctantly followed his partner, but soon found his head spinning as he drew nearer to the edge. Slowly, he backed away and closed his eyes, trying to regain his sense of balance. "I think I'll try the stairs again. If you don't mind."

Bill watched, as Ken peered into the empty stairwell. Even though he could feel no wind, he knew it was still present. Confidently he placed both feet onto the first step. A smile spread across his face. "So far so good," he yelled to Bill, who watched with interest from the edge.

As Ken's foot crossed the extended plane of the first step, he could feel a strong force pushing upwards. Instinctively he lowered his body and sat on the surface, sliding his left foot onto the second step. He could feel the wind ruffling his pant legs, as he slid his right foot onto the second step. Grasping the corner of the first step he lifted his body, lowering himself down. The wind intensified, as he cowered against the wall for protection. When his left foot moved onto the third step, he began to lose control. The wind, fueled by some unknown force, lifted Ken off the steps, tossing him onto the surface of the cylinder. For a moment, he lay motionless, eyes tightly closed. "I think I'll go down the side."

"Take a breather and watch me," Bill said with a smile. He then tossed his spear over the edge, watching as it tumbled gracefully down to the ground. The weapon bounced once, then came to rest in the grass.

The scientist then sat down, only inches from the side, turning his body so that his legs were dangling over the edge. The gravitational force of the rock gripped his calves and feet, pulling them to the smooth rock surface. "It feels strong enough to support me," he said to Ken, who by this time had crawled over next to him. Bill's entire reserve of adrenaline was released, as he prepared himself to take the biggest leap of faith he had ever imagined. Slowly, he eased the rest of his body over the side of the four hundred foot structure.

"This is the strangest feeling I have ever experienced!" Bill exclaimed. The entire back portion of his body was mysteriously glued to the rock surface. He looked up and saw Ken peering over the side. "It is rather difficult to move in this position," he said, trying to roll his body over. Some effort was required, but he managed to turn his body so that his front was now in contact with the cylinder. Trying his best not to look down at the ground, he slowly pushed himself down the side of the strange rock.

"Come on. You are going to have to come down sometime," Bill yelled, after descending fifteen feet.

"I guess you are right," Ken replied. After gathering his thoughts, he followed the same strategy Bill used in lowering himself over the edge. After realizing that he was not going to fall, Ken actually started enjoying the sensation. The effort needed to move just one arm was tiring, but he allowed himself occasional glances at the surrounding area. A bird flew by, pausing just below him, before continuing on its way. "This is really something," he yelled.

The gravity of the earth could still be felt, leading Bill to surmise that it would slowly drag them down the cylinder if they chose not to help the process. As he approached the halfway point, Bill decided to get creative. He brought his knees up to his chest, then slowly tried to stand. Ken glanced down, not believing his eyes, upon seeing his partner standing on the side of the cylinder, parallel to the surface of the earth.

"Amazing," Bill yelled. He took a few backward steps, still choosing not to look down. It only took a few moments for him to master this awkward method of walking. "Try to stand, Ken, you can move much quicker this way."

Ken crawled a few more feet, then looked to see how much more progress Bill had made. Deciding not to prolong the agonizing descent, he also struggled to stand. He could feel the earth's gravity pulling him downward, but the rock clearly had enough power to prevent him from falling.

"There you go," Bill yelled, now walking rather smoothly.

"I would have never thought this possible," Ken replied, turning his body to face the ground. His faith in the rock's power had dispelled all his phobias, at least temporarily. He quickly caught up to Bill, coercing him to turn around and face the ground as well.

As the duo approached the eight foot mark, the earth's gravitational forced suddenly seemed to grow stronger. In actuality, it was the rock's magnetism that had stopped. The two scientists found themselves in a free fall, descending the last several feet in a hurry. Luckily, the long plush grass cushioned their fall.

"Ouch!" screamed Ken, laying face down in the grass. "I think the stairs would have been better." He struggled to his feet and rubbed his neck.

"Look on the bright side," Bill said, rising to his feet. "At least we are down."

After tending to their minor bruises, Ken said, "I left my jacket up there."

"You really don't need it in this heat," Bill replied, not wanting to take the time to retrieve the garment. "If we have time later, we'll pick it up. Right now, I want to get to the time machine."

Bill lead the way to the path he had spotted from the top of the rock. Unfortunately, this path hadn't been traveled upon as much as the others they had followed. At times, the grass and vegetation rose up to their waists, slowing their progress considerably. As Ken noticed earlier, there were very few trees overhanging the path to offer shade. The broiling sun beat down on the time travelers, while the temperature continued to rise, draining energy from their weary bodies.

"This may sound strange, but this reminds me of the creatures caves," Ken said, wringing the moisture from his shirt. He glanced back at the rock, noticing the dog standing on top watching them. The animal held Ken's jacket in its mouth, while it wagged its tail in hopes that the humans would return.

"I guess it doesn't matter where you are around here. Your clothes are always going to be drenched," agreed Bill, doing the same to his clothing. "I sure hope Andy is all right."

"Me too," Ken added, turning back from the cylinder. "What do you say we rescue Andy and leave his brother here. He is no use to us. I'm sure those creatures would have a great time with him."

"There's a thought," laughed Bill. "But we should probably rescue him, too. I think we might have some sort of moral obligation. After all, we brought him here."

"I don't know. Those creatures seem to be his type. I think he would fit right in."

Their casual conversation was interrupted by the sound of an animal running through the thick jungle to their right. Taking guard with their weapons, the scientists grew nervous. Bill expected to see the shiny creature bolt from the foliage and resume its attack, but that was not the case. Several yards ahead, a large horse-like animal casually strolled out of the forest, stopping in the middle of the path.

The animal featured a bright orange tail and mane, as well as a brilliant orange horn growing out of its head. Pure white hair covered the rest of the animal's body. An unseen aurora radiated from the animal, causing the humans to stand motionless in awe. The beast stared bewildered at its audience, as if remembering some gratifying memory from the past. Then it jumped up on its hind legs, let out a pleasant sounding cry, and disappeared into the forest.

"Wow!" Ken exclaimed, truly astounded by the beauty of the animal.

"You know what that reminds me of?" Bill asked.

"No, what?"

"It reminds me of a unicorn. I have read about them in a book called 'Myths and Legends'."

"I thought myths were supposed to be false," Ken said, as they resumed walking. For some unexplained reason both felt quite relaxed, no longer threatened by the ancient jungle.

"I did too, but maybe there is some truth to them after all."

Just as he finished, he heard a yell from Ken, who had been walking a step behind. Spinning around, he was greeted only by the tall grass swaying in the wind.

"Ken, where are you?"

"Right here," replied a voice. A hand stuck up out of the grass, then Ken's head appeared. "I tripped over a tree stump." He rolled up his pant leg, revealing a large red welt. "I think I should have stayed home. Soon I'll have more bruises than I can count."

Now grimacing with every step, as he tried to shake off the effects of his encounter with the tree stump, Ken was thankful that the rest of their hike proved uneventful. That attitude soon changed, however, as Bill stepped from the path into the field, his actions making it obvious to Ken that something was wrong. The hobbled scientist, who had fallen several yards behind, quickly caught up to his partner, who stood only one step into the field.

Bill glanced around the field in obvious disappointment. No time machine could be seen, just long wet grass bent by the wind. "This must be the wrong field," he called to Ken.

"That's not possible. We never left the path," Ken answered, limping up to Bill. The two made their way over to the spot where the time machine should have been.

"Look at this," Bill yelled angrily. His face turned a bright red, as he studied the freshly made marks gouged into the soft soil. The tracks led off into the forest.

"Someone has dragged the time machine away," Ken said, stating the obvious. He looked around the area, but no sign could be seen of the thieves.

"We have to follow the tracks. Whoever took it can't be more than fifteen minutes ahead of us. Without that time machine we will never get out of this place," Bill offered in a serious tone. For the first time since landing in the ancient time, he was truly afraid of what might happen to them.

Hurriedly, the scientists followed the tracks through the tangled jungle. The seriousness of the situation forced Ken to fight through the dull thumping pain in his leg. It did not appear to the humans that the thieves had followed any established path through the forest. The gouges in the dirt wove their way haphazardly around trees and bushes. Countless pieces of vegetation had been torn from the ground by the large machine. More than once a hidden thorn bush stabbed Ken. He gave a feeble look into the sky and rubbed his mounting wounds.

"Do you think the creatures from the caves took it?" Ken asked, picking a few thorns from his already bruised leg.

"I doubt it. The tracks are leading away from their caves. Besides, I think the time machine would be too heavy for them to move. Someone else must have taken it."

"Someone much bigger?" Ken asked rhetorically.

To their relief, the tracks soon joined with a well traveled path. Bill and Ken were able to quicken their pace considerably, now that the tangles of the jungle were not conspiring to slow them down. They made good progress on the path, pressing their tired bodies to the limit, but still could not see any sign of the thieves.

The events of the past two days finally took their toll on Ken. He slowly stumbled over to the side of the path, sitting down in the shade of a large yellow leaved tree. "I can't go any further without rest and some water," he said, wiping the sweat from his face. "This heat is just too much for me."

"I agree. A short rest would do us good," Bill said, also taking refuge in the shade. "In a few minutes I'll go look for something edible. Maybe we will get lucky and find a lake or stream. After all, there must be a water source around somewhere with all this vegetation."

Ken glanced around the jungle. Everything looked so peaceful. The temperature seemed to have stop rising and even drop a few degrees, since stopping their pursuit. The tree he had chosen to sit by gave off a sweet odor. An odor that made him drowsy. In a matter of seconds, unable and unwilling to fight the feeling, he was fast asleep.

He did not often dream, at least dreams that he could remember. But this dream filled his head as soon as he dozed off. He dreamt of finding the time machine and rescuing Andy, but finding out that they were too late to save his brother. Joe had met an untimely and gruesome demise at the hands of the little creatures.

Bill did not notice that Ken had fallen asleep. This is because the pleasant relaxing odor of the tree had the same effect on him. Bill also found himself dreaming of finding the time machine. Unlike Ken, in his version everyone was rescued. With the time machine now safely in his hands, he returned to his laboratory to find Jim still alive. Jim had convinced the officials that Bill had been working against the Protectors without his knowledge. Bill knew, however, that in reality Jim would have been killed minutes after the time machine disappeared. The Protectors rarely gave their prisoners a chance to defend themselves.

Bill's dream did not end after the happy reunion with Jim. The pictures in his mind continued, allowing him and the others to complete their goal of overthrowing the Protectors. With the Protectors gone, the land was once again free. People could walk the streets without fear of being chased and killed by the menacing spheres.

Bill woke suddenly, a smile still on his face, only to discover that they had been asleep for hours. The sun had all but disappeared over the trees, showing the amount of time that had passed. He woke Ken, reluctantly telling him that they had allowed the thieves to get even further ahead. The sleep did do them some good however, as both felt refreshed.

Although the sun was setting, the temperature remained high. It did not take long for their clothing to once again become soaked with sweat, after drying off the shade. As the composition of the soil slowly changed, the outline of the thieves footprints could be seen in the clay-like dirt. To their dismay, the webbed footprints were approximately fifty percent larger than that of a human.

"I guess this eliminates the creatures who captured us. They had small feet," Ken said, trying to make conversation. Both scientists were depressed at the thought of losing the time machine.

"Yes, and by the looks of these prints the thieves are much larger."

"I've noticed," Ken replied, not trying to sound as concerned as he actually felt.

The traveler's shadows grew long behind them, as they walked toward the western horizon. The jungle grew dark and the strange sounds of the ancient time seemed to grow louder. Even though they had heard and seen evidence of a large animal population, they had only come in contact with the inhabitants on four occasions. The encounters with the small creatures and the shiny beast turned out to be rather hostile, while the brief meetings with the dog and unicorn were passive.

Though it appeared that not all of the creatures in this time were hostile, the humans were not about to let their guard down. The time machine lay ahead, pilfered by some unknown thieves. It was their only hope of leaving, and with every step they took, their only hope of seeing Andy and Joe again.

The fiery sun had disappeared behind the tree line, casting the jungle into an eerie dusk. The human's weary eyes, concentrating on spotting animals in the surrounding foliage, failed to notice a vine slithering silently along the ground. Moving with surprising accuracy, the vine burst from the jungle, deftly wrapping itself around Bill's right leg. Before the scientist knew what had happened, the vine yanked him to the ground. A second vine instantly followed the first from the camouflage of the murky forest, attaching itself to Bill's left leg. Not even straining under the scientists heavy weight, the vines proceeded to drag Bill into the jungle.

Ken was slow in reacting, thinking that Bill had only tripped over a rock. By the time Ken grasped the situation, Bill had disappeared between two bushes.

"Help!" Bill screamed. He tried to grab onto bushes and trees, anything to stop the vine's progress, but his hands were quickly torn away.

If the vines had been able to pull Bill at a quicker pace, Ken might have not been able to catch up to his partner. But the vines, although forceful enough to drag Bill's two hundred plus pound body effortlessly over the ground, were not very swift. Ken managed to reach Bill, but all efforts to stop his movement failed.

"Try to cut them off," Bill gasped, grabbing hold of small tree. He was able to maintain his grip long enough for Ken to race to his feet, before a sharp searing pain in his shoulders forced him to let go.

Ken cut savagely at the vine around Bill's left leg. The blade of the knife easily sliced into the flesh-like surface of the vine, but soon met with a stronger inner layer. The vine seemed to stop momentarily with the initial cut, as if trying to assess the damage, but quickly resumed its tugging.

Ken didn't let the toughness of the vine deter his efforts. Giving off yells of rage, he concentrated his attack on a six inch area of the vine, hacking and slicing wildly. Soon, a dark green liquid began to ooze out of the numerous wounds.

"It's loosening," Bill yelled, feeling the vice-like grip on his left leg relax.

Once the knife penetrated the tough inner layer, the thick green liquid spilled out even faster. Ken stabbed furiously at the gaping wound, until finally the vine released its grip, slithering away badly battered. The vine on Bill's right leg stopped pulling for a moment, giving Bill a chance to sit up. Only fifteen feet away sat a large pit, the obvious destination of Bill's journey through the jungle. The reprieve as short lived. The vine was not about to lose its prey.

Feeling a mighty tug, Bill was yanked back to the ground. With the pit visible and so close, Ken wasted no time resuming his attack. Finding that stabbing was more effective than slashing, he was able to sever the vine, before it could drag Bill within ten feet of the pit. The segment still wrapped around Bill's leg went limp and was easily removed.

"Are you okay?" Ken asked, offering Bill a hand.

"I think I'm fine," Bill replied. Lifting his pant legs revealed two dark bruises. The vines held such tight grips, that deep impressions were left in his skin. Bill grimaced, as he gingerly walked toward the pit. "It felt like they were crushing my legs."

The scientists cautiously inched to the rim of the pit, where they were stunned at what they saw. Sitting at the bottom of the twenty foot drop was a large plant-like creature. In the center of its cabbage looking head a large mouth opened and closed frantically, showing multiple rows of green teeth. A thin green liquid drooled out of the mouth onto the mass of surrounding leaves. Several other vine appendages were visible, but the creature evidently had no intention of risking their damage. It had lost its meal and suffered major wounds. The hunger it felt would have to wait to be satisfied, until other less dangerous prey wandered by.

"That is definitely not the way I picture myself dying," Bill said, with a sigh of relief. He backed away from the pit, not knowing if the creature would try another attack.

The scientists easily found their way back to the path, after their brief diversion. For all they knew, the few minutes spent fighting off the mysterious pit plant could have allowed the time machine thieves enough time to avoid capture forever. High thin clouds now moved swiftly through the sky, although very little wind could be felt on the floor of the jungle.

The amount of productive travel time remaining in the day was rapidly decreasing, as the sun continued is descent toward the horizon.

"I think we should try to find some water," Bill said, aware of his parched mouth. "I'm shocked that we haven't found any yet. You stay on the path. I'll go into the forest a bit and walk parallel to you."

"Just keep an eye out for any more man eating plants," Ken said, half joking, half serious.

"Don't worry about that," Bill said. "From now on I'll be watching the ground closer than ever."

Bill found moving through the jungle to be more difficult than anticipated. After battling through thirty feet of underbrush, he turned to the west. Several times he felt a branch tighten around his ankle, causing him to jab at the ground with his spear, only to find that he had decimated a wiry bush that he had happened to step upon. Occasionally he would stop and listen for water, but he never heard even a single drop or ripple. After an agonizingly slow hike through one hundred yards of jungle, he returned to the path. The sky had grown even darker, making another venture into the forest too dangerous to attempt.

"No luck?" Ken asked, as Bill emerged from the foliage.

"Not a drop of water anywhere," Bill replied. He looked down at his pant legs, which were covered by various prickly branches and pods. "I didn't even see anything that might be edible."

"I don't think we can go much longer tonight," Ken said, motioning to the floor of the path. "The tracks are still visible. We should be able to follow the path through the night, but if the thieves turned off the path..."

"We might not notice," Bill finished.

The scientists walked on slowly. Their bodies were tired and sore, having not been nourished for some time. Water was the main concern. They figured that they could survive several weeks on the scant offerings of the jungle, but without water they would surely die in a day or two in the oppressive heat.

The sun had now completely left the sky, casting the jungle into a darkness only brightened by the full face of the moon. The late afternoon clouds had also left, letting the countless stars shine down upon the lost time travelers. The rapidly declining temperature lifted the spirits of the humans, but only enough to keep them trudging forward. Their encouragement, low as it was, started to decline as Bill noticed the jungle had begun to thin.

"This is not good," Bill said, stopping to catch his breath. "It can only mean that water is becoming more scarce. If we had trouble finding water in the thick of the forest, I doubt that we will find any now."

"Do you think we should turn back?"

Bill stood in silence, staring down at the fading grooves leading toward the time machine. In his heart, he knew that everyone who journeyed through time in his time machine, with the exception of Ken, needed him in order to survive. Ken could operate the time machine in his absence, but no one else would even know where to begin. Preserving his life was crucial, if anyone was going to leave this time. Already three lives were out of his control. The rebel removed himself upon landing in the ancient time. There was no telling where he was, or if he was still alive. The same held for Andy and Joe. If the brothers had survived and escaped the little creatures, they would naturally try to find the time machine. He could not predict their actions, upon finding that the vehicle was missing. Everything, it seemed, depended his ability to recover the stolen time machine.

"No, we must find the time machine. It is the only hope any of us have," Bill said solemnly. "We can only hope that we last long enough to find some water."

"I can go look," Ken offered, realizing that they wouldn't make much progress in the dark. "The time machine will have to wait until morning."

"No, you stay here," Bill replied, taking the brunt of responsibility. "This looks like a good place to set up for the night. See what you can do to make things comfortable for us."

"Sure."

With that Bill turned and wandered into the thinning jungle. Ken stood for a moment, not sure what to do. The trees here were well spaced, and the underlying brush was almost nonexistent. He spotted a small clearing several feet off the path and began to cut down small branches to build a lean-to. It did not take him long to build a makeshift wall. Feeling that he at least protected himself from attack from one direction, he sat down to wait for Bill's return.

A cool breeze now filtered through the jungle, rustling leaves and carrying far off cries of unknown animals. Ken stared up at the sky, marveling at the crystal clear view he had of the cosmos. It was a rare night back in his own time when he could see the stars, never mind taking the time to study them.

His dry mouth cried out for liquid, as his eye happened to catch the glimmer of leaf nearby. He was desperate, ready to try anything. Eagerly he plucked the leaf from the tree and popped it into his mouth. As he chewed, a light liquid drained from the leaf, caressing his tongue. It was not water, but it served the purpose. After chewing on a dozen or so leaves, he returned to the shelter and fell into a light sleep.

Fifteen minutes later, Bill rushed up to him, startling him awake. "Ken, wake up," the scientist yelled. "I found some food."

"Food?" Ken mumbled, his eyes opening wide. His stomach began to growl at the mention of the word. "Where? What kind?"

"I found them in the forest, about a quarter mile from here," Bill said, holding out a handful of small round berries.

Ken took a berry and held it up to the moon light. It appeared to be dark blue in color. The small crater, surrounded by a ridge of thin skin, made him think of one thing. "A blueberry?" he asked cautiously.

"That's what I think," Bill responded. "I tried one, and it sure tastes like a blueberry."

Ken popped the berry in his mouth, squashing it against the roof of his mouth with his tongue. The savory insides of the berry exploded in his mouth in an eruption of flavor. "What are we waiting for? Lead the way."

Bill lead the rush though the jungle. Both ignored the occasional branch slapping them in the face and thorn digging into their calves. The thought of finally satisfying their ravaged bodies, gave them the reserve strength needed to press on. Within minutes, they were standing in the middle of a small patch of blueberry bushes.

"This is amazing," Ken cried, picking a handful of berries and tossing them into his mouth. "Of all the strange plants and animals we have seen, it takes something as simple as a blueberry to save us."

Though they had never seen blueberry bushes before, blueberries were one of the more plentiful fresh fruits available under the Protectors regime. Most of the berries were fully ripe and delicious, but the hungry scientists didn't allow the occasional sour berry disrupt their enjoyment. As they ate, a renewed burst of energy flowed through their bodies. They sat in the patch for a half hour, laughing and talking. For a while, they were removed from their predicament. Thoughts of their friends, lost amongst the mountains and trees, were placed into the back of their minds.

After eating his fill, Ken removed his shirt and proceeded to tie knots at the end of each sleeve.

"What are you doing?" Bill asked, cramming another handful of berries into his mouth.

"You don't think that I'm going to leave the only food I have seen in the last two days, without taking a supply?" Ken replied, plucking a few berries and tossing them into his shirt. Bill immediately followed Ken's lead.

Feeling somewhat refreshed, but still rather sleepy, the scientists made their way back the lean-to. The area seemed quiet and peaceful. The temperature had fallen to a comfortable level, allowing the men to relax.

"The creatures who stole the time machine must be hours ahead of us by now," Bill stated, trying to map out a strategy for the following day in his head. "We should try to rise early and make as much progress as possible, before the temperature gets too hot."

Ken nodded in agreement, but his thoughts were not on the time machine or the thieves. The adventure of the past two days seemed like a dream come true. Excitement was found around every corner. But somehow it didn't seem real. One moment he was working on experiments in his laboratory, the next he was roaming a jungle with nothing more than a knife for protection. The surrealistic appearance of the journey so far made the adventure seem temporary. Many times he felt sure that it would end and he would find himself back in the laboratory toiling over a new project. But as he sampled a few more berries from his shirt, he suddenly felt full. His stomach knew that he would not be returning, at least to the life he knew. If all went well, he would return to his home, but not as a scientist for the Protectors. Instead, he would be a scientist for the revolution. The adventure he found himself in now would end, eventually. He did not know how, but he was sure it would. What lay in his future was difficult to see. The only outcome that he could realistically see was his death in this strange time. Or maybe later, while fighting the Protectors.

"Do you think they killed Jim?" Ken asked.

"I hope not," Bill replied. He had stopped thinking about his strategy for the morning. "The Protectors kill even at the slightest sign of a problem. I don't think his chances are very good."

"How about the rebel that burst into the apartment? Do you think he is sill alive out there?"

Bill didn't say anything for a minute. His mind had wandered into the past. His thoughts cycling through a time, a time not long before they made the trip into the past. But the memory couldn't form and he was returned to the present. "Yes, I think he is all right. After all, he had a machine gun."

After that they stopped talking. Their muscles cried for rest, as did their drooping eyelids. Soon both were sleeping, dreaming of places far away from where they were. The night passed quietly, except for the howls of distant animals. Both slept comfortably on the sandy ground, fortunate that no hostile animals crossed their path during the night.

CHAPTER V "ANOTHER ESCAPE"

Andy slowly woke from his drug induced sleep, only to find himself surrounded by darkness. A putrid mouldy odor found its way into his nostrils, causing him to gasp for fresh air. Panic quickly spread through his body, as he found himself unable to move. Fighting hard to shrug off the effects of the knock out gas, he finally realized that his immobility was caused by ropes rather than paralysis. This fact helped the panic subside, allowing him to regain some rational thought. He found the binds to be very tight, causing his hands and feet to feel numb. Attempts to flex his fingers were met by a swollen resistance, allowing the digits to bend at only a fraction of their normal range. His eyes made every attempt to accustom themselves to the darkness, but his surroundings would remain a mystery. There was absolutely no light present, just darkness.

"Bill, are you in here?" he whispered in a cold scratchy voice. The taste of the knock out gas lingered in his throat, bringing back the memory of the attack. "Ken, are you in here?" he paused, but no response came. He closed his eyes, trying to collect his thoughts.

"Aren't you forgetting someone?" whispered a low voice from the opposite side of the room.

"Oh, sorry," Andy replied. He looked in the direction of the voice, even though he could not see.

"You yell for Bill and Ken, but forget about me," Joe snapped, as was his usual manner when talking to his younger brother.

"Sorry, I forgot you were with us," Andy replied, smiling to himself. He hadn't really forgotten that Joe had accompanied them on their time travel. It was just that if someone had to be in the room with him, he wished it to be one of the others.

Just then the sound of footsteps, walking over crunchy gravel, entered the chamber from some unseen doorway. The humans stopped conversing, as the owner of the footsteps clearly entered the room where they were being held. A tiny flame appeared out of nowhere. Soon a small fire was burning at the far wall. The orange flames gave off enough light for the prisoners to see their captor and the chamber they were occupying. The visitor was obviously one of the creatures who had attacked them near the cave entrance.

Given that they were in a cave, the humans found the chamber to be unexpectedly large. Most of the volume of the room was filled with long slabs of rock, which were scattered about in no orderly manner. A thick layer of moisture on the wall near the fire began to dry almost instantly due to the growing heat.

Andy was able to position himself so that he could examine the area near the fire. Next to the pit, where several logs were burning, lay a pile of broken bones. A sudden thought of terror rushed through his mind, hoping that they weren't the remains of his friends. After taking a longer look, he was relieved to see that the bones were old and cracked. The only exit to the chamber stood five yards to the left of the fire pit, where a pile of spears sat neatly arranged. Outside the door nothing could be seen and no sounds could be heard.

Andy rolled his body to the left. He estimated that the wall was about fifty feet away. Only slabs of rock could be seen in that direction. The binds made it impossible to see what was behind him, but he could see where the ceiling met the wall, about twenty feet back. As he finished examining the chamber, he suddenly became aware of the cause of the unpleasant odor. A large pile of what appeared to be dung sat rotting to his right. Strangely, a circle of white pebbles had been constructed around the pile of feces. The white pebbles were in turn surrounded by four sticks in the shape of a square. Beyond the strange display, he could see his brother, also bound and lying on a rock slab.

The lone creature, picked up an odd shaped rock, then found a spot to sit several feet from the fire. Without so much as a glance at the humans, it started chiseling at a rock slab. Small sparks jumped off the rock with every stroke the creature took.

"Hey, you," Andy yelled at the creature. "Where are we?"

The creature paused from its work to look at the prisoner. Its facial features were dark, due to the shadows. Andy could see the creature open its mouth slightly. A soft sigh followed, before the creature returned to its chiseling.

"Well aren't you going to answer me? I asked you to tell us where we are," Andy said a little louder this time.

The creature stopped, tossed its tool against the slab, then walked over to Andy. For the first time, and up close, Andy saw the ugliness of the being. He had briefly noticed in the field that they weren't very appealing to look at, but didn't have enough time to absorb all their homely features. The creature began to mumble, a strange language flowing from its lips, as it waved its arms in the air. It stopped, standing motionless, as if waiting for a response. Andy did not reply. In fact, he was suddenly not sure if trying to communicate with the creature was in his best interest. Not seeing any movement from its prisoner, the creature moved even closer. After a brief examination, the chiseler returned to its work.

"It's no use talking to him," Joe said, with a trace of laughter in his voice. "He can't understand you. Even if he could, you can't understand him."

Andy didn't reply. He felt slightly embarrassed at the futile attempt to communicate. Not dwelling on the failed attempt, he returned the focus of his attention to the characteristics of the room. This time his eyes were better adjusted to the dim light. From what he could see of the floor, long parallel cracks ran through it. In some places the cracks appeared to be a half inch wide. A greenish slime covered several areas of the grey floor. Andy guessed that the abundant moisture in the cave was a haven for such growths. The walls were dull and rough, sporting several animal hides. The hides were hung by the fire, evidently in order to dry out the skin. It didn't appear as if the creatures minded breathing the sooty smoke, as the lack of ventilation quickly clouded the air in the large room. After a while, another creature entered the chamber carrying a thin rock tray. It placed the small slab next to Andy, then proceeded to yell some mysterious order. Five armed creatures entered the room, forming a wall between the prisoners and the door. The five guards gave quizzical glances toward the humans, while mumbling quietly amongst themselves.

The head creature looked at the guards disgustedly, but did not discipline them for their unwarranted talking. The creature deftly untied Andy's hands, pointing to the tray. Andy struggle to a sitting position, cautious not to move too quickly and raise alarm. It felt good to have the pressure on his wrists removed. Immediately he could feel the blood course into his fingers, as the swelling slowly withdrew. On the tray he saw several globs of a colorless substance. He tentatively poked at the globs with his finger, looking at the head creature with a puzzled expression. The creature pointed to the tray and then to Andy's mouth.

"I think he wants you to eat it," Joe said.

"That's what I'm afraid of," Andy replied. He kept massaging his hands and fingers, not knowing how long his sore digits would be allowed to move freely before being tied up once again. Under the prodding of the creature, Andy picked up a small portion of the mush and held it to his nose. The mixture had an earthy odor to it, but nothing too repulsive. Gingerly, he placed the food into his mouth, bracing for the unknown taste.

Once inside his mouth, the food disintegrated into a sandy substance. Andy struggled to swallow the first few mouthfuls, which scratched his already dry throat. The food proved to be bland and relatively tasteless. It was the smell of the dung, which reached his nostrils once again, that caused him to stop eating.

Seeing that Andy had finished his scant meal, the head creature retied the prisoner's hands, thankfully not nearly as tight as the first time. The creature then moved over to Joe. Mechanically the creature untied the prisoner's binds. Joe eyed the creature intently, feeling that he could easily overpower the smaller being. But the guards were armed and they did have that powerful knockout gas. His escape attempt would have to wait. Joe picked up a small portion of the food. Placing the substance into in his mouth, he quickly spat it out.

"Why didn't you tell me it was so gross?" he yelled, spitting repeatedly to rid his mouth of the stale taste.

"You didn't ask," Andy replied, with a trace of satisfaction. His brother had always given him such a hard time that it was a special moment when he had the chance to even the score. "Besides, it's the only food we have to eat. So if you don't want to starve, you had better eat some."

"I'll take my chances with starving," came the reply.

The head creature did not seem to mind that Joe refused to eat. It only took a few moments for the creature to retie the prisoner's hands. The guards were then ordered to leave. The creatures continue to mumble amongst themselves, as they disappeared into the darkness outside the chamber. The head creature then walked over to the one chiseling. As far as the humans had noticed, the chiseler hadn't even raised its head during the entire feeding session. The head creature pointed to the rock the other had been working on and began to yell. The head creature then punched the chiseler square in the face, knocking him to the ground.

The head creature turned briefly to the humans, then left the room. The injured one slowly rose. A dim red glow radiating from its eyes, as it stared toward the exit. The creature wiped away a stream of yellow blood, which dripped from the corner of its mouth, then returned to work.

"I wonder what that was all about?" Andy whispered. not wanting to disturb the creature in its angry state.

"I have no idea. Maybe he chiseled a little where he shouldn't have," Joe answered trying to be funny.

The large rock slabs the brothers were lying on proved to be very uncomfortable. Their back and leg muscles ached, due to the inhospitable accommodations the creatures had provided. The chiseler stopped its work, but only long enough to toss a few more logs onto the fire. The growing pile of embers began to dry out the moisture in the air and in the human's clothing.

A sudden outburst of yells and screams, from outside the chamber, interrupted the quiet. The chiseler, obviously hearing some language that did not bode well, immediately dropped its tools and fled the room. Before Andy or Joe had a chance to speak, the creature returned. While it had been cautious in its first encounter with the prisoners, this time it showed no such inhibition. The creature rushed up to Andy, yelling uncontrollably. The red glow had returned to its eyes, this time directed at the humans rather than a fellow creature. After carrying on for some time, the creature stopped its ranting. It pointed at the prisoners, then toward the door. A puzzled look came over its grotesque features, as it stared quizzically at Andy. Several tense moments followed, as countless creatures rushed by the doorway of the chamber, obviously in an angered state. Clearly disturbed that Andy did not respond to its yelling, the creature turned away, resuming its work. Andy and Joe were left speechless, not knowing that Bill and Ken had caused the commotion with their escape.

"What do you make of all the yelling?" Joe asked. He kept a keen eye on the doorway, but corridor outside had grown quiet. "It looks like these creatures lose their tempers easily."

"I don't know what's going on, but I don't like the way that thing yelled at me. For a second, I thought it was going to attack. I think it is about time we started to think of a way out of here."

"I think you're right," Joe agreed. "I'm beginning to hate this place. Do you have any ideas on how to escape?"

"First, I have to figure a way out of these ropes," Andy said, struggling to pull his hands apart.

"Is that all you're worried about? Getting the ropes off?" Joe said, glancing over to the chiseler, whose back faced the prisoners. He rolled onto his side, so that Andy had a clear view, then simply pulled his hands apart. The binds fell silently to the ground.

"How did you do that?" Andy whispered, trying to duplicate the feat.

"It's a trick I learned while training for the Protectors," he answered with a smile of accomplishment. The creature looked up to see why the prisoners were talking, but quickly returned to its work, not wanting to risk another reprimand from its superior. Joe pulled his knees up to his chest, untying the binds around his ankles. "The problem is, how to get away from this guy. All he has to do to stop us is knock us out again with that gas."

"I have an idea," Andy said. "I'll get his attention, then you come up behind and strangle him."

Joe picked up one of the discarded ropes, stretching it between his hands. "I hope they have windpipes that are as vulnerable as ours," he said, taking a prone position on the slab.

Andy began to moan, as if in pain. The creature looked up for a moment, its eyes still glowing red, then returned to its work. Andy gave a questioned look over to Joe, who just shrugged in response. Andy moaned again, this time a little louder. The creature angrily threw its chisel against the wall, before rising to its feet. As it moved closer, Andy could see a stream of blood still flowing from its mouth.

The prisoner raised his hands in a manner to show that the binds were too tight. But the ploy was unnecessary. Joe had already slipped off the slab and had begun his silent but rapid sprint toward the creature. The chiseler was taken totally by surprise, as Joe wrapped the rope around its neck and slammed it to the ground. The creature seemed quite strong for its size, as it struggled to free itself. Andy immediately slipped off the slab, flopping onto the creature's legs, not knowing if this he was actually helping his brother. The stunned creature turned its head to yell, its eyes burning a deeper and brighter red, but no sounds came out of its mouth. When it became apparent that the creature could not match Joe's strength, the former member of the Protector's police force grabbed his victim's head, snapping its neck.

"It's kind of an old fashioned way to get somebody's attention, but it always works," Andy said, while Joe untied him.

"Let's just hope we don't have to try it again," Joe replied. He hurriedly dragged the body behind a slab, hiding it out of instinct rather than purpose.

The brothers each picked up a spear from the pile by the door, before fleeing the room. Unfortunately, there were no light sources in the hallway. By the feeble flames of the fire in the chamber, they were able to make out that the crushed rock floor of the passage sloped down to the left and rose to the right. Making an instant decision that it would be wiser to go up rather than descend deeper into the caves, the duo made off in that direction.

Once away from the fire, the darkness was total. In order to keep some sense of direction, one hand was kept on the right wall at all times. Like the chamber they had just left, the walls and floor of the corridor were moist, housing numerous patches of slime. The escapees scampered as fast as possible over the irregular floor of the tunnel, spears raised in case they happened to run into one of the creatures in the dark. The brothers stopped several times, listening for pursuers, but the passages were silent. After rushing through the tunnels for approximately fifteen minutes, they slowed down to a brisk walk. Their escape, aided by the fact that most of the creatures were outside chasing the other two time travelers, proved to be very effective.

The tunnel seemed to twist at unpredictable intervals. Occasionally they would come across a branch or intersection, but they continued with their strategy of keeping one hand on the right hand wall. The higher they rose, the drier the passages became. Soon they could feel no moisture at all on the walls. A half hour into their escape they slowed to a casual walk, sensing that they were going the wrong way.

The slope of the passage had leveled somewhat, but continued along a gradual incline. After making another right hand turn, the brothers found themselves in a medium sized alcove, with no exits. Wishing to regroup their escape effort, they decided to take refuge in the chamber.

The floor of the room, elevated slightly over the passage outside, was dry and covered with a thick layer of dust. Old fragile cobwebs cluttered every corner of the chamber. An eerie glow, seemingly emanating from the walls, lit the room enough for the brothers to study its features.

Off in a far corner, they discovered a rotten wooden table, covered with a hard layer of mould. The wood was so decomposed that it appeared that the integrity of the object was preserved entirely by the fungus. An assortment of broken arrows and torch stubs were piled up under the table, as if hastily swept there many years ago. Every object they saw was buried deep in the dust.

"It looks as if no one has been in here for a long time," Joe said, rummaging through the pile of debris. With the help of the mysterious glow, which was not visible while they were in the corridor, he was able to pick through the items with little difficulty.

"I wonder what's in that chest?" Andy asked, moving toward the object, glancing around defensively as he did so.

Hidden in one corner of the room sat an old metal and wood chest. He noticed that the metal corners and reinforcements of the object depicted intricate designs. If the light had been stronger he would have been able to make out more detail, but it appeared that different animals were etched into the once polished surface. A single rusted spike, dangling from a latch, held the lid closed. With little effort, Andy removed the rudimentary lock.

The wooden lid of the chest crumbled under Andy's touch. He let out a soft gasp, as he saw what lay inside. A skeleton, which looked remarkably close to that of a human, lie in a near fetal position. Decayed cloth, draped around the bones, showed the age of the chest's contents. Several inches of black ash partially buried the skeleton, making the perfect background for the tarnished gold pendant, which hung from its neck.

"I wonder how long he's been in there?" Joe asked, bending down to look at the decaying skeleton. The bones were obviously discolored due to the length of time that had passed since the owner died.

Andy gently removed the pendant from the skeleton's neck. A small crystal-like globe had been secured to the chain by several strips of gold. Not wishing to damage the fragile object, he gently polished the pendant with his shirt, removing some of the tarnish. "This looks as if it is real gold," he said, trying to study the details of the object.

As he spoke, the yellow globe on the chain began to glow a pale amber. For a moment, Andy thought his eyes were playing tricks on him, until the image of an old man appeared. Only the face of the figure fit into the sphere. The man had long grey hair combed straight back over his head, while several long wrinkles creased the his forehead. After a few moments the image disappeared.

"Who do you suppose that was?" Andy asked in astonishment. He looked at Joe, who also witnessed the sight. "It almost looked as if he were human."

"You know that can't be. According to your friends, we are one million years in our..."

The sound of creatures walking toward them in the passage interrupted Joe. A genuine fear spread across his face, as he pushed his brother. "Quick, hide behind the chest."

The brothers crouched in the corner, holding their spears tightly in front of them. A creature stopped by the doorway, peering into the room. The dark outline of another stopped next to it, said something, then started to enter the chamber. The first creature violently pulled his companion back, before it was able to cross the threshold. They briefly exchanged words, then continued up the passage. The escapees stayed behind the chest for several minutes, until they were sure the creatures were out of hearing distance.

"That was close," Andy said, walking back to the front of the chest. He fished through the ashes with his hand looking for other artifacts, but found none.

"We have to find a way out of here. We've been running through these tunnels for half an hour, and haven't come close to finding an exit," Joe said, peering out into the passageway. "I don't know whether we should turn around and go back the way we came, or keep going this way."

"Maybe we should rest here for a while," Andy suggested. "The creatures have already passed us, so they probably won't check back here again. Besides, did you see how that creature pulled the other one out of here. I think they are afraid of this room."

"Maybe so, but I don't want to hang around too long," Joe replied. He found a clean spot on the floor and sat down. "If we don't find a way out of these caves, we're going to end up like that guy in the chest."

Andy sat down next to his brother to study the pendant. A moment or two later, the image of the old man appeared again. This time the picture was not static. The man's facial expression seemed to change from a happy one to sad. Then, as before, the image disappeared without warning.

Andy awakened from his daydream, slapped back into reality by a dripping sound. He was stunned by the noise, positive that it had not been present when they entered the room. The slow dripping quickly hastened. When he rose, he found a small stream of water flowing through a hole near the ceiling of the opposite wall. The water quickly formed a puddle on the previously dry floor.

"Should I?" Andy asked his brother. His mouth felt dry and parched.

"Maybe test just a little," Joe said, moving over to the puddle. "We are going to need water."

Andy allowed the stream to cascade into his cupped hands. The liquid felt cold on his skin. He sniffed the water, but no smell made its way into his nostrils. Allowing himself a small sip, he smiled as he returned his hands under the stream.

"It tastes great," Andy informed Joe, filling his hands a second time.

Joe followed, but only drank enough to wet his mouth. "Even if it is safe, I've learned that strange foods and drink can cause havoc to our digestive systems. We're going to need to be as fit as possible to escape from these creatures," Joe said, as if drawing his words in part from a government training manual.

Before leaving the safety of the chamber, Andy rummaged through the chest one last time. Hoping to find something that would indicate why the skeleton was buried in the chest or why the pendant sporadically displayed a picture of an old man, he reached his hand all the way to the bottom of the makeshift casket. As with his prior search, he found nothing.

Joe reasoned that if they continued to follow the passages upward, sooner or later they would exit the mountain. The twists and turns of the tunnel seemed to become more frequent, as they blindly navigated through rock outcroppings and low ceilings. Several times they were forced to squeeze through very narrow openings. Ten minutes after leaving the mysterious skeleton room, they came upon a Y-intersection. Low voices could be heard down the right hand passage, probably the voices of the two creatures who they had seen earlier. A cool inviting breeze blew down the tunnel to the left.

"This doesn't seem to be a tough decision," Joe said, immediately moving toward the left. "I don't want to be captured by those creatures again. I have a feeling they won't be too kind to us next time around."

Though the humans could not see the creatures in the pitch black of the tunnel, the creatures were able to spot the escapees. The sudden yelling and quickly closing footsteps were all that was needed to spur Andy and Joe forward. As the fleeing pair turned a corner, their eyes were momentarily shocked by a dim white spot of light in the distance.

"I think it is an exit," Andy yelled over his heavy breath.

"I hope so. I think those creatures are gaining on us," Joe answered. With a sudden burst of speed, he ran past the tiring Andy.

As the duo closed in on the faint spot of light, the force of the wind increased. The gusting wind circled through the many cracks and crevices of the cave walls, causing a disenchanted melody to echo through the tunnel. The slope of the passage suddenly increased, as the humans found themselves scaling an almost vertical wall of rock. The voices of the pursuing creatures were definitely louder, but neither brother took the time to glance back.

Even in the darkness, Andy and Joe were able to find the necessary foot and hand holds to climb the wall of rock. Careful not to lose grip of their only weapons, they used all of their remaining strength to pull themselves up to the platform, where they hoped to find an exit. An array of twinkling stars greeted them, only ten feet away through a wide tunnel.

Joe glanced down the rocky cliff, spotting two creatures only several yards behind. "We'll get them outside," he said to Andy, who had already moved toward the exit.

A moonlit sky and bitter cold greeted them, as they stepped from the protection of the cave. The cold was the least of their worries, as they were surprised to find themselves high atop the mountain range, with sheets of ice littering the steeply sloped landscape. Andy was the first to slip on a patch of the frozen liquid, causing him to tumble down the sharp incline. He slid about twenty feet, before managing to grab hold of a large bush.

The pain he felt was instant. The bush he had chosen to stop his slide was covered by half inch thorns. The sharp spikes dug into the flesh of his hands, instantly covering them with blood. The pain shot up his arms into his head, but he had to hang on, or risk sliding down the mountain side to his death.

Joe had no time to react to Andy's misfortune. Though he was a step behind his brother, his momentum carried him onto the same patch of ice. Joe also managed to stop his slide, luckily grabbing hold of a bush without thorns. The danger was not over, however, as he looked up to see five creatures exit the cave.

"They brought some friends," Joe said, anticipating only two.

The creatures quickly spotted the humans, who were struggling to stabilize themselves on the slippery ice and snow. The creatures had no problem navigating the ice, as their rough sticky feet prevented them from slipping. Evidently the creatures were in no mood to recapture the humans. The quintet raised their spears, obviously in a manner to kill, then slowly edged down the ice covered slope. Sinister grins appeared on each of their sullen faces.

A quick glance down the mountain revealed that sliding down the slope would indeed be suicide, as a deadly cliff lay several hundred feet away. Andy, sensing death, buried his head in the frozen ground, waiting for the first spear to enter his body.

Just then, like the sound of thunder, machine gun fire filled the air. The stunned creatures were pelted by a barrage of bullets. One by one, the dead bodies slid down the slope of the icy mountain. After hearing the shots, Andy lifted his head, just in time to see one of the creatures cascade directly into his face. The beast's scaly skin scratched his exposed flesh, while its foul yellow blood oozed into the wounds.

The machine gun fire lasted only a few seconds, before returning the evening to a peaceful quiet. Andy slowly removed a hand from the thorn bush, pushing the dead creature away. The corpse slid down the mountain, catching onto a bush several yards below. Andy then turned his attention to his hands. The thorns had severely sliced through his fingers and palms. Blood flowed freely from the gashes.

Joe steadied himself with a bush and struggled to a safe location near the cave entrance. "Hey, are you all right?" he shouted to his brother.

"Yes, except for my hands. They are badly cut. What happened?" he asked, looking at the yellow blood stained ice.

"I don't know, but there is only one person in this time with a machine gun."

Andy found that the yellow blood was quick to freeze, which added much needed traction to the ice. He crawled up the slope on his side, trying his best to protect his badly injured hands. Joe met his brother halfway and helped him to his feet. Together they were able to reach the level terrain near the cave entrance.

Safe for the time being, they were afforded the luxury of scanning the side of the mountain in detail. Leafless bushes were scattered across the landscape. Off in the distance they could see the shadows of a forest. Joe looked up at the peaks of the mountain, which loomed only a couple hundred feet above. A freezing wind blew into his face causing him to turn away. The cold temperature quickly began to freeze the moisture on their clothing, sending shivers through their bodies.

"I don't like this," Joe said, eyeing his surroundings. "It is too dark for us to try to get down tonight. Maybe we should rest inside until morning."

"Do you see the rebel anywhere?" Andy asked through chattering teeth. His hot breath turned to fog as he spoke.

Joe scanned the mountain side again, but found no sign of the rebel or anyone else. "No, I don't see him. It's too dark to get a good look around. He could be hiding anywhere. Come on out," Joe yelled, but as expected there was no reply.

"I guess we should go in," Andy replied, cringing at the pain shooting through his arms.

"It even looks too dangerous to go about collecting brush for a fire."

"Yes, but it wasn't too cold inside," Andy said, moving toward the tunnel. "Hopefully morning isn't too far off."

The brothers walked into the tunnel, finding a spot near the wall of the rocks they had only moments before hurriedly scaled. Blocked from the chilling wind, they were able to find a comfortable place to rest during the remainder of the night. Though neither actually fell into a deep sleep, they were able to doze lightly and refresh their energy.

At the first sign of daylight they returned to the entrance of the cave. The dangerous and painful slide down the mountain the night before could have been avoided had the brothers known the landscape. A narrow path, partially formed by carefully aligned rocks, to the left of the cave entrance led up to what appeared to be a gigantic staircase leading down the side of the mountain. As the duo navigated over the ice covered path, they could see a complete line of rock slabs zig-zagging down the side of the mountain, disappearing into the green forest far below.

"I dropped my spear," Andy said, trying to fight through the pain in his still aching hands. Although the weapon would be no use to him now that his hands were damaged, he felt slightly guilty.

"Don't worry about it," Joe answered with sincerity. He had never seen his brother is so much pain. "We'll be okay. I still have mine. Luckily, I dropped it by the cave entrance."

"It sure is cold up here. I think we would be better off in the cave," Andy said in a faltering voice. The severity of the pain mounted in his hands and arms.

"If we go back in there, we might never find our way out again. I think we should try the stairs. If we can make it to the forest, we should be all right," Joe stated. Together they inched over to the top step.

"So this is what they do with the rock slabs. They make stairs out of them," Andy observed. The wry grin on his thin face would have been humorous, had it not been mixed with a grimace of pain. "There must be thousands of them to make such a long stairway."

"If you want, you can count them on the way down," joked Joe.

The stairs were six feet long, three feet wide, and one foot thick. A mysterious heat radiating from the slabs benefited the humans in two ways. First, it offered them minor relief from the bitter cold. Second, it prevented any ice from forming, allowing the escapees to travel rather quickly.

Andy followed a step or two behind his brother. He held his arms crossed about his chest, keeping his hands elevated at shoulder height. While Joe scanned the surrounding forest, in search of the field where they left the time machine, Andy just concentrated on his brother's feet and trying to minimize the pain in his hands. To Joe's surprise, not only could he not find the field in question, he couldn't see any fields at all. The thick forest continued unbroken in all directions.

"We must have wandered a long way in those caves," Joe said, fighting off a mild panic. Without a location to aim for, he suddenly felt lost. "I don't even see the cliff where we entered the caves."

"We traveled to the right the whole time we were in the caves, so the cliffs must be somewhere to our left," Andy suggested, struggling to lift his head and look in that direction. The pain now throbbed throughout his entire body, causing him great discomfort. The flow of blood from the wounds had stopped, but the significant amount he had lost was still wet on his hands and arms.

"We can't go by that," Joe objected. "Just because we went to the right the whole time doesn't mean the time machine is to our left. We could have been walking around in circles most of the time. Plus, we don't even know where we started. The creatures could have taken us anywhere, while we were unconscious. I'm afraid the time machine could be anywhere out there," he finished with a wave of his arm in the general direction of the forest. Andy silently agreed.

Even though the slabs generated heat, they offered no protection from the whipping winds. As the cold seeped into their muscles, they were forced to slow to a more moderate pace. The stairway ahead rose and fell over small hills and troughs, swerving to the left and right, following the terrain of the mountain. The shelter of the forest seemed miles away from the frozen time travelers.

"I think my whole body is frostbitten. I can't feel a thing in my feet," Andy said, with another grimace of pain. The throbbing made even speaking difficult. His neck had swollen and his frozen arms had very little movement.

"I'm pretty cold myself, but there is nothing we can do about it. We just have to keep on walking. The forest doesn't seem that far away anymore," Joe said, trying to lift the spirits of his brother. He exhaled into his cupped hands trying to warm them, before shoving them back into his pant pockets. "Now that I think of it, maybe we should have gone back into the caves," he whispered to himself.

Twenty minutes into the journey down the slab steps, the forest still appeared to be an eternity away. A quick glance back up the mountain revealed that they had indeed covered significant ground. Joe estimated that they were halfway to their destination.

"This might be a good time for a rest," Joe said, as he helped his brother lie down.

A refreshing warmth spread through Andy, as his body made full contact with the rock slab. In an ironic twist of fate, the same rock slabs that he had been placed on upon capture were now vital to his existence. Once providing an unwanted cool damp moisture to his aching muscles, they now provided much needed warmth to his frozen body. He breathed a sigh of comfort, as he curled up to rest. The ice and snow had long since disappeared from the mountain side, but the temperature, although warming slightly, still presented a problem. The sun sat high in the sky, but gave little relief to the two frozen bodies.

"We better not stay too long," Joe warned, as he flattened his weary body against the rock slab. "If we fall asleep up here, we will freeze to death for sure."

After a brief rest, the two struggled to their feet, continuing their march toward the forest. Soon after resuming, Andy's entire body turned numb. His arms especially were tingling with a pins and needles sensation. He actually welcomed the numbness, however, as it almost completely masked the pain in his shredded hands. Only the sight of the forest, and the burning desire not to fail in front of his brother, kept him moving.

The trek was no picnic for Joe either. He had given his leather jacket to his brother, after their brief rest. His hands and feet quickly succumbed to the cold temperature, while a thin layer of ice formed on his light weight clothing. Even his training for the Protectors had not prepared him for battling mother nature's extreme weather. More than once, eyes closed to only a slit to fend off the wind, he tripped. Too tired to stop himself, he let his weary body tumble down the steps, until it came to a rest on its own.

Although it seemed like it would never end, the bitter journey down the stairs did not last forever. After forty-five minutes of walking and falling they finally reached the fringe of the forest, where the stairs continued unabated into the depths of the trees. Though warmer air now surrounded them, their frozen bodies were not able to fully appreciate the moderate heat that the vegetation held. Joe led the silent march for several more minutes, before deciding to take another rest. He found a tree with low lying branches and climbed underneath to gain maximum protection from the elements.

"Now that we made it here, what do we do?" Andy asked. His words were soft and choppy. The numbness had begun to subside, returning the pain to his battered body.

"Here, take a cigarette. It will warm you up," Joe said, fumbling to remove one from the package. His fingers were swollen and very white. "I just hope my light has enough energy in it."

He pulled out a small odd shaped object. The base of the device was in the form of a circle, which quickly tapered off to a point at the top. Joe pushed the point to one side. After a few seconds delay, a small flame appeared.

Andy looked at the lighter with an angry stare. Bill had invented it many years ago, long before the time machine was even a thought. The most important element of the lighter was the small energy cell located in the base of the object. The cell was designed specifically to absorb heat energy, provided by the owner's body. The self charging characteristic of the cell allows for the lighter to be operational for nearly a decade. Andy's anger was directed at the Protectors. As was their practice, inventors were given no credit for the work they performed.

After lighting Andy's cigarette, Joe lit one for himself. As Andy inhaled the soothing smoke, he found that the many additives in the tobacco helped alleviate his pain, but not nearly as much as he would have preferred. Joe busied himself by pulling down several dead branches. Together with a handful of dried twigs, he was able to build a small comfortable fire. The flames fluttered in the light wind that was able to sneak through the drooping branches of the tree, but were strong enough to provide significant heat. The branch structure of the tree acted as insulation, allowing the brothers to enjoy a warm refuge.

Eager to warm the air even more, Joe continued to add branches to the fire. The warmth quickly began to offset the damage that had been done during their long trek down the stairway. But Joe's eagerness also showed his ignorance in the matter of campfires. As the flames leaped higher, they began to dance along the lower limbs. The fact that the live limbs were just as flammable as the dead ones he used for fuel didn't occur to him until several branches exploded into flames.

"Put it out," Andy cried, jumping up from his comfortable sitting position.

"I'm trying," Joe replied, beating the burning branches with a stick.

Unfortunately, the flames could not be stopped. As the flames jumped from one limb to another, the brothers were forced out into the open. Sensing that he could not stop the spreading fire, Joe dropped his stick and ushered his brother away from the flaming tree. Not content to destroy just one tree, the flames quickly spread to neighboring vegetation. Within several minutes, the fire had turned into a small inferno. The flames spread at such a rapid pace, Andy and Joe were forced to sprint down the slab stairs.

Huge billows of black smoke quickly filled the yellow tinted air, as hundreds of trees became engulfed in the flames. The wind whipped the smoke in circles, occasionally clouding the human's vision to the point where they could not see the next step in the staircase. The agonizing sound of burning animals, who were slow in escaping the sudden fire, could be heard from inside the blaze.

Joe and Andy found a comfortable speed, which allowed them to stay a safe distance ahead of the fire. The wind, aiding the spread of the flames, also carried warmed air to their bodies. As the brothers exited a cloud of thick smoke, they were shocked to find the end of the staircase. Even more troubling was what they saw scattered about. Four of the small creatures were lying in pools of their own yellow blood. They were apparently in the process of extending the stairway, as a pile of slabs could be seen a few yards away. Numerous bullet holes were visible all over the carcasses. One of them had been shot in the eye, allowing an orange jelly to spill out onto the ground.

"It looks like the rebel came this way," Joe observed, bending over a corpse. Hundreds of small insects had gathered on it, some of which were clearly devouring the flesh. But it was another type of insect that caught his attention. Small insects, no larger than a flea, were sucking up the spilled blood. The insects grew to the size of a golf ball, before taking flight. Joe estimated that at least fifty of the insects were struggling to fly away with their meals. "Never seen anything like this."

"Let's get moving. The fire is getting closer," reminded Andy.

The fire continued to spread and consume all that lie its path. The brothers watched in astonishment, as the flames rapidly jumped from tree to tree. Now that the stairway had ended, they were forced to make a decision on which direction to travel. Seeing that they did not recognize any landmarks, and for no other reason than the desire to leave the cold air as quickly as possible, they chose the route of greatest descent. The forest was not tightly packed and offered very little underbrush to slow their pace. The path they followed led them in a north-eastern direction.

Their sprint through the forest did not last long, abruptly ending at a gigantic fissure in the earth. The fissure stretched over two hundred feet across, running directly into the mountains and ending at a steep rocky cliff. To the right, the fissure ran out of sight into the jungle. In the depths of the massive crack, hundreds of feet below, they could see an inviting stream. The water cascaded freely down a steep waterfall, fueled by the snow capped mountain peaks, before slowing its pace along the meandering stream. Green vegetation grew in abundance at the bottom of the depression.

"I bet it's warm down there," Joe said.

"The water sure looks good, too," Andy added, remembering that the only thing he had to drink recently was the few mouthfuls of water consumed in the room where he had found the pendant. Just the sight of the vivid blue stream caused his mouth to grow dry. A quick glance showed that the walls of the fissure were plain and featureless, providing no obvious access to the bottom.

"What do we do now?" Joe asked, looking back at the fire. The flames were several hundred yards back, but closing fast. "We can't go back through that, and there doesn't seem to be a way across."

Andy gazed across the fissure, shocked to see the dark figure of the rebel standing on the opposite side. The rebel was waving one arm and pointing down the side of mountain with the other. After a few moments, the rebel seemed to become agitated, disappearing into the murky forest.

"There must be a way across," Andy said, looking into the fissure. "If he can get across, then we should be able to."

Joe carefully walked to the very edge of the fissure, looking lengthwise down the chasm to where the rebel had pointed. The air was clouded, due to the massive amounts of smoke billowing into the air, but the clear outline of a small bridge could been seen about a half mile away.

"Come on," Joe said, telling his brother about the bridge. "It looks like our only option. I hope we can reach it before the fire reaches us."

The fire had closed considerably upon the humans, while they were standing idle. As they pressed east, down a sloping terrain, they were suddenly hampered by a thickening underbrush. They scrambled as fast as they could, deviating their route as necessary to avoid patches of thorns and outcroppings of rock. Fifteen minutes later they arrived at the bridge.

The structure was not what they had expected, living their entire lives among steel, brick, and cement. Their lifeline, and perhaps only chance of escaping from the spreading flames, was constructed entirely out of vines. There were no walls or guide lines to aid in crossing, just a five foot wide fabric of woven vegetation. The condition of the vines, obviously dry and old, did not give much confidence that they could hold the weight of a human. At the opposite side of the bridge, a clear path could be seen leading into the forest.

Suddenly, the rebel appeared from the shadows of the forest onto the path. Obviously out of breath, he bent over with his hands on his knees, trying to recover from his sprint. Seeing the brothers, he lifted one arm, motioning for the two to follow. Joe yelled across the fissure, asking the rebel to wait, but the man disappeared into the forest as soon as Joe stepped onto the bridge.

"He is going to be sorry, when I catch up to him," Joe yelled angrily. He backed off the bridge, unsure of a crossing strategy. "I'll go first. I doubt it will hold the weight of both of us. If I make it across, then we will know it will be able to hold you."

"Joe, this looks awfully dangerous," Andy protested. "There has be another way."

Joe looked down the length of the fissure, not seeing any other bridges spanning the gap. To make the situation even more dire, the fire had spread down the mountain side past where they now stood. It did not appear that they could win a race against the flames. "I'm afraid this is it," Joe told his brother. "We're trapped."

"Remind me never to let you play with fire again," Andy said, eyeing the fragile bridge.

Joe slowly crept out onto the structure, deciding that walking upright was akin to committing suicide. The bridge began to sway gradually back and forth under his weight. Trying his best to keep his body weight centered, he used his fingers to find holds in the tight weave. The vines stretched and creaked with his every move, but they gave no indication that they were not up to the task. It did not take him long to find a successful crawling technique, allowing him to cover ground rather quickly. Thankfully, the weave of the vines was very tight, preventing him from seeing the ground so far below.

Progress was smooth, until reaching the middle of the fissure, where the wind began to swirl wildly. As if a puppet to the wind, the bridge began to sway. The movement was slow at first, quickly becoming violent. The bridge moved a bit too far to the right, forcing Joe's legs to slip over the left side. The muscles in his arms bulged, as he used all his strength to grasp onto the vines. Determined not to panic, he kept his thoughts focused on the task at hand. Counteracting the effects of the wind by shifting his body weight, he was able to stabilize the bridge, until the wind died down.

Once safely back into his crawling position, he glanced back at his brother, who eagerly watched from the edge. The flames of the forest fire appeared to be precariously close to Andy, who seemed not to notice anything except his brother crawling dangerously along an old bridge hundreds of feet above the ground.

The wind did not stir up any more problems, allowing Joe to complete his crossing safely. Upon reaching solid ground, he quickly sprinted along the path in search of the rebel, but found no trace of him. Returning to the fissure, he found Andy only five feet onto the bridge.

"Come on, Andy. It was easy. You'll have no problem," Joe yelled, but his brother gave no indication that he heard the words.

Andy was frozen, second thoughts running through his mind. He had seen the difficulty Joe had run into, when the wind had tossed the bridge about. Even if his hands were in perfect condition, he knew that he would have problems maintaining his balance in such a situation. But he had no choice but to proceed. The flames were dreadfully close. Turning around, he watched the flames engulf the trees nearest to the bridge. With his practically useless, battered hands as guides, he slowly crawled onward.

Joe cringed, noticing how slow Andy was moving. The flames were now tickling the bridge's moorings. For the most part the wind stayed calm, combining with Andy's slow methodical movements, to keep the bridge steady. But the wind was not about to stay friendly for long. As he neared the midway point of the fissure, the same spot where Joe encounter his problems, a gust of wind shook the structure. Andy was forced, in a sudden flood of panic, to grab onto the vines with his hands.

Pain screamed throughout his hands and arms, as the rough vine material scratched open his healing wounds.

Andy let out an ear piercing scream, which sliced through the wind like a knife. Joe stood in a helpless horror, as his brother's cries reached his ears. Andy's screams were not the only reason for Joe's horror, however. As if in slow motion, a flaming tree tumbled to the ground, landing squarely on the bridge. The fire instantly leapt from the tree to the dry vines.

Andy closed his eyes, holding on tight, as the wind died down and the bridge stabilized. He did not attribute the last rumbling of the bridge to the tree, but instead the wind. Once again, fright had frozen his muscles.

"Hurry," Joe yelled, not wanting to panic Andy even more by notifying him of the progress of the flames.

Andy slowly inched forward, totally unaware that the end of the bridge behind him was engulfed in flames. His body shook violently out of fright, tears streaming down his pain riddled face. Andy glanced up at his brother, noticing the concern on his face. Something deep in Andy's mind told him he was in trouble. Not wanting to, but knowing that he must, Andy looked back at the fire. His heart almost stopped, as he saw the flames dancing along the bridge.

With the face of death lingering even closer, Andy quickened his pace. The pain in his hands reached an unbearable stage. He actually contemplated letting go, allowing his tortured body to sail through the air to the ground below, thus relieving himself of the pain. Before he could make that fateful decision, a loud snap of fire filled the air. Hearing this, Andy instinctively clutched to the bridge with all his remaining strength, waiting for the inevitable. He was only twenty feet from safety, when the bridge burnt away from the earth, swinging poetically into the fissure.

Time seemed to alter itself, now progressing in slow motion. Andy felt the breeze whistle through the tiny holes in the woven vines, as the flaming bridge and his body floated through the air. From up above he could hear the screams of his brother, also in slow motion. Time righted itself, as Andy slammed forcefully into the rock cliff. His grip on the vines was strong, however, and his will to live suddenly even stronger. Both his arms became covered by bright red blood, as the rough vines ripped open new and old wounds. Andy felt a weightless sensation, as he bounced off the cliff, only to return moments later with another forceful jolt.

The bridge immediately stopped swaying, leaving Andy only yards from safety. But the flames were still there, eating ravenously at the vulnerable vines. Billows of smoke floated up through the air, finding their way into his lungs, causing him to gasp for fresh air. He could feel the heat creeping closer, but dared not look down at the flames. His thoughts of death were interrupted by a yell from above.

"Hang on while I pull you up," Joe yelled, tugging fiercely at the burning bridge. Adrenaline pumped through his body, offering him the assistance needed to lift his brother toward safety.

Andy held on, his body stiff and rigid. Blood flowed freely from his wounds, but he didn't notice. Joe's pulling caused the bridge to rock back and forth from the cliff, rattling Andy's body with every tug. The fire had already consumed half the bridge, and would reach Andy in a matter of seconds. With one final burst of strength, Joe pulled Andy over the edge and safely to the ground.

The younger Marshall lay motionless, his bloodied hands still clutching to the vines. Flames began to poke over the edge of the fissure, as Joe rolled his brother off to one side. Andy looked up to the sky, still not fully comprehending that he had survived the ordeal. The flames leaped over the edge of the fissure for several seconds, before consuming all the fuel available. White smoke continued to rise from the roasted bridge, but there was no threat that the inferno, still raging on the far side of the fissure, would cross the gap.

"I knew you would make it. Didn't I tell you it would be easy?" Joe said, helping his bother to his feet. "That was nothing compared to some of the stunts we did while training for the Protectors."

"I'd rather not hear about them," Andy managed to say through tight lips. His face cringed with every movement he made. The pain in his arms was excruciating, while Joe's apparent lack of concern over his pain disturbed him greatly. Did Joe really care about his well being, or did he view everything that was happening to them as just a game.

"The rebel is gone," Joe said, placing his hand on Andy's back, as a gesture of support. "I suppose we will catch up to him sooner or later. I doubt he will want to stay isolated in a place like this."

"At this point, I don't really care," Andy replied. "My hands hurt so bad."

"I know," Joe answered, taking a closer look at the injuries. "There is nothing we can do for them now. We need to find some water to clean the dirt out. After that we can dress it with a shirt. But we need to find the water first."

The cool mountain air seemed refreshing, now that the temperature had warmed significantly since their exit from the cave. The slight breeze actually numbed the pain of Andy's injuries, soothingly caressing his hands. Once again, the painful wounds began to dry. Andy couldn't believe the streak of bad luck that descended upon him. Getting captured by the little creatures was bad enough, but he escaped them with little harm. The painful events started them moment he slipped on the ice and became acquainted with a thorn bush. After the thorns, the bitter cold ravaged his body, only to be followed up with a hectic ride on a burning vine bridge. He doubted very seriously if he would be able to survive any more life threatening encounters.

The small path they followed hadn't been used for some time. They passed single file over the moderate vegetation, with Andy lagging several yards behind. The fire still raged on behind them, casting huge billows of smoke into the once clean air. While grey puffs of smoke still clouded their vision, it was not nearly as bad as the constant pollution they were subject to back in their own time.

A few multi-colored birds could be seen circling the two travelers. They were squealing violently, undoubtedly because they had just been burnt out of their nests. The birds made several passes, flying closer with each attempt, until their boredom carried them off to other places. The path ran along a north eastern route, gradually descending the slope of the mountain. Joe kept expecting to see the rebel dart from the trees, attempting an ambush, but that did not happen.

A half hour of walking led them to a large rock, where they decided to stop and take a much deserved rest. The sun seemed to be lowering itself over the mountain tops, a clear signal that the brothers were on the wrong side of the mountain; but this went unobserved by both. Andy was too caught up in his pain to give any significant thought to where they were heading. Joe, with all of his military style training, failed to even consider using the sun to aid with direction. His battles were fought in the cluttered city streets he once called home, not out in the vast openness that surrounded them. As they sat in silence, they noticed that the forest had grown silent as well.

"Why do you suppose the rebel keeps waving to us?" Andy asked.

"He wants us to follow him, but I have no idea why. If I were him, I wouldn't even come close to us."

"Well he hasn't come close to us yet. Every time we see him he runs away."

"He'll get his," Joe said with bitterness. "You know, it's actually his fault that we are here right now. If he hadn't burst into the apartment, we wouldn't be here."

"Where would we be, Joe? In prison?" Andy snapped, remembering the events that led up to the time travel.

Joe stared up at the yellow tinted sky, not caring to respond. The snow capped peaks were just visible over the trees. He took a deep breath of the slowly clearing air, then rose to his feet. "I think we had better get moving."

"Yes, I can't wait to get back to the time machine and have my hands fixed up. I think Bill has some first aid material stowed away somewhere."

A short distance later the path branched. One route slanted off to the left on an uphill slope, while the other continued along a gradual descent. There was no mistaking which direction the rebel intended the brothers to follow. A huge arrow, formed out of tree branches, pointed to the left.

"Should we follow it?" Andy asked.

"Sure," came the reply, "we have nothing else to do."

From that point on the slope of the path increased steadily. The higher they climbed, the cooler the air became. They soon began to question the wisdom of following the trail set out by the rebel, especially since the temperature would drop markedly once the sun set. After struggling up hill for a half hour, they exited the forest into a barren low ridge between two mountain peaks. A stiff cold wind blew down the depression directly into their faces. The brothers were not totally surprised to see a stairway, built out of the familiar rock slabs, leading both up and down the ridge.

"It's that creep again." Joe said, noticing the rebel. The dark outline of the unknown man stood at the top of the ridge, waving his gun in one hand, an obvious signal for the brothers to follow. "When we catch up to him, I've got an introduction he'll never forget."

"He still wants us to follow."

"But why does he want us to go over to the other side of the mountain?" Joe asked.

"I don't know why we didn't think of this sooner," Andy replied, as the revelation hit him. "We might be on the wrong side of the mountain. I bet that we passed all the way through, while we were running through the caves. That is why we couldn't see any fields or the cliff. We are on the wrong side of the mountain."

"That's not going to save him from me," Joe replied, breaking out into a sprint up the slab stairs.

The rebel was in no immediate danger from Joe, as he stood several hundred feet away, up a steep climb, but he disappeared over the mountain top none the less. Andy watched for a few moments, taking in a deep breath, before gathering enough strength to follow. As he climbed along the ridge, there were no trees to block his view of the large black cloud of smoke rising off in the distance. All he could wonder was how many trees would be destroyed, before the fire burnt itself out.

The slabs turned out to be identical to the previous steps they had walked upon, as they also emitted a subtle heat. The air was not nearly as cold as that during their descent, but the persistent biting wind gnawed at their unprotected faces sending a chill through their bodies. At times, the brothers resorted to climbing the steps backwards, in an attempt to foil the wind.

The top of the ridge was significantly lower than the surrounding peaks, allowing Andy and Joe to reach it in only fifteen minutes. From their new vantage point, they could see that the mountain range was much larger than either had imagined. The field where they had landed stood off to the north, identified by the massive cliff where they had been attacked. The land to the west actually sat on a large plateau between another much smaller mountain range, which ran parallel to the one they stood upon. Beyond that range, it appeared as if the ground dropped off into a gigantic canyon. The fact that they could see no sign of the rebel made Joe all the more angry.

A glance back down to the base of the mountain at their rear revealed that it had already begun to darken with shadows. The thickly grown jungle ahead of them stood in complete sunlight. To their liking, the heat emitting stairs lead straight into the vegetation.

"There's the cliff over there," Joe said pointing to his right. The sun reflected brightly off the broken rocks. He quickly estimated that their destination lie two miles away, through a tangle of trees and vegetation. From where they stood, they could see no paths leading in the direction they wanted to follow.

"We must have gone a long way in the cave. I mean, we have already walked what seems like miles, and look how far away the cliff is," Andy noted. The thought of hiking the additional distance sickened him.

"Well, there is only one way to go," Joe added, as he started down the stairs. The swirling wind now blew at their backs, almost giving them a lift down the mountain.

It did not take long for the travelers to reach the bottom of the stairs. The strange slabs ended, just as the murky jungle began. The brothers welcomed the trapped heat of the jungle, after spending so much time battling the cold. The fact that no paths were available, coupled with the small amount of light able to filter through the tangled vegetation, made traveling quite difficult.

Once again the Joe was upset at not finding any trace of the rebel. Keeping in mind the general direction of the time machine, he led the struggle through the densely packed forest. Several times they had to take a detour to bypass a patch of land that was so tangled that passing was impossible. More time was lost, as they had to stop frequently to free themselves from thorny vines and prickly bushes. The first half mile of their journey took well over an hour and a half.

"Why would those creatures build a stairway leading into a tangled mess like this?" Andy asked, trying to squeeze his body through a wall of vines, without using his still aching hands.

"Maybe they're still working on clearing a path," Joe replied, carefully lifting a thorn covered branch, allowing his brother to pass.

"I don't think we are going to make it to the time machine before dark," Andy said, noting the dimming light.

"You're probably right. Let's keep an eye out for a place to spend the night."

After another hour of battling the jungle, they came to a small clearing. The clearing was not large by any stretch of the imagination, but there was enough room for both to find a comfortable place to sleep. Through the opening in the canopy of branches and leaves they could see the cloud filled sky darken with every passing moment. Though there still appeared to be ample daylight left, the low level of light reaching the floor of the jungle made traveling too dangerous.

Joe found a supply of dead wood to build a fire, hoping that it would keep the animals away. Learning from experience, he took the precaution to build the fire far enough away from the surrounding foliage, as not to start a sequel to his first inferno. Relief from the humidity came from a cool comfortable breeze blowing lazily through the jungle, carrying with it distant howls.

"You know this place is very strange," Andy said, taking a cigarette from Joe. "Not only are there creatures here that we have never heard of before, but the days seem to be much shorter than in our time. Did you notice that?"

"Yes, now that you mention it, they do seem shorter. It seems like it should be mid afternoon about now, not sunset," Joe replied, tossing a stick onto the fire.

"Joe," Andy said, pausing slightly before continuing, "I still don't understand why you work for the Protectors. After what they did to our parents, I'd think you would hate them."

"The Protectors didn't do anything to them," Joe replied, beginning a speech he had giving many times. "They were causing trouble. I looked the other way a million times. I kept warning them what would happen if they didn't stop, but they didn't listen to me. Besides, I really don't have much of a choice but to work for the Protectors. I can't quit. They have people watching me all the time. I have to stay loyal to them, or they would have me killed. And they don't just kill insiders like me, they torture them for weeks, just to prove a point to anyone else with a treasonous idea."

"How did they really find out about them, Joe? Did you turn them in?"

"No, I would never have done that," Joe snapped angrily. He silently thought back to the incident. "Someone else stumbled onto them. I did all I could, but it was too late. The Protectors had all the evidence they needed. They should have listened to me. I think I was starting to make progress with Mom, but Dad thought he could really change things."

"You could have gone underground. I'm sure the rebels would love to have someone with your knowledge on their side."

"I'm sure they would. But the way the underground runs their operation, I would be dead in a matter of weeks. The Rebels don't go more than two days without losing somebody. They are foolish to think that they can destroy the Protectors. I have seen how strong they are. They have more weapons and technology than your friend Bill could even begin to understand. But let me tell you something. I do have a hate for the Protectors. I have just never had the opportunity to do anything about it," he paused and threw another stick on the fire. "I don't want to talk about it any more."

The pain in Andy's hands had subsided considerably. Most of the wounds had dried up nicely, but the thickening scabs left relatively no mobility in his fingers. He counted seven serious wounds on his left hand and only four on his right, all caused by the initial confrontation with the thorn bush. Other less threatening wounds were scattered over his palms and fingers, mostly caused by the rough vines of the bridge. With great effort, he managed to pull out the pendant from underneath his shirt. "What do you make of this?"

The globe on the pendant gave off the same amber glow they had seen earlier. Within moments of Andy removing the piece of jewelry, the mysterious image of the old man appeared. As before, just a picture of his head filled the sphere. The man's two melancholy eyes were blank, as he stared and smiled at the two observers. A few moments later, he disappeared.

"It is probably just a picture of the person who used to be the skeleton," Joe suggested. "Although I have no idea how people in such a primitive place could have the technology to make something like that."

"Yes, but I know I saw his expression change before," Andy said examining the object. "If he is human, where are all the people. If this man used to live here, why aren't there any people here now?"

"I don't know, and I'm not worrying about it. The man is dead and nothing can change that. You can stay up looking at that thing if you want, but I'm going to get some sleep. We are going to have a long trip through this jungle, before we reach the time machine." With that, Joe turned toward the fire and fell asleep.

Curiosity still nagged Andy about the pendant. In the orange light of the fire, he took a closer look at the piece of jewelry. The yellow sphere, approximately three quarters of an inch in diameter, gave off a constant dim amber glow. The globe was attached to the chain by fragile looking gold leaves, apparently glued to the flawless surface. The leaves were covered by etchings, but the light was insufficient for Andy to comprehend the minute details. The gold chain had no clasp and no markings.

Andy found that he was strangely fond of the artifact. A fear of losing the piece of jewelry inexplicably spread throughout his body. Feeling protective, he replaced the pendant around his neck, tucking it into his shirt. The moment the sphere came to rest on his chest, the globe began to glow intensely. The light was so bright that Andy could see the illumination through his clothing. He quickly pulled the object free, ignoring the sudden spikes of pain in his hands. The image of the old man once again filled the sphere, his facial expression beaming with happiness. The man raised his fist in front of his face, waving it back and forth. He then extended his index finger, pointing it directly at Andy.

A frightful feeling came over Andy. He could have sworn that the man in the sphere was actually behaving in response to his presence. This was total nonsense, as Andy fully understood that no one could actually live in a piece of jewelry. But still, the eeriness of the situation caused Andy's heart rate to increase. The image slowly faded, returning the globe to its persistent dim amber state. Cautiously, Andy replaced the pendant under his shirt. He waited patiently for a few moments, expecting another outburst of light, but none came. The weary time traveler then curled up next to the fire, trying to fall asleep. The thoughts of the mysterious man in the sphere kept him awake for some time, but his exhausted body finally won out. Instantly, a dream filled his head. In it, he met the man inside the pendant.

The night passed peacefully. By the time the brothers awoke, the fire had long since burnt itself out. The sun had just risen over the snow capped peaks, though they could not see this due to the thick foliage. A few singing birds, along with the fact that no intruders stumbled upon them during the night, was all that lightened the travelers situation.

Joe relit the fire, then looked into the sky through the small openings in the trees. Dark rain clouds were sweeping through the atmosphere, carrying with them a silent threat of drenching rain. A passive search of the area revealed no small animals or any recognizable plant life to satisfy their breakfast hunger.

"How long do you think it will take us to reach the cave?" Andy asked, finally pulling a root from the ground with his right hand. He tapped the root against his leg to knock the loose soil free, before biting into the soft fibrous material. The juice inside made him cringe at its bitterness.

"I don't know. I would guess no longer than a couple of hours. It would take no time, if we could just find a clear path to follow," Joe answered, munching on a similar bitter root. He spat it out on the ground, before looking for a more promising food.

"Why do you think the rebel won't come out in the open with us? Surely he can't be afraid of us."

"No, I don't think he's afraid. He has the upper hand. We don't even have our spears anymore," Joe answered gritting his teeth. "Just wait until I catch up with him."

Abandoning their futile attempt to find food, they resumed their trek to the cliff. As with the previous day's travel, they were forced to struggle through thick tangled vegetation. Thorns and vines blocked what often appeared to be promising paths. The hungry sounds of the wild animals also dictated their route, but none of the creatures ever showed themselves. The temperature quickly rose, due to the greenhouse effect of the jungle, with the humidity level following. The thickening dark clouds, slowly floated over the mountains, darkening the entire sky.

As the brothers broke through a barrier of vegetation into a small clearing, a large bushy tree immediately caught their attention. The appearance of the tree was not nearly as interesting as what the tree was doing. The twenty foot tree was covered by rich green leaves and a multitude of bright purple flowers. The colorful flowers were what caused the tree to stand out amongst the rest of jungle plant life. The flowers were rapidly forming from small buds, opening their petals to the early morning sun. But as soon at the flowers were fully formed, the entire blossom dropped from the tree, floating gracefully to the ground. Another bud would immediately grow in place of the dead flower. The new bud would flower and also fall to the ground. Once on the ground, the petals seemed to decay at an accelerated rate. The process continued endlessly. The humans stood entranced, watching the sight in silence.

Andy awakened from his daydream, as a sharp pain rifled through his right leg. He glanced down to discover razor sharp shoots quickly growing from the soft ground.

"Move!" Andy yelled, pushing his brother, who was still caught in the trance of the flowering tree.

Joe looked down to see the six inch shoots sprouting ever taller. Struggling to pick their way through the living mine field, the shoots seemed to alter their growth pattern to follow. The humans were too quick for the shoots, however, making it to the edge of the clearing suffering only several minor pin point wounds on their lower legs.

"I've never seen anything grow so fast. Those sprouts would have skewered us like a couple pieces of meat" Joe said, with a heavy breath. The sprouts had surpassed twelve inches in height, with no signs of slowing.

Andy lifted up his pant legs, revealing numerous spots of blood. "We were lucky to make it out in time," he said, rubbing the wounds, with the back of his hands.

"It looks like they got you pretty bad," Joe observed. His heavy leather boots had protected him from all but two of the shoots.

"I'll be okay," Andy said, lowering his pant leg. "This reminds me of the hypnotic leaf Bill found. Just like the leaf, the flowering tree kept us occupied. If we hadn't been so alert, we would have been an easy meal for some animal. I wouldn't be surprised if the tree was planning to eat us itself."

"Well, we're not dead, so let's not talk about it," Joe said, proceeding in the direction of the cliff.

"I wonder if those creatures are our ancestors?" Andy asked, as his train of thought returned to the small creatures.

"I hope not. I wouldn't want to have ancestors as ugly as they are," Joe answered, ripping down several vines to clear a path. "I doubt they are though, because of their yellow blood."

An hour after foiling the attempts of the shoots to skewer them alive, the brothers were relieved to find a refreshing mist falling from the cloud filled sky. With the sun now totally blocked and a cool breeze cascading down the mountain, the temperature dropped markedly. Within minutes, the drizzle turned into a heavy downpour. The plants of the jungle were obviously as interested in the rain as the humans, as all seemed to open their leaves to receive the water supply.

"This feels great," Andy said, spreading his arms, allowing the water to cascade off a large leaf onto his body. His parched skin welcomed the moisture, as the layers of dirt and blood washed away.

Joe also found a natural shower and busied himself scrubbing his face. He then took several long drinks from the tumbling water stream. "You'd better drink up, Andy. We don't know how long this rain is going to last."

Traveling became even slower, as the brothers had to navigate running streams and slippery mud puddles. But the refreshing nature of the rain storm set their minds at ease. The holes in the jungle canopy were growing more frequent, allowing them to see the ominous cliff grow slowly over the tree tops. With their destination in sight, the travelers pressed forward. The rain continued its drenching of the jungle, while the travelers soon found themselves at the edge of the field where they were captured two days earlier.

From their clandestine hiding place, they could see two armed creatures guarding the cave entrance. The rain seemed to be falling in sheets now, blurring their vision. The creatures stood motionless, seemingly oblivious to the storm. Joe silently nudged his brother, pointing to an opening across the clearing. The two slowly edged toward the path that led to the time machine.

Once on the path, they quickened their pace to a jog. The excitement of reaching the time machine soon pushed them to an all out run. The sprint through the forest was quick, as an opening appeared in front of them. The duo emerged into the field, stopping short, mouths open in shock. The wind tossed rain battered their sullen faces. The field was empty. Andy could feel his heart skip a beat, realizing that the time machine was missing.

"Where is it?" cried Andy, looking into the rain filled sky. The clouds were thick and black, showing no sign of breaking.

"I don't know," replied his brother. "But what's that over by the forest."

Barely visible over the long bent grass, lay a crumpled black object resembling a body. The two rushed over to the object, quickly recognizing it to be the rebel.

"Do you think he is dead?" Andy asked, bending down next to the motionless figure.

Joe rolled the body over uncovering the rebel's face. The long brown hair and thick mustache, which covered the young man's face, were both matted with mud. His black jacket, with the insignia of the rebels on the shoulder, had several tears in it. Not surprisingly, the man's pants and shoes were also black. In his right hand, he still clutched the machine gun. Joe promptly plucked the weapon from his grasp, then checked for a pulse.

"He's alive," he said disappointedly.

The rain washed the mud away from the rebel's face revealing several deep gashes. One wound was under his left eye, another along his chin. Blood streamed down the rebel's face. Andy and Joe looked at each other quizzically.

"What happened to him?" Andy asked, bending over to get a better look at the wounds. A frightful shiver traveled up his spine, as he remember the initial pain in his hands after they were shredded by the thorns.

"I guess he ran into the creatures on the way here. They saved me the trouble of doing this myself," Joe said smiling.

"They sure did a number on him," Andy added. He glanced cautiously at the surrounding jungle, to see if the culprits were still around. Nothing could be seen.

At Andy's request, they dragged the rebel into the forest to protect him from the drenching rain. Andy attempted to clean the wounds with a handkerchief he found in the rebels jacket. When only minutes before it appeared as if the storm would last forever, the rain suddenly stopped. The ominous black clouds slowly broke up and drifted off to the west. The powerful heat of the sun once again beat down on the humans.

The moisture in the grass quickly dried, causing a light fog to rise from the ground. As if notified by some master source, the plants and trees closed their leaves in an attempt to store the water they just received. The brothers, who were standing by the edge of the field watching the fog roll in the wind, were startled as the rebel started to groan. Joe immediately raised the weapon, but the rebel still lie incapacitated on the ground. Andy moved closer, astonished to see that the facial wounds were already starting to heal. In fact, he could actually see the gashes shrink.

"Look at that. The wounds are only small scratches now," Joe said in astonishment. The scratches soon disappeared, not even leaving any scars. The rebels' face looked as perfect as the day he was born.

"I have never seen anything like it," replied Andy. He glanced down at his hands. To his amazement, the wounds he had suffered were no longer visible. He flexed both hands, feeling no pain what so ever. "The rain must be healing water. Look at my hands. They are completely healed."

The stranger slowly awakened, grasping his head, which still pounded with discomfort. As his eyes cleared, he noticed the brothers standing over him. He started to rise in an attempt to flee, but stopped when Joe pointed the gun at him. The rebel then allowed his battle weary body to collapse to the ground. Joe demanded to know who he was and why he burst into the laboratory.

"I'm Dave Albert," the man said, obviously feeling no need to keep the information a secret. "I am an officer for the REBELS. A group of us were planning to assassinate the leader of the Protectors. Before we could act, soldiers raided our hiding place. I was able to escape the initial attack, and ended up running into your building and apartment. The next thing I knew, I was in that machine and surrounded by a forest. That's enough about me. Why don't you tell me something about you?"

Joe looked at the rebel in disbelief. He had never had anyone reveal so much information without force. "I'm Joe Marshall and this is my brother Andy. I work for the Protectors. I find rebels and have them killed." A childish grin grew over his face, as he said the those words. He waved the barrel of the gun at Dave. "Do you think I have told you enough?"

Dave felt a lump in his throat, realizing that he may have said too much to the wrong person. He quickly looked around the forest trying to plan an escape, but Joe blocked his way with the aid of the machine gun.

"Not so fast. Why don't you stick around for a while?" Joe said, feeling the thrill he had often experienced while interrogating prisoners.

"Sure," Dave said dejectedly. He knew it would suicidal to try an escape now. He rose to a comfortable sitting position. "What are you going to do to me?"

"I don't know what we're going to do with you, just yet," Joe retorted with a sinister laugh. He thoroughly enjoyed the feeling of power he held over the rebel. "What do you think we should do with him, Andy? He is a threat to the Protectors. Do you think we should execute him? After all it is my job. I took an oath to 'kill any and all persons who pose a threat to the Protectors'."

"No, not yet," Andy quickly answered. He gave a secretive smile toward the rebel; not wantirig anything to happen to him. For he himself disliked the Protectors and worked toward their overthrow. "I don't think we should kill him. He is no threat to the Protectors here. Besides, we might need him for something."

"I guess you lucked out. If it wasn't for him, you would be a dead man," Joe said with disappointment, as the truly wanted to kill the man. "Why don't you tell us what you did with the time machine."

"Time machine?"

"Yes, the time machine. What did you do with it?" Joe asked for the second time.

Dave gave another puzzled look.

"You mean you don't know where you are?" Andy asked.

"No, but I do know where I'm not. I'm not in New York City," Dave replied, still puzzled at the mention of the time machine.

"We are one million years in the past," Andy informed.

"Now that he knows he's one million years in the past, he can tell us what he did with the time machine," Joe ordered. He tapped his finger on the trigger of the gun as a warning.

Dave gave a worried glance at the surrounding forest. "I don't know what happened to it. This is the first time I've seen this field since we got here. I expected to find some of your group here today, but when I arrived the field was empty."

"You weren't attacked by the creatures?" Andy asked.

"No, I haven't had any problem with them," Dave replied. "When I arrived here and found the field vacant, I walked over to the edge of the forest to rest. No sooner had I sat down, a bunch of funny looking birds attacked me. First they swarmed around my head, then they flew down at me. They had rally long beaks, which came to a sharp point. They began jabbing their beaks at me. It felt as if they were sucking the blood right out of my body. I managed to fire off a few rounds. I guess I scared them away. That's all I remember," he finished with a deep breath.

Joe gave a nod, as if accepting the story. "That only explains what happened in the last thirty minutes. What have you been doing, since you ran off? Better yet, how did you get to the top of the mountain, and why were you signaling us?"

The thought of killing the rebel still ran through Joe's mind. He had not fully comprehended the fact that he no longer worked for the Protectors, nor would he ever be allowed back into their privileged circle. He was considered as much an enemy to the Protectors regime as Dave. Joe found a comfortable tree and sat down against its truck. The barrel of the gun remained pointed at Dave's chest.

"I can tell you the whole story, if you want."

"Amuse us," Joe replied.

"As soon as I ran off into the forest two days ago, I realized I was lost. I found my way back here and followed the four of you to the cave. I was hiding in the forest and saw you get captured by the creatures."

"You saw us get captured, and didn't even try to help?" Joe said angrily. His face turned red and his eyes narrowed.

"There really wasn't anything I could do."

"You had a machine gun," Joe yelled, raising his voice even louder.

"There were too many of them. You saw how many there were. It would have been impossible for me to kill them all. And it really would have done you no good anyway. They would have still been able to capture you," Dave said, defending his actions.

Joe released the tension in his face, realizing that the rebel was correct. There were far too many creatures for one man fight. Calmly he told the rebel to continue.

"After they carried you into the cave, I stayed low in the jungle for a while, not wanting to get captured myself. I was hoping that they would leave the cave entrance unguarded, but they never did. I could have shot my way in, but I figured that might put your safety in jeopardy."

"You were actually concerned for our safety?" Joe laughed. "You don't even know us."

"No, but I know without you I would never get out of this place."

"He's got you there, Joe," Andy said, giving the rebel another friendly smile.

"Eventually, I found my way back to the time machine. Although, I didn't know it was a time machine at the time. I found the door open, so I went inside. I quickly realized that I had no idea how to operate anything. I spent a few minutes rummaging through everything, but found nothing useful." Dave paused to catch his breath. He looked at Joe to see if he had dropped his guard, but he hadn't.

"I wandered around the base of the mountain and found the path that led to the ridge. I had nothing else to do, so I climbed up to the top. I followed the stairs, then the path, ending up at the bridge, which you two burnt. I crossed the bridge and found the second set of stairs. That is when I killed the little creatures. It looked like they were in the process of building the stairs, but I didn't take the time to actually confirm that. I climbed the stairs and was just about to enter the cave, when I heard your voices. I retreated, then I saw that you were being chased. The rest you know."

Joe looked at Dave, not quite believing the coincidence needed for the rebel to accidentally end up at the precise location and time where he and Andy needed help. "If you weren't there, we would be dead now," Joe said. Dave just nodded in acknowledgment.

"You said that you followed a path to the ridge?" Andy asked.

"Yes, but on the way back I couldn't find it. It was the strangest thing. I walked into the jungle to where I knew the path to be, and the trees seemed to move aside and open up for me as I walked. I really can't explain it."

"Wait a minute," Joe said, eyeing Dave suspiciously. "You expect us to believe that you climbed that staircase in the bitter cold, at night, just because it was there?"

"No. At that point I was no longer just wandering around. After I ran across the creatures building the stairs, I suspected that if I followed them I would come across another entrance to their caves. I thought maybe I could help you."

"When we climbed back up to the cave, after you shot the creatures, we couldn't see you. You couldn't have walked back down the stairs that fast," Joe asked, again with suspicious overtones. Rationalization of the situation proved difficult.

"It was rather dark," Dave replied. "And I am dressed in black."

"Why were you waving to us? Why didn't you just wait somewhere for us to catch up to you?" Andy asked, who by this time had also reserved a spot next to a tree.

"I didn't know what kind of reception I would get. I didn't know that we weren't in our time. I thought that maybe I had been unconscious and taken out into the country," Dave explained.

"How much ammo do you have for this thing?" Joe asked, marveling at the gun. He had lost all interest in the conversation. Machine guns were a big fad in his time. Even though there were more advanced weapons, such as lasers, most people preferred to use old fashioned guns. The thought of killing Dave had left his head, at least for the time being.

"I have a few more clips in my pocket, but I don't have as many as I would like," Dave answered, beginning to feel safe with his new acquaintances. He relaxed and stopped looking for a chance to escape.

The balmy sun had done its job, drying up all of the water from the storm. The trio walked out into the field to see if they could find any sign of the time machine. Unfortunately, the rain had washed away all the tracks and foot prints that led in the direction of the time machine, Bill, and Ken.

"Are you sure this is the right field?" Joe asked.

"Yes, I'm positive," Andy replied.

"Me, too," Dave added. "I remember it distinctly from the day we arrived."

"What do we do now?" Andy asked, walking back into the forest. "The time machine is gone, and we don't know if Bill and Ken took it or if they are still in the caves."

"I doubt that they are still in there; alive at least," Joe said. "With all the creatures we've killed, they would be dead by now if they haven't already escaped. We would probably be dead now, if we hadn't escaped when we did. I think it is reasonable to assume that one or both made it back here and took the machine to find help in rescuing us."

"I say we find a safe place to stay. We're going to need it when night comes," Dave said, after hearing an unfriendly howl of a nearby animal.

The brothers eagerly agreed. A brief search revealed a group of three trees, growing side-by-side, not far from the field. It was decided that the trees would be used for structural support of their shelter. Luckily, the day was still young, leaving plenty of sun light for them to complete their project.

The forest provided ample supplies for the time travelers. Small branches, which were either torn down or cut with Dave's knife, were bound together with vines collected from various trees. The trio constructed three panels of branches and vines, leaving one a bit short, in order to allow room for an entrance way. Once attached to the tree trunk foundation, the three walls formed a perfect shelter. Long leaved branches were then gathered and tied tightly together, forming the ceiling of the structure. The ceiling filled a dual purpose. First to protect the humans from any future rain storms. Second, to protect from aerial attacks, most notably the birds that attacked Dave.

As was their experience, time in this ancient jungle seemed to pass at an accelerated rate. Dusk arrived just as they were securing the ceiling to the walls. Feeling a well deserved sense of accomplishment, they built a small fire just outside the door of the shelter, then sat down to rest.

"Did you notice that some of the trees let off cries when we cut them? It's as if they're really alive, more than just ordinary plants," Andy said, making himself comfortable next to the fire.

"Yes," Dave answered. "This is a very strange place. Have either of you noticed that the days seem shorter here? By several hours at least."

"Yes, we were talking about that last night," Andy answered.

"Dave, why are you against the Protectors?" Joe asked. After being away from their rule, and being with people that hated them, second thoughts about his loyalty were running through his mind.

"Because they cause too much violence. The Protectors want everything their way, no matter what the consequences are to anybody else. The people have no rights. They had plenty before the war, and even more before the previous war. I've read books about the people and governments before that war. Everyone had the right to vote for what they thought was right, although many of them didn't. That I will never understand. Maybe they should spend a day with the Protectors to learn what freedom is all about."

"I thought the Protectors destroyed all the books when they took power," Joe said, thinking of what he had just heard. Indeed the Protectors ran a sweeping campaign to destroy all literary items in their realm immediately after taking power.

"That's what they thought, or what they wanted people to believe. They did destroy most of them though, but not all. It's a shame. Most of the books I've read were interesting and useful."

Joe had heard enough about his time. He felt confused. On the one hand, he had practically been raised by the Protector's organization. It was the only way of life he knew. But when he listened to what the others were saying, thoughts of doubt lingered. "I think it's time we get some sleep," he said staring out into the dark forest, not that any of them were overly tired. "We can only hope that your friends get back here tomorrow. I'm sick of this place."

Joe mapped out a schedule for Andy and himself to stand guard. He purposely left Dave out of the rotation because he didn't trust the rebel enough to leave him up alone with the gun. Joe had drawn the first watch, but Andy and Dave did not retreat into the shelter immediately. They moved to one side of the fire, as far as they thought safe, to isolate their conversation from Joe. The two exchanged brief life stories and philosophies. By the time their stories wove themselves together for their untimely meeting in the laboratory, darkness had taken a firm grasp of the jungle. It was then, that they turned in for the night.

Joe, now alone, sat in silent thought. His world and all the protection it offered was shattered. He felt alone and vulnerable. Many times he thought he heard the trees whispering to one another. To him, it sounded as if they were laughing at the sight of the humans. He was only able to stifle the whispering sounds, by concentrating on scanning the jungle for any signs of attack.

Inside the shelter, Andy almost immediately fell into a deep sleep. His small body was not used to the heavy physical demand placed on it since landing in the past. He dreamt that he was in the laboratory, a time shortly before the police raid. This time the events unfolded differently. When the police barged into the dream laboratory, they entered with guns blazing. Andy did not escape the assault. He was shot repeatedly in this scenario, screaming wildly as each bullet entered his body. Then all went black. This was not the end of the dream, however. Andy's dream self awoke from his nightmarish murder, trapped in a dark wooden coffin. Sharp nails had been driven through the lid to secure it shut, some had been misguided into his limbs. A dull pain ripped through his body, whenever he tried to move.

One by one the nails were removed from the coffin. Bright intense rays of light filtered in through the cracks, as the cover was slowly pried open by a disembodied hand holding a crow bar. Andy rose from his casket, unaware of what was happening. To his surprise, thousands of people surrounded him, sitting on benches in the form of a circle. The people were segregated by the color of their clothing. The darker the color, the lower they sat on the rows of benches.

One by one, the people rose, walking toward the center of the circle. They stopped for a moment at table, scribbled something on a piece of paper, then dropped the folded paper into a slot on top of a large wooden barrel. Andy looked around, confused by the sight of the strange people. While some were orderly walking up to the barrel and then returning to their seats, others were scrambling about in an undefined manner. Many yells, both of approval and disapproval, filled the air.

Then a disembodied head floated up to Andy in a jerky motion, as if it were still attached to its body. Arteries and veins hung loosely from where it used to be attached to the neck. Its mouth moved and choppy words came out, "AREN'T YOU GOING TO VOTE?" Then its eyes spun rapidly around inside its head, stopping on Andy. Andy closed his eyes, terrified by the sight. When he opened them, the head was gone.

Andy glanced around for a few moments, hoping to find someone that he knew. A man in a red shirt walked up to him, tugging on his arm.

"Come," the man said, assuming that Andy's blood stained shirt included him in his group. "It is time to vote."

Andy obeyed, joining the man in line. Once at the table, he found a piece of paper and a pencil. Just as he lifted the pencil to write, a group of the Protector's special police entered the room. They yelled simultaneously in the same choppy voices, "YOU CAN'T VOTE!"

The police raised their guns, firing endlessly into Andy's body. Their evil laughs dominated the noise in the crowded room. Even while lying on the floor, with blood spilling out of a hundred different holes in the dream Andy's body, the police still fired at him.

The real Andy woke from the dream sweating. Finding himself inside the shelter, he quickly relaxed. Joe, noticing his sudden awakening, rose from his sitting position by a tree, and entered the shelter.

"I had a dream," Andy explained, pausing to catch his breath. "I was killed repeatedly by the Protectors." A confused feeling raced through his head, as he tried to piece together the fragmented dream. "I'll tell you more in the morning. I want to go back to sleep."

"Whatever," Joe replied.

The rest of the night passed quietly, except for the never ending cries and howls of distant animals.

CHAPTER VI "TREEMEN"

The loud cawing of a large colorful bird simultaneously woke Bill and Ken from restful dreams. The bird, perched directly over the two, glanced down at the humans between cries. The early morning sun cast its light brightly over the towering mountain range, causing the yellow tint of the air to reflect dully off the pale sand that the scientists used for bedding.

The serenity of the morning only lasted until their eyes adjusted to the daylight. Intermingling with the songful cries of the bird was an irritating buzzing sound. A quick glance around revealed that several armies of small flying insects had invaded the area during the night. The trees, from which they cut the branches to make the lean-to, were covered by millions of tiny black insects. The invading armies showed little interest in the humans, however, as access to the exposed wood was all that they wanted.

Not wanting to risk a possible attack, Bill and Ken cautiously wandered a short distance down the path. There they stopped and commenced with breakfast, which consisted entirely of blueberries. They discussed the strangeness of their new surroundings. The topics covered ranged from man eating plants, hypnotic leaves, savage little creatures, and the one thing that really bothered Bill, no water. Of all the land they had covered, they hadn't even seen the slightest sign of a drinkable water supply.

The scientists quickly consumed the remainder of their blueberry reserve. Several minutes later, black clouds began a steady march over the mountains, blotting out most of the sun. The thought of being soaked by a refreshing rain appealed to the travelers, but they knew they couldn't stand still waiting for the event. They had more pressing concerns to worry about.

"We had better find the time machine, before the rain washes the tracks away. If that happens, we'll be stuck in this time permanently," Bill told Ken. The idea of being marooned in the ancient past sickened both scientists.

"I definitely don't want to spend the rest of my life here," quipped Ken. "Out of all the places I can think of, this is probably one of the worst."

"Worse than our time?" Bill questioned.

"In our time we knew what to expect," explained Ken, with a relaxed laugh. "I've survived nearly four decades there. I'm only working on a few days here."

The steady nighttime wind had already done a good job of erasing the time machine tracks, although they were still easily traceable. The daytime temperature rose sharply, as did the humidity brought in with the clouds. Without the protection of the jungle canopy, the travelers quickly tired. Pressing onward, they found the once bountiful vegetation continued to rapidly disappear. For all intents and purposes, the lush forest had turned into a desert. Large trees were nonexistent. The small bushes and plants that were left had few leaves and were widely spaced over the sandy soil. The duo dutifully followed the tracks, tracing the subtle hills of the terrain.

As the morning dragged on toward afternoon, thirst began to slow their progress. Just as thoughts of retreat were coming to the forefront of their wandering minds, they were encouraged by a thick cluster of trees on the horizon. The tracks leading to the time machine continued in a westerly direction, but the scientists departed from that route in order to explore the green oasis, with the prospects of finding water.

The dry wind was playing with the loose desert sand, whirling it around the large collection of plant life, which drew closer with every step. As Bill and Ken approached the trees, it became apparent that they would be able to find needed shelter from the elements, while they rested for the next leg of their journey.

Except for the wind rustled leaves, no sounds could be heard from within the circle of trees. The isolated patch of vegetation appeared to be deserted, causing the scientists some concern over the unnatural silence. Ever since arriving in this strange time, they were constantly bombarded by the sounds of the animal population. Now they would welcome the single cry of a bird or howl from an unseen animal.

"Something doesn't seem right here," Ken said, approaching the outer wall of trees.

The vegetation did not gradually build from the vacant desert. It started abruptly, as if some mystical line formed a border between sand and trees. Adding to the strangeness of the area, long silky strands of a clear material were strewn around the ground in an unruly manner. Each strand measured approximately one half the thickness of a human forearm. None of the translucent objects were present outside of the invisible boundary line, but they seemed to grow more abundant the deeper the scientists looked in to the forest.

The coolness of the vegetation lured the time travelers inside, but their fears kept them only several feet from the openness of the desert. The sweet odor of mingling plant life drifted into the human's nostrils, allowing them to relax slightly. Bill turned to look out toward the western horizon, where the time machine had been taken. A small mountain range could be seen poking its peaks over the sand dunes of the desert. The scientist could not estimate the distance to the mountains, but he knew that they were far away. Much too far to walk without first finding water.

"I haven't seen anything like this before," Ken said, lifting the end of a strand. To his surprise, a powerful adhesive instantly bonded to his skin. Frantically he tried to pull his hand free, only to find his other hand stuck as well.

"Ken. Ken, calm down," Bill yelled, trying to keep his partner from slipping into an uncontrollable panic.

"I can't get it off!" Ken said, struggling with the mysterious object. He held his arms outstretched in front of his body, pulling first with one hand then with the other.

"Just calm down," Bill repeated. He scanned the area, finally focusing his attention on a fallen tree branch. "Let me try to pry it off with this."

Bill inserted the branch between Ken's hands, then began to pull. Ken concentrated his strength, pulling in the opposite direction. A loud ripping sound filled the air, as Ken's right hand separated from the strand. A moment later his left hand was also free.

"Ouch!" Ken screamed, examining his hands. From what he could see, none of the skin had been torn off by the adhesive.

"That stuff is pretty strong," Bill observed.

"My hands are still sticky," Ken complained, holding his hands in front of him, afraid to touch anything or even allow his fingers to touch each other.

"Rub them in the dirt," Bill suggested. "That should offset the adhesive, until it has a chance to wear off."

Ken followed Bill's advice, covering his hands with a layer of the powdery soil. "That was a little scary," Ken said, rubbing his now dirty hands together. "I had no idea those things were that sticky. I mean, they don't even look wet."

"I hate to say this," Bill said, lifting the branch, which was now firmly attached to the strand, "but it's my guess that these strands are webbing from a large spider."

"That's impossible," Ken replied, but his face grew worried none the less. "The spider that could leave a web strand this large would have to be huge."

"And from what you've seen so far?" Bill asked, allowing Ken to draw his own conclusion.

"I really don't think we should hang around here much longer," Ken said, shaking his hands in the air in an attempt to dry the adhesive.

"Well, it doesn't appear that were are in any immediate danger," Bill said, ignoring Ken's plea to leave the area. He looked out at the distant mountain range. "Besides, we need to find water. There has to be some in this cluster of trees. We can't go too much further in the desert without something to drink."

At first, the scientists just traveled along the outer edge of the tree line, deep enough to find protection from the heat, but close enough to the desert to make a quick escape. The trees were not packed so close as to prevent them from watching the blanket of black clouds slowly float by. The high humidity level caused each of them to break out into a drenching sweat.

"There is no water out here," Bill said, as the duo reached the western most point of the forest. "We are going to have to walk in a little deeper."

"You first," Ken said.

The deeper the humans ventured into the trees, the more difficult it became to find clear paths to walk upon. Some areas were covered by piles of strands two to three feet high. Bill silently pointed deeper into the forest, noticing a large clearing. The thought of a lake or pond gave him energy to proceed. His excitement was quickly dashed, as he struggled through some low lying branches to the edge of the opening. There was no water.

The scientists found themselves standing at the edge of a large circular crater, which stretched out well over a hundred feet. The depression in the earth only measured ten feet, but that is not what worried the time travelers. An intricate maze, comprised of hundreds of the sticky strands, spanned the hole.

"This doesn't look good to me," Ken said, raising his weapon.

Adding to the troublesome sight were the many white sacks hanging from the strange web work. Bill poked at the nearest sack with his spear. The package, large enough to contain a human, made him even more nervous. Incredibly, the contents of the sack began to squirm, rocking the sack back and forth.

"Look over there," Ken yelled, pointing to the center of the depression.

A large hole entered the earth at this point. As if sensing the human's intrusion, massive spiders were quickly scurrying out of their underground home. The bodies of the insects were a full two feet in diameter, with their wiry legs spreading out in all directions. They quickly located the humans, beginning a swift march toward the intruders.

Bill gave a surprised glance into the depression. His eyes bulging at the sight of the gigantic spiders. "I didn't think they would be that large. Run!"

Bill and Ken rushed through the forest, skipping and jumping over the littered ground, knowing that one false step could easily result in a gruesome demise. The spiders quickly jumped up on the webbing and began pursuit. Fortunately, the insects were not very swift running over the forest floor. The scientists easily reached the fringe of the forest without confrontation. It was there that another problem quickly surfaced.

A steady rain began falling the moment they exited the patch of trees. While the cool water refreshed their tired bodies, other thoughts pressed them into a sprint toward the tracks left by the time machine. They found some barely visible marks in the sand, only to see them wash away a moment later. The two stared dumbfounded toward the peaks of the mountain range off in the distance.

"We should have never gone into the trees. It was just a waste of time," Bill yelled angrily.

"We are so far behind, it probably won't matter much," Ken consoled. "The rain would have washed the tracks away regardless."

"I suppose you are right," Bill said, quieting his voice. "We just have to hope the thieves didn't change direction."

Ken refrained from comment. He looked over his shoulder into the trees, spotting a group of spiders staring out at them. Apparently they were satisfied that the humans had left, as they gave no further pursuit.

The rain felt cool, drenching the weary time travelers. The dirt that had built up during the past two days readily washed away. A soothing feeling could be felt, as the cool liquid cascaded down their parched throats. But the rain didn't last very long. The sun soon poked its way through the thinning black clouds, leaving the travelers somewhat refreshed, but still quite thirsty. The sandy soil quickly absorbed what few puddles had formed during the downpour, leaving the ground dry once again.

The trek into the patch of trees indeed proved useless. Once again, the peculiar features of the ancient time disrupted the human's progress. Though the rain greatly improved their chances of surviving the desert elements, it significantly lowered the odds for them to find the time machine. If they had stuck to the tracks and avoided the spider's habitat, they would have been that much closer to the time machine, before losing the trail.

Occasionally the marks of some small animal crossed the path they were following. The ground had taken on a rough texture, due to the pelting rain, only to be disheveled with every footstep taken. With their supply of blueberries having been finished at breakfast, their stomachs growled with no promise of being fed.

The scientists trudged forward, hoping that the last few remaining clouds would stick around to block the searing rays of the sun. The fiery ball in the sky won the battle, however, evaporating the clouds and focusing its energy unabated on the two lonely beings crossing the desert floor.

The seemingly endless stretch of desert, each hundred yards looking the same as the last, allowed Bill to let his mind wander. Though his thoughts were off, weaving their way through hypothetical situations, they would have done him no good had they stayed at home. The elder scientist stumbled, suddenly finding himself waist deep in sand. The water from the storm had found its way into a small trough, liquefying the ground in the process. Ken, instantly realizing that Bill had stumbled into an undesirable location, stopped dead in his tracks. Bill turned his body to face Ken, but found that he had sunk several inches in the process.

"Don't move," Ken said, inching forward, trying to find the edge of the quagmire. "Stick out your spear, and I'll pull you in."

Bill reached out, with the weapon in his right hand. His body sunk another inch, but Ken managed to take hold of the weapon. Fortunately the quicksand was rather loose, offering little resistance to Ken's efforts. Several moments later, Bill was standing on solid ground.

"It figures," Bill said, skimming globs of muddy soil from his clothing, "just as I get cleaned up by the rain, I fall into a mud puddle. You know, I'm beginning to get annoyed with this place."

"Just beginning? I've been annoyed with this place since we arrived."

The occasional small leafless bush soon turned into the occasional dead leafless bush. Not long after, the terrain turned into a barren desert. The sand on Bill's clothing had long since dried and fallen off, though he still felt dirty and uncomfortable. On the bright side, they had made much progress. The small mountain range on the western horizon loomed larger than ever. Even though the mountains reached several hundred feet into the air, they didn't compare in size to the little creature's mountain range far back to east. Thankfully, it appeared as if their destination lay only a couple miles away.

"I hope the time machine is there," Bill said, struggling to climb a small sand dune. "I wouldn't know where to look, if it isn't."

"That reminds me of a question I have," Ken said, reaching the peak on a sand dune. "What do we do with the time machine once we get it? We can't go back to our time."

"Obviously we will have to go to another time to find help in rescuing Andy and his brother. But I think we can wait to discuss that, until we find the time machine."

The sun reflected off the pale sand, partially blinding the travelers. Their exposed skin had already begun to turn red, but as of yet they had managed to avoid any serious burns. Bill walked face down, occasionally looking up to check the distance to the mountains. It was during a jog down a small incline that his eyes began to play tricks on him. The sand in front of him appeared to move away from his foot forming a footprint, before his foot actually hit the ground.

"This is impossible," Bill said, leaning over to scoop up a handful of sand. His brain was slow in acknowledging, but half of the grains of sand actually jumped out of his grasp.

"Hey, I think the sand is alive," Ken said, observing the performance. He stomped his foot repeatedly on the ground, watching the top layer of sand move away before his foot struck. "The sand must be little animals that don't want to get crushed," he laughed. A moment later he stopped, now afraid of even taking a step and crushing the small creatures.

"You could make up the wildest story and tell me that you saw it in this place, and I would believe you," Bill said, tossing the handful of ordinary sand remaining his palm to the ground.

"Do you think we are killing them?" Ken asked, still not willing to move his feet.

"At this point, I don't really care," Bill replied. "It is either them or us. It does seem that they are able to get out of the way though."

"Maybe the sand in our time is just the shells or fossils from these animals," Ken suggested. He started to run to catch up to Bill.

"It is a possibility," Bill conceded, not really hearing what Ken had to say. His attention had shifted to the terrain that lie ahead.

With the majority of the empty desert now behind them, thoughts of actually reaching the mountain range safely ran through their heads. Small clumps of trees could be seen scattered around the base of the bluff they were heading toward, again offering the prospects of water. The entire ridge of mountains appeared to be just a strip of wind blown rock, housing inhospitable jagged cliffs.

As the scientists reached the top of a small sand dune, they stopped short, quickly dropping to the ground. The now expected phenomenon of the sand moving away from their bodies did not phase the humans. Instead, they were shocked to realize that some of the objects they had assumed to be vegetation, were actually living beings. Lifting their heads just high enough to clear the desert floor, four large creatures could be seen walking around what appeared to be a cave entrance. Bill and Ken stared in excitement, feeling that they had successfully tracked down the time machine thieves.

"I hope it's there," Ken said, shifting his body in an attempt to relieve himself from the tremendous heat of the sun.

"If these creatures took it, I doubt that they will just hand it back over to us," Bill responded, sliding halfway down the sand dune, apparently having seen enough. "We need a plan."

"It looks like there is a large cluster of trees and bushes a short distance from the cave entrance. If we can make it to there, we might have a better perspective," Ken said, watching the dark colored objects move in and out of the cave. The size of the creatures sent a shiver up his spine.

Bill crawled back up to the top of the dune to survey the situation. "If we stay in the ditches and circle out to the left, I don't think they will spot us," he finally said, after a few moments of thought.

In a humorous attempt to remain concealed, Bill lifted his overweight body over the peak of the small hill, clumsily sliding into the next ditch. At the same time, a sudden gust of wind swept across the desert floor tossing sand everywhere. When the wind died down, hundreds of the small sand creatures simultaneously jumped off the scientist's body. Still, he found himself half buried.

"It looks like you enjoy playing around," Ken laughed, sliding down the slope after his partner. "First, you take a bath in quicksand, and now this."

"Actually, I'm beginning to like the feeling of sand covering my body," Bill joked. He rose to his feet, offering a half hearted effort to dust himself off.

The scientists stopped at every sand dune peak, eyeing the entrance of the cave carefully, but the large creatures did not even take a passing glance in their direction. Twenty minutes of covert desert crawling brought the two to the base of a bluff, several hundred yards south of the cave entrance. The scattered vegetation provided ample camouflage for them to quickly scamper north to the cluster of vegetation Ken had spotted earlier. The trees offered a solid wall of concealment, as their long leafy branches drooped all the way to the ground. It was at the edge of the cluster, peering silently through small openings, where the humans got their first good look at the guards.

The creatures were tall, averaging eight feet in height. The rest of their bodies appeared to be proportionally correct, except for their huge circular heads. Thick veins protruded from their skulls, offering a contrast to the eyes deeply embedded into their sockets. The hands of the guards were webbed and scaly, while their feet were long and flat with short thin toes. An apparently useless thin tale, much darker than the rest of the lanky creature's skin. hung from behind. The guards seemed to be conversing freely amongst themselves, roaming aimlessly around the clearing in front of the cave. Two of the creatures apparently finished their guard duty, as they entered the cave, leaving only two at the entrance.

"Only two left," Ken said, revealing the obvious. "Do you think we should make a move?"

"No, I don't think we would have a chance fighting them. They must be at least two feet taller than us. Besides, those huge axes they carry could probably cut us in half with one swing."

For the first time Ken noticed the axes that each creature held. The fact the weapons blended in perfectly with color of their skin, was the perfect camouflage. The scientist's eyes widened, as he studied the long wooden handles and large sharpened stone blades. Strangely, all of the blades appeared to be discolored by a black stain.

"Wow! I missed those. I suppose they are used to fight off intruders," Ken said, drawing a conclusion as to why the guards were armed. "But then again, they might not object to us just walking in and searching for the time machine."

"If you believe that, go ahead and try to get inside. If you find the time machine, you can come back here and get me."

Ken looked at the guards once again, quickly changing his mind. "It was just a thought," he said, retreating deeper into the shadows of the trees.

"And not a very good one," Bill remarked, following Ken into the tree cluster.

The scientists found a couple of rocks to sit upon. Their new vantage provided several small openings through which they could spy on the guards. The inactivity did not bother duo, though they were very anxious to find the time machine. The physical exertion expended crossing the desert warranted such a reprieve.

The creatures milling around the entrance never wandered more than a few yards from the opening, leaving no opportunity for the humans to sneak into the cave. The actions of the guards were similar to what humans might do, if they were expecting something interesting to happen.

"You know, they look like trees with arms and legs," Ken said with a laugh. They had allowed their whispered voices to grow louder, as it appeared that the creatures did not possess astute hearing.

"Yes, I suppose they do look like living trees," Bill agreed, after taking a good look. "They are strange looking though. I mean, their heads are way to big for their bodies."

"That could be what happened to all the trees around here," Ken said, after thinking for a few moments. Once again, he let his limited scientific knowledge run amok. "A ship from outer space or a radio active meteor could have crashed here releasing deadly radiation. The radiation caused all the trees within a certain radius to come to life. Those dead trees we saw could have been at the fringe of the radiation cloud. During the years, the trees evolved into these things."

Bill frowned, shaking his head as he absorbed Ken's theory. While both were keenly adept with the technologies of their time, much of the mundane scientific knowledge had disappeared during the time since the first big war. "Your hypotheses are getting way out of hand."

"It is possible," Ken said in a dejected voice.

Two treemen exited the cave, returning the total to four. The guards greeted each other and continued to converse, giving the impression that the treeman society was quite civilized. The scientists listened with interest, but neither could understand the language. The original two guards entered the cave, leaving their weapons leaning against a rock near the entrance.

"I've got an idea," whispered Bill. "Those axes they left could help us even the score. If we can use the element of surprise, we might be able to grab the axes, rush, and kill the guards."

Ken mulled over Bill's idea for only a second before protesting, "That doesn't sound safe to me. They must be experts with those things. We've never used an axe before, for any purpose. The blades are so large, we probably won't even be able to lift them."

"It might be the only way we can get in. This isn't a game we're playing. Retrieving the time machine is a matter of life and death," Bill said, moving himself into a position for attack.

Bill crouched near the edge of the tree cluster, waiting for Ken to join him. For a moment Ken stayed sitting on his rock, not believing that Bill was about to commit suicide. Knowing that he couldn't let his partner attempt to enter the cave by himself, he reluctantly scooted up next to him. As the humans watched in silence, waiting for the appropriate time to act, two huge mounds of sand suddenly grew from the desert floor, only several yards in front of the guards.

The scientists were stunned by the occurrence, instinctively retreating deeper into the safety of the trees. The mounds grew at a astounding pace. As the granules of sand slowly fell to the ground, two large tick-like animals were revealed. The treemen instantly raised their weapons, preparing for battle, but the ticks had the element of surprise on their side.

Before even fully emerging from the sand, the first tick scampered forward grabbing a treeman in its huge pinchers. The helpless treeman writhed in pain, giving out an ear piercing cry of death. A dirty brownish-yellow liquid dripped from the dying guard's wounds, staining the white sand.

The remaining guard managed to scream out an order, before engaging battle with the attacker. Four additional treemen promptly emerged from the cave. The dumbfounded scientists moved even deeper into the patch of trees, not wanting to be seen. Safe for the time being, they watched with keen interest as the deadly battle unfolded.

Three of the new treemen pounced on the second tick, who was busy parrying with the original guard, savagely hacking at the creature with their axes. As if following some unheard rhythm, they took turns slashing at the hard shell of the overgrown insect. The obviously wounded combatant bled a deep black blood, which mixed with that of the fallen treeman, forming an unsightly stain on the desert floor.

Sure that its victim was dead, the first tick released its pinchers and grabbed for another. As it darted forward, another pair of mounds grew from the desert sand. A second treeman screamed, helpless in the grasp of the enemy. He let out a second silent scream, before his body went limp.

By now, the scientists had lost count of the number of participants in the battle. Treemen and ticks were scurrying about, kicking up a fog of dust in the process. Only yards from Bill and Ken's hiding place, a fierce battle took place between two treemen and a single tick. The tick had its pinchers firmly imbedded in one of the treemen's legs. The insect shook its head violently from side to side, trying to tear its victim apart, but the treeman fought back with its axe. The second treeman attacked the assailant from behind, scattering pieces of the tick's shell into the air with every blow.

Meanwhile, near the cave entrance, a tick lay in waiting, as four treemen rushed from the cave. The insect squirted a clear liquid from its mouth at the unsuspecting treemen. All but one fell victim to the substance. The liquid instantly hardened, leaving its subjects immobilized. One by one, the helpless treemen were ruthlessly torn apart. Their screams of horror and pain filled the air, as their blood mixed with that already spilled on the sandy ground.

The small war lasted nearly fifteen minutes. The attack had been well planned, as the ticks effortlessly lashed out at any treeman that wandered too close to their clutching jaws. The treemen soon gained an edge, however, as new recruits were readily available. Finally, all four ticks lay crushed and shattered on the desert floor. Ken and Bill counted seven dead treemen. Brown and black blood covered the once white sand and pale grey rock of the mountain side, giving the site a well deserved sense of death.

Two of the surviving treemen entered the cave, returning several minutes later carrying a long rug constructed of vines and skins. It took six treemen to load all the corpses onto the rug. As if practiced in this ritual, the group immediately began to drag the carpet out toward the center of the desert, where the dead would be left for hungry animals to consume. The humans could do nothing, except look on in awe.

"They don't even give their own kind a decent burial," Ken said, watching as the caravan grew small on the horizon.

"I think it is because they don't want any rotting bodies around to attract unwanted visitors," Bill whispered, not wanting to be heard by the group of treemen cleaning up the battle site. "It seems like they have enough hostile visitors as it is."

"You're probably right," Ken agreed, not really paying attention to Bill's answer. He leaned back against a tree, making himself comfortable. Breathing a sigh of relief, he felt thankful that they had not foolishly attacked the treemen, as Bill had planned. The battle proved that the creatures were highly skilled fighters. "What are we going to do now? Wait for things to quiet down, before we go on with the plan?"

"Yes," Bill whispered, still crouching behind a branch watching the clean up process. He, too, was impressed by the treemen's battle skills, but the need to find the time machine drove his every thought. "The treemen seem very angry right now. We might have a better chance, after they let off some steam."

"While we wait, I suggest you think of a safer plan," Ken warned.

An hour passed. The bodies of the dead had been dropped at some location out of eye sight from the cave. The escorts of the caravan had returned and order had been restored. Luckily for the humans, none of the treemen wandered close enough to the patch of trees to detect them. Two fresh guards were placed outside the cave entrance, apparently waiting for the next attack. A pile of axes, most broken in battle, lay nearby.

The minutes dragged on, as the humans waited and contemplated their strategy for recovering the time machine. They watched intently, while a third treeman exited the cave carrying a small wooden bucket. The treeman pulled a long curved leaf from the bucket, then began splashing a clear liquid onto the blood stained sand. The scientists were puzzled by this bizarre behavior, until the soiled sand slowly returned to its natural color. After the creature had finished *cleansing* the battle site, it stopped to chat with the guards. Several minutes passed, until the cleaner reentered the cave with one of the guards, leaving only one at the post.

"Wow! That's some formula!" Ken exclaimed. "Throw it over blood and there's no sign of a battle. I bet the Protectors would love to have some of that stuff."

"Never mind that. Now's our chance," Bill replied. He rose from his comfortable sitting position, cautiously moving to the edge of the trees, not even looking back to see if Ken was following. "We should have no problem killing just one of them."

"I just hope we don't get sliced up like the ticks. You don't suppose they take prisoners, do you?" Ken whispered, following Bill out of the camouflage.

The treeman stood staring out toward the northeast, unable to see the humans scurrying along the base of the bluff. The scientists stopped once, behind a lone bushy plant, to make sure they had not been detected. The guard remained still, apparently lost in thought. Bill then led a tip-toed scamper to the pile of axes. He easily found two intact weapons, handing one to Ken. A nervous sweat formed on Bill's forehead, as he closed to within ten feet of the unsuspecting guard.

Ken followed a step behind, but did not possess his partner's stealth abilities. The moment Ken placed his foot on the ground he knew he was in trouble, as his weight snapped a dry twig breaking the silence. The treeman spun around, his weapon already moving up to an attack position. Its eyes opened wide, expecting to fend off another tick attack, but instead seeing a rotund human rushing toward him. With a mighty groan, Bill swung his axe at the surprised creature. The scientist maneuvered the axe with such accuracy that an observer might have thought him to be an expert with the weapon. The large scaly head of the creature fell to the ground, staining the freshly cleaned sand.

Bill was utterly surprised at the effectiveness of his attack. Although he felt sincere remorse in killing the treeman, he had no time to stop and pay his condolences. He had not created the time machine with the intent of running a murderous rampage through time, which he has successfully commenced upon during the past several days, but his survival was at stake. He had no proof that the treemen had stolen the time machine, but there was no turning back now. He darted into the cave entrance, with Ken close behind.

The entrance tunnel, wide and spacious, ran straight into the mountain. The short passage soon merged with a cross tunnel, running north and south, Wooden supports were located on each wall of the new passage, spaced out every fifteen feet. Torches fixed to the supports gave off an amiable light. To the scientist surprise, no treemen were present. The cave seemed deserted.

"Now where?" Ken asked, eyeing each direction with a fearful glance.

"I didn't think it out this far," Bill confessed.

An arbitrary decision led the intruders along the north passage. Unlike the caves they were in before, these were dry and well lit. The stone walls looked smooth and unblemished, as if hours of demanding work had been spent perfecting them.

The serenity was broken, by the voices of several treemen walking toward the time travelers. The humans immediately pulled an about face, fleeing to the south. The scientists were not as evasive as they had hoped. The treemen had spotted the intruders and began a lanky sprint in pursuit.

"It would be nice if you thought things through a little better," Ken huffed, feeling weighed down by the heavy axe he carried.

"I think better on the run," Bill replied, also struggling under the weight of his weapon.

The three treemen steadily gained on the short legged humans, who soon spotted a lit doorway ahead to the right. Ken paused at the opening, hoping it would lead to a possible escape route. The room was large, but offered no sanctuary. The chamber was lined with long rows of tables, covered by hundreds of axes, meticulously stacked into piles. Two treemen inside the room noticed the humans, immediately joining the chase.

"I hate to say it, but things aren't looking too good," puffed Ken. He dropped his weapon at the doorway, resuming his frantic sprint down the passageway.

"They sure aren't," Bill agreed, also dropping his axe. At this point speed was of the essence.

The scientists were now running side by side down the corridor. The treemen closed the gap to about twenty feet, as the humans cut a sharp right down an intersecting corridor. Angry yells boomed through the cave, echoing off the smooth walls. The continuous noise was loud, pounding the human's ear drums. The fleeing time travelers sprinted forward, not looking back, expecting at any moment to feel the blade of an axe slice through their bodies.

"Quick, duck into the next room," Bill ordered, as the two made a turn to the left down another passage. "Maybe we can lose them."

The two literally dove into the next chamber, but they had no such luck in losing the treemen. The room was not an out of the way storage compartment or dark tunnel, as hoped. The brief jaunt through the treemen's caves ended, as the humans looked up to see a mob of startled treemen staring down at them. The scientists quickly scrambled to their feet, in an attempt to retreat back into the hallway, only to be stopped by the five treemen who had been chasing them.

The treemen did not attack, as feared. In fact, it seemed as if they were mollified by the sight of the humans. Realizing that any attempt to fight the creatures would be suicidal, Ken and Bill just stood motionless.

"Caught again," Ken said, looking around the room.

Broken bones were scattered across the far end of the forty foot square chamber. A small door to their left led into a dark room, from which a loud periodic grating sound could be heard. The sound of crushing bones mixed with the grating, forming a hideous melody. Neither human could imagine, and had no desire to find out, what caused the noise.

"It looks like these guys are a lot tougher than the first ones," Bill said, referring to the small creatures who caught them earlier. He studied the treemen, who were talking amongst themselves, not liking the situation he and his partner had stumbled upon.

"At least they don't seem to be too disturbed by our presence," Ken said, trying to find a bright side to their predicament.

"Just wait until they find the dead guard. I'm sure that will change their opinion of us."

"Maybe if we just casually walk toward the exit, in a non-threatening manner, they will let us go," Ken said, hopefully. He stepped toward the exit, but the four treemen blocking his way made no attempt to move.

The treemen conferred for a short time, then motioned the scientists to the door. Six treemen then escorted the prisoners through a maze of tunnels, each looking quite identical, making any chance of a fleeing escape impossible. The twists and turns were so frequent that Bill and Ken felt as if they were being led in circles. They realized they were wrong, however, when their tour ended in a vast chamber.

A river of water fell from a large waterfall, located on the left wall, and flowed through a six foot wide channel in the floor. The water exited the chamber through a hole in the opposite wall. Two treemen were on their knees leaning over the stream. Bill assumed they were drinking, but he couldn't tell for sure.

"So this is where all the water is," Bill said, gazing at the falls. His parched mouth ached, wanting only to drink from the crystal clear river.

One of the treemen suddenly pushed Bill to the floor, kicking him in the small of the back for good measure. The blow, only meant as a warning, still caused quite a bit of pain. Ken, not wanting to be treated to the same, didn't speak or make any attempt to help his partner.

At the far end of the chamber a large rock slab had been laid against the wall at a forty-five degree angle. A very tall treeman, dressed in a multitude of multi-colored leaves, lay motionless on the rock slab. Hanging on the wall, one on each side of the creature, were two large shells, unmistakably those of the giant ticks. Ken noticed that the veins in the reclining treeman's head stuck out at least twice as far as the others.

One of the escorts crossed a stone bridge spanning the channel, respectfully approaching the one on the slab. The creature then bowed, waiting for acknowledgment, before rising. The escort stood completely motionless, as it spoke to the decorated treeman. The language resembled that of the little creatures, but had distinct differences. More vocal components were present in the speech of the treemen, as opposed to mostly gurgling sounds used by the little creatures. When the treeman finished speaking, he turned with precision movement, pointing one of his large webbed hands at the prisoners.

At this point, Bill struggled to his feet and walked toward the treeman on the slab. "Look, we are only here for our time machine. If you would..."

He was interrupted by the forearm of one of the guards. Bill crashed to the ground and let off a low groan. This time the treeman had given him a solid blow. Ken could tell that Bill was hurting, but decided it best to leave him alone.

Bill slowly rose, gradually returning to where Ken stood. "I guess they don't want to listen," he whispered in his softest voice, not wanting to be slammed to the ground for a third time.

"I wouldn't listen to you either, if I were them. You smell terrible," Ken whispered in return.

For the first time, Bill noticed the stench. The foul odor of the quicksand, not to mention the sweat and grime that had accumulated during his travels, had bonded to his clothing. Apparently he hadn't noticed the strong odor earlier, since they had been traveling out in the open.

The treeman on the slab slowly raised his head, as if consuming all of its energy in the process, then stared at the scientists. It became clear to the humans that this treeman was very old and ill. Every time the creature moved, a painful grimace fell across its face. A subtle smile slowly formed, as if the elder treeman was remembering some long lost memory. Slowly the creature lowered its head to its resting position and in a scratchy voice whispered to the guard. The guard repeated the order for all to hear. The prisoners were then escorted out of the room.

"That was rather peculiar," Bill whispered.

"What around here isn't," Ken replied. The guards hurried the scientists along with gentle shoves to the back. "I wonder why all the creatures in this time have twisting caves? It would be much easier to find one's way around if they were all straight."

"Yes, but this way it would take a person forever to find his way out," Bill replied. A treeman interrupted him with a shove, but the act was only a formality. The treemen obviously did not care that the humans were communicating with each other, now that they were no longer in the presence of their leader.

After traveling a safe distance from the elder treeman's chamber, the guards slowed their pace slightly. They chatted casually amongst themselves, paying only the slightest attention to their prisoners. The humans, Bill in particular, had no intention of riling the treemen with an escape attempt. The scientist's back was still sore from the abusive treatment he had received earlier. In fact, the casual mannerism of the treemen actually led the time travelers to believe that their hosts did not have a deadly fate in store for them.

The second journey through the maze of passages lasted several minutes, before the scientists were escorted into another large chamber. An abundance of torches lined the walls, giving the room a near outdoor appearance. Bright yellow sand covered the floor, unbleached by the suns rays. As the humans raised their sights from the ground, through the spaces between the guards, a glimmering of metal and glass caught their eyes. The time machine stood before them, standing alone in the center of the room.

"I wonder why they brought us to the time machine?" Ken asked, trying not to sound too excited in front of the treemen. His heart pounded in his chest, with the realization that all the time they had spent trailing the tracks had come to a fruitful conclusion.

"Obviously they must link us to it. I just hope they didn't cause any damage. I have no way of fixing it here," Bill answered, eyeing the machine. He began to outline in his mind the events that would allow him and his partner to escape. All he needed was for the guards to be distracted for the briefest of moments.

Lining the walls of the chamber were various sized rocks of every color in the rainbow. A few large wooden barrels were arranged neatly off in one corner. Upon further inspection, it became apparent that the barrels were placed under stalactites, hanging from the high domed ceiling. Even the intense power of the many torches had trouble illuminating the distant crevices that loomed above. A dripping sound could be heard, as a clear liquid occasionally fell from the stalactites into the containers. Next to the barrels were stacks of wooden buckets, identical to that used by the treeman to bleach the battle stained sand of the desert.

The moment Bill was waiting for did not come. Before he had a chance to make a break for the time machine, the treemen quickly surrounded the prisoners. In a matter of moments, the humans were bound by dry vines. Even though the vines were frail in appearance, they had a strength that neither human could over come.

After securing the prisoners, who were now seated on the sandy floor, the guards stood around casually talking amongst themselves. This quiet conversation lasted several minutes, until another treeman entered the room. This late arrival carried a stack of blue and red feathers, which he painstakingly attached to the human's bodies with a thick white substance. Moments after the feathers were secured, another creature entered carrying colorful skins of unknown animals. The skins were carefully draped around the scientist's immobilized bodies. A third bearer of gifts adorned the stunned prisoners with stone necklaces.

"They sure go all out. Rocks and feathers. I'm really impressed," Ken joked.

"These costumes do look foolish," Bill agreed, trying to hold back from laughing at Ken.

"What do you think they are going to do to us?" Ken asked, his voice turning worried. His vocal cords quivered, trying to hide his fright.

"I don't know. I have read about some cultures that make sacrifices to rid themselves of evil spirits and the like. That would explain the costumes."

"I was hoping for something less severe."

Bill and Ken talked freely now. In fact, the guards weren't even paying the slightest attention to the prisoners. They were off in a corner, letting the costume designers have their go at the humans. Though they were unattended for several minutes at a time, the scientists could make no attempt at escape. The vines and significant weight of the rocks inhibited all movement. Bill and Ken could do nothing at the moment to change the fate the treemen held in store for them. Sensing that they had completed their jobs, the bearers of the feathers, skins, and necklaces left. Only the five original guards remained, still talking and paying no attention to the prisoners. Several long uncomfortable minutes passed, before a single treeman appeared in the doorway. The treeman stood for a moment, observing the guards chatting off on a corner, then ordered them to follow.

Two treemen carried each prisoner through another array of twisting passages. The scientists paid no attention to their surroundings, as they had long ago lost all sense of direction. The walls of the circular room they were brought to glowed a bright yellow. Eight small statues, of unrecognizable beings, were equally spaced around the chamber. Countless torches lined the perimeter of a square pit, located in the center of the room. Bills' theory was correct, the treemen were going to make a sacrifice.

Bill and Ken were carefully placed at the edge of the pit. Stairs led down all sides of the depression, stopping at a five foot square platform. By the order from an unseen treeman, the scientists were shoved into the pit. Each tumbled painfully down the stairs, landing hard on the rock bottom.

Ken struggled furiously to free himself, with the realization of his fate becoming clearer with each passing second. "We can't let these guys kill us."

"I don't see that we have much choice," Bill said quietly. He stopped tugging at his binds, then looked toward the surface. One thought raced through his mind, had all his work to free his people from a tyrannical government been for not?

One treeman stood at each side of the square pit, holding a large wooden bucket over its head. A shrill splash of a gong echoed through the chamber, signaling the treemen to commence with their ceremony. One by one the contents of the buckets were tossed onto the horrified humans, covering them with a bright red liquid. The thick sticky substance splattered everywhere, but the prisoners were helpless to even wipe the liquid from their eyes.

A dull chanting made its way down the many steps, sending a chill through the time traveler's spines. The four treemen stepped back from the edge of the pit in unison, only to be replaced moments later by four others. The gong sounded for a second time, grating at the human's ears. This time the buckets contained a yellow liquid, resembling the blood of the little creatures. This substance mixed with the red forming a vivid orange.

"I wonder what kind of ceremony this is? I've never had blood thrown on me before," Ken said. He attempted to wipe the mixture from his face with his shoulder, but all he succeeded in doing was smearing a large orange streak. Bill remained silent, sitting calmly and facing the wall.

"As long as they don't throw any weapons down here, we should be all right," Ken continued, trying to keep his composure. He stopped talking, closing his eyes and mouth, as the third splash of the gong filled the room.

A deep purple liquid followed the yellow. The prisoners were now struggling to keep their bodies upright in the slippery concoction, the depth of which now measured over a foot. The original chanting continued nonstop, as a second melody was added. Ken could vaguely see the heads of treemen dancing around the pit, waving their arms wildly. Several minutes later the second melody stopped and four more treemen stepped up to make an offering. The gong sounded again. Four buckets full of a black liquid, which Ken guessed to be the blood of the ticks, were added to the collection.

"Hey, what are you trying to do drown us?" Ken yelled to the surface. No one even acknowledged his screams. The weights of his costume made it difficult to keep his head above the rising level of the mixture. "We're sorry we killed one of your guards. We just want our time machine, then we'll leave."

Yet another group of treemen approached the pit. The now familiar sound of the gong echoed through the chamber. Four buckets of a clear liquid were emptied into the basin. Within moments, the entire mixture turned transparent. The clear liquid reminded Ken of water, which he had tasted only a few mouthfuls of during the past few days. Fortunately he restrained himself from the temptation to drink.

Throughout the entire ceremony, Bill remained calm. He kept his eyes fixed on the stairs just above his head, his mind off in some distant thought. The sudden sound of grinding rock, reverberating through the ground, didn't even break him from his solitude. Some unseen mechanism caused the vibrations, but more importantly it opened four drains, previously unseen in the bottom of the pit. A different second melody overlaid the first, as the clear liquid slowly flowed away. Two guards then walked down the stairs, hoisting the prisoners over their heads. The treemen carried the soggy humans up opposite stairways, displaying them proudly to the audience. The gong sounded one more time, signaling for the various chants to stop. Rows of treemen looked on in silence, as the time travelers were taken from the chamber. Moments later, the prisoners found themselves back in the chamber that housed the time machine.

Ken was surprised to see two treemen standing guard by the time machine door. His curious glance at Bill revealed that the elder scientist was still lost in his own private thoughts. The time travelers were unceremoniously stripped of their feathers, furs, and jewelry; but were left tied at the wrists, with their arms still bound to their torsos at the elbows. The same two treemen who carried the prisoners from the pit, once again lifted them off the ground. With an effortless motion, both men were literally thrown into the time machine. The tumbling scientists slammed into a wall of computers, where they let off muffled cries of pain.

The treemen forcibly closed the time machine door. Eight of the creatures then surrounded the machine, lifting it several feet off the ground. The treemen were obviously strained by the feat, but were quick to carry the machine and its cargo from the chamber.

Ken paid no attention to the twisting tunnels that passed outside the clear glass of the time machine. He instead struggled furiously to free himself from the binds. The multitude of liquids that had been dumped over his body acted as a lubricant, allowing him more flexibility. But despite all his efforts, he made no obvious progress.

Bill, on the other hand, sat in the same silence he had fallen into since being tossed into the pit. The rotund scientist's eyes looked glazed, offering no recognition of the calls from his partner.

The time machine was carried past the entrance the scientists had used to infiltrate the treemen's domain. Ken caught a passing glimpse of another battle between the treemen and the ticks. He was shocked to see that the treemen carrying the time machine didn't even slow or make an attempt to help their comrades.

Ken could only hear his own heavy breathing inside the time machine, as the thick glass of the vehicle blocked out all sounds from the outside. The treemen were now marching along a steep incline, slowing their once quick pace. The tunnel alternated between left and right turns, but did not diverge from its upward slope. By this time, Ken had conceded the fact that the treemen were taking them to the top of the mountain. For what purpose, he did not want to guess.

The tunnel finally leveled. Ken could see a sense of relief in the treemen's faces who were carrying the time machine. Even though the creatures were obviously very powerful, the massive weight of the lead floor had taken its toll. The escorts were tired, but continued to move onward. Passing a chamber, Ken caught a most peculiar sight. A large treeman was in the process of whipping another with a long vine. The time machine lingered in front of the doorway long enough for Ken to see the vine wrap around its victim, before tearing off a thick layer of skin. Though Ken could not hear, he was positive that the recipient was crying out in pain.

"I'm sure glad they didn't decide to do that to us," Ken said, trying to initiate a conversation with Bill, who remained focused on some unknown thought. Ken shuddered at the thought of the pain the whipping must be causing. "Of course," Ken continued, "we don't know for sure that they don't have that in store for us."

The time machine passed a few more chambers on its journey, but Ken had become too entrenched, struggling once again with his binds, to pay any attention to their contents. His muscles, beginning to ache and stiffen, cried for relief. He accommodated the silent request, relaxing his limbs.

Just as thoughts of surrender, giving in to his deadly fate, flooded through his mind. Red hues of the sunset brought him back to reality. The treemen had finished their exhausting journey to the top of the mountain range. Another sigh of relief could be seen, as the group lowered the time machine to the level ground of the bluff. Ken watched as the escorts disappeared back into the tunnel.

Had the situation not been so dire, Ken would have allowed himself more time to take in his surroundings. The time machine sat on a small plateau at the exact apex of the mountain. On the eastern horizon, he could see the larger mountain range, which seemed to run parallel to the one he found himself on, where they had begun their journey. He assumed that somewhere in its depths Andy and Joe were still being held captive. The thick jungle they had traveled though blanketed the area closest to the huge mountain range, before gradually thinning into the barren desert, which he found to be most unfriendly.

To the west lay a vast canyon. The depression was so deep, that the vegetation at the bottom could barely be seen. Lost in the broken layer of low lying clouds, which hovered over the canyon like a blanket, stood the far boundary of the magnificent natural wonder. Several large pinnacles could be seen rising from the canyon floor to elevations higher than the bluff the scientists now sat upon. The immeasurable size of the canyon made Ken feel small and insignificant. Occasionally a bird or two would rise through the cloud wisps, circle once or twice, then plunge back into the mysterious depths. Ken's mind spent several moments imagining the vast variety of plant and animal life that must live on the canyon floor. But he knew that his life would not last long enough for him to ever see the mysteries that lie there. While Ken absorbed the beauty surrounding him, Bill broke from his trance.

The rotund scientist struggled to his feet, frantically trying to manipulate the controls of the time machine. Panic spread through his body, as he realized that the restrictive vines would not allow him to reach the necessary controls. Thinking quick, he dropped to the floor, wildly kicking the soggy shoes from his feet.

"Ken, bite the end of my sock and pull it off," Bill ordered, suddenly bursting with energy. He slid across the floor, with his black filthy sock pointed at Ken's mouth. The fabric, soaked from the strange ceremony, reeked an unearthly odor.

Ken looked at the foul sock and grimaced. "What, are you crazy? You want me to bite that thing?"

"Just do it, or do you want to be squashed like a bug?" Bill yelled. He stuck his foot closer to Ken's mouth. "In case you haven't noticed, they are planning to throw us off this mountain."

"I noticed a long time ago," Ken snapped, "while you were off in dreamland." Ken took a look at the treemen, who stood quietly surrounding the time machine. Then he took another look into the gigantic canyon. Reluctantly, he bit into the end of Bill's sock, pulling the article of clothing from his foot. He spat several times trying to rid his mouth of the foul taste.

"Now the other foot," Bill commanded.

Ken knew it would be useless to argue. The muscles in his face tensed, as he prepared to remove the second sock. The stomach churning odor reached into his nostrils, causing his head to spin. Not wanting to prolong the torture, he savagely tore the second sock from Bill's foot, biting into his partner's big toe for good measure.

A moment later, six treemen emerged from the cave entrance, carrying the elder treeman on a rock slab. A few more colored leaves had been added to his attire, since the humans last saw him. The sweat covered treemen carefully lowered the slab to the ground. Unlike the treemen who had carried the time machine to the bluff, these did not allow themselves the satisfaction of a sigh of relief, as that would have been an insult to their leader.

With his feet free, Bill wasted no time in scurrying across the floor to the main computer bank. Struggling to maintain his balance, he stretched to reach the controls with his toes, desperately trying to prepare the machine for a life saving trip through time. Unfortunately, his legs were not quite long enough to accurately manipulate the buttons and dials. The awkwardness of his situation kept causing his feet to slip from the panel. Meanwhile, eight fresh treemen walked up to the elder and bowed. They then spaced themselves around the time machine, lifting it from the ground.

"Hurry up with those controls," Ken said nervously. "They are bringing us toward the edge."

The head treeman gave a swift gesture. The eight pallbearers gathered their strength for one massive joint effort, heaving the time machine over the side of the plateau and into the vast depths of the canyon. Bill had run out time. Without knowing if he had even set any of the controls properly, he kicked at the control panel. The time machine tilted, as it plunged toward the ground. The thick plate of lead scraped against the side of the mountain, tossing the scientists against a wall of computers; knocking both unconscious.

CHAPTER VII "ANTS"

Dave woke with a start. For the past several years he had spent every conscious moment looking over his shoulder, worrying that the police might catch him. The routine was now a permanent part of his daily life. It took a few moments for him to recognize his surroundings and piece the situation together. Before the unexpected trip into the past, he was forced to relocate every two or three days, in the constant battle to stay one step ahead of the Protectors. The sight of the trees calmed his racing heart, telling him that he was safe.

Several feet away, Andy slept in a fetal position, knees drawn up tight to protect from the slight chill that crept through the jungle during the night. Dave snickered, as he spotted Joe propped up by a tree several yards away. The tough member of the Protector's police force had fallen asleep while on guard duty. The machine gun lie under one of his arms, available for the taking, but Dave had no interest in trying to obtain the weapon. He had no need to fear Joe now. They all knew that they needed each other to survive in this wilderness. Quietly, the rebel stepped outside the shelter, taking a deep breath of fresh air. For the first time, since he and the others had landed in the strange time, the air didn't contain a yellow tint. Instead, a familiar blue filled the sky. High white clouds floated overhead in the warm comfortable breeze. His stomach cried out, leading him to wander the area in search of food.

The jungle seemed peaceful at this early morning hour. There were no cries of wild animals, just the pleasant sound of birds chirping a soothing melody. As he walked, he kept glancing toward the sky through the trees. The clouds danced freely in the blue vastness of space, seemingly playing tricks on him. First he thought he saw the body of an official dressed in a combat uniform. A couple of holes in the white puffs formed blue eyes, which beamed down angrily at the rebel.

The figure in the sky slowly rearranged itself in the wind. The clouds now took on the formation of a flying sphere. Human legs protruded from the top of the death machine, while the rest of the body had already been shredded to dust. Another gust of wind broke up the form, leaving the sky full of countless white specks.

Dave reached the field, where they had landed three days earlier. He thought that by some miracle the time machine would be sitting there, with Bill and Ken lounging around in the tall grass waiting for him to arrive. Reality set in, as he viewed the empty meadow. The wind whistled through the grass, mimicking the sound of evil laughter. Several colorful birds flew by over head, squealing as they settled in the branches of a nearby tree. The birds stopped all activity upon seeing Dave. The rebel paused, fearing that they might be the same birds that attacked him the previous day, but they were not. These birds did not appear hostile, as they sat on the branch, staring intently at the human. The staring match lasted several minutes, before the feathered creatures took flight, disappearing over the treetops.

On his way back to the shelter, Dave spotted a small white animal curled up under the branches of a large bush. The growl in his stomach returned with a vengeance. The rebel carefully removed his knife from its scabbard, hurling it silently at the unsuspecting animal. The blade stuck into the animal's back, killing it instantly.

To Dave's surprise, red blood oozed out of the fatal wound, as he removed the knife from its victim. He had expected to see yellow blood, like the creatures in the caves, but the sight of red was entirely welcomed. He picked up the small rabbit-like creature and rushed back to the shelter. The brothers were still deep in sleep and he had no intention of waking them. Within moments, he had fashioned a primitive skewer from some branches. Using some dry twigs to fuel a fire, he began to roast his breakfast.

It did not take long for the odorous smoke to float into the shelter, wakening Andy from his restful sleep. Though he couldn't recognize the smell, his growling stomach knew it to be food. His nose led him outside, where he found Dave leaning over the fire. "What are you cooking?" he asked.

"Breakfast," Dave replied, without looking up from his task. He smiled, as he rotated the meat over the fire.

"I'd be careful," Andy said, moving closer to the fire. He watched the flames dance, as the fat drippings splattered onto the hot coals. His eyes slowly moved up to the meat on the skewer, causing his stomach to growl again, a reminder that it had been some time since his last meal. "We don't know what that yellow blood will do to us."

"I'll take my chances with this one," Dave said, turning to face Andy. "This animal had red blood."

"Really?"

Dave picked his blood stained knife up from the ground, proudly showing it to Andy. He then wiped the blade in a clump of grass, in an attempt to clean it, before placing it back into its sheath. Still smiling with a childish grin, he returned to rotating his food over the jumping flames.

"I can't wait to taste it," Andy said, finding a comfortable spot on the ground to watch the meat cook.

"Who said you were going to have a chance to taste it?" Dave questioned. "If you want something to eat, you should go out and find it yourself. I'll even lend you my knife, if you want to use it."

Dave's reply left Andy speechless.

"I'm only joking," Dave said, after a few moments of silence. "I just wanted to see how you react to such things. Obviously, you don't do much reacting."

The two chatted freely, while the meat cooked. The conversation took on the appearance of two life long friends catching up after a long separation. They talked about their individual involvement in the attempt to overthrow the government. Andy's stories seemed boring and practically meaningless compared to the life threatening missions Dave described.

"The news just doesn't get out," Dave said, poking a stick at the meat. "We have made a major dent in the Protector's organization. Several of their leaders have been assassinated recently, but they continue to carry on as if nothing has happened. The public thinks these people are still alive."

"I'm almost ashamed. I don't have any exciting stories," Andy conceded. "My involvement has been limited to the work I do for Bill. I deal with the black market and stuff like that."

"That's important work," Dave replied earnestly. "We need to keep the pressure on from all sides."

The aroma from the roasting meat finally woke Joe, which caused the conversation about the government to stop. He didn't seem too disturbed by the fact that he had fallen asleep on guard duty. In fact, no one even brought the subject up. Dave decided not to joke with Joe about finding his own food, since Joe held the machine gun and could easily over react to such teasing.

It did not take long for the meat to turn a golden brown. Andy found three large, relatively clean looking leaves, which they used as plates. Dave sliced the animal into three pieces, keeping the largest for himself. The succulent juices tingled their taste buds, as each devoured his portion in a matter of minutes.

"This thing not only looked like a rabbit, but it tasted like one, too," Dave said, licking the grease from his fingers. He closed his eyes to savor the flavor, before changing his expression to a more serious one. "I looked around the area and found no trace of the time machine or your friends."

"I hope that they both escaped from the caves," Andy said, trying not to think of the worst.

"We could go back and look for them," Dave suggested. "Since we now know what we are dealing with, we should be able to complete the mission with only the machine gun."

"No," Joe said, speaking for the first time since finishing his breakfast. "I can't believe that you would voluntarily go back into those caves. I think it is obvious that they escaped and took the time machine. The only question is whether or not they plan on returning to get us."

Dave looked at Andy, "It sounds as if your brother is a bit scared."

"That's not true at all," Joe retorted. "The probability that the time machine was taken by someone else and that your friends are still alive in the caves is so small I couldn't even begin to guess. We killed a whole bunch of those creatures. It's not unrealistic to think that they would retaliate."

"An assumption based on the practices of your bosses?" Dave cracked. "I don't think you can apply their actions to this instance."

"Maybe not," Joe replied, staring Dave in the eyes. "But I'm not willing to risk my life over the slim possibility that they are both still in the caves. It only stands to reason that at least one of them has escaped and taken the time machine."

Dave nodded and averted his glance into the jungle. He had challenged Joe on purpose. Joe did not fly off the handle at the first sign of conflict, but rationally defended himself. A sign that gave Dave some comfort, especially since Joe would be the one wielding the machine gun.

After several moments, Andy broke the awkward silence. "Do either of you think that we will ever get out of this place?"

"I hope so," Joe quickly answered. "I really don't like it here. I can't imagine spending the rest of my life in a place like this." He looked out into forest in disgust.

Dave said nothing. He just stared blankly into the cloud filled sky. The crystal blue atmosphere he had enjoyed earlier was no longer present. Once again, the yellow tint polluted the air. A sudden gust of wind disturbed the branches of the surrounding trees, breaking the peaceful silence of the jungle. The unseen creatures of the forest had also awakened, offering the sound of distant animal calls for all to hear.

"I can't stand just sitting around like this," Joe said. He rose from his sitting position to rub the cramps out of his legs. "We aren't going to find anything, or help ourselves out, by sitting around here."

"What would we go out and look for?" Andy protested. After all the traveling he had done already, he felt like staying put and resting. "We'd just be looking for trouble wandering around the jungle."

"We might be here for a long time," Joe insisted. Nothing had changed he realized. He had never seen eye to eye with his brother, arguing over every little point. "I'm not going to sit around, until I die."

"But..." Andy started, before Dave broke him off.

"Joe is right. There is no one here to take care of us, except for ourselves. We have to go on the premise that we are going to be stranded here for the rest of our lives. At the very least, searching the area will help kill some time."

Realizing that he was outnumbered, Andy reluctantly agreed to accompany the other two on the search. Wishing to explore as much of the region as possible, they decided to travel in a new direction. Uncertainty filled their minds, as they trudged across the field heading west, away from the mountain range. The sun quickly warmed the morning air, causing a small drop of sweat to trickle down Andy's face. It was then that he knew he was in for a long journey.

The crunching sound of the dry leaves underfoot and the occasional cry of a nearby animal were the only sounds in the ancient jungle. They followed a route that resembled a path, but it had no defined boundaries. Trees and bushes randomly sprung up through the soft soil, forcing the travelers to weave around them.

"Maybe we will be lucky and find another rabbit for lunch," Joe said hopefully. The small portion he consumed for breakfast didn't even begin to satisfy his appetite.

"That would be nice," Dave agreed. The bitter distaste Joe and Dave had for each other had greatly subsided, but they still weren't about to carry on a lengthy friendly chat. "I could go for another roasted rabbit. Even though we didn't use any seasoning, it was very tasty."

Dave started marking the trees, in order to find his way back to camp easily. Surprisingly, as soon as he cut into the bark, a new layer would begin to grow over the wound. After puzzling over the situation for a while, they decided that the healing rain worked on plants as well as humans.

"Why do you suppose we haven't seen any animals?" Joe asked. "By the sounds of things, I would guess that there are hundreds of them out there."

"I think it is because of the heat. They probably stay in the shade of the jungle during the day and save their hunting and traveling for night," Dave answered. "Actually, they are very smart. We on the other hand, are tiring ourselves out by traveling in the heat."

"It's not too late to turn back," Andy said, wiping his forehead free of sweat. "We could take a lesson from the animals and go back to the shelter and rest. I'm not used to all this walking."

"Nice try, Andy," Joe said, giving his brother a slight shove forward. "Those animals live here, we don't. And I want to get out of here as fast as I can."

The trio followed the ill defined path for over an hour and a half. Many times losing sight of it all together, only to stumble across what they presumed to be a continuation several yards later. To their surprise, the path ended abruptly, leaving the adventurers standing at the edge of a small clearing. Large boulders were scattered about, apparently forming some strange pattern. Filling the space between the boulders, were several large piles of sand, each standing nearly five feet high.

"I was getting ready to turn back anyhow," Joe stated, eyeing the contents of the clearing.

"Just when we find something interesting, you want to turn around," Andy said, walking over to the nearest hill. The loosely packed sand made climbing the hill difficult. After taking two steps, he lost his footing, tumbling to the bottom.

Joe and Dave gave a few chuckles, as Andy brushed himself off. He gave a mock bow to his audience, then attempted the climb again. With a grim determination, and the fact that he scaled the incline on all fours, he was able to make it to the top.

The summit of the hill was relatively flat, allowing him to stand. But it was the large hole he saw, which fell into the earth's secret depths, that gave him some cause for alarm. As he turned to tell the others of his discovery, a large red tentacle slid across the sand toward his feet.

"Hey, there's a..." was all that he could say, before the tentacle tightened around his left leg, hauling him to the ground. A surprised Andy struck the ground hard, with sand entering his open mouth.

The tentacle released its grip on Andy's leg, allowing his body to begin a slow slide down the side of the hill. An instant later, a giant red ant emerged from the hole. It stood three feet tall and three times that long. Its two black eyes frantically scanned the jungle, as its clutching jaws snapped furiously at Andy's moving body.

Joe rushed forward, firing several blasts from the machine gun into the ant. The creature instantly slumped to the ground, crumpling into a ball, before sliding down the hill. Orange liquid oozed from the ant's many wounds, but the humans did not stay long enough to analyze the giant insect.

Dave rushed to help Andy to his feet. "I think we should leave, before more of them come out," he said, nervously looking around the clearing. "I've never heard of an ant hill with only one ant."

"I can't believe the size of that thing," Joe said, watching Dave and Andy make their way away from the ant hill.

Just as he finished his sentence, a second ant exited the hole and let off a high pitched shrill, barely audible to the humans. Joe casually raised his gun, firing a couple rounds into the ant. The insect instantly shriveled into a blob of red flesh and died.

The three trespassers turned to flee down the path, but another ant had emerged from the jungle to block them. As the humans turned toward the surrounding jungle, Joe silenced the screeching ant with a short blast of bullets. Dave led the dash through the trees, knife drawn ready to attack. Andy huffed several steps behind, while Joe protected the rear. The trio soon slowed to a walk, as it became apparent that the ants were not in pursuit.

"We had better keep an eye out for more of their holes," Dave said, bent over gasping for air. He stared intently back toward the clearing, but could see no movement. "They could have hundreds of holes around here."

"How come they are so big?" Andy asked, recovering from his fright.

"I don't know," Joe answered in a heavy breath. He kept the barrel of the gun raised, ready to fire at any attackers. "Maybe they shrunk over the years. In any case, I don't think we will be able to survive in this time for too long. We only have a limited amount of ammunition."

After a brief rest, the trio continued through the jungle at a much more comfortable pace. Their heavy breathing slowly returned to normal, but their eyes remained alert. Their frantic sprint through the jungle left them absolutely lost. A brief search for the path that led them to the ant hills, proved fruitless. Deciding that they had explored enough for the time being, they headed east toward the towering mountain range.

The idea that any of them could sustain several hours of hiking would have seemed ludicrous several days ago, but now their bodies were becoming accustomed to the physical exertion. A half hour after their encounter with the ants, the trio stumbled upon another clearing. This one was very small and almost barren.

The sight of the clearing sent chills up each of their spines, but the reason was not obvious. From the safety of the jungle, they peered in to the twenty foot square area. No matter how hard they looked, they could find no trace of life in the rocky patch, safely hidden in the vast green of the jungle. Not even a single blade of grass grew in the inhospitable soil. Strange as it seemed, the trees even knew enough to keep their branches out of the region.

But the lack of vegetation was not the only surprising characteristic of the clearing. In the precise center of the desolate square stood the strangest sight the humans had ever seen. Four white bricks were placed on the ground in the form of a five foot square. Four black bricks, positioned six feet off the ground, were floating directly over the white bricks. The fact that black bricks had no visible means of support puzzled the onlookers. Together, the eight bricks formed a perfect rectangular cube.

If the floating bricks alone were not enough to impress the time travelers, the white semitransparent mist filling the cube certainly did. As the mist rotated and swirled, within the confines of the surfaceless structure, the rays of the sun were refracted into a rainbow of colors. The particles of the mist were so fine that the opposite side of the clearing could be seen, although somewhat distorted.

"I wonder what that is?" Andy questioned. He cautiously stepped into the clearing, bracing for something, but feeling nothing. He inched his way toward the object, stopping five feet from the nearest brick. He held his hand out, feeling the air in front of him, when an internal coldness spread through his body.

"I don't know, but it sure has gotten cold all of a sudden," Joe said, rubbing the goose bumps on his arms. The surprisingly cold temperature reminded him of his experience on the slopes of the mountain range.

Dave picked up a small rock and hurled it at the mist. The rock struck the invisible barrier containing the mist, before bouncing back and landing at his feet. Surprisingly, the rock made absolutely no sound upon contact with the cube. "I've never seen anything like it," he said, in a whisper under his breath. Upon touching the stone, a sharp coldness shot up his arm. He quickly dropped the rock and backed away.

"What's wrong?" Andy asked.

"That rock is freezing cold," Dave replied. He placed his fingers in his mouth in an attempt to warm them.

"No wonder nothing wants to grow here," Joe said. With his patience for this strange time growing thin, he raised his gun and smiled an evil grin. "We may not know what this thing is, but I know a sure way to open it."

Before the others could react, Joe squeezed the trigger of the machine gun. The striking pin struck the next bullet in the cartridge, sending the slug of lead down the long barrel of the gun. As the bullet exploded into the air, a small puff of smoke formed, quickly dissipating into the atmosphere. It took but a fraction of a second for the bullet to race across the short distance separating the gun and the cube. As soon as the round struck the mist, the entire structure burst in a spectacular explosion. A strong force of bitter cold air emerged from the cube, lifting the humans off their feet and hurling them toward the fringe of the jungle.

The mist, now dispersed, quickly gathered itself into a spiral funnel, swirling around the clearing for a few moments. A sudden frost appeared on all nearby vegetation. The translucent mass paused briefly, as it passed over the humans, then sped off toward the mountain range. The frigid temperature left with the mist. Within a minute, the frosted vegetation began to melt.

As the dumbfounded humans rose to their feet, checking for any injuries, they began to notice subtle differences in the jungle. To be sure, the temperature had returned to normal. But the jungle had become suddenly quiet. The mild breeze had stopped, along with the distant animal cries. No birds could be seen. Not a single branch or leaf moved. An eerie silence had blanketed the jungle.

"What ever it was, I don't think we should have fooled with it," Andy said with a shiver, this time caused by fright not cold. "Did you see the way the mist took off toward the mountains? You would think it was in a hurry."

"I don't think I even want to know what it was," Joe said. His face had turned pale and his eyes looked glassy. "From now on I'm not going to shoot at anything, unless its attacking."

"I think we had better get back to the shelter," Dave said, looking around at the emptiness of the clearing. Only the eight bricks, the black ones had strangely fallen straight down and come to rest on top of the white, lay on the ground.

No paths led from the clearing, so the trio decided to follow the direction taken by the mist. At least, they reasoned, they will end up near the mountain range and the shelter. The water from the melting frost dripped from the trees, casting the illusion of rain over the jungle. The travelers were correct in their assumption that this water was not the same healing water that fell from the sky earlier. The artificial rain smelt old and mouldy and did nothing to make them feel refreshed.

"Even the animals turned quiet, after the mist left," Andy noted, as the moisture on the trees dried up.

"For every minute we stay in this place, I hate it more and more," Joe said, showing his discomfort for the ancient time. Most of his anxiety was not caused by his surroundings, but rather the fact that the security blanket provided by the Protectors was not available to protect him.

"I hope we find Bill and Ken soon," Andy said, as the three fought their way through the tangled jungle. "I have a bad feeling about this place."

Their progress through the jungle seemed slow. The tremendous heat from the sun quickly dried the vegetation, but soaked their clothing with sweat. While the mist remained on their minds, all physical traces of the mysterious object had evaporated. To add to the strange sights they had already seen, they noticed that the trees in this section of the jungle had predominately blue leaves. If this was caused by the chilling effects of the mist, they did not know. To make matters even more peculiar, all of the leaves were slowly curling up into the buds from which they grew.

CHAPTER VIII "DISCOVERIES"

Joe fell to the ground inside the shelter, exhausted. Andy collapsed several feet away, while Dave found a comfortable spot outside the structure. The hike from the clearing, where they had released the mist, proved to be long and bruising. The route they followed had been tangled and riddled with thorns. No matter which direction they tried, they were unable to find a clear path to walk upon. That struggle was in the past now, as a cool comfortable breeze blew in through the jungle, relieving them from the heat.

"I am so sore," Andy complained. Even the workout he had hiking up and down mountain sides, did not compare to the dull pain that ached his muscles. He stared up at the leafy ceiling, allowing his heavy breathing to slowly subside.

"Me, too," Joe added. He had collapsed to the ground on his stomach, but now squirmed over to the tree wall trying to find a comfortable position for his aching back. "I'm more hungry now than I was before breakfast. I wish I had saved some of my rabbit for now."

"I have an idea," Dave yelled through the shelter doorway. The talk of food had sent his brain to work. "Why don't we make a trap? That way we will almost be sure to catch something before dark."

"Sounds like a good idea to me," Joe agreed. He had stopped fidgeting, since he had found the perfect position to sit. His eyes were closed, allowing the cool breeze to soothe his body. "We will need some sticks and vines to make it. Andy can go look for them. I've got to stay here and rest."

Andy started to object, but stopped, rationalizing that the time spent arguing with his brother would be time spent hungry. He did not immediately embark on his mission, rather he lay on the ground resting. The sounds of the jungle were so pleasant that he actually began to doze off. A distant howl woke him from his light slumber. Several minutes later he slowly rose to his feet. While not entirely rested, the short pause has restored some of his expended energy. Since he didn't know how far he would have to wander to find all of the supplies needed, he decided to take the knife with him for protection.

Stepping out of the shelter, Andy stared down at the sleeping rebel. A slight snoring sound could be heard from Dave's nostrils. Andy stared off in all directions, not knowing which area of the jungle would offer the most supplies. He noted that the late afternoon shadows were growing long and the brutal midday heat was subsiding. To his relief, the animals in the forest seemed to have returned to normal, after the mysterious silencing caused by the mist.

Although Andy had seen plenty of vines during his travels, none were available near the shelter. He scrambled through the thick jungle heading south, keeping the fiery sun to his right. Several minutes passed, before finding the first suitable candidate. As the knife sliced through the fibrous structure of the plant, Andy felt suddenly at home in the ancient jungle. The animal cries were as loud as ever, but he did not feel threatened by them any more. The jungle appeared dark and crowded, yet he only thought of it as home. As a result of his new found confidence, he allowed himself to wandered freely. The search for sticks and vines carried him further away from camp with every step, but this did not bother him in the least.

Though he felt at ease, his body was still recovering from his tiring experiences earlier in the day. A felled tree caught his attention and he picked his way through a tangle of thorns to rest upon it. He wondered briefly at what might have caused this massive tree to break from its stump two feet above the ground, but soon consumed his thoughts with other concerns.

Deciding to manage his load a bit more efficiently, he divided the sticks into bunches, tying them together with the vines. It took several attempts to master this technique, but he soon had four easily manageable bundles.

As he rose to continue his mission, a subtle movement out of the corner of his eye startled him. His comfortable feeling quickly disappeared. He dropped his bundles to the ground, grabbing for the knife. His eyes focused on the tree stump, then he laughed out loud. The laughter was directed at his own jittery actions, rather than what he saw.

Hundreds of small objects were hopping back and forth between the stump and the felled tree. The objects were so small, that Andy had to squint to see them. Though individually tiny, together they created an obvious blur of movement. As far as Andy could tell, the objects had no definitive shape or color. Both appeared to be in a constant state of change. After further study, he realized that the objects were actually carrying small pieces of the felled tree back to the stump.

The time traveler found this hard to believe, though the evidence sat before him. The minuscule objects were actually rebuilding the tree. Andy made a quick scan of his surroundings, remembering the fast growing bamboo shoots, but found nothing out of the ordinary. The miniature creatures were not a part of some scheme to attract food. They were simply rebuilding part of their world which had fallen apart. Andy marveled over the ambitious creatures, before picking up his belongings and continuing with his search.

Several minutes later Andy finished tying his fifth bundle of sticks together. By all estimates he had accumulated more than enough materials to build the trap, but he did not want to return to camp just yet. The darkening jungle enthralled his imagination and senses, as he wandered almost aimlessly through the vegetation. The cement and brick buildings, which had formed his previous environment, were now gone. Though only a few days removed, the life that he had known seemed an eternity in the past.

As he pushed his way through a wall of leafy branches, a putrid odor caused him to wince. The odor, he quickly discovered, came from a large pool containing a thick black liquid. The powerful stench caused his eyes to water and lungs to cry out with every breath, but he did not flee. He even toiled with the possibility that the vapors were poisonous, but still he did not back away. The black pool drew him closer, until he was standing only inches from the edge.

Out of curiosity, he tossed a stick into the thick quagmire. The stick struck the surface with a hollow splat, then slowly started to sink. Just before the stick surrendered to the liquid, it suddenly burst into flames. The quickness of combustion startled Andy, backing him away from the edge of the pool. Curious, he tossed a several more sticks into the mysterious liquid, just to make sure his eyes weren't playing tricks on him. These sticks also burst into flames, only seconds after striking the surface.

The substance in the pool intrigued him, but he realized that he did not have time experiment with his new discovery. The patches of sky visible through the trees revealed that evening was quickly approaching. Andy was not yet ready to head back to camp, however. The afternoon's exploration did not yet seem complete. He continued heading south, tossing aside stray branches and circumventing large rocks. It was only when the rays of light filtering through the trees turned to orange, did he decide it was time to reverse his direction.

Only Andy could complicate the simple operation of turning his body one hundred eighty degrees. His awkward motor skills caused him to catch his right toe on a stray root. As he stumbled forward and began tumbling to the jungle floor, the realization that he had slung the bundles over his shoulders in such a way as to prevent him from breaking his fall with his hands flashed into his mind, but only briefly. His head hit the ground with a solid thud, knocking him unconscious.

When the youngest Marshall woke, he was greeted by a dark sky and the multiplying sound of animals howling in the evening air. The adventurer rolled onto his side, then into a sitting position. He rubbed his hand over his head, feeling a small bump on his forehead. A sharp pain spread through his upper body, as his fingers reached the center of the bruise. Small spots of blood could be seen on his fingers, but nothing to cause an alarm. He tried to stand, but the jungle instantly began to spin in circles, forcing him to lower himself to a kneeling position. He remained motionless for several minutes, waiting for his vision to clear.

Finally, he made a second attempt at standing. Finding some success, he began to gather his dropped supplies. It was then that he noticed a large hole in the ground, only a few feet from where he had fallen. Once again, a wave of curiosity raged through his body. Barely recovered from his previous encounter, he inched toward the edge of hole, peering into its dark depths. With the aid of the scant moonlight, he could see the glimmering of a small object far below. Upon further examination, he recognized the object to be a pendant, his pendant. Somehow, even though it had been securely placed under his clothing, the piece of jewelry had fallen from his neck.

Andy rubbed his hand along the walls of the pit, which felt smooth and flawless. Seeing no way to the bottom, save jumping, coupled with the fact that he still felt quite woozy from his fall, he quickly rejected the idea of immediately retrieving the pendant. He had confidence that it would be safe until daylight.

Once again, Andy piled the bundles onto his back, making sure to keep his arms free this time. He gave one last look into the pit, before trudging off into the forest. The return trip to camp proved very slow, since he couldn't see more than several feet ahead in the dim light. A comforting sigh of relief slipped out of his pursed lips, as the putrid odor of the black pool reached his nostrils.

It only took seconds for the time traveler to realize that by plunging a stick into the pool he could create a torch. The newly formed flickering yellow light danced in the breeze, filling the jungle with a warm glow. With his sight now restored, Andy quickly found his way back to the dead tree.

The stump, now a few inches taller, made him laugh silently at the small creatures performing the work. The dedicated creatures seemed to be constantly working, but of course he had no way of knowing if they were the same ones he had seen earlier or simply the graveyard shift. Whatever they were, he thought, it would take them a long time to rebuild the entire tree. Even when they did finish, it could easily be knocked down again; forcing them to repeat the entire process.

The remainder of the trip back to camp took only several minutes. Andy welcomed the sight of the camp fire flames dancing freely in the evening breeze. Dave sat by the shelter, machine gun clutched in his hands. The rebel looked up suddenly, startled by Andy's movement. The barrel of the weapon rose with swift precision, leveling on Andy's torso. Andy stopped suddenly, frightened by the unexpected action. With a concerned look he scanned the camp area, looking for his brother. Joe was nowhere to be seen.

"Where have you been?" Dave asked, allowing his facial muscles to relax. "We thought you had been recaptured or killed by something. Joe is out looking for you now." Dave slowly raised the weapon, pointing it off into the jungle. Three short blasts echoed through the dark forest, a signal to Joe that Andy had returned safely.

"I couldn't help being late. While searching for the vines, I tripped and knocked myself out," Andy said, embarrassingly pointing to the black and blue lump on his forehead. "I woke up only about fifteen minutes ago. Then I found a large pit, which I almost fell into when I tripped. When I looked into hole, I realized that the pendant had fallen from my neck. I couldn't reach the bottom, so I came back here," Andy said, finishing with one of his awkward smiles.

Dave listened to the rambling explanation, not fully following the course of events. His eyes had focused on the torch Andy held in his right hand. Recognizing Dave's quizzical expression, Andy opened his mouth to explain, but didn't have a chance to speak. Joe interrupted by noisily barging through several branches. Andy looked up at his brother, only to be greeted with an angry stare.

"Where were you? I bet you were having yourself a great time, while I was running around this place looking for you. With no weapon, I might add," Joe yelled. He paused to catch his breath, before continuing his tirade. "Hey, where did you get that?" he asked, in a somewhat relaxed tone, referring to the torch.

"I was just about to tell Dave about it, when you came in here yelling like a mad man," Andy snapped back. "I'll start from the beginning."

"On my way out, I saw a very strange sight. Hundreds or maybe thousands of small microscopic insects were rebuilding a tree which had fallen down. It was simply amazing. Naturally I watched them for a few minutes, but they gave no indication that they knew I was there. Later I came a across a pool of awful smelling black stuff. When I threw a stick into the pool, it just burst into flames. The black stuff is what I used to make this torch." He waved the torch in front of his brother's face, before continuing. The brief review was finished off with a description of the hole where he dropped the pendant.

"This place is getting stranger by the minute," Joe said softly. He glanced out into the forest, smiling and shaking his head in wonderment.

It took several hours for the trio to construct an operable trap, seeing how none of them had any experience building such devices. They located the trap about twenty yards into the jungle, hopefully far enough away so that potential food wouldn't be scared off by their scent. A medium sized rock, fastened to the top of the cage, was intended to prevent the captured animal from freeing itself. Dave had collected several sweet tasting roots, while Andy had been out gathering vines, which were used as bait. The remaining roots were nibbled on by the adventurers to tide their hunger over until morning.

"Now that the trap is complete, and we have nothing to do, tell us more about the pool and the hole," Joe said, making himself comfortable against a tree. A cool wind blew through the jungle, causing the leaves to dance across the moon's face. "Do you think we can reach the pool in the dark? It would be nice to have some torches for the night. The one you have looks like it is ready to die out."

"I wouldn't risk it," Andy answered. Although he believed he could find his way in the dark, his eyelids were growing heavy and he had no intention of wandering through the jungle anymore today. "I think we should wait until morning. I don't know my way around here too well, yet. Besides, in the morning we can go to the hole and retrieve the pendant."

"I agree," Dave added. "Waiting for daylight sounds like the best idea. If we get lost out there, I doubt we'll find our way back in the dark."

"Well in that case I might as well show you what I found," Joe said, as a wry grin spread across his face. He rose and stood by the fire. "At first I thought that Andy had been captured by the creatures again, so I wandered over to their cave entrance. Two of them were standing guard. Being unarmed, I decided to leave them alone.

"I then wandered around the base of the mountain south of the entrance and discovered a small cave," he paused to take a bite out of a root. Andy squirmed, angry that he left off at that particular point. "The entrance to the cave was hidden behind a large thorn bush. I managed to squeeze by the bush, with only a few pricks. The passage was only five feet tall, so I had to walk hunched over." Joe demonstrated by drooping his shoulders. "About ten feet in, I found an entrance to a side chamber. I was surprised to find that enough light filtered in from the outside to allow me to see."

"Hurry up and get to the good part," complained Andy. "What did you find?"

"Okay, don't get hostile," Joe said. He stopped talking and turned toward the jungle. His steps were slow and methodical, drawing out the suspense as best he could.

Joe disappeared into the foliage, only to reappear a moment later concealing something behind his back. Andy jumped to his feet to try to catch a glimpse of what he carried, but Joe turned away. Sensing that he would have to wait and play by Joe's terms, Andy relaxed and sat back down. Joe slowly made his way back to the fire, dropping a large sack made of a small metal mesh onto the ground.

"When I returned and saw that you were okay, I decided to hide this stuff until later," Joe said with a smile. He fell to his knees and opened the sack. Secretively, he peered inside. Acting cautiously, he placed his hand inside the metal container, slowly fishing it around to purposely torture his intrigued brother. With a sudden yell, he unexpectedly pulled his hand from the sack, startling Andy, who gave a frightful scream. Joe then thrust medium sized skull into his brother's face. Andy screamed again. His eyes met Dave's and the same terrible thought ran through both their minds.

"That looks like a human skull," Dave noted. "Don't tell me that it is Ken or Bill's." His voice died off into a whisper.

"No, it doesn't belong to them," Joe explained. He held the skull closer to the flames. "But that is what I thought at first." With his free hand he reached into the bag, producing two more skulls. "You see, when I found these two, I realized that there must have been other humans around here. There were more than just these three in the cave."

Dave took the skull from Joe to study it closer. It quickly became apparent that it could not possibly belong to Bill or Ken, seeing that the bone was cracked and obviously in an advanced state of decay. When finished with his cursory examination, he passed the skull to Andy, who immediately dropped it to the ground. Even though the person it belonged to had long since died, he felt awkward touching the remains.

"When I entered the chamber, I saw just the one skull on the floor. At that point all I could think about was getting out of there. I turned to flee, but then saw three headless skeletons hanging by their ankles. Another much larger skeleton lay on the ground in front of the headless ones. This large skeleton had two broken spears lodged in its chest. I don't think it was human. I am guessing that he was an executioner or something."

"How did you arrive at that?" Dave asked, picking up the dropped skull from the ground.

"Because of this," Joe answered. He rose to his feet once again. This time he did not attempt to keep his audience at bay, as he hurried off into the forest. He returned, proudly displaying a large axe. Both edges of the two sided metal blade were still razor sharp. A few flaking blood stains were all that soiled the blade's silver complexion. "I found it buried in a human skull."

"It's strange that this blade is made of metal," Dave observed. He held his hands out to accept the weapon for examination, but Joe ignored the silent request.

"Why is that?" Joe asked, trying to remove some of the blood flakes.

"It seems out of place," Dave replied. "The creatures who captured you didn't have any metal tools. They were still using rock instruments and wooden spears."

"They're just stupid," Joe replied.

"Yeah, that doesn't mean anything," Andy agreed, rising to examine the weapon. "Did you find any other weapons in the cave? We could use some more protection. The bullets for the machine gun won't last forever."

"No, there is no use in returning there. I saw nothing of value to us," Joe answered, handing the axe to his brother. He gathered the skulls, placing them back into the mesh sack. The trio then entered the shelter in search of a restful sleep.

* * * * * * * * * *

The fire died down, leaving the jungle almost pitch black. A cloud cover had rolled in, blocking most of the light cast down by the moon and stars. Joe wakened from a light sleep and tossed a few twigs into the ring of stones, trying to keep the coals burning. He had been chosen for the first watch, but had negligently fallen asleep. A ball of sparks rose from the dying embers, as the dry twigs crashed upon them. The small specks of light danced in the still night air, before drifting away and burning out.

Joe's eyelids were still heavy, but he was alert enough to spot a small dot of light out in the distance. At first he thought the light to be a run away spark, but more of the tiny dots appeared. One by one the forest filled with the small yellow lights. After a few minutes, Joe began to worry.

He ran into the shelter, waking the others. Together they watched the mass of lights slowly drift through the jungle. With their number increasing and distance from the shelter decreasing, the lights had become a threat to the humans.

"Who's out there?" Dave yelled. His voice echoed amongst the vegetation. He knew that his warnings would not be understood by the intruders, but he hoped that the sound of his voice would scare them away. "Answer or retreat, before we open fire on you."

"They are still coming," Andy observed. The lights were still too far away for him to see who or what was there. "Maybe you should get the remaining cartridges."

"I think you are right," Dave replied, momentarily slipping into the shelter. He returned with the remaining five machine gun cartridges. "I'll give you one more chance. Retreat or I'll open fire." Dave's warnings did nothing to slow the lights from moving though the jungle.

"It looks like they are heading off to the southeast," Joe said, watching the string of lights grow longer.

"I don't think we have the luxury of waiting to see if they will pass us by," Dave replied. "There are too many of them. We could be over run in a matter of seconds."

Dave knew that by using the weapon the possibility of an attack would be increased, but he felt that a preemptive strike was their only hope. Reluctantly, the rebel fired a few rounds into the jungle, several yards ahead of the first light in the growing line. A few yells could be heard, filtering in through the vegetation. The lights slowed for a moment, but then continued their movement.

"You are going to have to shoot at them to stop them," Joe said, observing the action.

"I was afraid of that," Dave responded. "I just hope Bill and Ken are not among them."

"They would have answered our yells," Andy replied.

"If they were capable," Joe said, not taking his eyes off the mysterious lights. "It is possible that they are incapacitated."

Dave fired another blast into the forest, making sure that this time some of the bullets hit their target. Several screams of pain could be heard, as several of the lights fell to the ground. A bush ignited into flames, but was quickly snuffed out by the light bearers. The procession stopped, as the unknown beings paused to take account of the situation.

"They probably don't even know what hit them," Joe said, standing ready with his axe. "I'm sure that something as common a bullet to us, is a complete mystery to them."

"I wonder what they are," Andy added quietly. The other two were too engrossed in the action to pay him any attention.

The group stared eagerly into the forest, where the lights seemed to hover in place. Some moved forward a few feet, while others moved back. But as a whole the group did not move. After the initial cries of pain, nothing could be heard from the intruders. The minutes passed slowly, before the mass of lights began to move once again.

"That didn't stop them," Dave said, raising the gun for another assault.

"It still looks like their path is not heading toward us," Andy said, studying the movement. Though he had grown up amongst routine violence, he did not wish to be witness to the possible massacre that stood before him. "Maybe we should give them a chance to pass."

"Do you really want to take that chance?" Joe asked. "For all we know they could be the little creatures out looking to recapture us. Just because they aren't heading our way now, doesn't mean that they might not surround us first, before attacking."

"I don't think that they are the creatures," Dave surmised. "They're carrying too many torches."

"The creatures did have a few torches lying around," Joe replied.

"It really doesn't matter," Dave added, his finger tightening around the trigger. "Whoever or whatever, they will not encroach on our camp without a fight."

A barrage of bullets cracked through the jungle, tearing through leaves and branches. A few more lights dropped to the ground, followed by yells of pain. The wind rustled some leaves behind the shelter. Dave spun around, expecting to see an unfriendly creature, but nothing was there. The lights, once again, seemed to circle amongst themselves, but none ventured any closer to the human's camp.

The trio sat patiently watching for any sign of movement. Several small bush fires were scattered about the jungle. One by one they were extinguished. Fifteen minutes passed, with the lights still showing no indication that they were going to continue on their march.

"You two can go and try to get some sleep," Dave finally said. He found a comfortable spot on the ground and placed the gun down beside him. "I'll take the next couple hours watch. They don't seem to be doing anything right now. I'll call you, if they do,"

Joe and Andy watched the lights in silence for a few more minutes, before retiring to the shelter. Neither of them could sleep for more than a few minutes at a time, stirring at the slightest sound.

Dave watched the lights for well over an hour. As the minutes passed, their number slowly decreased. His heart felt truly relived that the bearers of the lights were retreating back in the direction from which they came. The second lethal blast of bullets had done its job. At one point, during the slow retreat, Dave thought he saw the reflection of two small eyes staring at him. The evil yellow glow from the two round circles made him so uneasy that he wanted to shoot at them, but the dwindling ammunition supply prevented him from doing so. Finally all the lights disappeared and no further threat was made on the shelter during the night.

When Joe woke, he found Andy feeding the fire with the remaining sticks. The sun shone brightly through the cover of the trees, filling the air with the now familiar yellow tint. The tranquil chirping of the birds made the ancient time seem like paradise.

Andy, still paranoid from the events of the night before, heard Joe's footsteps and spun around with weapon raised. "Oh, it's only you," he said with a sigh of relief.

"Don't point that thing at me," Joe yelled, shaking his head. "That would be a fitting end to this misguided trip through time. Joe Marshall shot by his kid brother."

"Sorry," Andy said in a soft voice. "I'm just a little tense. Look, I found a rabbit in the trap. You startled me, just as I was about to skin it." He held the dead animal up by its ears.

"Have you ever skinned an animal before?"

"No, have you?"

"No," Joe admitted. He was proud of the military style training he received from the Protectors, but they had never prepared him for survival in the wild. "By the looks of things, we are going to be here for a while. We might as well get used to doing everything for ourselves."

"I'll skin this one. You can do the next," Andy suggested.

"Sure, but make it quick. I'm starving," Joe said, finding a comfortable spot on the ground next to his brother. "By the way, how long have you been on watch? I figured you would wake me for another shift."

"I've only been up for a couple hours. Dave spent most of the night out here. He said he couldn't sleep, so he decided to stay up. I think he was just too interested in the lights," Andy explained.

Andy soon had the animal cleaned, even with the persistent supervisory instructions from Joe. Carefully, he placed the meat on the spit to roast over the fire. Dave woke a short time later, joining the brothers in conversation.

"Have either of you checked out the area where the lights were? I'd like to know if there are any bodies," Dave said, gazing in the direction he spoke about, hoping that there would be some evidence as to who he had shot. The possibility that he had killed innocent beings weighed heavily on his conscience. While he had a hand in killing many humans, and would readily admit the fact, all were members of the Protector's organization and thus easily justified. Before last night, all the creatures he had killed since his arrival in this strange time had been in self defense. But for some reason he did not feel that way about his last murderous spree.

"No, why don't we walk over now. Andy's the chef for the day. I just hope he can cook," Joe said, with a laugh.

"You better be back in time to eat. I can't guarantee that there will be any food left, if you're late," Andy said, spinning the meat over the fire. "I'm so hungry I could eat this whole thing myself."

Dave and Joe slowly made their way through the tangled forest. Dave carried the machine gun, while Joe armed himself with the axe. Both were alert, but neither really expected to run into any trouble. All indications suggested that the intruders had left the area. While the mysterious light bearers posed no threat, the low lying thorn bushes were nagging to say the least. The sharp thorns stabbed Joe's legs, making the short trek a painful one. When he bent down to remove one of the bothersome branches, he spotted a small charred torch half hidden in the underbrush.

"It doesn't appear as if they were very tall," Joe surmised, lifting the torch through the vegetation. "This thing is only a foot and a half long."

"They may not have been tall, but they sure had us out numbered," Dave said, kicking through the underbrush in search of more torches.

"It smells as if they used the same black stuff Andy found to ignite the torches," Joe said, after further examination of the artifact. "There must be more than one pool of that stuff around here. The one Andy found is located on the other side of the shelter."

The two continued their trek, soon coming upon a small patch of trampled plants and bushes. Large spots of red blood covered the rocks and trees surrounding the area. Several burnt torches were strewn about, giving the site a sense of death. To their disappointment, there were no signs of dead bodies. They were sure that Dave had killed some, however. The amount of spilled blood proved that. But there were no clues as to the identity of the intruders.

"I guess these guys weren't from the caves after all," noted Joe, after spotting the red blood. "I wonder why they were traveling at night? There were so many of them, that they had to have a place to live somewhere around here. Why would they move?" he asked the last sentence to himself in a whisper.

"They weren't from the caves, but we had to shoot at them none the less. We really can't take any chances, if we expect to get out of this time alive. If we didn't shoot when we did, they would have been close enough to overpower us," Dave said, still trying to rationalize his actions, more for his own benefit than for Joe's. He continued to look over the site in disappointment. A few small animals wandered by in search of food, but quickly fled into the jungle upon seeing the humans.

The delicious odor of roasting rabbit found its way through the forest to their nostrils. Growling stomachs proved more powerful than inquisitive minds, starting the two on the return trip to the shelter. Joe found the path back to the camp just as painful as the route they originally took, which puzzled him since his boots had offered adequate protection in the past. Now, however, the thorns seemed to be guided into his legs, striking the most vulnerable areas. The two arrived, just as Andy removed the rabbit from the spit.

"What did you find?" he asked curiously.

"Not much. There were a few torches lying around. We didn't find any weapons, so we don't know if they were dangerous. The only thing we are sure of is that they had red blood, lots of it. It appears as if Dave killed some, even though we didn't find any bodies," Joe said, tossing the charred torch into the fire.

"That's what they must have been doing after we shot at them," Dave said, as the thought suddenly entered his head. "They were probably gathering the wounded and dead. No wonder they were out there for so long."

Neither Joe nor Andy remarked, as their attention changed focus to the rabbit. It was slightly larger than the one Dave had caught the day before, meaning they could go that much longer before growing hungry again. Andy cut the meat into three pieces. Each starving time traveler devoured his portion in a matter of minutes. A small piece of meat was spared for use as bait, although the humans had no idea if it would provide better results than the roots. After the filling breakfast, the three returned to the battle site for a second look. They spent several minutes searching for any missed artifacts, but found none.

"Now, what about the hole you found yesterday?" Joe asked, as the group arrived back at the shelter. "Do you think it would be worthwhile to check it out?"

"Well, I do want to get the pendant back, if nothing else. Like I told you before, it looked as if the hole led to a tunnel, but I can't be sure. It was too dark."

"I say we check it out. We have nothing else to do around here," Dave said, waving his hand around the forest. "We don't know where the time machine is and the last time we looked for it we almost got killed."

"Let's make sure the trap is set properly. I want another rabbit for lunch," Andy said, licking his lips in remembrance of his tasty breakfast. "As long as we are here, we might as well eat."

"Yes, and I think I'll bring the axe. You never know when we'll need the extra protection. Besides, now we'll each have a weapon," Joe said proudly. He popped into the shelter, returning with the axe draped over his shoulder. The weapon weighted slightly more than he would have preferred, but he could handle it if needed. "Okay, show us the way."

CHAPTER IX "THE HOLE"

Andy led the trio along the same route he had followed the night before. After a short walk, the group found themselves standing next to the felled tree. The tiny repairmen had worked throughout the night, as evident by the increased height of the stump. Andy estimated that the workers had restored nearly a foot of the damaged tree, since the last time he passed by. Dave knelt down close to the stump, squinting to watch the tiny objects. He looked on in amazement, as the mysterious objects transported pieces of the dead tree, reassembling them into their original positions.

"It's amazing that they are so accurate," Dave said, as he rose. "They seem to effortlessly break the wood away from the tree."

"I'm still trying to figure out why they do it," Andy said, smiling his awkward grin. "One tree is as good as another."

"Maybe they are some kind of caretakers," Joe suggested. "It could be that their job is to wander through the jungle looking for damaged plants and things."

"At the rate they are going, it is going to take them a few weeks to finish this tree," Andy said. "I sure hope for their sake that not too much gets damaged around here."

"Enough with these things. I want to check out that hole," Joe said, urging the other two to leave the dead tree.

A few minutes later they found themselves standing at the edge of the black pool. Every few seconds several bubbles would rise from the center of the pond, where they popped with a low gurgling sound. With the help of the axe, Joe cut several three foot branches from a nearby tree. Dave dunked the branches into the pool creating three torches. The translucent orange flames danced freely in the warm breeze.

"What do you think it is?" Andy asked, taking a torch from Dave.

"It looks like some sort of petroleum deposit. But I have never heard of any that self ignite materials," Dave answered, rising from the edge of the pool.

"What ever it is, it sure smells disgusting. Let's get out of here before I get poisoned," gagged Joe. He moved away from the pool, holding his breath.

"For being a ruthless killer, you sure have a weak stomach," Dave joked. Joe smiled, but moved on without speaking.

Andy pointed off into the jungle, signaling the direction to follow. A short jaunt later, the time travelers reached the hole Andy had discovered the previous night. Its diameter measured just over four feet, while the depth fell ten feet into the ground. The smooth walls Andy had felt during the night were formed of a highly polished marble.

"It looks like a tunnel down there to me," Dave said, gazing into the pit.

"How are we going to get down?" Andy asked, leaning over the edge of the hole. The walls offered no means to aid in descent.

"Getting down is not the problem," Dave said, running his hand around the surface off the wall. "We could easily jump that distance. Climbing out could be tricky. We would have to boost one of us out, so he could help from the top."

"Or we could just use a rope," Joe said. He swung his axe at a nearby tree cutting a vine free. Deftly he tied the vine around the donor tree, depositing the free end into the pit. "Pass the gun down to me, when I reach the bottom," he told Dave.

Joe gripped the vine, quickly dropping himself into the hole. Upon reaching the bottom, he immediately verified that tunnel extended into darkness. A brief inspection revealed that the pendant had not suffered any damage from its fall. Joe tossed the piece of jewelry up to Andy, who felt a sense of relief pass through his body.

The instant Andy replaced the artifact around his neck, the man in the globe reappeared. The image wore a smile, which spread clear across his face. Andy couldn't be sure, but the figure seemed to be younger than in any of its previous appearances. The man's hair looked darker and less wrinkles were visible in his pale skin. Andy's thoughts were broken by a voice from below.

"Okay, throw down the gun," Joe yelled to the surface. Dave obeyed, carefully dropping the weapon into the hole. "Now pass down a torch. I can't see a thing down here." Joe had no intention of trying to catch the torch, so he let it fall to the ground. The orange flames billowed, as the torch landed, but continued to burn. Joe picked up the torch, then glanced toward the surface. The flickering light cast an evil glow over his features.

"Don't get careless with the ammunition," Dave warned. "We only have four cartridges left. If you run into trouble, get back here as quickly as possible. We'll be ready to pull you up."

Joe nodded in agreement, before disappearing into the darkness of the underground passage. Andy tried in vain to watch his brother walk off, craning his neck into the pit. The light from the torch was visible for a while, before fading away. The few minutes that passed seemed like hours to Dave and Andy, who waited impatiently on the surface. Suddenly the faint glow of orange returned and Joe's face reappeared.

"The walls definitely look as if they were constructed by intelligent beings," he said, taking a breath of fresh air. "The passage goes straight and slants downward. It ends at a set of stairs, which descend even deeper underground." He paused to take another breath, as the air in the tunnel tasted stale and musty. "I didn't go down, because I couldn't see well with only one torch. But I think I heard the sound of running water."

"Water!" exclaimed Andy. "What are we waiting for? Let's go find it."
Andy and Dave wasted no time in joining Joe at the bottom of the pit.
The thought of water, after almost five days without more than a mouthful
of rainwater, suddenly made them more thirsty than they actually were.
Once away from the light of the sun, the orange glow of the torches took
over, glimmering off the polished rock surrounding the explorers. The
walls gave the appearance that they were constructed out of a single
piece of marble, as no creases or seams were visible in the blue and
white swirls.

The trio quickly reached the stairs, cautiously beginning their
descent. Even though the five foot wide stairwell offered ample room,
they decided to pass single file. Dave led the way, with the machine gun
aimed straight ahead. Joe kept to the rear, armed with the axe.

Thirty-three steps later, the adventurers found themselves standing
at one end of a vast hall. The feeble light cast off by torches was not
nearly strong enough to illuminate the far end of the chamber. Andy
looked up at the arch shaped ceiling, which loomed twenty feet above.
The torches did offer enough light, however, to reveal intricate art work
carved into the rock ceiling. The fancy art work stopped where the ceiling
met the walls of the hall, which were formed from the same marble
composite found in the tunnel.

Thirty feet out into the hall two rows of columns appeared, dividing
the room into three long corridors. A small alcove was located on either
side of the staircase that they had just descended. A quick examination
revealed that each alcove contained a set of stairs, which led further
underground.

"Look at this place," Joe said, walking toward the nearest column. "It
is huge. It must have taken years, for whoever built it, to complete."

Dave followed several yards behind Joe. He waited for Joe's voice to
stop echoing, before speaking. "As long as its creators don't come back,
while we are here, I don't think we should have any problems."

"I don't think we have to worry about being intruded upon," Andy
said, pointing to the set of stairs in the right alcove. "This stairwell is
clogged by cobwebs. For that matter, just look at the floor. We're
standing in nearly an inch of dust."

Andy's observations were correct. For the first time they realized that
the hall was actually quite deserted. The sparkling walls even a had a
thin coating of dust upon them. A potent patch of the stale air reached
their nostrils, adding further proof that the hall had not been used for
many years.

Andy burned away several yards of cobwebs in the alcove. He
entered the passage to the first step, peering down into the darkness,
before moving out to join the others at the base of the first column. As he

moved closer, the form of a large creature slowly became apparent, fighting its way through the shadows behind Joe and Dave. Andy was momentarily stunned by the size of the beast, its height reaching nearly to the ceiling. "Look out! Behind you!" he screamed.

The surprised Dave and Joe turned quickly, ready for battle. The tense expressions, which had suddenly appeared on their faces, just as suddenly turned into smiles and then laughter. As Andy stepped closer, he too began to laugh, albeit a most humbling chuckle.

"I thought it was a monster or something," Andy said, as his red face went unnoticed in the darkness.

"It's only a statue," Dave confirmed, looking up at the column.

Joe and Dave had not previously noticed, but the column was actually a complete carving of a human. The detail of the workmanship was remarkable. The creases in the figure's clothing and position of all his limbs looked as natural as if he were standing there breathing. The gaze from the somber face stared dutifully toward the exit.

"This is truly amazing," Joe said, marveling at the statue. "I have never seen anything like this."

"Look, all the columns are carved to look like humans," Andy said, as he approached the second row of supports.

Dave glanced down at the floor, where a metallic glint caught his eye through the thick layer of dust. He bent down, picking up the blade of a sword. The handle to the weapon could not be found. "It looks as if it was broken in combat," he commented, after examining the markings on the piece. The silver metal contained several outstanding dents and chips.

Joe's sensitive ears, once again, picked up the faint sound of running water. The delightful sound of splashing came from the far, yet unseen, end of the hall. All other thoughts were lost.

"Quiet," he ordered, as he listened closer. "I can hear the water."

The other two immediately stopped talking to listen. The fascination with the statues was abandoned, as the trio broke out into a jog toward the refreshing sounds of splashing water. Joe led the way, only taking the precaution of making sure there were no obstacles on the floor ahead. As the thirsty humans ran forward, the sound of rushing water grew louder.

Even in his excited state, Dave had an uneasy feeling that the eyes of the statues were watching him, as he raced by. He kept glancing up at the figures, expecting them to suddenly move and chase after him, but they were as lifeless as the rock from which they were carved. Andy, however, had no such fear. Eager as he was to quench his parched throat, he still found time to zigzag through the two rows of columns, taking a quick look at each statue's face.

The columns ended and only a thirty foot stretch of dust covered marble floor separated the humans from a refreshing drink of water. The water, cascading over a tall waterfall on the left wall, ran through a ten foot wide fissure in the floor, before disappearing into a hole in the right wall. The fissure was obviously created to be a feature of the hall, as colorful blocks of stone were built into the floor along the edge of the water. A cool breeze blew in through the drainage hole, where only darkness could be seen.

"I think Andy should have the first drink, since he found the hole," Joe said, eagerly awaiting his share of the precious liquid.

"As long as he makes it quick," Dave teased.

Andy carefully placed his torch on the floor several feet from the fissure, then knelt down next to the water. He dipped his hand into the rushing fluid, allowing the cool temperature to soothe his parched skin.

"I said, as long as he makes it quick," Dave said, placing the machine gun and his torch on the floor. "You better hurry up and take a sip, because I'm not waiting any longer."

Andy quickly withdrew his cupped hand, slurping at the water it contained. His throat relayed to his brain an immediate voice of satisfaction. "It's great!" he informed the others. "It's the best water I have ever tasted."

Dave and Joe immediately joined Andy at the edge of the fissure. A few moments later, Dave dove into the water. Not accustomed to water sports, a sudden panic took hold of him, as the current swept him toward the gaping hole in the right wall. After a brief struggle with the rushing water, he was able to grab onto the marble floor and stabilize himself.

"Sure, now you contaminated the water," Joe said. He had been drinking downstream of Dave.

"Just move up closer to the waterfall," Dave replied.

"Maybe later," Joe said, placing his belongings on the floor. He dove into the water, purposely only inches from Dave, making sure to splash as much water as possible in the rebel's direction.

Andy quickly followed. Soon all three were splashing and swimming, completely forgetting their situation and the fact that not too long ago they were on opposite sides of a deadly political battle.

"It sure feels great to have a bath," Andy yelled over the thunderous waterfall. He splashed some more water on his faced, trying to scrub the layers of dirt away.

"I for one can vouch for the fact that you needed a bath," Dave laughed.

"Just don't get too close to the hole," Joe warned. "You might get sucked into it and we have no idea where you might end up."

After a glorious ten minutes of splashing and swimming, the refreshed humans decided to leave the fissure and return to the surface to dry off. The festive mood proved to be short lived, however. While Joe, the last to leave the water, struggled out of the fissure, he accidentally knocked the axe into the swift current. The heavy weapon instantly plunged to the bottom, where it remained for only a second. Without reason, the roar from the waterfall intensified, as the volume of water flowing into the fissure rapidly increased. Joe, poised to reenter the water to retrieve the axe, stopped short, suddenly worried about the changing environment. The momentary delay was all the time the water needed to carry the axe off into the unknown darkness that lie beyond the right wall. Joe watched in partial horror, as his prized possession vanished. Surprisingly, as soon as the axe disappeared from sight, the flow of the water returned to its previous state.

"That's strange," Andy noted. "It is almost as if the water didn't like having the axe in it."

"It's no use worrying about it," Dave said, as a cool shiver ripped through his wet body. "Right now I could use some of that sun to warm me up. It's too cool down here to stay dripping wet like this."

"Come on, Joe," Andy said to his brother, who was still staring into the void. "We'll find you something else. That thing was a bit big for you anyway."

Joe turned away from the fissure, took two steps, then stopped. He turned back to the water for a moment, positive that he had heard a voice. The words, 'Joe, save me', were repeated in a soft whisper. Dave and Andy evidently did not hear the voice, as they continued their stroll toward the exit. Joe was positive that the whisper came from the void in the right wall. He waited several moments, hoping the voice would return, but it didn't.

"It's just the water," Joe mumbled to himself. "No different than the whispers of the wind."

Joe turned from the fissure and hurriedly ran to catch up to the others. With their damp clothing sending a bothersome chill through their bodies, the trio walked briskly through the hall. The statues were ignored, as the thoughts of the warm sun drew them to the stairs. Still cautious of a surprise attack, their worries subsided slightly, upon reaching the access tunnel. Moments later they were helping each other climb to the surface, where the midday sun immediately began to dry their clothing.

"I don't know about you two, but I want to explore this place some more," Dave said, after a refreshing rest. He stared down in to the pit. "If nothing else, It will help pass the time."

"Don't you think we should check the field first? We should keep an eye out for Bill and Ken, for when they return," Andy said, wondering what had happened to his friends. The group was continuing with the premise that the scientists had taken the time machine and would return to try to rescue them from the caves.

"We can check later," Dave said, eager to return to the mysterious hall. He looked over at Joe, who sat with a dejected expression on his face under a tree. "Don't fret over that axe, Joe."

"I know I shouldn't be upset," Joe replied, deciding not to mention the voice he thought he heard. "It's just that... I really can't explain."

"Come on," Dave said, extending a hand to help Joe to his feet. "I have a feeling we are going to find so much stuff down there, that you are going to forget that you even found that axe."

"Depending on what we find, you might be right," Joe replied, with a smile.

This time the trio felt at ease, as they walked through the dark tunnel that led to the descending staircase. They spent a few moments studying the marble walls, but still could find no seams or creases in the blue rock. When they reached the hall, Joe tried to cheer himself up by commenting that at least they had a water supply now. But that just caused him to flashback, witnessing in his mind's eye the axe being swept away by the water all over again.

With only two passages visible, they decided to follow the webbed staircase in the right alcove. The torches easily burned through the numerous cobwebs, casting a grey smoke into the air. The cracked stone steps bent inward at a sharp angle, soon merging with another set of stairs, obviously those of the second alcove. The two formed a larger staircase, which continued to lead down into the earth.

After descending another twenty cobweb covered steps, the passage made a U-turn, where the stairs continued to descend even further. The stairs finally came to an end, leaving the visitors at one end of large hall. This hall appeared to be identical in size to the previous, except that only one row of columns were used to support the ceiling.

"I wonder how far down this place goes?" Joe asked, taking in his surroundings. The cool temperature caused him to rub his arms in an attempt to warm them. "We must be at least eighty feet below the surface already."

"Maybe it goes all the way through the earth," Andy suggested. Joe just shook his head and laughed.

"I sure wish I knew if humans really built this place," Dave said, absorbing the details of the second hall.

Andy walked up to the first statue and studied it for a few seconds. "Hey, guess what?" he asked the others. "This statue looks exactly like the image in the pendant."

Andy removed the mysterious pendant from his neck, hoping to compare the two. But to his disappointment, the pendant did not produce the image he sought. He gently shook the amber globe, but nothing happened. Reluctantly, he returned the pendant to its home underneath his shirt. Closer examination of the column revealed lettering around the base.

"It must be the guy's name," Dave surmised. "Each of these statues must depict an important person to the people who used to live here." He stopped and stared at the strange markings, trying to decipher them. Some of the letters were similar to his own, but most were quite different. He did notice that none of the lines forming the letters were consistent in thickness. One end was always thicker than the other, or the middle of the line would be larger or smaller than the ends. "Very strange," he mumbled to himself.

This hall, unlike the first, had many side passages. Joe quickly grew bored of the statues and made his way into the nearest side chamber. The large rectangular room was populated by stone tables, neatly arranged in three rows. The rows unmistakably led up to a giant altar. Several of the tables were broken, intentionally destroyed by some unknown force, while others seemed to have deteriorated naturally. No other exits were visible.

A life sized statue of a human, dressed in a long robe, was proudly displayed on the altar. Joe found it strange that the vandals had destroyed some tables, but had left the center piece of the chamber unscathed. The art work, carved out of a bright red marble, held a sun in one of its outstretched hands. Yellow rays of stone diverged from the sphere, almost lighting the room themselves. The other outstretched arm held a yellow carving of a crescent moon.

"That must have been their god," he said, as the others entered the room. Each of them had an eerie feeling, imagining how the ancient humans lived their lives.

Dave walked up to altar to study the statue. He found the workmanship to be as precise and detailed as that of the columns. As he turned away from the statue, the table nearest the altar caught his attention. The adventurer cupped his hand and scooped off the layer of dust, which wasn't nearly as thick as that found in the upper hall. Cleared of the camouflaging cover, the red polished marble revealed the same odd lettering found on the column in the hall. He spent a moment more clearing the remaining dust of the off the table. Once again, he found it useless to try to decipher the language.

"Look at this," Andy said, as he finished brushing the dust from another table. "More writing."

"It looks to be the same as the first," Joe said, glancing between the two tables.

"It looks like each table is inscribed with the same words," Dave said, after wiping clean a third table. "This one looks identical to the others."

"Too bad we can't read it," Andy added.

"If Bill and Ken never come back for us, we'll have plenty of time to decode it," Joe said, moving toward the exit.

Andy and Dave remained behind, making one final examination of the chamber. Finding nothing of interest, they left the altar room, joining Joe at the base of a column.

"Getting bored?" Dave asked.

"No," Joe replied, gazing up at the column's figure. "It's just that there are so many questions, and no one here to answer them."

"We'll just have to keep looking for them," Dave said, leading the way to the next doorway. "The answers, I mean. I'm not sure I want to meet the people who used to live here."

As the light from their torches displaced the darkness, they could see that the second doorway did not lead to another chamber, but rather a corridor. The passage stretched out for more than a hundred feet and measured nearly twenty feet wide. Both walls were lined with what appeared to be humans skeletons. The sight of the remains reminded Joe of the cave he had discovered, but this corridor was obviously meant to be a shrine rather than a place of execution. Embedded in the wall under each skeleton was a silver plaque, engraved with the now familiar lettering. Stone shelves under the plaques were used to display an array of silver swords.

"This is a strange way to honor the dead," Joe said, walking amongst the skeletons.

"I wouldn't want to be put on display like this," Andy added, standing in the exact middle of the corridor as to maximize his distance from the frightening bones. "Do you think they let the bodies decay here? That must have been gross."

"I wonder how they died?" Dave asked, picking up a sword. The blade of the weapon measured just over three feet long. A notch was present in the finely crafted handle and the point had been broken off.

"It looks as if they died in combat," noted Joe, picking up two pieces of another sword. The skeleton the sword belonged to was missing its right arm, plus several ribs. The bones were worn and discolored. "I hope this guy died quickly."

The group walked along the corridor, with Dave stopping at every skeleton inspecting the weapons that lie below. He was discouraged to find that each sword had been damaged in some fashion, until he reached the middle of the long corridor. There he found one that was not only undamaged, but appeared untarnished by the passing of the years. He picked up the weapon and started to fray with an invisible opponent. The razor sharp blade sliced silently through the stagnant air.

"You look as if you've had some experience with those things," Andy said, as he watched Dave maneuver the weapon.

"No, as a matter of fact, I've never touched one before," Dave answered, surprised himself at how comfortable the sword felt in his hand. "Swords aren't very effect when dealing with flying spheres." With little effort, Dave removed the remaining arm from a nearby skeleton. The body of bones fell to the floor, breaking into countless pieces.

"Let's see those little caretakers put that back together," Joe laughed, pushing the bone fragments up against the wall with his foot.

"I don't think we should be messing with these things. It gives me the creeps," Andy said, eyeing the skeletons, afraid that they might come alive and exert revenge for the desecration.

"Yeah, you're right," Dave said, now feeling sorry that he had destroyed the skeleton.

Joe searched the remaining swords, hoping to find another undamaged, but found none in operable condition. They were either broken in half, or severely damaged by chips and cracks.

"Look at this," Joe said, grasping the handle of a broken sword. He held his outstretched hand to Dave, who immediately turned over the blade he had found in the upper hall. The two pieces fit together perfectly. "I wonder how the blade found its way upstairs?"

"Some animal probably took it up there," Andy suggested, still keeping the maximum distance possible from the skeletons. "It has probably been up there for some time, considering the amount of dust it was buried under."

Dave examined his sword, then looked up at the other two in amazement. "Hey, I can read the markings on this thing." Both Andy and Joe studied the markings, but they appeared as jumbled and meaningless as the other inscriptions they had seen.

"You can't read that," Joe said, annoyed by Dave's joke. "It's just like everything else, a jumble of funny marks."

"But I can," Dave protested.

"Well, what does it say?" Andy asked, not sure whether to believe Dave, but eager to find out what the markings read, none the less.

"It says 'DUZIC'," Dave told the others. Andy and Joe looked at each other, clearly disappointed.

"Are you sure you can read that?" Joe asked sarcastically. "I think you are just making it up. I'm sure that if I look at the markings long enough, I can make up a word that looks similar to the letters, too."

Dave didn't reply. He silently walked over to the plaque, from where he had taken the sword. To his surprise he could read it also. "Listen to this. 'Duzic, the fighter, died in battle. With his powerful sword, he has contributed to the cause more than can be mentioned here.'" He stopped and looked at the others.

"That's why you could handle the sword so well," Andy said. "The inscription says that it is a powerful sword. It must make the user an expert swordsman."

"Yeah, right! Just like it gives its user the ability to read this language," Joe added, still unconvinced by Dave's sudden new abilities. "Here, let me hold it for a minute."

Dave handed the sword to Joe, who found the inscription to be as jumbled as ever. "Nothing yet," he said, looking up at Dave. When he looked back, the letters were there. DUZIC. "I don't believe it," he said, staring back and forth between the sword and the plaque. "I can read this stuff."

"Let me try," Andy cried, leaving his secure spot in the middle of the corridor, for a chance to read the plaque. He, too, found that he could read the ancient language with the aid of the sword. "This is amazing." He handed the sword back to Dave, and once again found the plaque to be unreadable.

"Just another mystery," Dave said, flicking the blade of the sword through the air, once again.

"A mystery we will never know the answer to," Joe added.

The trio followed the corridor to its end, where they found themselves standing at the top of a very large, and very dark, stairwell. Plump rats ran for shelter, as the light from the torches fell upon them. An earthy odor rose from the stairs, making the underground air even more potent. The orange glow from the flames reached twenty feet down the staircase, but no end could be seen.

"Do you think we should go down?" Andy asked, clearly worried that the reply would be yes.

"It looks too dangerous to me," Dave said. "Our torches are starting to burn out. I wouldn't want to be too far underground when they die. Besides, there is still quite a bit more to explore on this level."

"We know that this place has at least three levels," Joe noted, as the group turned back toward the hall.

"I have a feeling we are going to spend quite a bit of time exploring this place," Dave said, as he passed Duzic's skeleton for the second time.

The moment Andy stepped out of the skeleton passageway, a burning sensation spread across his chest. The intense heat was concentrated precisely where the pendant made contact with his skin. Frantically he fumbled with his clothing, grasping the pendant's chain, and pulling the globe free from his shirt. The once pale amber sphere now burned a fierce red. Andy held the sphere away from his body, trying to protect himself from the heat.

"Break the chain, if you have to," Joe said, noticing that Andy was having difficulty lifting the chain over his head.

The red glow suddenly disappeared, with it the intense heat. Andy, still holding the sphere out in front of him, watched as the image of the old man returned. This time, however, he did not appear as an old man. All of the grey in his hair was gone, as were the once numerous wrinkles in his pale skin. The image appeared to be that of a young and vibrant man. But the change in the image's age was not the most striking attribute. The man no longer wore a jovial expression. The friendly grin and warm eyes had been replaced by a serious, stone cold stare.

Feeling that the heat had dissipated, Andy allowed the sphere to be cradled in his palm. Dave and Joe gathered close to watch the image. The man in the pendant slowly faded into a white fog. As the fog cleared, a tightly clenched fist could be seen, filling the sphere. The hand wore an amber colored ring, which housed a clear stone in a gold setting. The display gradually enlarged. Inside of the clear stone, another fist could be seen. The image continued to enlarged, revealing a similar ring on the second hand. The rate of change hastened, as the images quickly cycled through a loop of fists and rings.

Suddenly, instead of another fist, a lightning bolt appeared in the stone. The white bolt traveled through a black cloud filled sky, before crashing into a tree. The tree immediately cracked in half and burst into a ball of flames. Then, without warning, the pendant exploded. A small crack ran through the glass globe and a yellow mist seeped out, leaving the sphere black and imageless.

"What do you suppose that was all about?" Joe asked.

"I have no idea," Andy replied, gingerly poking at the pendant with his finger. The globe felt surprisingly cold. He unbuttoned his shirt to examine his chest. "It's funny, but I don't seem to be burnt. The pendant was really hot, but my skin is not even red."

"It doesn't surprise me," Joe said. "Just the fact that you found the pendant in this time explains everything."

"Look at the hall. It is lighter than it was before," Andy observed, looking around the hall in wonder.

The hall indeed seemed to be brighter. For some inexplicable reason, the vast chamber was giving off its own light, from an unseen source. The new light was so bright, that they no longer needed the torches to see.

"When the pendant burst, all of its energy must have gone into the hall. They are definitely connected in some way," Dave said, taking a second look around the newly illuminated hall. Unknowingly, his grip tightened around the handle of the sword.

The trio walked through a few more side chambers, now that they were no longer in a rush to leave before the torches burnt out. They found them all to be empty, except for the dust. As they prepared to head back to the shelter, Dave decided to stop back into the altar room to see if he could read the markings on the tables.

The source of light in this chamber was clearly evident, as they stepped through the doorway. The sun in the statue's hand glowed an intense bright yellow. Dave found that he could only stare at the sun for a few seconds, before the intensity forced him to look away. Shielding his eyes, he approached the table closest to the altar. Joe and Andy stood silently by the door, as Dave read the ancient text.

"I guess their god's name is Gotte Sonne Mond," Dave said, pointing to the words. His face grew puzzled, as he tried to continue. "For some reason, I can't make out the rest of the words. They appear to be written with the same lettering, but no words are forming."

"It figures. Even after we can read the language, we can't understand it," Joe said shaking his head. "Let's go. I'm getting tired."

The group left the altar room, but Dave delayed the trip to the surface, by stopping at the statue which resembled the man in the pendant. "This guy's name is, or was, Konig Chaz," Dave said, translating for the others. "From what it says here, I guess he used to be the leader of the humans. He was responsible for building the halls. And, I guess, this place is called Plebiscite."

"I wonder why there is only one statue of a woman?" Andy asked, referring to the statue directly behind Chaz.

Dave read the lettering and relayed to the others, "Her name was Konigin Claibe. She was Chaz's wife."

"I wonder if there is a statue of Duzic down here?" Andy asked.

"I don't know, but it won't do us any harm to take a quick look," Dave said, realizing that his torch had burnt out. He dropped the charred stump onto the dust covered floor. "I just hope this place doesn't stop giving off light, until we are gone."

Joe gave a sigh, as he watched Dave and Andy walk deeper into the hall. "I'll wait here for you two. My legs are too tired." Joe sat down at the base of Chaz's statue, staring at the stairwell, which led to the hall above.

Dave and Andy returned a few minutes later. None of the statues in the hall depicted an image of Duzic. Joe groaned, as he rose to his feet. His obvious attempts to hurry the others along, went unnoticed. After climbing the stairs to the upper hall, Dave and Andy immediately headed toward the columns.

"I'll just wait here," Joe said to himself, sitting on the stairs, which led to the surface.

Dave read the inscriptions aloud. "'Pristine - Although he fought like a primitive warrior, he helped keep order in Plebiscite.'" Dave and Andy looked at each other and shrugged their shoulders.

"I guess that was important to them," Andy said, as he followed Dave to the next statue.

"'Racontuer - kept the people amused by telling them old stories of life before Plebiscite.'"

"At least that one made some sense," Andy commented.

"'Proselyte - found him wandering through the jungle. Converted him to our colony. Never did speak a word.' He doesn't look too much like a human," Dave observed.

"Not at all," Andy agreed.

Dave paused, before reading the next statue. "Here it is. 'Duzic - helped colonize the people. Plebiscite's best warrior.'" Dave stopped and glanced up at the statue's face.

"Hey, he looks like you," Andy stated, looking back and forth between the two. The statue had slightly longer hair than Dave, but no moustache. Besides the lack of facial hair, the two looked exactly the same. "Maybe you two are related. He could be your ancestor."

"I don't think so," Dave said, slightly embarrassed at the suggestion. "It's just a coincidence. There are no humans left here. How could he be my ancestor?"

The two argued the point, as they walked back toward the exit. Joe was mildly impressed by the fact that Duzic and Dave had similar appearances, but he was more interested in ensuring that Andy and Dave didn't find any more excuses to remain in the halls. The fact that the two were now just as exhausted as Joe, allowed the latter to lead the group up the stairs without complaint.

Now that Dave had the 'Sword of Duzic' for protection, Joe was able to carry the machine gun. As they struggled out of the hole, they were greeted by the late afternoon sun. A short hike brought them to the edge of the black pool.

"I guess we spent more time in the halls than I thought," Dave said, lighting the last of three torches.

"You can say that again," Joe said, as a cramp tightened his leg muscles.

"But I think it was worthwhile," Dave added.

"We even found one of Dave's ancestors," Andy joked, taking a torch from Dave. As he did so, a bitterly cold wind blew over the mountain peaks through the tangle of the jungle, as if an evil force had been revived.

"It's cold all of a sudden," Joe said, staring intently into the jungle.

"A storm is coming, that's all," Dave said, as the group continued their walk toward the shelter.

To the surprise of no one, the tiny objects were still busy reconstructing the dead tree. Their efficiency hadn't let up one bit, as the stump stood several inches taller than it had in the morning. The sporadic breeze did cause a disruption though, momentarily scattering the small flying creatures.

The only thought on Joe's mind was a long refreshing nap. His muscles ached for a reprieve, but none would be forthcoming. As the travelers pushed through the last cluster of vegetation, they were met by a terrible surprise. The shelter had been completely destroyed by fire. Several of the nearby trees were also scorched, but the limited area of the fire indicated that it had been deliberately set. The remnants of the shelter had been haphazardly tossed around the area. A stunned silence followed, as the humans stood in disbelief.

"I bet those creatures we attacked last night did this," Andy said, kicking through the charred remains. The burnt wood crumbled under his foot, leaving only a pile of ash.

"I think you're right," Dave said angrily. He swung the sword at a small tree. The blade sliced through the trunk, as if it were made of paper, dropping the sapling to the ground. "If I had one of those guys here right now, I'd do the same to him."

"You can't blame them. After all, we attacked first," Joe said, trying to rationalize the situation. Another gust of chilling wind sent a shiver through his spine.

"Yes, but we had to fire upon them," Dave said, angrily looking out into the jungle. His thoughts returned to the events of the previous night. "We were greatly out numbered."

Andy's hungry stomach led him to the trap, which he found to be intact. He also noticed that the trap had been sprung, meaning that they would not go hungry this evening. While happy that they had food, the three prepared, cooked, and ate in silence. They were not upset so much at the fact that they had lost the shelter, as the feeling that they had been violated by the intruders.

"It looks like we will have to spend the night in the halls. It seems to be the safest place." Joe said, after finishing his dinner. "I sure wish we could find something else edible around here."

"Staying in the halls shouldn't be too bad," Andy said, sitting back to relax. "At least we will have water."

Dave said nothing. He just stared blankly out into the forest. Without his knowing, the strange powers of the sword had begun to take control of his mind, planting seeds and suggestions. The sword compelled him to go to the caves of the small creatures and destroy them. Suddenly, he stood up and started to walk toward the mountains.

"Where are you going?" Andy asked.

"I'm going to the caves. I feel as if I have to vent some frustration and those creatures are going to feel the brunt of it," Dave said in a dark voice.

"Remember what happened the first time we went over there," Joe said sternly. He felt leery about reentering the caves, especially with no apparent purpose.

"I don't think we should go either," Andy added. "Why do you want to bother with them?"

"I don't know. I think the sword wants me to," Dave replied, shocked by the words that he had just uttered.

"I think you are cracking up," Joe stated flatly. "This place is starting to get to you. If you go into those caves, you're asking for trouble. We already went through this."

"I am not cracking up," Dave yelled in defense.

"This is silly," Andy said, trying to defuse the situation. "It is too late in the day to be running around."

Dave tightened his grip on the sword. He could feel a strange sensation running up his arm and into his head. A sudden realization came to him. "The sword can communicate with me. I don't know how, but it can. It has told me that the creatures are called Blieins and that they helped overthrow the humans. All I want to do is help the sword get its revenge. It has waited a long time for this opportunity."

"You are talking as if the sword is alive," Joe argued. He stood, with the gun in his hand, just in case Dave's erratic behavior worsened. He had seen the cutting ability of the sword and wanted to protect against an assault.

"How can you talk to a sword?" Andy asked. "Are you saying that you can carry on a conversation with it?"

"I... I don't know," Dave replied. He walked back toward the ruined shelter and crashed to the ground. "It is so confusing. Most of the conversation is one way. It is talking to me. But I think, if I concentrate hard enough I can communicate with it." He suddenly jumped back up and started to maneuver the sword, as if fighting an invisible foe. The cold wind continued to blow down the mountain and whistle through the trees.

"If you can talk to it, ask it what the mist was that froze all the trees," Andy told Dave. Thoughts of the mist still ran through their minds.

Dave nodded and closed his eyes. He let his mind wander into a deep meditation. He stood silent, with the sword grasped tightly in both hands. Slowly he raised the weapon, until he held it above his head, with the tip pointing straight up. A few moments later he opened his eyes. A large smile crossed his face, but quickly eroded into a troubled glare. "The sword is both pleased and troubled."

"What?" Andy asked, totally perplexed.

"The mist was not captured before Duzic died, but the sword knew of the cube. It says that freeing the mist was the worst thing we could have done. The humans never intended for the contents of the cube to be released. It was designed to forever contain the spirit of the Minomassa, the leader of the human's greatest enemy; the Ubeleutes. They live on the other side of the mountain. They were the major force against the humans during the war."

"Wait a minute," Joe said shaking his head. "You are jumping all over the place. You're telling us about the human's enemies and about revenge. Why don't you fill us in on what they are getting revenge for? For that matter, who is getting revenge? They are all dead."

"Okay, I'll try to explain it the best I can. The Ubeleutes controlled the land, before Chaz and the humans settled in Plebiscite. The Ubeleute's hatred slowly built over the years, until finally they started a war with the humans. Under normal circumstances, the humans would have been able to defeat the Ubeleutes. In fact, the Ubeleutes had attempted to destroy the humans several times, only to be thwarted. The Ubeleutes then became resigned to coexist with the human population, or at least that is the impression they gave. For the most part the two sides stayed away from each other, allowing everyone to live in peace. But the Minomassa would not rest until the humans were all dead. The Minomassa used its powers to convince the Blieins, along with many other creatures, to fight against the humans. The Minomassa's forces staged a surprise attack on Plebiscite, causing severe casualties. The humans were able to hold off the aggressors for almost a year, but they were slowly battered. The last recollection the sword has was when there were approximately thirty humans left. It does not know what happened after that. After Duzic was killed, the sword was placed in the hall where we found it, and has had no contact with any human for many centuries."

"That makes things crystal clear," Joe said sarcastically, as he tried to follow the story. He felt leery about Dave's sudden ability to communicate with the sword, and was not ready to place his fate in the hands of a centuries old piece of forged metal.

"Yes, and it also means that Duzic could still be Dave's ancestor," Andy said, still trying to logically connect Dave and Duzic. "The sword does not know what happened to the remaining humans. They could have escaped and set up camp somewhere else. If Duzic had some children..."

"It would be a long shot," Dave said, lowering the sword. He relaxed the tight grip he had on the weapon.

"This seems a bit far fetched to me," Joe said, still keeping a sharp eye on Dave and a ready finger on the trigger of the machine gun.

"But will you go with me to the caves?" Dave asked, returning to the desires expressed by the sword. "I will go by myself, if I have to."

"What exactly are we going there for?" Joe asked. "We already know that we are severely outnumbered. Just having that sword isn't going to change anything."

"And we don't have much ammunition left," Andy added. "By the looks of things we are going to be here for a long time. We need to conserve what we have."

"The sword does not expect us to totally destroy the Blieins," Dave said, trying to persuade the brothers to join him. "It just wants to cause some major damage and let the Blieins know that humans are back in Plebiscite."

"I think they know that already," Andy said. "In case you forgot, they did capture us."

"I didn't forget," Dave replied. "This strike will also serve to protect us in the future. The Blieins have been free from the Minomassa's rule for some time. If we can show them the strength we have, they might resist any attempts the Minomassa might make to ally with them again."

"Great, just what we need," Joe said shaking his head in disapproval. "The humans were wiped out by these creatures. There are only three of us. I don't think we want to provoke anything."

"It is too late for that," Dave answered. His expression grew stern. "From the time you released the Minomassa, we have been marked men. We might as well have an offensive showing, before our enemies become organized."

"What is he talking about?" Andy asked his brother.

"I don't know," Joe answered. A nervous tightness gripped his stomach, a feeling he had not felt since his first days on the job for the Protectors. "If he is right, we can't stay around here for long. If your friends don't come back for us soon, we are going to have to leave on our own and try to find a safe place to stay."

"Are you coming?" Dave asked. He rose and began walking toward the mountains.

"I suppose so," Joe answered. He checked the cartridge in the machine gun. "As long as you promise to make it quick. Tomorrow we are leaving this place, whether you join us or not."

"Fine," Dave yelled, slicing the sword through some bothersome vegetation. "Follow me."

The sun had just about set, when lightning lit up the darkened sky. The light flickered through the jungle, casting shadows in all directions. Dave led the brothers along the path, which they had followed upon first landing in the ancient time. The lightning continued to flash across the sky and the humidity rose drastically, but no rain fell. A sudden gust of wind pushed the humans backwards, but they forged ahead none the less.

Upon reaching the cave, they found two guards standing by the entrance. Not even waiting for the others to ready themselves, Dave burst from the cover of the vegetation, surprising the two creatures. With a single swipe of the sword, Dave parted one guard's head from its body. The Bliein instantly dropped to the ground.

The other guard had no time to react. Before it could process the information it had just witnessed, Joe fired a few rounds into its body. The creature slumped to the ground, yellow blood leaking out of its wounds. In its dying moment it looked up to see Dave's face and the sword in his hands. A flash of lightning filled the sky, as the creature let out a mumble. "Duzic," it said, then died.

Joe stared into Dave's eyes, puzzled by the comment made by the dying Bliein. It was the first word he had heard and understood from the little creatures. Dave stared back, with an expressionless glare. Though Joe had only known the rebel for several days, he knew that at that moment it was not Dave staring back at him. Whether it was the sword or Duzic himself, he did not know. But for sure, Dave was not in control of his body.

The sword led Dave, like a magnet, into the cave. It guided him down several passages, directly to a group of five Blieins, who were running to get their spears. Before they could arm themselves, Dave killed two, while Joe shot the other three. Andy stayed clear of the fighting. The youngest brother observed the fighting with a torch in one hand and the knife in the other.

Another Bliein entered the chamber, hurling a spear at Dave. With the help of the sword, he knocked the missile aside. The creature looked stunned, its eyes opening wide upon seeing the sword. Before the Bliein could react, Dave dropped it to the ground. The rebel gave off a victorious yell, as he held the vibrating sword over his head. After hundreds of years of waiting, the sword was finally having its revenge. Even so, it was not satisfied. The sword still had control over Dave, compelling him to kill more.

The trio left the murder site, heading for the exit, now that the element of surprise had been neutralized. Because of their sheer number, the now organized Blieins were sure to gain the upper hand. As the fleeing humans passed a chamber, Dave beheaded another creature, just as it stepped from the room. Joe kept a constant eye on the rear, killing any creature that happened to walk into his sight.

The humans easily found the exit from the caves and fled into the jungle, but the Blieins were in close pursuit. The time travelers stopped at the edge of the forest, where Joe placed a new cartridge into the machine gun. Just as the first wave of creatures exited the cave, he plastered them with a barrage of bullets. Dozens fell to the ground, before the cartridge emptied. He looked at Dave with disdain, tossing the empty ammunition case to the ground.

"That's enough," Joe said. "Let's get out of here."

A brilliant flash of lightning cracked through the cloud filled sky, but still no rain fell. A deafening roar of thunder followed the lightning. Moments later a bright flash of green light lit the jungle, silhouetting the peaks of the mountain range. The sword, now cold in Dave's yellow blood stained hands, told him that the Ubeleutes have been aroused. The spirit of the Minomassa had regained a physical body, and once again was out to destroy all humans.

Strange sounds filtered in through the forest, as the animals also sensed the danger. Joe placed another cartridge into the gun, leaving only one in reserve. The humans quickly retraced their steps along the path. With their chests heaving, trying to grasp enough oxygen, the trio emerged into the field where they had originally landed. As expected, there was no sign of Bill or Ken. They had not returned. For a moment the thunder and lightning stopped, leaving the jungle of the ancient world peaceful and serene.

Dave stood in silent meditation. A crack of lightning filled the sky, breaking the silence. A second flash of green light followed, just as the thunder echoed through the dark jungle. Suddenly, Dave popped out of his meditation.

"What were you asking it?" Andy inquired. He kept a nervous eye on the path, just in case the Blieins were following.

"I was asking it how powerful the Ubeleutes are," came the reply. "The sword told me that they were experts with arrows and axes during the war. It thinks they might be stronger now, but there is also an equal chance that they are weaker, since they have been inactive for so long. Apparently the Minomassa has great mental powers, as well as physical."

"It doesn't sound too promising," Joe laughed. "If all those humans couldn't beat them, what does it expect us to do?"

Before Dave could answer, a loud noise from the far end of the field startled the trio. The Minomassa had contacted one of its old allies; the giant red ants. They had been given orders to attack the humans. Three of the massive insects burst through the vegetation, pausing momentarily to assess the situation. With their antennae waving rapidly, the trio rushed forward.

A moment later, the Blieins reached the field. The creatures also stopped, surprised to see the ants. But the Blieins did not wait for long, before flooding into the field. Dave led Andy and Joe to edge of the forest, where he hoped they could defend themselves more effectively.

"We have to make a run for the halls," Andy said, above a roll of thunder.

Joe fired at the group of Blieins, killing most of the creatures. The others paused, almost as if they were considering a retreat, but a green flash filled the sky compelling them forward. More ants had emerged from the forest, but they seemed to have been misinformed. They were attacking both humans and Blieins, more frequently the latter. Dave joined into a battle with an ant, quickly dropping the insect.

"Come on," Andy yelled again. "We can't stay here."

"Forget him," Joe said, referring to Dave. He moved toward his brother, in an attempt to flee into the forest, but stopped short as two Blieins jumped from the foliage. The small creatures were quickly killed by a short burst from the machine gun.

"We'll never make it in there," Joe said to his brother. "It's too dark. Too many places for them to ambush us."

"We can't stay here," Andy yelled in return.

Joe returned his attention to the center of the field, where another group of Blieins were gathering for an attack. He waited until the creatures had closed to within twenty feet, before firing a blanket of bullets at them. As the last creature fell to the ground, the cartridge emptied. Joe held his breath, as he slipped the last clip into place. He knew that he had to shoot accurately and selectively, for once this cartridge emptied, they would be helpless.

"Actually, trying to make it to the halls might not be such a bad idea," he said, firing at several creatures.

"We are lucky that the ants are helping us," Andy said. By this time he had picked up a stray spear. He jabbed at an ant, as it charged by. The creature instantly crumpled into a ball and died.

"They aren't exactly on our side, but they are helping," Joe yelled back. Another burst of green lightning filled the sky. A rumble of thunder followed, mixing with the yells and screams of the warriors. "Dave, let's make for the halls," he yelled, but Dave was too engrossed in the battle to hear.

The rebel was not merely defending himself, but actually seeking the offensive. Mindlessly he jumped from foe to foe, dropping each to the ground almost effortlessly. The sword, of course, was dictating his every move. The centuries of inactivity did not diminish the weapon's power in the least.

"It's no use talking to him," Andy yelled. "We have to stay and help."

"No, we don't," Joe replied. "This is not our battle. It's not even his. Our only chance is to make it to the halls."

Joe fired at another group of Blieins. The gauge on the cartridge read half empty. He turned to flee into the forest, but once again a wall of creatures blocked his path. This time there were far too many to kill. The closing ranks forced the humans into the center of the field, where they were now vulnerable to attack from all sides. Joe dodged an array of spears, then dropped several Blieins to the ground. He picked up a spear, ready to use it when the machine gun emptied.

Another group of Blieins closed in. Joe fired the remaining bullets at them. He then began to swing the gun like a club, striking anything that came within arms length. He looked up just in time to see Dave finish off another ant.

"We have to try to make it to the halls," Joe yelled over the noise to Dave.

Dave nodded in agreement. "You two start for them. I'll do the best I can to protect you from the rear."

More lightning filled the sky, as Joe and Andy raced for an opening into the jungle. A handful of Blieins quickly blocked their path. After successfully fending off the attack, the brothers made another attempt to reach the jungle, but were blocked once again. A strong gust of wind carried the putrid odor of burning flesh from the other side of the mountain. The Minomassa was sending the humans a message, forecasting their demise.

Andy was busy dodging spears, when an ant burst out of the jungle behind him. Before he even knew the insect was there, it grabbed him in its clutching jaws. A timely rumble of thunder drowned out Andy's yells and the crunching sound of his breaking bones.

CHAPTER X "CIVILIZATION"

The darkness slowly dissipated. Colorful streaks converged on a spot of white light, waking Bill from his unconscious state. The scientist opened his eyes wide, only to fall victim to a sharp pain pounding through his head. He closed his eyes once again, while taking inventory of his person. All fingers were present and operational. He moved his left arm, only to find his right following along in unison. The treemen's ropes were still intact. Both legs were cramping, having been twisted in some inhumane angle for an unthinkable length of time, but he knew that a relaxing walk would bring them back to normal. He opened his eyes once again, but the pain instantly returned.

Bill tried to push himself up into a sitting position. The binds made the effort much more painful, but he managed to crawl to the door of the time machine and look outside. To his surprise, the air proved to be free of the familiar yellow tint. Through the numerous trees, he marveled at the sight of the bright blue sky. Several white cotton clouds hovered high overhead, slowly rolling away with the wind. At that moment he realized that they had escaped from the ancient past. The only question in his mind was, what time frame had they landed in?

His vision momentarily wobbled, as he spun his head toward Ken. The elder scientist did not wait for his eyesight to stabilize, before crawling over to his partner. Ken lay crumpled and unconscious against a bank of computers, but his chest rose and fell in regular intervals, easing Bill's mind.

"First things first," Bill said, managing to remove a panel from the computer. Upon the sharp metal edge, he sliced through the binds that bound his wrists. The restrictive ropes fell to the ground and a sigh of relief came from his parted lips. After rubbing the soreness away, he used the metal panel to cut through Ken's binds.

"Ow! I feel like I have been run over by a sphere," Ken said, finally returning to the conscious world. The fact that his binds had been removed did not immediately strike him, as his hands instinctively moved to rub his aching head. His swollen fingers traced a small cut that had opened on his forehead. The blood had already dried, giving evidence to the length of time they had been unconscious. Memory of the events that led to their time travel filled his head, as he massaged the deep yellow impressions left behind by the grimy ropes.

"Welcome back," Bill said, with a painful smile. He struggled to stand, using the computer as a crutch. His legs were understandably weak and wobbly. The aching scientist leaned over the controls and pushed a few buttons. To his surprise and liking, the date on the computer screen indicated the year to be nineteen sixty-seven. The twentieth century was the precise time he had chosen as a model for his revolutionary government.

"Where are we?" Ken asked, managing to rise to a kneeling position. "Or should I say, when are we?" He reached for the controls and opened the door of the time machine. A rush of fresh air bombarded the occupants. The chirping of several birds, who were comfortably perched on top of the time machine, greeted the time travelers.

"We are in the year nineteen sixty-seven," Bill informed. Ken nodded, also happy with the outcome of their time travel. "We are still in New York, of course. The time machine only travels through time, not distance."

"I know," Ken replied, "I did help design this thing."

"Forgive me," Bill replied, not turning from the controls. The excitement he felt was overwhelming. The thoughts of Andy, Joe, and the rebel were lost. The realization that he was one step closer to his goal of overthrowing the Protectors set his mind wandering along that track.

"At least we are away from the treemen," Ken said, still easing the soreness out of his wrists. "I can't believe that those creatures actually lived on earth. What could have happened to them, to leave no trace of their existence?"

"I don't know. Maybe some day we will find out why," Bill replied. "But before we do, we have to explore our surroundings. We have to find some allies here to help with our revolt."

"Don't you think we should rescue Andy and his brother first?"

"Hmm?" Bill questioned, as the remembrance of Andy filtered back into the forefront of his mind. "Yes, of course. I was just jumping ahead a bit. But there is no reason we can't work on both tasks simultaneously."

The time machine had landed in a plush forest, sparse when compared to the dense jungle of the past. All of the plants and trees were fully blossomed and green. A refreshing breeze blew into the open door of the time machine, carrying with it the sweet odor of the vegetation. Most of the trees were recognized as pine by the scientists, with a sampling of oak and maple scattered about. All senses of danger were gone, allowing the scientists to feel at home.

Bill ran some diagnostic tests on the computer, revealing that the time machine had suffered some minor damage while in the possession of the treemen. After scouting the immediate area, and finding the forest deserted, the scientists began repairs. In less than an hour, the computer indicated that all of the problems were fixed.

"I can't wait to see what the people in the twentieth century were like," Ken said. He stepped outside the time machine, taking a deep breath of twentieth century air.

"We can think of this as an experiment," Bill said, following Ken outside. "From this point on we are on a research mission. Our goal is to determine if we really want to copy the present form of government."

"Sure," Ken replied, losing some interest in the battle with the Protectors. *After we rescue Andy, there is no reason to return to our time,* he thought to himself. *We have already escaped.* Bill and Ken attempted to camouflage the time machine, using branches broken from nearby trees. Even so, the pyramid shaped machine was easily identifiable and distinctively out of place. A layer of pine needles softened the ground, giving some relief to the over worked feet of the travelers. A pleasant feeling spread through Bill's body, as the sounds of the birds mingled with the rustling of leaves. His heart began to pump faster, sensing the victory over the Protectors. *It will not be long,* he thought, *the Protector's time is ticking away.*

It did not take long for the time travelers to stumble upon a dirt road. Six inch blades of grass grew wildly between two dirt tracks, which twisted out of view in both directions around trees and boulders. A short walk along the road led the scientists to a small paved street. A wooden sign, nailed to two wooden posts, read 'GEORGE WASHINGTON STATE FOREST, PUBLIC PARK'. In small letters on another sign the words 'New York Forest Department' were printed.

The scientists found a third sign several feet away which displayed a list of warnings. 'NO CAMPING, NO MOTOR VEHICLES, NO FIRES, NO UNAUTHORIZED PARTIES ALLOWED BEYOND THIS POINT.'

"For a free country, they don't let you do too much. No this and no that," Ken said, after reading the sign.

"No, I guess not," Bill said, eyeing a group of small buildings across the street.

"I don't remember any farms in New York City," Ken said, noticing the same buildings.

"A lot of things have changed in two hundred years," Bill remarked. "I just hope the people are hospitable."

The buildings were surrounded by a small stone wall. The main farm house was located off to one side, while two other buildings balanced the landscape. Outside of the stone wall, stretching out of sight in all directions, stood endless rows of corn stalks, swaying lazily in the warm breeze.

Bill found the dashed yellow line dividing the street to be quite interesting. The same feature was also present on streets in his time. *Maybe things really haven't changed that much,* Bill thought. The scientist paused momentarily, following the line with his eyes, until the road disappeared over a small hill. As the two stepped off the pavement, the sound of an approaching vehicle momentarily frightened him, bringing back the memories of the flying spheres. The sound was not from a sphere, of course, but rather a blue convertible. The car approached and sped by in a blur of sounds. Music blared from the vehicle. 'All you need is love', were the only words the time travelers could decipher from the song.

"There is nothing like that in our time," Ken said, as the convertible reached the peak of the hill and disappeared from sight.

Bill said nothing. He was thinking of the words he had just heard. 'All you need is love'. If all the people in this time felt that way, he thought, it would be a perfect time to copy.

"They must have been done away with during one of the wars," Ken said in a low voice. He imagined himself driving the vehicle, looking as relaxed as the driver who just raced by.

"Yes," agreed Bill, who didn't hear a word Ken said. He was lost in thought, imagining a world without the Protectors. "Right now I just want to go over to that house and see what the people are like."

A rock littered dirt road led from the paved street to the small farm house. Thin metal wires, secured to wooden posts, separated the driveway from the rows of corn that filled the fields. Occasionally, the scientists were forced to dodge potholes full of muddy rain water, but considering the ragged condition of their clothing the effort was not needed. The stalks of corn cast a sweet odor into the air. An odor neither could compare to any other they knew.

Upon stepping onto the flagstone walkway, Bill's heart rate skyrocketed. Each step took him closer to the small cement stoop, which rested at an odd angle underneath the front door. Wooden buildings were something rarely seen in the future, with most of the forests being destroyed during the war. Bill and Ken were from a world dominated by brick, metal, and concrete.

The farm house had obviously seen better days. Shingles were missing from the roof, while the peeling paint suggested that the building was in dire need of maintenance. A faded United States flag hung next to the door, shifting effortlessly in the wind.

"What's that?" Ken asked, as the duo stopped at the bottom step of the stoop. "I've never seen anything designed like that before."

"It is the flag of the United States of America," Bill answered, his eyes brightening. "I have seen pictures of it in books, but I've never seen a real one."

"You act as if it is important," Ken stated, as he climbed the first step.

"It is," Bill replied. "It's the symbol of freedom."

Bill struggled to keep his balance on the slanted stairs, then raised his hand to knock on the door. But something stopped him. Not only was the paint on the door peeling, but the wood was beginning to splinter. Fearing that his knock might further damage the door, possibly upsetting the owners, he took a moment to search out an area that still seemed to be solid. A brief silence followed his light tapping, sending his heart rate even higher. Countless thoughts ran through his head, most of which were negative as to the outcome of the encounter.

All his worried thoughts ceased, when a lady in her early fifties opened the door. She stood about five foot seven inches tall. Her shoulder length hair was strewn about, showing that she had recently woke. A blue and white plaid shirt and a pair of old dungarees confirmed the fact that the battered farmhouse was not owned by wealthy individuals. An awkward silent stare greeted the two men, dressed shabbily in their battered and soiled clothing. The dirt smudged and caked over their bodies gave them a definite transient appearance.

"Hello," Bill said in a polite voice, not knowing the proper introduction for the twentieth century. The lady smiled, but said nothing. Bill continued in a hopeful voice, "May we come in?"

The lady looked at Ken, who stood at the bottom of the stoop. He smiled, hoping to break the tension, but remained silent. The woman then opened the door a bit wider, looking around to see if others were nearby. "What for?" she asked with a stern face.

"Who's there?" yelled a man from inside.

"A couple of bums," the lady replied. "I think you'd better handle them." The woman backed away from the door, then disappeared out of view.

Bill stood in confusion, not knowing if he should enter the house. He could hear the sounds of dishes and running water, but could not see or hear the residents.

"What do you want?" the man yelled, after several moments.

"Go in," Ken encouraged.

Bill slowly pushed the door open and stepped into the house.

The tiled floor entryway was small, no more than five feet square. The faded color of the tiles indicated a once bright and cheery entrance to the aging farm house, but Bill saw nothing that looked overly inviting. To the immediate right sat a dark and dreary living room. Straight ahead, a partially sunlit hallway led to the rear of the house. But Bill gave all a cursory glance, instead focusing his attention to the left, where the farmer and his wife were preparing to eat breakfast in a small kitchen. The scientist moved forward, stopping just inside the doorjamb. Ken followed a step behind, remaining hidden in the shadows.

The morning sun shone brightly though a window, giving the room a serene appearance. The man, also in his early fifties, sat at the kitchen table, reading the morning paper. He carefully folded the paper and placed it aside. The farmer's clothes were, as expected, old and worn. The man studied the visitors for a moment, before speaking.

"What do you want?" he asked in a semi-harsh voice. "I'm very busy and don't have time to entertain strangers."

Bill hesitated, not knowing how to respond. A quick glance around the kitchen revealed an old gas stove, by which the woman stood frying eggs. A small round clock, the plastic face yellowed with age, hung on the wall over the table. The hands of the clock indicated that it was seven o'clock. Bills eyes widened, as he noticed what hung from a rusted nail, embedded in the wall directly below the clock. The pages of a calendar shifted gently, due to a breeze entering through the open window. The calendar, opened to August nineteen sixty-seven, appeared to be the only new object in the prosaic kitchen.

"My name is Bill. This is my assistant Ken. I'm..." Bill paused, taking a nervous look back at Ken. "I'm not sure if you will believe us, but the urgency of our situation suggests that I should get right to the point. We are scientists from the year twenty-one eighty-six. That is to say we are from your future. We are in dire need of help in order to rescue a couple of our friends," Bill finished with an impish smile. The grin, however, soon disappeared.

The woman burst out in laughter, as she tended to her cooking. "And we are a couple of fools," she said, removing the eggs from the pan and placing them on a plate. She walked to the table, placing the food in front of her husband, before whispering in his ear. "Humor them while I call the police."

It was not her intention for the scientists to hear her statement, but they did. If the word police meant the same in nineteen sixty-seven as it did in twenty-one eighty-six, Bill knew they were in trouble.

"I don't think it is necessary to call the police," Bill said, growing very concerned over the situation. "We truly are from the future. As I said, we left New York City in the year twenty-one eighty-six, in order to escape an invasion by the Protectors police force." He stopped and watched helplessly as the lady dialed the telephone.

"Look, if you two just want food or something, we never turn your kind down. We know it is tough for people like you, so you don't have to make up stories," the farmer said, picking up a forkful of eggs.

"We would appreciate any food you could spare," Ken said, as his growling stomach reminded him of its lack of nourishment over the past several days. He stepped forward, eyeing the plateful of food with a sinister greed.

"I knew it," the farmer said, turning to his wife. "You can put that down, Mary. They just want some food."

Mary grimaced at her husband's offer of hospitality and replaced the phone into its cradle. She walked back to the stove and reluctantly cracked open several eggs for her guests. The transparent substance of the raw eggs sizzled, as it hit the hot pan. A moment later the yellow yolk was surrounded by an opaque white.

"We do appreciate the food," Bill said. He glanced at Ken, who had moved to the middle of the kitchen to watch the woman cook. "But food is not our main concern. We really are from the future. And we really need assistance to rescue our friends. Our time machine is in the forest across the street."

"Is that so?" the farmer remarked. He looked casually at his wife, who stood with her back toward him. The farmer then motioned for the scientists to sit. "I hope you boys like eggs. It's something we eat a lot of around here, since we don't have to buy 'em."

Bill and Ken had never eaten fresh eggs. The Protectors tight control of all food supplies, provided almost exclusively processed foods to the general population. Each scientist found an empty chair, which consisted of a gold metal frame with inexpensive vinyl covered squares for the seat and back rest.

"I never tasted a real egg," Ken said, "but I'm so hungry I'm sure I'll like it."

"Really?" Mary questioned, as she walked up the table and placed a plate in front of each visitor. She gave a disgusted snort toward her husband, before leaving the room. This act made Bill even more nervous. The scientist wished that his hostess would have stayed in the kitchen, where he could keep an eye on her. For all he knew, she could be going to fetch a gun or make the threatened call to the police.

"Back to this time machine," the farmer said, picking up another forkful of eggs. He smirked a little as he continued, "Just where did you acquire a time machine? Did you just go down to the store and buy it?"

"No. Seeing how this is the very first time machine ever built, it is quite impossible for it to be sold in a store. I made it," Bill replied. Ken cleared his throat in protest. "Actually, we made it," he corrected. "Along with a couple of my assistants." Bill started to become even more discouraged, as the farmer smiled and nodded.

"You don't look like a scientist to me," Ronald said, passing a forkful of food through his smiling lips. "To me, you look like a very old unemployed hippie." With that the farmer laughed out loud.

A frustrated Bill looked over to Ken, who apparently was more interested in his meal than with the conversation. "I'm afraid I have no idea what a hip..."

Bill didn't have a chance to finished his sentence. Mary, who had obviously been listening from the other room, reentered the kitchen. "Let's assume you really are from outer space. Why did you come here?"

Bill shook his head in wonderment. "First of all, we are not from outer space. I never said we were from outer space. We are from earth, just like you. The only difference is that we come from a time that is in your future." The expression on Mary's face didn't change. Bill began to wonder if all the people in this time were as dense as she.

"Our laboratory was raided by the Protector's police..."

"The Protectors?" laughed the lady. "That sounds like something from a cartoon."

"Yes, the Protectors," Bill snapped. He had a few choice words for Mary, but decided to hold them back, not wanting to offend his hosts. "Luckily, we had enough time to reach the time machine and escape. Since the process was so rushed we were not able to fully program the computers. As a result, we ended up one million years in our past. If the police had caught us, we would have certainly been killed. I'm afraid one of my assistants met that fate."

"Oh, I see now. You traveled one million years into the past. That means you are from the year one million nineteen hundred sixty-seven," the woman began to laugh even harder. Several tears formed in her eyes, causing her to excuse herself from the room. "This is the best joke I have ever heard."

The man also laughed, but not quite so hard. He rose from his chair and looked out the window toward the forest. Everything he knew told him that Bill and Ken were lying. There was no such thing as a time machine. But still, he wanted to believe their story. Though clearly fictitious, their story was interesting, nothing like his boring life.

"She was not listening to us," Bill said to the man. He rose from the table and approached the farmer. "We are not from the year one million nineteen hundred sixty-seven. We traveled one million years into our past. Since then, we have traveled almost one million years into the future. We..."

"No need to explain to me," the man replied. "I was listening. I know what you were saying. But you must understand. Your story is ridiculous. It is impossible for what you have said to happen."

"What I have been telling you is true," Bill replied. "If you can not help us, we will find someone who will."

"Wait a minute," the farmer said, eyeing the serious expression on Bill's face. "I thought you said the time machine was across the street? I don't see a time machine. What does it do, turn invisible when you're not using it?"

Ken remained quiet during the entire conversation. Instead of wasting what little energy he had left arguing, he observed in silence and refueled his body. He found the eggs to have a very unique flavor, which he liked very much. While Bill had his back turned, Ken secretly exchanged plates and resumed eating.

"No, it does not turn invisible," Bill said in disgust. "It is some distance into the forest."

"I want to see it," the farmer said.

"You want to see it?" Mary laughed, as she reentered the room. She dabbed at her tear filled eyes with a tissue. "I can't believe you, Ronald. How can you possibly believe that there is a time machine in the forest. These two are just plain crazy. They're probably just hallucinating on drugs."

Bill ignored the woman and returned to his chair. He took a sip of his orange juice, noticed that his eggs were gone, and gave a knowing glance toward Ken. "We will be happy to show you the time machine. It's probably the only way we can convince you of our story."

"Are you coming, Mary?" Ronald asked, as he ushered the scientists toward the front door.

"Sure, why not?" Mary replied. "This should be good for an even better laugh than I had earlier."

Bill led the group along the dirt driveway. The farmer followed a half step behind. Ken busied himself with culinary questions for Mary, clearly impressed with the breakfast offerings. "Three others were transported into the past with us," Bill resumed. "Andy is one of my assistants. He has worked with me for quite some time. Then there is Joe, Andy's brother. Joe works for the Protectors and was following Andy at the time of the incident. The third person... Well we just don't know who he is. He barged into our laboratory, followed by a swarm of police. We were very fortunate to escape. Upon materializing in the past, the stranger fled into the jungle. We haven't seen him since." Bill paused and looked at the farmer, who seemed to be interested in the story. His wife, however, half listening to the story and half answering Ken's questions about eggs, still had a smirk on her face.

"After realizing what had happened and where we were, we decided to search the surrounding area," Bill continued, as the group crossed the paved road and entered the forest. "To make a long story short, we were captured by some little creatures. We managed to escape, only to find that the time machine had been stolen. We tracked down the thieves, which we labeled treemen, because of their appearance. The treemen captured us and as part of some sacrificial ritual tossed us off the top of their mountain range, while were tied up in the time machine. Needless to say, we were successful in reaching the controls, just before the time machine struck the ground. When we woke up, we were in this forest," Bill finished, once again looking at the farmer's face for any indication of acceptance.

"Nice story," Mary said, clapping her hands in a mock applause. "I can't wait for the movie."

"So where is this time machine," Ronald asked, looking around anxiously.

"Over this little hill," Bill said, pointing up a small rise.

As the group reached the top of the hill, the unmistakable shape of the time machine could be seen nestled amongst the foliage. The farmer's jaw fell and his eyes opened wide. Mary seemed to be astonished by the sight as well. The scientists quickly tore down the branches they had used for camouflage, revealing the glistening glass and metal machine.

"So this is a time machine," Ronald said, standing nose to the glass, peering inside at the banks of computers. "How do I know this is real and not just some trick."

"You'll have to take our word for it," Bill replied, relieved that he had finally broken through the initial wall of skepticism. Mary also approached the time machine, staring inside with awe. Her laughter had stopped, but she hadn't fully bought the scientist's story. "If you like, you can return with us, when we go back to rescue our friends."

Ronald's curiosity became aroused at the thought of traveling through time. Still, he was not convinced that the feat was possible, but the thought of actually seeing all those creatures that Bill had talked about was clearly an opportunity he did not want to pass up. "I'll have to think about," he said, although his mind was already made up. "First, you had better do some more convincing."

Ken opened the door of the time machine, allowing the four to walk inside. Bill began to explain the different components of the machine, but he quickly lost the farmer and his wife in a myriad of scientific names and acronyms. Ken, noticing that his partner was speaking on a very high technical level, cut in and tried to give a simplistic overview of the time machine and the theory of time travel. Ronald nodded continuously, as if understanding, but in reality only knew that a time machine traveled through time, nothing more.

Understanding or not, Ronald became more enthusiastic with every word. Clearly, he thought, no one would go through such an elaborate scheme just to pull a joke on a farmer and his wife. Mary did not share her husband's enthusiasm, however. After a few minutes of listening to Ken talk, she stepped outside. It was more the cramped confines of time machine that bothered her, rather than anything that the scientists had been saying. A claustrophobic whisper, deep in her mind, kept telling her that she was going to get trapped in the machine.

The brief tour of the time machine ended shortly there after, and the group casually strolled back to the farm house. Over a cup of coffee, which Bill and Ken drank only when they could afford to purchase it from the black market, they talked about the scientist's time and the Protectors.

Bill told of how the Protectors originated, and how they finally won the long bloody war. He also told the farmer and his wife about the spheres that flew through the streets, killing anyone caught outside after curfew. Finally he told them about Andy, and what little he could about Joe. Ronald's attention hung on every sentence. The farmer kept asking questions, trying to piece the entire story together.

"Don't take what I am about to say too seriously. I'm still not totally convinced. But just out of curiosity, what kind of provisions will you need to rescue your friends?" Ronald asked, pouring Bill and himself another cup of coffee.

Ken, in the mean time, became obsessed with the writing printed on the coffee can. He drank his coffee very quickly, saving one drop. Then he drank it, trying to see if the last drop really tasted as good as the rest of the cup. After six cups, he gave up with inconclusive results.

"We'll need some weapons and perhaps a few men," Bill replied. He started to like the farmer, but didn't care too much for his wife. She kept laughing at them and asking what he considered to be stupid questions. "It doesn't appear as if any of the creatures in that time are too sophisticated. The group that captured us only had primitive spears for weapons."

"Don't forget the knockout gas," Ken reminded.

"Oh, and a powerful knockout gas which they secrete from their fingertips."

"That's something," Ronald mumbled.

During the conversation, Bill found out that Ronald's last name was Kelly. He also learned that the farm was approximately fifty-five miles from the outskirts of New York City. This, of course, proved to be a problem for Bill, since he assumed that the time machine stayed in the same place as it traveled through time. Guessing that they couldn't have walked more than twenty miles from the landing site, while in the past; how could they be over fifty miles from the city? The only explanation that he could come up with was that the earth had grown appreciably in size over the previous million years. But even this did not satisfy his curiosity.

"Your story is very hard to believe. I've heard many sales pitches and sweet talking scam artists. If I hadn't seen that machine across the street, you wouldn't be sitting here right now," Ronald informed. "Mind you, if you are trying to pull something over on me, although I can't think of anything that you could gain from doing that to me, I'll have you arrested," he ended the last sentence with a smile, but Bill didn't find the statement too humorous.

"I still don't believe a word of their story. It is totally ridiculous. I think they are trying to pull off some sort of hoax," Mary interjected. "I bet they are in it for the money. Of course, we don't have any, but if enough people buy into this story..." She rambled on with her statements, but Bill and Ken had learned long ago to just blank her out.

"I know this fellow who owns a gun shop," Ronald whispered to Bill, not wanting his wife to hear. Currently, her back was turned, washing dishes at the sink. "He owes me a rather large favor. I'm going to trust that you are telling me the truth. I think I can get the kind of fire power you need."

Bill looked at Ken with a smile and a sigh of relief. "Thanks, you won't regret this," Bill said excitedly.

"Just remember what I said. If you are lying to me, I'll call the police. I have a few friends in the department, too," Ronald warned, this time there was no trace of a smile. "Mary, I'm going to take the boys into town. We'll be back in a while."

"If you're going to take them into town, you might as well let them have some clean clothes and a shave. They look terrible," Mary said, shaking her head at the two. "Even though I think they are lying crooks, I can't let them walk around in those rags. People will see them with you and start talking."

"She does have a point," Ronald agreed. "You two look terrible."

Mary ushered the scientists through the hallway Bill had noticed upon entering the house. Without speaking, she brought them to the bathroom, where she produced a can of shaving cream and two razors. She eyed the room, as if taking inventory, before leaving the men alone. Several minutes later Mary returned carrying a stack of clothes. The faded work pants appeared to be ancient, as did the matching flannel shirts.

"This is the best I can do on such short notice," Mary said, almost ashamed of the quality of clothing she was presenting to the time travelers.

"They are fine, I assure you," Bill said, with a smile. Mary returned the smile and left to two to their business.

"These clothes are worse than the ones we have on," Ken said, after his host had left. He looked out the bathroom window at the rows of corn stalks stretching toward the horizon.

"Yes, but at least they're clean," Bill commented. He held the shirt up to the window and counted three holes. "My clothes smell so bad I think it would be appropriate for them to be burned rather than washed."

The two guests took turns showering and shaving. The caked on grime of the past several days reluctantly parted from their skin, leaving the time travelers refreshed and energetic. With neatly combed hair and a clean shave, they actually looked liked the scientists they claimed to be.

"That's more like it," Ronald said, as his guests entered the kitchen. "You'll fit right in."

"I'm feeling more at home all the time," Bill joked.

The three men then moved off to the barn, where Ronald kept his old pickup truck. "It barely runs, but it gets me to where I'm going," the farmer said, opening the passenger side door. Moments later he was sitting behind the steering wheel, sliding the key into the ignition. Several failed attempts followed, before the engine roared to life.

Ken and Bill found the ride along the driveway to be very bumpy and uncomfortable. But as soon as they hit the paved road, the ride became bearable. Ken rolled down the passenger side window, sticking his head out into the breeze, taking frequent breathes of the fresh air and savoring every lungful. In a way, he wished he had lived during the nineteen sixties, without the burdensome presence of the Protectors. The farmer and his wife seemed happy enough, seemingly free to come and go as they pleased. At the same time, he found himself missing the life he had known. His work especially. He had no family left. Unfortunately, his parents had died during the most recent war, while his brother had simply disappeared a few years later. The life style was gone, but maybe his time could be saved.

The ride to town was short. As Ronald brought the vehicle to a stop in front of a small brick building, the engine choked and coughed, shaking the passengers. The engine even continued to chug for a few moments, after it had been turned off. "Can't start it and can't get it stop," he laughed. "I think you two had better wait for me here. I don't want my friend to get too suspicious. I don't ask for high powered weapons everyday."

"Just once a week?" Ken laughed.

"Ha, ha," Ronald laughed back. "You didn't tell me you had a sense of humor."

Bill and Ken watched, as Ronald pulled open the door to the building. Not knowing how long this 'business deal' as Ronald called it would take, the scientists decided to take in their surroundings. Several other businesses were located nearby. A gas station sat to the left of the gun store. To its right stood a small two story office building. The sign outside said the occupants were attorneys, a term totally unfamiliar to the time travelers. A bit further up the road they could see a cluster of buildings, but they were too far away to read any of the signs. Across the street was a large field covered by endless rows of corn stalks.

"It seems peaceful here," Ken said, comparing the small town to the hectic and oppressive life he had lived in New York City, twenty-one eighty-six.

"Yes, it is," Bill agreed. "But I don't think all people in this time live in such surroundings. From what I have read, there are large impersonal cities here as well."

Bill and Ken returned their attention to the gun store, where they could see Ronald talking to the clerk through a large picture window. Various types of guns could be seen in the many display cases that decorated the interior of the store. Apparently guns hadn't changed much in appearance during the two hundred year span between the two times, as most of the weapons looked frighteningly familiar to the scientists.

The casual conversation between Ronald and the clerk soon turned into a heated argument. Both men were yelling adamantly, with arms flailing about, but only muffled sounds filtered out to the truck. The quarrel was short lived, however, and Ronald returned a few minutes later carrying a large package wrapped in brown paper.

The farmer climbed into the truck and looked at the two scientists, as if trying to decide if he wanted to speak what was on his mind. "I can trust you two, right?"

"Of course," Bill replied, wondering what the farmer was leading up to.

Ronald started the truck, on the first try this time, and began the trip back to the farm. "If I find out that you two are lying to me, some of my friends are going to be very angry. What I have here, is not necessarily legal," Ronald said, with a straight face. "During my years, I have made friends with a lot of people. Some of them aren't exactly model citizens. But sometimes one needs to have the right contacts. Anyway, I got a machine gun, two rifles, and plenty of ammunition. You have to promise me that you won't say anything about the guns to Mary."

"No problem." Ken replied, as he had little regard for the laws of the twentieth century.

"You said that your friends were in caves," Ronald said, returning to the mission at hand. "We should probably stop and buy some flashlights."

Bill and Ken had never heard of the term flashlight, but when they saw one they recognized it simply as a lightsource. Deciding that flashlights would not be powerful enough for the creature's caves, they purchased three very powerful hand held flood lights. Bill and Ken did find the concept of a department store to be quite novel, but the situation prevented them from examining the goods of the twentieth century in detail. The trio engaged in an interesting conversation about life in the nineteen sixties on the way back to the farm.

The men found Mary sitting at the kitchen table, playing a game of solitaire. Ronald confirmed his intentions to return to the past with Bill and Ken. As expected, Mary laughed at her husband's gullibility, although she did agree to walk across the street and wish them farewell. Fortunately, she made no inquiries into the contents of the brown paper parcel, saving Ronald the trouble of lying about the guns.

Bill and Ken entered the time machine, while Ronald hugged his wife good bye. "Don't worry about me," he said, kissing her on the cheek. "I'll be okay. From what they say, we should have no trouble overpowering the creatures that captured their friends."

While Ronald spoke with sincerity, Mary had to struggle not to burst out laughing. "I know you'll be okay, Ronald. You're not going anywhere. These two are pulling one over on you."

"Maybe," Ronald replied, "but just in case."

"Okay," Mary said. "Just in case. Take care of yourself." She pushed her husband into the time machine and stepped back a few feet.

"What does it feel like to travel through time?" Ronald asked with enthusiasm, after the door closed behind him.

"It doesn't feel like anything out of the ordinary," Ken explained. "You're just standing here, and poof you're in another time."

"Oh," Ronald replied sadly. He had been anticipating the experience to be quite thrilling.

"Are you ready to go?" Bill asked. Both passengers nodded in the affirmative. Bill pushed the button, but nothing happened. No sparks. Nothing. The screen indicated that they were still in nineteen sixty-seven.

Ronald looked out the thick glass at his wife, who stood with her arms crossed staring into the time machine. His suspicion of the scientists story began to grow once again. "Well, this can't be the past," he said. "I can still see Mary."

"We didn't go anywhere," Bill answered, wondering why the time machine did not work.

"I told you two that this had better not be a hoax. I wasn't bluffing when I said I would call the police," Ronald yelled. "If you don't get me into the past, then I'm going right back to the farm to make a phone call."

"Take it easy," Ken said, trying to soothe the irate farmer. "The time machine had been damaged by the treemen, maybe some of the controls are not set properly." He walked over to Bill and whispered, "What happened? I thought we fixed all the problems."

"I thought so, too," Bill answered, scratching his head in perplexity. "Maybe we should try again." He went through all the motions, but nothing happened.

Ken ran another test of the computer. After a few minutes, the computer indicated that all systems were operational. Bill looked at Ronald, who stood with his back toward his wife, not able to face her and the 'I told you so' look she wore. The scientists proceeded to remove the front panel to the computer, revealing scores of circuit boards. Several minutes were consumed, while they examined the equipment. Inexplicably, nothing seemed out of place or damaged.

"Everything looks fine," Bill said with a sigh of disappointment.

"We are going to have to do a complete circuitry check, aren't we?" Ken asked, recalling how long and tedious past checks had been. "It could take hours."

"Not only is it going to take a long time, but I don't have the check list. It is still on the desk in the laboratory. We're going to have to do it from memory," Bill replied solemnly. He looked up at the farmer, who stood in silence. "Luckily, we have our electrical equipment on board."

"Yeah, lucky," Ronald answered. "I can't believe I let you two make a fool out of me. Let me out of this thing right now. I'm going to call the police and have you arrested."

"We're not lying to you," Ken said, watching helplessly as Ronald pick up the parcel of guns.

Bill reluctantly opened the door of the time machine, letting Ronald storm out. The farmer walked right past his wife, barely giving her a passing glance. Mary stood for a moment, glaring at the scientists, who immediately began to work on the time machine. She was no longer in a 'see I told you so' mood. While she had totally expected nothing to happen, she now shared the hurt and humiliation Ronald was feeling. Mary turned from the time machine and followed her husband back to the farm.

"Maybe we will be lucky and find the problem right away," Ken said hopefully, staring at the countless circuits that sat before him.

"I doubt it. I have learned over the years that you never get things done quickly when you're in a hurry," Bill replied in a hollow voice.

As the hours passed, again and again the scientists came up empty handed. Everything they tested turned out to be in perfect condition. Every computer chip sat firmly in its socket. Every wire securely soldered in place. The afternoon sun soon fell to tree level, casting long shadows across the forest floor. The scientists stared out into the trees, clearly reminded of the jungle in the past.

After four hours of monotonous tests, the problem suddenly presented itself. Apparently a small wire, held in place by a screw rather than solder, had come loose. The affected system monitored outside atmospheric conditions. Since the computer program executed earlier to diagnose problems only considered primary systems, the problem had not been detected.

"Why didn't the computer notify us of the problem?" Ken asked, securing the last computer panel in place. "Obviously it knew there was a problem, since it aborted our time travel."

"If we had left a week later than we did, it would have. All of the software hasn't been installed yet," Bill explained. "I wasn't expecting to actually use the time machine as soon as we did. Actually, we are very lucky to even be alive."

"What do you mean?"

"It is possible that the wire became disconnected before the treemen tossed us over the cliff. In order for the time machine to work, the machine had to have been tilted at the proper angle in order for the wire to make contact. If at the time when I hit the button the time machine was at any other position, the time travel would have failed and we would have crashed into the ground."

"Dumb luck is just as lucky as any other kind of luck," Ken said, staring out into the forest. "Maybe some of that dumb luck will rub off and we'll be able to convince the farmer to come with us again. And maybe he'll give us some more food. I'm starving."

"I don't think that we have any other choice, except to try and get on friendly terms with him again," Bill said, as he closed the door of the time machine. This time they did not bother to camouflage the machine, seeing that they had not seen a single person during the entire time they spent solving the mystery of the aborted time travel. "Even if we can't convince him to go back with us, we need those guns. We can't expect to battle those creatures successfully without them."

Upon reaching the paved road, the scientists were treated to a magnificent display, as the setting sun cast a rainbow of colors throughout the sparsely clouded sky. A refreshing breeze stirred the rows of corn, casting the sound of rustling leaves into the air. Once again the time travelers found themselves standing on the slanted stoop leading to the front door of the farm house, not knowing if the occupants were going to be hospitable. Bill raised his hand, this time knocking without hesitation on the old splintering door.

After a short wait, Mary opened the door. She wore a near hateful expression on her face. Without speaking a word, she motioned for the two visitors to enter. They found Ronald sitting at the kitchen table, as with their first visit. This time, however, there were four settings on the table.

"I was expecting you," Ronald said, pointing to the extra place settings. "Mary thought you weren't going to come back, but I knew you would. I must confess I didn't think it would take you so long to fix the problem, but I knew you would show up for dinner."

Bill and Ken looked at each other in astonishment. "You mean you still believe us?" Ken asked in a surprised voice.

"Of course. From the first time I saw that machine, I knew you had to be telling the truth. No one, except a man from the future, would go through the trouble to build something like that and then try to pass themselves off as people from another time."

Evidently Ronald wasn't the least bit disturbed by the delay. He treated the scientists to a steak dinner, complete with potatoes, bread, and corn on the cob. Bill and Ken had their first taste of wine, an ancient beverage that had disappeared from the diet of New Yorkers under the Protectors regime.

"I called my son Steve. He is going to arrive in the morning and join us on the trip. I figure the more people that go with you, the better chance we have of finding your friends. I hope you don't mind," Ronald said, with a questionable look on his face.

"What if he tells someone? They might come out here and interfere with us, or steal the time machine during the night," Ken said nervously. Even though he liked the atmosphere of the nineteen sixties, he still felt uncomfortable and leery of the time's inhabitants.

"Don't worry about it," Ronald replied reassuringly. "I didn't tell him about the time machine. I didn't even hint at it. For that matter I didn't even tell him about the two of you. If I started telling him about traveling through time, he probably would have me committed to an insane asylum. And I'm sure Mary would be a willing accomplice."

"You've got that right," Mary replied.

"I just asked him to stop by and help me move some equipment," Ronald added.

"Bringing him along is probably a good idea, but we were hoping to leave as soon as possible. We aren't sure what kind of trouble Andy and his brother might be in," Bill explained, as he finished his last piece of meat.

"I don't see why that would matter," Ronald said. "If you can travel through time, why don't you just travel back to the time right after you left. Or even earlier."

"It might not be as simple as that," Bill replied. A genuine look of concern creased his brow. "We are inexperienced at the laws of time travel. Because of that, we are reluctant to cross over the constant time frame. For example, if we were to travel back in time to the exact moment when we were captured by the little creatures, would there be two Kens and two of me?"

The farmer shrugged his shoulders.

"We don't know either," Ken said, cutting into his second serving of steak.

"If we were to travel back to the point ten minutes after we were tossed over the cliff by the treemen, obviously there would be only one Ken and Bill in that time frame. But we would be one day removed from the constant time frame that Andy and Joe would be in. We are not sure if this would cause any problems."

"I think I understand," Ronald said, nodding in agreement. "I think."

"We just don't know what to expect if we deviate from the constant time frame pertaining to Bill, Andy, Joe, and myself," Ken said. "By the simple fact of us arriving in your time when we did, we have initiated a constant time frame with respect to you. If keeping the time frames synchronized is important, trying to maintain that constant time frame while traveling through time could become very complicated."

"But I think we can wait until morning," Bill said, after a slight pause. "Andy and Joe have been on their own for several days now. If they are still alive in the caves, then the odds are that they will still be alive in the morning. I think we can wait, but we must leave first thing."

"I'm used to rising with the sun," Ronald said, with a smile.

"Maybe ten years ago," Mary chided.

That evening the scientists were exposed to several twentieth century American television shows. Bill found it amazing how people could openly criticize the government and other powerful organizations without fear of reprisal. If someone in his time openly, or sometimes even privately, spoke out against the Protectors, they would be killed and dumped into the ocean.

For the first time since they abruptly left the twenty-second century, Bill and Ken found sleeping easy. They did not have to struggle to find a comfortable position on a rock or amongst jungle vegetation. The farm house had two spare bedrooms. Both beds were soft and clean. Bill found his muscles to be relaxed, not tense waiting to fend off an unwelcome predator. Despite this, he had the worst nightmare of his life.

He dreamt that when the rescue party reached the caves, he found Andy and Joe's bodies in a pile, all cut up into little pieces. A separate spot had been reserved for their eyeballs, which had an unmistakable look of horror in them. The little creatures then recaptured Ken and himself. Ronald and Steve, who were present only moments before, were nowhere to be seen.

The creatures held Ken down and began to cut into his right arm with a knife. Bill tried to turn away, but his head was yanked back. He closed his eyes, but to his horror he could still see. The creatures were forcing him to watch the murder of his partner. One of the murderers picked up Ken's dismembered arm and wiped it across Bill's face, blood spilling into his screaming mouth.

Bill woke suddenly, sweat covering his face. He jumped from the bed and dashed to the mirror secured above the dresser. Huge dilated pupils stared back at him through the dust covered glass. He listened for a few moments, as the silence gradually gave way to the voices of the Ronald and Ken. His dream was only a nightmare and nothing more.

After taking a few moments to wipe the sweat from his face, the well rested scientist made his way to the sunlit kitchen. There he found Ken eating breakfast with the Kelly's. Their son Steve had arrived an hour earlier and had already been informed of the rescue plans. Bill sat down and enjoyed a hearty breakfast of bacon and eggs.

"I've been thinking," Bill said, after finishing a cup of coffee. "I think we should move the time machine toward the city, before we try another time travel. We don't want to end up next to the treemen's caves, which is where I expect us to land if we leave from here. I'm sure that if they capture us again, they will destroy the time machine and us along with it."

"I have also been thinking of moving the time machine, but for another reason," Ken stated. He sat back in his chair to relax after his meal. "We originally left from the city and landed in a field near the creature's cave. Then we left from the treemen's caves and ended up almost sixty miles from the city. We know we couldn't have traveled that far back in the past. Assuming we walked twenty miles in the past, every three miles closer we can get to the city here, is one less mile of walking we have to do back there."

"I know of a place where we can bring the time machine," Steve said, eager to become a contributing member of the rescue team. He was a young man in his early twenties. His long brown hair reached his shoulders and his patched clothing was a sign of the times. "There is a small plot of wooded land about fifteen miles from the city. A couple of years ago a friend and I were hoping to buy it, but the deal fell through. It is still vacant as far as I know."

Bill nodded in acknowledgment. "Now that we have a place to leave from, how are we going to move the time machine? Ronald's truck is much to small to hold it."

"We can load it onto the trailer I have in the barn. I haven't used it for a long time, but I think it will hold the time machine. We can cover it with an old tarp that I've been meaning to toss out. That way no one will get suspicious," Ronald suggested.

"That should work out fine," Ken said, rising from the table. "Let's not waste any time."

An old rusted steel platform, with no sides, turned out to be Ronald's idea of a trailer. Upon first glance, it was apparent that the vehicle's best days were far behind. The wheels and axles were so rusted, that the truck had to use all of its remaining horse power to move it from the barn. Once free of the caked on oxidation, the trailer rolled effortlessly across the street and into the forest.

Lifting the massive time machine onto the trailer was not a simple task, but with the creative use of some farm equipment the task was quickly accomplished. Under the weight of the time machine, the eight wheels of the trailer appeared as if they would explode at any second. As it turned out, they were fortunate that the trailer had no sides, since the base of the time machine proved to be several feet wider than the rusted platform.

After storing their provisions inside the time machine, several pieces of mouldy, spider web covered tarp were used to cover the device. Though observers would not be able to see the contents of the machine, the pyramid shape was clearly evident. The aging engine of the truck initially rejected the command to pull the heavy load. With a little coaxing, and several choice words from Ronald, the truck inched forward.

The occupants settled in for the forty mile drive, but comfort would not be accompanying them on the journey. If the scientists thought the earlier ride in the aging truck was rough, they would now call it luxurious. Though one could not expect four adult men to fit any other way than cramped inside the cab of the vehicle, the frequent lurches and engine spurts made their ride even more miserable. The passengers quickly became immune to the queer stares that came from every car that passed, all centered on the huge pyramid shaped object hidden under the tarpaulin.

More than an hour after the journey began, the straining whir from the engine stopped, as Ronald turned off the ignition. He had driven the trailer a short distance into the camouflage of the trees to protect from any curious passers-by.

"I sure hope this thing works this time," Ronald said, as the group massed around the time machine.

Yeah, me too," Steve added, helping Bill climb up into the time machine. "I still don't believe there is such a thing as a time machine, but I hope it works anyway."

"I just hope that the smooth ride you gave us didn't jostle any wires," Ken said, laughing at Ronald.

"I'm open to any offers you might make to buy me a new truck," Ronald replied.

Bill immediately shuffled over to the controls, leaving the others to struggle into the time machine on their own. He did not bother to look, but a warning light indicated that the time machine door had been closed. "Cross your fingers," he said, before pushing the button.

As hoped, the time machine departed from the twentieth century. The passengers inside could clearly see the bright white sparks bouncing off the outside surface of the glass. The farmer and his son instinctively gravitated toward the center of the machine, in an attempt to stay as far away as possible from the mysterious happenings outside. Several moments later the sparks stopped. The four found themselves standing in total darkness.

"Hey, it was morning when we left, now it is dark," Steve noted in a puzzled tone.

"We think it has something to do with the days being shorter in this time. As a result the night and days are not synchronized," Bill explained, as he loaded his rifle.

"Who is not going to carry a gun?" Ken asked, eyeing the two remaining weapons. "There are only three of them and four of us."

"I don't really need one," Ronald quickly offered. "You three can carry them. You can probably use them better than me, anyhow. I haven't been out hunting in years and didn't hit anything the last few times I tried. If anything happens, I'll stay right close to you."

Ken took the remaining rifle, as Steve had already appropriated the machine gun. Upon exiting the time machine, they noticed a path only several feet away. In the dark, the ancient time did not seem very different to Steve and Ronald. For all they knew, they could be standing in the forest across the street from the farm. But the peaks of the mountains, barely visible over the treetops, indicated that they were not in their forest. Several feeble rays of moon light reflected off the peak's snow cover, before a cloud blocked them from sight. As soon as the group began their hike, thunder echoed from the mountains they were heading toward.

"I sure hope it doesn't rain again," Ken commented, remembering the rain storm that he and Bill trudged through two days earlier.

"That is something we can do without," Bill agreed. "Although the rain was a blessing in the blistering sun."

Bill and Steve led the way with weapons in one hand and a lightsource in the other. The long shadows of the jungle vegetation seemed to dance in harmony with the thunder, causing a bewildered look of fear to spread over Steve's face. Ronald, carrying the third light source a step ahead of Ken, found the atmosphere of the past to be equally mysterious.

Though the towering mountains to the east indicated that they were heading in the right direction, they had no way of telling if they were north or south of the creature's caves. The path they followed ran east with a slight slant to the north. Bill kept a keen eye out for the jagged cliff near the cave entrance, but could not see any significant markings in the dark.

Again and again, lightning filled the sky, freezing the image of the jungle. Without fail, the deafening roar of thunder followed each lightning strike.

"It can't be more than three miles to the cave," Bill informed the others, after estimating the distance to the mountains. Another flash of lightning zigzagged across the sky, followed by a stiff wind, which pushed the group forward. "We should get there in less than an hour."

Both Ronald and Steve felt as if they were in a dream, caught up in events that they were helpless to alter in any way. The fact that they were walking through an ancient jungle didn't fully register in their minds. The air seemed different and the actions of the scientists suggested that they were indeed in the past. But up to this point, they had seen nothing which would indicate that they were in another time, just another place.

Thirty minutes passed, causing Bill to quicken his pace. The others dutifully followed. The rotund scientist began to jog toward the mountains, his chest rising and falling heavily with every breath. His body screamed for leniency, but Bill knew that they were only a short distance from the caves. The rocky cliffs were now visible, when the lightning streaked across the sky. His mind kept reminding him that he was entirely responsible for Andy and Joe's welfare. That burden made him shuffle along even faster. Just then a green flash filled the sky, drenching the jungle in its eerie light. The foursome stopped in fright.

"I never saw anything like that before," Ronald said, as a nervous sweat formed on his forehead.

"Neither have I," answered Bill, still in shock over the sight. The following few minutes were filled with an unparalleled silence. No sounds could be heard throughout the dense jungle. Even the lightning and thunder stopped.

"What's happening?" Ronald asked, starting to question his decision to go with the time travelers. The group had resumed their jog, not letting the troublesome silence deter them.

"I don't know," Ken answered. "This is the first time I've seen this place so quiet."

Suddenly, another flash of lightning, followed by a second flash of green, broke the silence. The wind reversed direction, directly into the human's faces. Bill struggled to quickened his pace, but the stiff head wind actually slowed his progress. A low buzzing sound made its way through the tangled foliage to the ears of the rescuers, growing louder with every step forward. The buzzing droned on, pounding through the thick night air. Without warning, the buzzing stopped, as the unmistakable sound of machine gun fire crackled through the darkness.

"Do you think that is..." Ken began to ask, before the thunder stifled the remainder of his sentence.

"I hope so, but I don't remember them having a machine gun," Bill replied over the thunder, anticipating the rest of Ken's question. But then something jogged its way into the forefront of his mind. Andy didn't have a machine gun. Neither did Joe. But the rebel had one. For some reason Bill had totally repressed the memory of the rebel, but now it all came back to him. The rebel was the wild card in the situation, but not wild enough for Bill to have second thoughts about forging ahead.

The group rushed forward, entering the war ridden field. Ronald and Steve stopped short in astonishment. The bloody battle site was augmented by the giant red ants and small human-like creatures. Even though they had been warned, words could not prepare them for the sights surrounding them.

In the center of the field the four rescuers could make out three dark figures desperately fighting for their lives. Bill and Ken immediately began firing into the surging mass of warriors, clearing a path to the stranded humans. As the rescuers drew closer, it became apparent that one of the figures was trapped in the clutching jaws of a giant red ant. The scientist's yells were completely drowned out by the horrid combination of the ant's buzz, little creature's mumbled cries, howling wind, and roaring thunder.

Dave slashed fiercely at the ant, until it loosened its grip on Andy. The insect turned to flee, but stumbled to its death only feet away. The rescuers quickly made their way to the center of the field, where a continuous barrage of bullets kept the attackers at bay. Bill reached the stranded party first, despite his short stumpy legs. The scientist surrendered his gun to Ronald and immediately attended to Andy.

"It's about time you showed up," Joe yelled over the ruckus, as he helped Bill lift the mutilated body of his brother.

The path to the forest remained clear, as the group immediately retreated toward the time machine. To the dismay of all, the ant had left a gaping hole in the middle of Andy's chest. Blood flowed freely from the wound. From first sight, Bill held little hope that Andy could survive such an injury. The four weapon bearers kept the warring creatures at bay, as the humans left the battle field behind. Several flashes of lightning filled the sky, followed by roars of thunder much louder and stronger than any that had preceded. For the time being, it appeared that neither the ants nor the Blieins were interested in following the humans into the jungle. Feeling safe, Ronald took a moment to examine Andy. The gruesome sight of the bloody exposed organs made him quickly turn away, reminding him of a horrible farm accident he had witnessed many years ago.

The group hurried as fast as they could along the dark path. After several minutes, Joe and Bill passed Andy to Steve and Ken. Everyone, except Ronald, took turns carrying the lifeless body. Just as Bill and Joe lifted Andy for the second time, the skies opened and buckets of rain fell on the fleeing humans. Joe, for one, felt relieved that the rain finally came, knowing that it was the only chance his brother had to survive. If only it was the same healing water that worked its magic on Dave's facial wounds.

Joe tugged at Andy's shirt, now ragged and soiled, pulling it away from the injury. He wanted as much of the cool liquid as possible to fall into the gaping void. An abundance of rain did find its way into the wound, but no change occurred. The blood stained water simply rolled off Andy's body, as if someone were spraying him with a hose. At this point, Joe became terminally worried. Maybe the wound was too serious for the rain to heal.

The miles to the time machine seemed to stretch on forever. Ronald kept glancing behind, expecting to see a red ant or Bliein attacking from the vegetation. But no assault came. The Blieins were to slow to keep up with the humans, even though they were burdened with a fallen comrade. The ants did not care that they escaped, since they had not been given specific orders to kill the humans. They were told just to kill whatever they found at the field. Just as Bill was ready to pass Andy off, the pyramid shape of the time machine appeared through the trees.

Joe, still staring eagerly into Andy's chest hoping that the rain would heal his brother, used his last ounce of strength to haul his body into the time machine. Moments after the door closed, he collapsed to the floor in exhaustion.

Ken quickly reset the controls for Ronald's time, wishing that he had done so upon arriving. It was then that the first Bliein was able to catch up to the humans. Now safely behind a wall of glass, Ken casually pushed the button, waving good-bye to the stunned Bliein as he did so. The time machine disappeared into a wall of sparks, only to reappear square on the back of Ronald's trailer several moments later.

Steve and Dave carried Andy from the time machine, carefully placing him on the ground. It quickly became apparent, in the bright sunlight, that no amount of medical attention could save his life. Several blades of green grass poked their way through the ugly wound, making the situation all the more bleak. In addition to the massive blood loss, it was unclear what organs might have also been damaged. Bill walked away in disgust, clearly distraught over his decision to leave in the morning rather than the preceding evening. Joe sat on the edge of the trailer, letting all the thoughts of his life scramble through his brain. The others just stood in silence.

But their grief was premature. Andy's body had not given up the fight, and neither did the miraculous rain. The tissue near the edges of the wound began to move ever so slightly. To the passing glance it might have looked as if the wind was cruelly playing with the dead. But the wind was silent. The rain water was working. It had only taken longer to start because of the severity of the wound. Dave yelled to the others, upon seeing the unmistakable healing process speed along. The group gathered and watched in surprise. New bone and muscle began to fill the void in Andy's chest. In a matter of only five minutes, the wound was completely healed. No trace of the incident remained. Everyone, except for Dave and Joe, wore the most stunned expression on their face.

"How did he do that?" exclaimed Steve. "Just a few minutes ago I saw him lying there with a hole the size of a football in his chest."

"Yes, I would like to know how he did it also," Bill said, looking at the smiling faces of Joe and Dave, who were trying their hardest not to burst out laughing. "Well, Dave? I'm waiting."

"Okay, the rain in that place is healing water. It heals all wounds almost instantly. I'm just glad you arrived when you did. If you were any later, all the Blieins and ants we injured would have been healed. Then we would have been in big trouble."

Hey, wait a minute," Joe yelled. He suddenly stopped laughing. "How did you know his name?"

"Yeah," Ken added, also puzzled at the situation. For the first time he recognized the stranger as the rebel who barged into the laboratory, which they were forced to leave five days earlier. "How did you know his name, Bill? You told us that you didn't know who he was."

Bill's facial muscles instantly relaxed, caught in a lie. But the seriousness of his expression softened, as he realized that the secret was no longer important. He was not in his time. The Protectors could not do any harm here. A sly smile slowly grew on the scientist's face, while the others waited patiently for an explanation. "First of all, I don't believe that I ever said I didn't know him. And if I did, you can't prove it. Secondly, I'll tell you how I know him on the way back to the farm. Right now I want to get the time machine out of here." With that they piled into the trailer and headed back to the farm house.

CHAPTER XI "MIKOKIL"

The stories were long and detailed, as everyone involved proudly described their experiences in the ancient past. The Kelly's listened intently, only interrupting to have some point clarified. As the stories unfolded, Bill revealed that he had actually known Dave for some time, as both shared the same goal of overthrowing the Protectors. The two decided long ago to keep their friendship secret, in order to protect each other and their respective organizations. Bill sat with a wry smile, still reluctant to reveal how he and Dave actually met, only assuring the others that they would find out at the appropriate time.

As the stories unraveled, it became known that Dave hadn't planned on bursting into the laboratory when he did. It turned out to be just a matter of bad timing, which quite possibly may have been good timing as far as Bill, Ken, and Andy were concerned. "If you consider that Joe was ready to turn us all in," Bill said, with a now friendly smile toward the former Protector's policeman, "this seems to be a much better scenario."

The eight continued to talk over a filling lunch of cold cut sandwiches and beer. Even Mary showed some interest in the stories of the past, now that both her husband and son had first hand proof that the time machine actually worked. She now claimed that she believed the scientist's story all along. The lunch was the first filling meal Dave, Andy, and Joe had eaten for a long time.

Bill showed great interest in the story of the halls. No matter how he tried to rationalize the existence of the structure, he could not understand how the humans of that time period could have acquired the technology necessary to construct the halls as described by Dave. The description of the mysterious underground building was only the appetizer, however. Dave's detailed recollections of the of the Minomassa and Ubeleutes, provided by the sword of course, were so detailed, that his audience could practically envision the creatures standing only feet away.

After lunch, Bill and Dave quietly slipped out of the kitchen and into the living room. The others were too busy exchanging stories of their respective times to notice. One thing about the past still bothered Dave. He was able to think of little else, since arriving at the farm. The sword, a seemingly harmless piece of metal, was still using its unexplained power on him. Using its powers of communication, the sword was compelling Dave to return to the past and defeat the enemy. This time permanently.

"So you can see why I must return," Dave explained. He balanced the sword on his palms, as he and Bill sat on the farmer's worn sofa. "All I ask is that you bring me back. You can leave as soon as you drop me off."

"You realize that the sword is making you want to return," Bill stated, not liking the idea of returning to the troublesome time. The numerous problems encountered during his first trip saturated his appetite for any further excursions. "I can't see how you would have any interest in what happened so long ago, except for what that sword is placing into your head. I don't even understand how it can be communicating to you."

Dave gazed out the window at the rows of corn swaying gently in the breeze. "I don't know how or why the sword is communicating with me, but I do know that I want to return. I feel as if I have a vested interest in this matter."

"What kind of vested interest could you possible have in anything to do with that time period? If you would just throw that sword away, you would forget all about this desire to return. The Protectors are your enemy, not the Minomassa."

"I can't throw it away. I have a strange feeling that I was supposed to find this sword. It's almost like I was called from our time to find it."

"Come on, Dave," Bill laughed, but only briefly. "You know that can't be true."

"Why not?" Dave replied. "You don't know that there can't be communication across time."

"No, but..."

"Look," Dave said, leaning closer to Bill and making sure no one was in ear shot. "I wasn't supposed to be on your street that night. I started out a mile away. Something went wrong with our plans. Somehow the Protectors found out about our assassination attempt."

"You have a leak?"

"No way," Dave replied. "There were only four of us that knew what was going to happen. Before I reached the rendezvous, the police... They were waiting. I saw them murder three of my men. That is how I know there was no leak. Everyone who knew about the mission, except for me, is dead."

"Dave, that doesn't mean that the you were called to the sword."

"I didn't even know where I was, until I recognized your door, Bill. I was running through alleys trying to shake the police."

"It's just a coincidence."

"I'm not so sure."

"Your men must think you are dead now," Bill added.

"Yes."

Bill sat in silence for a few moments, absorbing all of what he had just heard. "I'll take you back, but I want to make sure that you are making the decision and not the sword."

"It's like we are one in the same," Dave said. "I must return. I must return the rule of the land to the human race. The Ubeleutes stole the rule from the humans. They must be made to pay the consequences. I feel as if I owe the sword this debt. It helped me."

"There are no humans left, Dave," Bill argued. "From what you told me, the humans originally stole the power from the Ubeleutes. As far as I'm concerned, you owe nothing to the humans or that sword."

"Chaz did every living creature a favor by overthrowing the Ubeleutes. They were tyrants. There was no peace before the humans took over. I need to do this for all the species of that time, not just the humans." Dave had clearly made up his mind. Not even a close friend like Bill was going to be able to sway his decision.

Bill thought of his world, his time. He thought of all the time Dave and he had spent together trying to overthrow the Protectors. He knew all that work would be for not, if he did not have Dave's expertise and leadership abilities to aid the cause. "If you must return, then I will go with you," he said at last. "After we kill these Ubeleute creatures, we will resume our war against the Protectors."

"No, you must go back to our time and continue the fight. We can't afford to alleviate the pressure we already have on the Protectors, even for a short time. Even now, both our organizations are probably confused by our absence. You have worked too hard to give up now. We can't risk the chance of the rebel force losing both of us."

"We have already taken that chance, by accident," Bill stated. "I don't think that the risks we will be taking now are any greater than the risks we took on our initial journey to the past. We know what to expect now, more or less. Besides, we lead two very different groups. I don't think our cause can stand even the loss of one of us. I will help you on your quest, even though I don't think you should do it. With the weapons we can get here, we should be able to destroy the Ubeleutes in short order."

Andy and Ken soon joined in on the conversation. Both had done their part in the effort to overthrow the Protectors, though neither had known of Dave's existence and the work he performed. It was clear in their minds that losing Bill would spell doom for the revolution. Based on their desire to protect Bill, they also decided to return with Dave.

"The sword's enemy, this Minomassa you talked about, must have been very powerful to destroy all of the humans. Now you are telling us that it could be even more powerful. Isn't it possible that it is too powerful for us to handle?" Ken suggested.

"Not with the weapons we have. I'm positive we will have little trouble fighting the Ubeleutes, once we find them. That will be the hard part. The sword can tell me all that it has seen and heard. That is its power. It will guide us safely to the border of the Minomassa's territory. After that, we will be without its guidance," Dave explained.

The news of the return trip to the past soon spread throughout the small farm house. Ronald and Steve were excited by the thought of a second visit. Now that they had first hand experience in the ancient land, they were anxious to go with Dave and explore some more.

Joe needed some coaxing though. He had seen enough of the ancient jungles and dreary caves. Having to live off the land was not something he wished to experience again. Only after they convinced him that his only other choice was to remain in the nineteen sixties, possibly forever if the mission failed, did he agree to go. Mary, the only one who had no desire or intention to time travel, scoffed at them.

"You two can go back there and fight those monsters, but I'm going to stay here where I know it is safe," she said to her husband and son. She really didn't care what the others did. As far as she was concerned, the sooner they left her time the better.

"Don't worry about us, mom. It will be a breeze. We are going to have guns and explosives and things like that. None of those creatures will have a chance against us. It will be just like hunting," Steve said, partially trying to coax her along.

"Good, but I'm not going. Besides, if it is going to be such a breeze, why go at all?" she said in a firm voice. "You guys are crazy if you think you can fool around with time. You can't change the past. If you want me to see the past so badly, then take some pictures and bring them back for me."

"So the seven of us will go," Dave said, not wanting to hear any more complaining from Mary. Actually, he was relieved she didn't want to go. He didn't think he could put up with her persistent whining for an extended period of time. "I must remind you, that you are all going on your own free will. I don't think this is going to be as quite as simple as Steve thinks. I'm sure the five of us who spent more than a few hours there will admit, there are many dangers."

"That is true," Bill agreed. "Ken and I found survival to be a challenge. And we didn't even run across one Ubeleute."

"But you have never been camping," Steve chided, sitting forward in his chair with pride. "I once spent two weeks in the wilderness. I had to do everything for myself."

"And you didn't have to worry about creatures who could render you unconscious with a gas secreted from their fingertips," Bill shot back. Steve contemplated the scientist's words, before sitting back in silence.

"No one could have been prepared for the first journey to that time," Dave said, trying to thwart any egotistic arguments. "But we are somewhat prepared now. Since this is my quest, I will make all final decisions on the matter. Of course, any of you will be free to set off on your own at any time."

"Ronald, I think you are crazy. You shouldn't be running around like this at your age," Mary pleaded.

"What about my age? I'm in excellent shape for my age. I can handle taking a trip like this," defended Ronald. Mary, with genuine concern on her face, decided that arguing would be futile. She rose and silently left the room.

"Ronald, we are going to need some money to purchase the equipment we need," Dave said, satisfied that Mary would not be disturbing their discussion for a while. "Of course, I will find a way to repay you. I'm sure I can find something of value back in our time, once we return there."

"I'll be able to buy some equipment, but I'm not very wealthy. I do know many of the merchants in town, however. Most of them owe me a favor or two. Maybe I can borrow some of what we need."

"That sounds good to me," Dave said, rising to his feet. "Let's get started."

The six others followed his lead and moved toward the front door of the house. Ken, trying to fill his insatiable appetite for twentieth century American cuisine, fixed himself a quick sandwich, as he passed through the kitchen. The one thing he definitely liked about this time was the abundance of food.

"I still think you are making a big mistake," Mary yelled from the kitchen door as the men crammed themselves into Ronald's truck. "Ronald, do you hear me?"

Ronald did, but didn't answer.

The group unanimously decided that fire arms was the most important provision, which lead them to their first stop. Ronald, Steve, and Dave were the only ones to enter the small brick building, which housed the gun store. The remainder of the party waited outside in the truck, not to raise more suspicion than was absolutely necessary.

"Hi, Ronald, back so soon?" the clerk asked, giving a curious look at Dave. As the trio walked up to the counter, the clerk didn't take his eyes off the stranger. Not being sure if Dave was with Ronald and Steve, he lowered his voice to a whisper. "By the way, you didn't tell me what the guns were for earlier."

"That's not important. I'll tell you about it later over a game of pool at Sharky's. Right now I'm in sort of a hurry. And don't worry about this guy, he's with me," Ronald said pointing toward Dave, who stood staring into a display case. The clerk eyed Dave one more time, before returning his focus to Ronald. "I need two machine guns, a rifle, and plenty of ammunition." Then lowering his voice, "I hope you can give me the legal stuff on credit."

"I suppose so," the clerk mumbled, before turning away. He unlocked the door leading to the basement, then took another look in Dave's direction. The clerk rubbed his chin in a contemplating manner, eyeing

Dave, trying desperately to piece together the little mystery Ronald was presenting. "It sounds to me that this is going to be a pretty exciting trip, with all these guns. How long are you going to be away?"

"It all depends. I really can't give an exact time," Ronald replied, trying to be as vague as possible. "I've never stiffed you money before, if that's what you're worried about. Mary will honor my IOU, you know that."

"Sure, I know that," the clerk replied. "This is just business."

"I'll be back in a few days, I hope," Ronald added, not wanting to leave his occasional pool partner completely in the dark. "And you won't be hearing about us in the news. We aren't doing anything illegal."

"Don't you think we should get something for Dave," Steve whispered to his father. "All he has is that sword. I know he said he didn't want anything, but we should get him something."

"I suppose you're right," Ronald replied. He yelled to the clerk through the open basement door. "Why don't you throw in a handgun, too."

A few minutes later the clerk returned to the counter. "Okay, here's your stuff. Just make sure you pay me as soon as you return. But I will need this much, before you go," he said, sliding a slip of paper across the counter to Ronald.

"Wow," Ronald said, as he counted through a wad of bills he had withdrawn from the bank.

"I'm giving you a great price, Ronald," the clerk said. "Just remember, I need the rest when you return. I have a lot of overhead in this business."

"Sure, no problem. I'll see you then," Ronald replied, rushing to leave the store.

Ronald's next stop was in a small shopping plaza, anchored with a department store on one end and a grocery store on the other, The five men from the future marveled at the row of shops, as nothing even similar was present in their time. The Protectors had complete control over all legal commerce, offering what they thought the population needed rather than what was wanted. The group briefly wandered through the department store, before purchasing three more flood lights, a couple of long hunting knives, and two hiking backpacks.

Back in the truck, Ronald roared the vehicle's engine to a life. As he shifted the transmission into drive, he mentioned that he knew a construction foreman, who just might have some explosives lying around. A short drive later, Ronald found himself assuring the foreman that the explosives would be replaced before they were ever missed. Ronald was granted twelve sticks of dynamite for his effort.

* * * * * * * * * *

A violent storm kept Andy awake most of the night. The horrible memories of the ant ripping open his chest kept repeating themselves through his mind. Though he only felt the initial jolt of pain, before lapsing into the unconscious, his mind extrapolated and filled in the rest. The thoughts of the biting pain and the grotesque feeling of the ant's saliva mixing with his blood made him squirm. After a few hours of fighting the thoughts, he finally fell asleep.

Morning came and the seven adventurers found themselves in the same wooded plot of land that they stood in a day earlier. The air was warm and a subtle breeze rustled the leaves of the massive oaks and maples that surrounded the time machine. Since there was no urgency to return to the past, the group spent several casual minutes arming themselves.

Each member of the party carried a canteen and a small amount of ammunition on their person. Dave carried the 'sword of Duzic', which seemed to have become an attachment to his body. It was rare that the weapon was not firmly grasped in one of his hands or resting balanced on his knees. After a half-hearted objection, he reluctantly took the pistol and tucked it safely into his clothing. Steve eagerly armed himself with the same machine gun he had used during the rescue, feeling thoroughly exhilarated by the thoughts of using the powerful weapon once again. The farmer's son also volunteered to carry a lightsource and a fifty foot rope.

Bill found his machine gun to be the perfect balance to the lightsource he carried. Neither object proved too cumbersome for the elder scientist. Strapped around Ken's shoulder was a rifle. A twelve inch hunting knife hung from his belt, while a backpack filled with dynamite and enough sandwiches for two days finished his attire. Joe insisted that he carry a machine gun, since he was the only one present with formal training for such a weapon. The former policeman complemented the gun with the remaining knife. He also carried a lightsource. Andy and Ronald both carried a rifle and a lightsource, with the former also lugging the backpack containing the ammunition store.

The time machine's third journey to the ancient past landed its passengers at the anticipated location. The late afternoon sky held no traces of the of the violent storm of the previous evening, although a strange sour ocean odor lingered in the air. While none of the time travelers had actually seen an ocean in this land, each had occasion to visit one in his respective time.

The all too familiar yellow tint still stained an otherwise clean atmosphere. The setting sun was trying its best to leave its mark on the jungle, filling the sky with a strange pattern of colors. The time travelers made a half hearted attempt to camouflage the time machine, realizing the task to be practically impossible in a limited amount of time.

"The sword says that the Ubeleute strong hold is on the other side of the mountain," Dave relayed, as he came out of a deep thought with the sword. He was finding that communication with the weapon was becoming easier and easier.

"How are we going to get over there?" Steve asked, looking up at the ominous mountain range. He momentarily studied the evil features of the mountain peaks, something he couldn't do in the darkness of his first trip. "They look awfully big."

"We could get lost, if we were to walk through the Bliein's caves," Joe added. "It was just blind luck that Andy and I found a way through."

"I don't suggest walking through the ridge," Andy flatly stated. A brief shiver worked its way up his spine and into he head. "Joe and I almost froze to death up there."

"We won't have to take any of those routes," Dave said, after contacting the sword. "There is a secret tunnel through the mountain about a mile and a half north of the main entrance to the Bliein's caves. The sword says that the Ubeleutes constructed it during the war. That is how they overthrew the humans so easily. By the time the humans found out about the tunnel, the enemy had completed it," he paused for a moment, as if listening to an unexpected communication from the sword. "I think we should fill our canteens with water from the halls. The sword has informed me that it is the same healing water as the rain."

"Sounds good to me," Ken said in agreement, clearly eager to experience the halls first hand.

The group followed the path that led to the field where Dave, Andy, and Joe battled the ants and Blieins. Surprisingly, there was very little evidence that a battle had occurred only a day earlier. The long grass was not trodden down and blood stains could not be seen. The only visible traces left of the battle was the occasional scattered bullet underfoot and the few broken branches still clinging to their respective trees.

"Not really surprising after what we have seen," Dave said, remembering the microscopic creatures Andy had discovered rebuilding the tree.

"Everything has its place," Bill observed, as the group waded through the flowing grass. "The caretakers don't like it when things get moved."

"Sounds like my wife," Ronald laughed.

After browsing the field for several moments, Andy led the group the rest of the way to the halls. The four humans, who were making their first trip to the structure, marveled at its vastness. The serenity and peacefulness of the underground chambers quickly caused the visitors to forget their troubles. Since the structure was still providing its own subtle lighting, the travelers were able to conserve the batteries in their lightsources. Disappointment quickly set in, however, when they reached the waterfall and found it dry. Not even the smallest drop of water remained in the fissure. A thin layer of dust had already settled on the rock bottom.

"What happened to it," Andy said in amazement. "Just yesterday it was overflowing with water. Now nothing."

"The Minomassa stopped it," Dave informed. "I've been told that the Minomassa did the same during the war, right before the Ubeleutes attacked. The humans couldn't heal themselves throughout the entire battle."

"I wish I took mom's advice and brought a camera," Steve said, not paying any attention to the conversation. He looked around at the statues and simply shook his head in wonder. "This place is fantastic."

"It's too late to think of that now," Ronald replied, as the group retraced their steps to the surface. He kept looking over his shoulder, trying to see if the halls were actually a dream.

"Without the water, we will have to be very careful," Dave explained. "While this is not the only supply, I doubt the Minomassa will leave any healing water available to us on our journey. If any of us become injured, we will only have conventional methods available for first aid."

"Which is an area we completely neglected," Bill said, as the group arrived at the bottom of the hole. "Dare I suggest that we return to purchase the needed supplies?"

"Do you really think that we will need any first aid?" Joe said, giving Bill a push to help him start his climb up the vines to the surface.

"I don't think that having first aid supplies will be critical," Dave said, watching the group struggle out of the hole. "Granted, we could have prepared better for this journey, but we would never be able to carry everything we would need or want. I say we continue with what we have now."

"Sounds good to me," Steve said, as the last of the group safely reached the surface. "I don't want to delay this action for one minute."

"Me either," Joe added.

The group found their way to the Bliein's caves with ease, but to their surprise no creatures could be seen. The entrance was completely unguarded. A few birds casually flew from the mouth of the cave, raising a brief alarm, but no other activity could be detected. Dave was slightly disappointed that the Blieins had gone into hiding, but the Ubeleutes were the real enemy. The Blieins were just pawns in the Minomassa's arsenal.

"Are we going in?" Steve asked.

"No," came the reply. "They know we are here and have no intention of fighting us. We could walk through their caves for days and not see a single creature."

Dave and Joe led the way from the cave through an overgrown path, which the enemy had used so many years before to fatally attack the human population. Now in an ironic twist of fate, humans were using the path to attack its constructors.

Steve and Andy followed a few yards behind, while Ken, Bill, and Ronald kept up the rear. Just two of the powerful flood lights were needed, illuminating the path as if it were midday. Dave used the sword to whisk away the light brush that clogged the route. After a twenty minute hike, the humans reached the spot where the sword indicated the entrance to the secret tunnel to be, but no entrance could be seen.

"Are you sure that thing is right? There isn't anything here," Steve said, placing his gun and lightsource on the ground. He rubbed a cramp out of his shoulder, as he surveyed the surrounding area.

The adventurers found themselves standing at the base of a sharp incline, which merged with a jagged rock cliff several hundred feet up the mountain side. Two rows of closely grown trees, approximately ten feet apart, stretched two hundred feet up the slope. A huge boulder blocked off the corridor between the trees. Ten yards of barren dirt and rock, surrounded the strange tree formation, before slowly mingling with the vegetation of the jungle. Besides the route they had followed, no other paths were visible. Dave checked with the sword again, just to make sure he had followed its directions. The sword confirmed that they were indeed at the proper location.

"It must be behind this rock," Joe said, trying to push the boulder aside.

"Don't waste your time. You can't move that thing. It must weigh tons," Andy snapped at his brother.

"He's right. I don't think that the tunnel will be that difficult to enter. Maybe if we walk up to the other end of the trees we might see the entrance," Bill suggested. "It could be that the other end is not obstructed."

"Yes, that's probably it," Joe said, backing off from the undisturbed rock. "We aren't going anywhere through that thing."

The time travelers were puzzled by the fact that the tree trunks had grown so close together that they actually appeared to have merged. The merging was so complete that they couldn't even get the slightest peek of what filled the space between the two rows. Fortunately, the rock-like roots of the trees made perfect steps for the group to climb, as they struggled up the steep incline. The combined power of their floodlights was so strong that they barely noticed that the sun had set.

"Maybe we should have left Ronald's time in the afternoon. Then we would have landed here during the day," Andy suggested, after the group reached the top the root stairs. A distant call of some unknown animal sent a chill through his spine, causing him to shiver. He let his gaze follow the slope of the cliff up to the mountain peaks and then to the cloudless sky. The stars were plentiful. Suddenly, the distant specks of light began to spin. Andy found himself stumbling dizzily toward a rock, which he used to stabilize himself. "It would have been more convenient."

"It really didn't matter what time of day we arrived. Once we enter the tunnel it will be pitch black; no matter how bright it might be out here," Dave said, watching Andy shake the dizziness out of his head. "This way, we might have more daylight to find the Ubeleutes, once we get through the tunnel."

"I hope we can find the entrance from up here. This equipment is becoming heavy," Steve complained. Once again, he placed his lightsource and rope of the ground. For the second time, he attempted to rub a cramp out of his shoulder.

"You had better get used to it. We still have a long way to go," Dave reminded.

"But I think a rest might do us good," Bill chimed in, only slightly out of breath. His stamina had increased magnificently, since he began this seemingly non-stop hiking trip through the ancient land. "It doesn't look as if we have a clear path to follow anyhow."

To everyone's dismay, a huge boulder also blocked this entry into the void between the rows of trees. Once again, Joe tried to push the massive rock out of the way. Once again, he found his effort wasted. Ken made a quick survey of the opposite side of the tree formation. It also featured a rough stairway formed from the tree roots, but no entrance was visible.

"We have only been here a little over an hour and we're stuck. What do we do now?" Ronald asked, looking at the trees in dismay. His line of vision slowly shifted to the peaks of the mountain. He could barely see the snow capped outline against the dark sky. "It would take an awful long time to climb over this mountain."

"There must be a way in," Dave said persistently.

"These trees don't even look natural," Steve said. "I've never seen trees that grew like this. I've seen maybe two or three trees form together, but never this many."

"It's obvious that somebody, probably the Ubeleutes, planted the trees in this formation," Bill said. "They are aligned perfectly. Dave, ask the sword if it knows how to get into the tunnel."

"Yeah, it told you of the tunnel and where it is. It only makes sense that it knows how to get into it," Andy said, rising from his rock. The lightness in his head had passed.

Dave went into meditation for several seconds, before focusing his attention back on his companions. "The sword says that it entered the tunnel by walking between the rows of trees. The problem is that the boulders were not here then."

"A lot of good that does us," complained Joe, sitting down next to Ken on a rock several feet from the hindering boulder.

"I bet the boulders were placed here after the war so no one else could pass through the tunnel," Steve said.

"If that's the case, then we will have to find another way to the other side," Bill commented, looking up at the frozen peaks.

Ronald studied the trees for a few moments. "There must be some way to get through," he mumbled to himself. "Maybe we can climb over them," he finally blurted out.

"They must be close to seventy feet high," Andy said, doubtfully. "There's no way."

"Hey, I have another idea," Ronald said, a few more moments of thought. His eyes lit up with excitement. "Why don't we cut through them? Dave can use the sword on the trunks."

"That might work. Remember how the sword sliced through that small tree back at the shelter," Andy recalled. "It should only take a few swings to get through a tree this size."

"It can't hurt to try," Dave replied.

The rebel walked a few steps down the root stairs, searching for an area with few branches. Unfortunately the branches were thick and evenly spaced along the tree wall. Finally settling on an area, he took a mighty swing at the first layer of branches. Several of the smaller limbs flew out, scattering leaves in all directions. The razor sharp blade sliced through several more branches with its second swoop. For a moment it appeared as if the sword would be able to break through the barrier, until the blade met the trunk of the tree. The sword feebly bounced off the trunk, not even making a scratch in the bark. Dave took an even mightier swing and a handful of sparks bounced from the trunk.

"These trees aren't even real," Dave said, taking a closer look at the trunk. "They seem to be made out of metal. The branches are just used for camouflage."

"There must be some way through," Ken mumbled to himself. "No one would create a barrier that could never be removed." He reclined his position on the rock, sliding his hand back as he did so, until his fingers found a small groove in the rock. Semiconsciously, he allowed his index finger to follow the indentation. All of a sudden he jumped up, as if something had bit him. The others in the group were immediately drawn to the frantic swoops of his hands, as he quickly brushed off a thin layer of dirt. What he saw caused a wide grin to form on his face.

Joe, who had been watching Ken, immediately identified the markings. "Hey, you guys come here. Ken found a message carved into this rock. I bet it tells how to get in."

Since Dave was the only one capable of reading the ancient language, with the help of the sword, he sprinted the short distance to the rock. "It says that in order to gain access to the tunnel there must be at least two people. One at each end of the trees. They must pull simultaneously at the base of each rock," Dave translated.

"I wonder why the Ubeleutes left a message telling how to enter the tunnel? I thought the tunnel was supposed to be a secret," Steve said.

"I don't think the Ubeleutes left the message. My guess is that a human wrote it," Bill theorized. "Most likely he saw how to access the tunnel and wrote the message in case he didn't return to the halls to warn the other humans."

"From the outcome of the war, it seems that he never did return," Ronald stated.

"I think I can safely say that he didn't," Joe said bluntly.

"What makes you so sure," Bill questioned.

Joe swung his light a few yards up the incline. The others soon realized why he made the remark. The unmistakable hand and forearm of a human skeleton protruded from the ground. A well worn dagger was still clutched in its hand.

"It's impossible for that to stay intact after all these years," Steve said.

"A message from the Minomassa no doubt," Bill observed. "I have a feeling it knows that we are here."

Andy cautiously approached the skeleton, half expecting it to rise up out of the ground and attack. But no such excitement was in store. He reached down and grasped the dagger, careful not to touch the decaying bones. The entire arm of the skeleton easily popped from the soft soil. The bones then proceeded to fall back to earth and shatter.

"He must have gotten killed right after completing the message," Ken said. "Lucky for us the Ubeleutes never found what he had written."

"Well, what are we waiting for?" Steve yelled, showing his eagerness to enter the tunnel. "Andy and I will run down to the bottom. When we flash our light off and on, start to pull."

"You got it," Joe said, already finding a position to tug at the boulder.

Andy and Steve rushed blindly down the root steps. Each almost tripping on separate occasions, but managing to keep their balance. Upon reaching the base of the incline, Steve tossed his gear aside and rubbed his hands along the bottom of the boulder, surprised to find a ridge which made the perfect finger hold. The farmer's son nodded to Andy, who flashed the light up toward the others. Steve began pulling at the boulder, lightly at first, then gradually increasing the force. Bill saw the light flash and told Joe to proceed. The instant he tugged at the massive rock, both boulders simultaneously tipped inward, sinking into the ground.

Steve rolled backward, afraid that the moving boulder might crush him, but the mechanism controlling the movement of the rock prevented such danger. From their position at the bottom of the incline, Andy and Steve could see the lights of the others rush toward them through the corridor between the trees. Steve hurriedly picked up his equipment and ran up to meet them.

Both parties stopped short, as they approached the middle of the tree lined passage. A deep black pit, stretching twenty feet across and as many feet down, separated the two groups. The void proved to be less of an obstacle than its first impression suggested. Blue rock stairs led down both sides of the pit, merging at the bottom.

"This must be it," Joe said, flashing a beam of light down the steep staircases. The light showed that after merging the stairs turned off to the side, continuing the descent into the earth.

"We have Ken to thank for finding the message," Dave said, eyeing the stairway. "But I'm afraid we are going to be faced with many more challenges, much more difficult than this one."

The group quickly descended to the platform that lie below. The steps were well worn in places, revealing the abundance of travel the stone had endured over the ages. After merging and turning off in a new direction, the stairs continued for only several yards. There the humans found themselves at the end of a very long dark tunnel, which disappeared into the heart of the mountain.

The passage was nearly ten feet wide and close to fifteen feet tall. Clearly the tunnel had been designed to allow for the effective movement of troops and weapons. The flood lights lit up the tunnel brightly, divulging walls of bright blue stone. The rock walls were similar to the steps they had just descended, with the exception of occasional rough and jagged areas. Several metal torch holders were still clinging loosely to the sides of the passage, but most had long ago fallen to the floor and begun the long slow corrosion process.

A musty stench was present in the air, indicating that many years had passed since the tunnel had been used. The stagnant air made each human gag more than once, but they soon became accustomed to it. As they cautiously proceeded through the tunnel, the sound of the massive boulders rising to their original positions reached the traveler's ears.

There the boulders would patiently wait for some other intelligent beings to find the message and the secrets of the tunnel.

"Just a thought," Bill said, as the group paused to listen to the rumbling. "We might not be able to reopen the boulders from the inside."

"Let's just hope that retreat is not in our future," Ken replied.

Steve and Andy flanked Dave, as he led the way through the gloomy tunnel. After traveling a couple hundred feet, the passage turned off to the right. The time travelers now found themselves traveling south, following the mountain range to some unknown end.

"Look at that," Ken said, glancing back down the tunnel. "The walls are glowing."

The others turned to view the sight. "This rock must have been purposely chosen by the Ubeleutes to aid in lighting the passage," Bill said in a scientific manner. "It appears as if the rock absorbs heat and converts the energy into this form of light."

Andy held his hand flat against the wall, keeping it in place for a several seconds. Upon backing away, a perfectly shaped bright blue image of his hand glowed on the rock's surface. "Not bad," he mumbled softly.

The passage ran in a seemingly straight line, descending at a gradual rate. Every so often the travelers would come upon a section of tunnel that had suffered some minor damage. More than likely caused by the effects of time, a small section of wall, floor, or ceiling would be missing and a pile of rubble scattered about. The damage was never serious enough to hamper progress, however.

After walking for approximately a half mile, the group found themselves at the entrance way to a small chamber. The twenty foot square room had only one exit, located directly across from where the party stood. In each of the four corners stood a large purple statue. The humans paused briefly, scanning the room for any danger, before entering.

Each statue reached nearly eight feet in height and stood elevated on a two foot platform. Although the features of the statues were practically identical, obvious differences were apparent, mostly in the positioning of limbs. The statues depicted creatures with huge muscular arms and legs, easily three times the normal size of a human. The faces resembled those of a bull, with a large horn growing from above each ear and short fangs protruding from a long snout.

The workmanship of the statues proved to be of the most expert craftsman, although all present assumed the work had been done by an Ubeleute. Evidence of the skill involved came from the countless fine lines representing hair that covered the entire body of each creature. But the exquisite detail of the statues was not what held the eyes of the visitors. While the large axes that the statues held were formidable enough, the fact that the creator of this art work had done a such magnificent job of giving the statues the appearance that each beast stood frozen in time ready to attack, caused some alarm.

"They sure are ugly," noted Ken, gravitating toward the center of the room. "I wonder who they are."

Ken's question was pointless, as they all knew that the statues were of Ubeleutes. But the frightening size of the creatures caused some doubt that the art work might not have been performed to scale. This doubt was short lived, as Dave confirmed that they were indeed looking at life sized statues of the enemy they were seeking.

"The sword informs me that they use those axes with deadly accuracy."

"Damn!" Steve exclaimed.

"Too bad they won't get close enough to use them," Joe said, clutching his gun and waving it at a statue.

Steve walked up to the nearest statue, reaching a hand out to feel the fine detail of the stone. He had but a moment to sense the intricacies of the work, for the instant his finger touched the rock, the statue exploded, rocking the underground chamber. A blinding burst of light filled the room, as Steve was hurled backward onto the ground by the force of stone turning to flesh. Fortunately his eyes were clenched closed bracing for the impact with the floor, else he would have seen the axe of the Ubeleute swipe only inches past his face. Steve opened his eyes just in time to see a live Ubeleute rush toward him, its axe cocked and ready to attack.

If the sword's description of the Ubeleute's skill with the axe was accurate, chances for two misses in succession would be low. Joe, however, was quick to react to the situation. Though he had been forced off balance by the explosion, his gun was still raised from his mock attack. This fortunate positioning, coupled with his years of training and actual combat experience, allowed him to quickly fire several rounds into the beast. The sound of the machine gun blasting bullets through the stagnant air was mild compared the previous violent explosion, but that did not take away from the deadly power of the lead slugs. The Ubeleute stumbled, feeling the rapid succession of bullets enter its body, then looked over at Joe with a clearly stunned expression. The creature fell to the ground. Determined to finish its attack, it tried to lift its axe. A second burst from Joe's machine gun stopped the attempt. The massive creature sprawled out on the floor and died.

Relief was not yet in the human's future. The instant the Ubeleute's life ended, the remaining three statues exploded simultaneously, once again shaking the chamber and blinding all occupants with a powerful burst of light. By this time all of the humans had their weapons ready for attack, but the lingering blinding effects of the explosion prevented an immediate response, from everyone except for Joe. He did not let the fact that his vision was blurred prevent him from assaulting the Ubeleutes. His mind had registered the exact positioning of all the rooms occupants and immediately turned to his right, firing into the corner where he knew a statue had been. He could hear a creature groan and crash to the floor.

Images began to form as the blindness subsided, allowing the rest of the humans to defend themselves. Ronald and Ken, who had just raised their weapons to fire at the first Ubeleute, now shifted their aim, killing another. Bill turned his machine gun loose on the remaining creature, but not before the beast released its weapon. The axe hurled across the small chamber, missing Ken's right shoulder by the width of a hair, before embedding itself into the rock wall.

A stunned silence followed, as the adventurers attempted to comprehend the events that had just happened. With their vision slowly returning to normal, they could see that the statues were gone, replaced by four dead Ubeleutes scattered on the dusty floor.

"That was close," Steve said, rising from the floor of the battle site. He took a deep breath and brushed off his clothing, as if he had accomplished something. He looked around for his lightsource, only to find that it had been crushed by the fallen Ubeleute. Suddenly a sharp pain rushed through his head, reminding him of his fall. "That floor sure is hard."

"Never mind the floor. Did you see how close that thing came to hitting me?" Ken said. His eyes lit up, as he noticed how deep the blade of the axe had penetrated the rock wall. He tugged at the weapon, but it would need a force stronger than he could provide to free it.

"If Steve hadn't touched that statue..."

Andy was cut off by Dave. "We can't go around blaming someone for every little thing that happens. Steve had no idea that touching the statue would bring it to life. I bet none of us expected that to happen."

"We had better be very alert from now on," Joe said, checking the amount of ammunition left in his gun. He looked at Steve, as he spoke. "The Ubeleutes are obviously no match for our weapons, but they could kill us if they gain the advantage of surprise again."

"These must have been guards left by the enemy after the war," Bill surmised, studying the bodies. "Any unwary person, such as Steve, foolish enough to touch a statue would be attacked, and most likely killed."

"I'm just glad we have the guns," Steve said sheepishly. His rapid heartbeat had begun to slow and return to normal, following his near fatal encounter.

"I think you should just keep your hands off things from now on," Ronald warned. He then cracked a smile and put his arm around his son. "I'm sure your mother would blame me, if you got yourself killed."

"Don't worry about me, dad," Steve said with a wry smile. "These creatures won't get close enough for another attack, now that I know how they operate."

While the farmer and his son were exchanging words, Bill busied himself by watching the rich purple blood stream from one of the Ubeleute's wounds. "I thought I had seen it all. Yellow, brown, and even black blood; but purple? This is getting to be too much."

"I wonder what happened to all the creatures with different colored blood?" Andy asked. "There is no record in our time of any color besides red. Dave, ask the sword why only the red blooded creatures survived."

Dave went into meditation, and remained motionless for such a long time that the others thought he had fallen asleep standing up. Finally his eyes popped open and he spoke. "The sword doesn't know what you mean when you say that only the red blooded creatures survived. It can only tell us what has happened in its life. Obviously there are still creatures with different colored blood," he said, motioning to the nearest corpse.

"Just another mystery that we will never know the answer to," Ken said, giving one more feeble tug at the axe embedded in the wall.

"Come on. Let's get out of this room, before some more of these guys come at us," Steve said, looking down the corridor they were to follow.

"Steve is right. We should be moving on. According to the sword, we have a long hike ahead of us," Dave noted. He paused briefly at the exit. "Like I said before, we can easily kill the Ubeleutes. Getting to them is the hard part."

With one last look at the dead bodies, the group resumed their march down the mysterious tunnel. As a result of the Ubeleute smashing Steve's light, the party was left with only four sources, which for the time being proved to be more than adequate. The stench in the air soon turned into a rich earthy odor and the tunnel offered no breeze to clear it away. As they walked, their feet kicked up inches of dust that had settled over the centuries. The dust clouded the air, significantly reducing visibility.

The travelers were pleased to find that the passage remained straight for the next mile, offering no side passages or any more small chambers full of statues. With each passing minute, Ronald became more and more paranoid of the roof caving in and burying him under tons of dirt and rock. Before taking each step, he would eye the ceiling ahead, trying to detect any oversized cracks that might trigger a cave-in.

At the end of the mile, the passage made a ninety degree turn to the left and the slope of descent increased dramatically. The sound of their lonesome footsteps, muffled by the layer of dust, echoed off the smooth walls. A soft dripping sound was the only other noise that could be heard. The group soon discovered the cause of the disturbing dripping sound. A small round opening in the ceiling allowed a drop of water to fall every second or so. The drop ran down the wall, four inches of which had been worn away over the years, and accumulated on a small ledge before dripping into a hole in the floor. The opening of the hole was no more than a foot across, but closer inspection revealed that the water had created a huge cavity underneath the tunnel. A rippled reflection indicated that a small pool had accumulated at the bottom of the ten foot pit.

"There's something that this mountain isn't impenetrable by," Dave said, watching a drop of water flow its course.

"Yes, I'm surprised that the tunnel hasn't caved in by now," Bill joked, aware of Ronald's fear. "Water does have a way of destroying things."

"Don't mention anything about the roof caving in," Ronald said worriedly. He stepped backward, trying to get as far away as possible from the pit. "I have enough trouble worrying about the roof caving in without you adding to the problem."

Bill smiled, as he walked to Ronald and gave him a pat on the back. "I'm only joking with you. If this tunnel has survived this many years, it will survive at least until we get out."

"I suggest passing by the far wall," Joe said, rising from his inspection of the hole. "It looks like the most of the supporting rock has been washed away. This floor might not be too stable."

"See, I have reason to worry," Ronald said nervously.

While the water had indeed structurally weakened the floor, it would be many years before the rock and dirt would collapse under the weight of a human. With the pit quickly forgotten and the dripping of the water long since faded, only the sounds of fourteen marching feet and seven hampered breaths filled the tunnel.

Dave had resumed his position at the front of the pack, when a short time later he kicked a small object buried under the dust. Though he had stumbled over many small rocks in the tunnel, he could tell immediately that what he kicked was something different. Cautiously he bent down to pick up the object, quickly recognizing it to be a broken arrow, brown with age. Two feet further along, lay something not nearly as old. A whole arrow, dripping with red blood, lay on top of the dust.

"It looks as if this place hasn't been deserted for as long as we thought," Dave said, spending a few moments examining the arrows. The broken one was obviously a remnant of the war, preserved somehow in the dry tunnel. The frail wood of the useless weapon crumbled at his touch. The second arrow had been left recently, as the red liquid hadn't even begun to dry.

"This could be a warning from the Minomassa," Ken suggested. "It might have been trying to get to the entrance before us and block it off. When it discovered that we were already in the tunnel, it left this instead."

"If they knew we were coming, why didn't they wait and ambush us?" Joe said sarcastically. "Obviously they don't have any military strategy."

"They are scared of us," Steve said. "They saw what we did to those statues and ran away."

"The statues might have been their attempt to ambush us," Bill explained. "We assumed that they were left after the war. They just as easily could have been placed there recently."

"The Ubeleutes don't think the way we do. They have strange customs that they follow very closely. Don't get the wrong impression. They are not scared. I'm sure they will be ready for us, when the time comes," Dave said. He tossed the arrows onto the floor, not giving the others a chance to examine them.

"How come there are no footprints here?" Andy asked. "If the Ubeleutes put the arrow here, there should be footprints. The dust isn't even disturbed."

"Maybe they can fly," Steve suggested.

"I wouldn't be surprised if they could," Dave commented. According to the sword, the Ubeleutes could not fly; but Dave wanted to keep everyone alert, so he let the misconception stay alive.

"That is just what we need," Ronald said, as they resumed their journey. "Eight foot tall flying creatures."

After another time consuming mile of walking, the group decided to rest. The humans eagerly removed their surprisingly burdensome equipment. Each took a sandwich from Ken's backpack. The tunnel, unlike the moisture laden Bliein caves, proved to be very dry. The only moisture they had come across was the water dripping into the pit. The sound of the humans chewing their food replaced the footsteps as the only sound in the lonesome tunnel.

"I don't know how much longer I am going to be able to put up with this foul smelling air," Andy complained. He tossed the plastic wrap which housed his sandwich onto the floor. "I thought the air in our time was horrible, but this is even worse. I hope the exit isn't too much further."

"The sword says that we are nearly three quarters of the way through," Dave informed, as he finished his sandwich. He also tossed his rubbish onto the floor.

"It seems as if we have walked through the mountain several times over," Ronald observed. The thoughts of a cave-in still ran through his mind, but they were slowly subsiding. "I figure we should be out of here by now."

"You must consider the fact that the purpose of the tunnel was not exclusively to by pass the mountain," Bill said, theorizing the intentions of the Ubeleutes. "If the purpose of the tunnel was to keep the Ubeleutes hidden for the longest possible time, then they would not necessarily end the tunnel just to the other side of the mountain."

"They would make the other end close to their base camp," Joe added. "That would be the smart thing to do for a surprise attack."

"I wish I knew how the creatures in this time made all these underground passages," Ronald said, marveling at the accomplishment. "I can't tell you how long it takes me just to plow my fields. Just imaging how long it took them to actually clear all this dirt and rock out of here."

"By the size of the creatures who attacked us, I doubt it took them very long," Steve said.

"I think we should start on again. If we pace ourselves, we should reach the outside within an hour," Dave said, urging the others to gather their belongings.

"The sooner we get there, the sooner we can do the killing we came here to do," Joe said, tapping his gun. He raised the barrel in a mock attack, then quickly lowered it, remembering what happened the last time he performed the act.

Soon after they resumed walking, a high pitched whining sound filled the tunnel. A few yards later the blue stone walls gave way to dirt. The earth was loose and moist, giving the walls the appearance that they could collapse at any moment. This, of course, renewed Ronald's fear of a cave-in. The travelers quickened their pace, only to be faced with their first major decision a few moments later. The tunnel forked. The two new passageways branched out in opposite directions.

"Which way do we go?" Ken asked, staring down the left hand tunnel.

"I don't care. Let's just get out of here, before the walls crash down on us," Ronald cried.

"I don't know," Dave answered. "I'll just ask the sword which direction we should take." The communication was brief, as Dave opened his eyes with a most disturbing look on his face.

"What's the matter, Dave?" Bill asked, stepping forward.

"I knew it, we are going to get trapped in here," Ronald whimpered. He looked nervously down each corridor.

"The sword says that there should not be a division in the tunnel. According to it, the rest of the way should be straight."

Bill flashed his light at the wall facing the humans. Sure enough, the outline of a passage became visible. Large rock blocks were carefully stacked, effectively blocking the tunnel. Fresh marks were visible in the dirt floor, apparently caused by the dragging of the boulders. "It looks as if the passage used to go straight. I'll give you one guess who barricaded it," the scientist said, kicking the barricade lightly.

"The Ubeleutes are sure making it difficult for us to get through this tunnel," Steve said.

"Were you expecting them to make it easy?" Ronald snapped. A nervous sweat had formed on his forehead. He paced quickly in a small circle, trying to quell his fears.

"I guess we will just have to pick a tunnel and hope it is the one that leads to the outside," Joe said, flashing his light down the right hand tunnel.

"That is, if one leads out," Andy added. His words drew angry stares from the rest of the party.

"Let's try this one," Ken said, still looking down the left passage.

Seeing that the group had absolutely no information on which to base their decision, they agreed with Ken and embarked on a journey down the somber tunnel. The width of the new passage was quite a bit narrower than what they had grown accustomed to in this underground environment, although they were still able to file two abreast. The whining sound now began to oscillate from a super high pitch, barely audible to the human ear, to a low bass-like hum. The haphazard markings on the walls supported the theory that the tunnel had recently been constructed. After a short walk, the corridor opened into a large chasm. Twenty-five feet across the void the passage continued into enigmatic darkness.

"It looks like a dead end," Joe said, staring down into the depths of the fissure. He nudged a rock over the edge with his foot. When it hit bottom, they could hear a soft splash followed by a bright light located at the point of entry. The light brightened the walls of the chasm for a brief moment, before restoring the chamber to its original darkness.

"It appears as if there is some sort of acid down there," Bill concluded.

"I think we should turn around and hope the other passage leads to the outside," Dave said, as it became apparent that there were no means for them to cross the fissure. "It doesn't look as if we can go any further this way."

Just as they turned from the edge of the chasm, the ground began to rumble. The stunned humans watched in horror as cakes of dirt fell from the ceiling directly over the entrance to the tunnel they had just traveled through. The size of the clumps quickly grew, until a shower of debris clogged the passage. The rumbling grew louder, as a massive boulder fell from the ceiling, rolling briefly down the tower of dirt, before coming to a rest square in the center of the entrance way. The shaking ground quieted, leaving the dust to settle at its own gradual pace.

"It doesn't look as if we are going any further that way either," Joe said, prodding the obstruction with his gun barrel.

"I knew the ceiling was going to collapse," Ronald yelled. "In a few minutes the rest of the ceiling is going to cave-in and bury us alive."

"Calm down, Ronald," Dave said in a soothing voice. "Don't get too excited. Just give a us a few minutes to figure out a way to get out of here."

After examining the blocked passage, they discovered the cave-in to be more than just another diversion by the Ubeleutes to slow their progress through the tunnel. The completeness of the avalanche convinced them that the event was supposed to kill them. Though it didn't manage to crush anyone, the avalanche would still succeed in its ultimate goal, if another exit couldn't be found.

"It seems as if the Minomassa finally recognizes us as formidable opponents. The Ubeleutes are actually trying to kill us," Dave said, examining the cave-in. "I figured they would have waited at least until we made it out of the tunnel."

"I don't understand these creatures," Joe said, shaking his head. "If they are actually trying to kill us, why play all these little games? Why don't they just attack us head on?"

"I told you," Dave replied, "they have certain practices or rituals that they follow. It is hard to understand."

"I guess we are going to have to find a way to get across this chasm," Ken said, peering into the murky depths of the void. Soft snapping sounds could be heard from the acid pool that lay below.

"Since the sword has never passed through this chasm before, it is going to be useless to us as an informant," Dave added.

Ronald opened his mouth, as if to say something, but Bill interrupted. "Don't say it, Ronald. The roof isn't going to collapse. And we will find a way out of here." The scientist looked down into the fissure, not sure about the validity of either statement.

The seven prisoners walked to the edge of the fissure and stared blankly into it. Even with the power of their flood lights, they could barely see a reflection off the black pool that lay below. Joe scattered a few rounds into the liquid. Small bursts of light appeared where the bullets struck, then quickly disappeared. The lethal liquid gave off a sulfurous odor, which mixed with the already earthy fragrance of the underground chamber, causing Andy to pinch his nose and walk away.

"It does look as if we are trapped," Steve said, turning his attention on the blocked exit.

"People in their time sure give up easy," Andy whispered to his brother. "All they do is talk about how we are trapped. They don't even try to find a way out." Joe acknowledged silently with a nod.

In the mean time, Bill walked the length of the chamber poking at the walls. His search for a concealed exit proved fruitless. The slightly sloped floor measured ten feet from the base of the wall to the edge of the fissure. The floor and walls, both rough and damp, were freshly dug. Hundreds of earthworms, or what he hoped were just earthworms, crawled slowly over the dank surfaces.

"If we could attach a rope to the other side, we could cross that way," Ken said hopefully. The humans examined the opposite side of the chasm, but found it to be just as featureless as the side they stood upon.

"Maybe if we tie one end of the rope to a rock, we can toss it over to the other side," Andy suggested.

"We could never throw a rock across the fissure large enough to support us," Dave said in a monotonous voice. He searched the far side of the chasm once again for an outstanding feature, but there just wasn't anything there that they could secure a rope around.

Joe soon became hostile. The idea of fighting an opponent that he could not see, irritated him to no end. "I didn't come all this way to become trapped in some stupid underground dungeon," he yelled, firing half a cartridge of ammunition in to the far wall. A few sparks could be seen, as the bullets struck rocks buried in the dirt.

"Take it easy," Dave said, trying to keep the group's emotions in check. "We are going to need all the ammunition we have, when we get out of here. We can't afford to waste anything. There are no stores nearby to buy more."

Joe yanked his now empty cartridge from the gun and hurled it across the fissure. It struck the wall, bounced several times on the floor, then plunged into the acid pool. A soft snap and a small spot of light was the cartridge's last farewell. Joe looked at Dave, shook his head, and walked over to the cave-in.

After tossing around several more ideas on how to cross the chasm, they gave up on the thought. It was obvious that the route out was not going to be found by crossing the fissure.

The Ubeleutes could not have made a chamber more featureless and bland than the one the travelers were stuck in. Even the ceiling was smooth and bare. The high pitched whining sound could still be heard through the blocked passage, giving some hope to the prisoners that they might escape back the way they came. Even more tempting was the fresh breeze that could be felt blowing through the passage just several yards away across the fissure.

"They sure know how to torture us," Ken said, taking a deep breath. "The air coming through that tunnel smells as if it is coming from the outside."

"It probably is," Andy said. "With our luck, the exit is probably less than a hundred feet away. And we're stuck here separated from it by a hole in the ground."

"Are you sure we can't clear the cave-in?" Ronald asked. He tossed a few rocks from the blockage into the acid, causing great bursts of light to silhouette the ceiling.

"You're wasting your time," Ken said calmly. "It will take a year to clear that out by hand."

"He's right, Ronald," Dave added. "It probably won't take a year, but we don't know much of the tunnel the cave-in destroyed. In all likelihood, the tunnel will collapse again before we can escape."

Ronald didn't stop. Ignoring the words of his companions, he continued to toss more rocks into the fissure. "At least I'm doing more than you guys. You're just standing around doing nothing." Steve moved toward the exit and also started tossing debris aside.

"The only thing he is doing more than us is complaining," Joe said angrily to Ken.

Ronald and Steve cleared away several more boulders, oblivious to the others. After removing the larger obstacles, they began using their arms to move away some dirt. They labored for several minutes, until some unstable soil shifted and fell from the ceiling. All the work they had performed had been negated in a split second.

Ronald looked at the blockage and whispered to himself, "We are never going to get out of here."

Steve put his arm around his father's shoulder. Together they walked off along the base of the wall. The rest of the group watched, saddened by the failed attempt.

"At least we have plenty of air," Andy said, breaking the awkward silence. The breeze from the opposite side of the fissure was weak but steady. "We should be able to last long enough to find a way out."

"Don't you understand? We aren't going to get out," Ronald yelled angrily, pulling away from Steve and staring violently at Andy.

"If you don't stop whimpering, I'm going to throw *you* into the acid," Joe yelled back, partly protecting his brother, but mostly out of pure anger.

Ronald realized that Joe had no intention of throwing him into the acid, but he turned away none the less. The farmer walked over to the blocked exit and sat on the ground.

"We might have plenty of air, but we are going to need water. We only have seven canteens, and most of them are half empty," Dave said.

He began to pace back and forth upon the strip of land they were stranded on.

"Maybe we can somehow tunnel a new passage around the obstruction," Steve suggested. One look at the rocky walls quickly killed the idea.

Joe, still restless, leaned over the edge of the fissure and peered into its depths. The void was black and seemingly boundless. He inched his way so far over the edge that the others thought that he might fall in. Andy quickly jumped to his feet, immediately grabbing onto his brother to balance his weight. Feeling more secure, even though Andy's weight was nominal, Joe allowed himself to lean even further over the edge, trying his best to calculate how far below the edge of the fissure the surface of the acid lay.

It was in this vulnerable position that Joe noticed that the inside walls of the fissure seemed to be made out of a metallic substance. Though the walls were as black as the acid, a faint glimmered appeared as the feeble rays of light reflected off the smooth surface. He could not be certain, but it appeared as if the metallic portion of the wall, which started five feet below the edge, was being ever so slowly eaten away by the dangerous liquid. The putrid fumes quickly made him dizzy, causing him to back away. *If the breeze entering the chamber were to stop,* he thought, we *won't be able to survive for long.*

"Did you see anything worth while?" Ken asked.

"I'm not sure," Joe replied, wiping some tears from his irritated eyes. "I think I saw a dark shadow about fifteen feet down. It could be a tunnel."

"A tunnel!" Bill exclaimed jumping toward the edge of the fissure.

"Hold on to me, Bill," Dave said, quickly dropping to the ground and inching his body over the edge.

"I don't see anything," Andy said, taking a quick glance into the fissure. The thoughts of falling didn't allow him to get close enough to actually take a decent look.

"I see the shadow, but it's too dark to tell if it's a tunnel," Dave said.

"Wait, I have an idea," Ronald said, eagerly rising from his sitting position. He grabbed two large rocks and tossed them simultaneously into the acid. The anticipated result lit up the chamber with a near blinding light.

"It's a tunnel," Dave yelled, as Bill pulled him back from the ledge. "I don't know how far it goes, but there appears to be plenty of room for at least one person to go down and take a look."

"How, are we going to get down to it?" Andy asked, not wanting to be the one to volunteer.

"I'm going to climb down and check it out," Dave said. "I'll need all of you to hold on to the rope from up here."

Andy quickly picked up Steve's rope and tied one end of it to the largest boulder he could find. The other end Dave secured around his waist. The fifty foot rope would have no problem reaching the tunnel. The remaining six travelers grabbed hold of the rope, backing up as far as possible from the edge and digging their heals into the soft soil.

Dave tugged on the rope, before looking up at the others. "What a group to place my life in the hands of," he joked, as he stepped over the edge.

"Just be careful," Billed warned.

Dave found sturdy foot holds in the dirt walls, but that only lasted for the first several feet. Gingerly, he tested the metallic portion of the wall, finding it to be quite smooth. Returning his foot to a safe position, he closed his eyes in anticipation of his next move. Calmly he listened to the gurgling of the acid, the only sound in the chasm.

Glancing down one more time to get a bearing on the tunnel, he again placed his foot on the slick surface, transferring half of his body weight. The sole of his shoe could not find a grip and began a slow slide downward. Dave did not like the feeling, but he knew that in order to reach the tunnel he would have to trust that the six on the surface could support his weight. Bracing himself for the imminent fall, he removed his second foot from the dirt, quickly replacing it onto the metallic portion of the wall. It proved to be a useless attempt to keep his balance, as he immediately dropped into the fissure. His surprised yell echoed through the chamber, raising some alarm from the surface. The sudden tug on the rope pulled the six anchors forward, but they were able to quickly regain control.

Dave opened his eyes, finding that he had fallen only a few feet. The inviting entrance to the tunnel was directly below his dangling body. He yelled for the others to lower him to his target. As he approached the tunnel, he could feel small drops of the deadly liquid bubble up and burn his unprotected skin. Missing a feeble attempt to grab onto the corner of the passageway, he rotated into an inverted position. The pistol slipped from his clothing, plopping into the acid. A natural instinct caused him to raise his head, just in time to avoid having his hair singed by the sudden ball of flames.

"Are you okay?" Bill yelled, concerned over the unexpected burst of light.

"I'm fine," came the reply. Just lower me a few more feet. Dave's second attempt at finding a handhold to the passage entrance was successful. His heart was beating rapidly, as he hauled himself safely to the floor of the newly discovered tunnel. He untied the rope from his waist and watched as it was quickly pulled back up to the surface.

"Hey, are you all right down there?" Joe yelled, moving toward the edge, after feeling the tension in the rope disappear.

"I'm fine, but I have a few holes in my clothes from the acid," Dave answered, taking count of the numerous singed areas on his clothing.

"Does it look safe?" Bill asked, looking down. He could see Dave's head sticking out of the tunnel.

"I don't know how safe it is, but it is a tunnel." With that he heard cheers of happiness from the surface. "Send down the sword and a lightsource," he ordered. A few moments later the requested items were dangling in front of him.

Dave quickly untied the objects and switched the light on. The powerful beam instantly filled the seven foot wide tunnel. The rebel was not surprised to see that the damp, rough cut features of the walls and ceiling appeared to have been hastily constructed. He followed the downward slant of the floor, with his eyes, into a black nothingness.

"Do you think we will be able to get through that way?" Ken asked, peering into the fissure.

"I hope so," Dave replied. "It is a good size passage. We should have no problem moving through it. See if you can secure the rope to something, so the rest of you can climb down."

Joe retied the rope to the boulder, while the rest of the group hurriedly searched for more rocks, piling them onto the rope. A few minutes later a massive pile of dirt and rocks stood near the wall, totally covering the boulder the rope was actually tied to.

"I hope it'll hold," Andy said to his brother. "Just to make sure, we'll send everyone else down first. Since I'm the lightest, I'll go last."

"If you want," Joe replied, tugging at the rope.

As a precaution the guns were lowered one by one down to the tunnel. Keeping with Andy's suggestion, Bill, the heaviest of the group, was lowered into the fissure. The rotund scientist bounced freely off the walls, placing a strain on the anchors, but he reached the tunnel safely and was pulled in by Dave. At this point a second lightsource was sent down. Ronald followed and then Steve. As the farmer's son reached the tunnel, the pile of rocks began to shift slightly, causing the remaining three to toss a few more rocks onto the pile, before lowering Ken.

"Are you sure you want to go last?" Joe asked, pulling the rope back to surface, after lowering the third lightsource. "Don't take this the wrong way, but my physical conditioning might make it easier for me to navigate down without anyone holding on from up here."

"I can make," Andy replied, only to finish off with a quick jab at his brother. "I hardly weigh anything compared to you."

"You do look a bit skinny," Joe laughed. He loosely wrapped the rope once around his right forearm.

Andy nodded, signaling to the elder Marshall that he was ready. The rope immediately drew taught, again rustling the pile of rocks. Andy strained, digging his feet in to the loose earth, using all his strength to fight the gravitational pull on his brother. A sweat began to form on his brow, as his muscles cried for relief. Moments later, the tension in the rope disappeared. Joe had safely reached the floor of the tunnel.

"Okay," Joe yelled to the surface. "Whenever you're ready."

Andy looked down at the pile of rocks, replacing several which had fallen during Joe's descent. He was positive that the rope had moved several inches during Joe's trip, but there were no large boulders left to reinforce the anchor. He would have to count on the existing structure to hold his weight.

"If you don't think you can make it with the last light source, leave it up there," Dave said, peering up toward the surface. "We don't want to take any unnecessary chances."

"I think I can handle it," Andy responded, tugging at the rope. With a heavy sigh, he glanced one last time into the fissure, before backing slowly into the void. As he removed his second foot from the platform, relief spread through his body. The rope was holding his weight. He paused to gather his thoughts, before stepping onto the slick metallic portion, remembering how the others had lost their balance as soon as they stepped from the dirt wall. The tunnel opening seemed so close, almost close enough that he could leap down to it by pushing away from the wall with his legs, allowing gravity to pull him down safely into the open passage. But in reality he knew it to be too risky. Andy held no illusions as to the awkwardness of his motor skills. The image that repeated itself over and over in his mind was that he would push off too far and fall to fast, plunging in to the acid pool.

Despite all of his mental preparation, his feet could not find a foothold on the metallic wall. A truly frightful scream leapt from his lips, when he lost his footing. Gravity instantly pulled him toward the wall, ramming his face against the cold black surface. Images of his earlier meeting with the rocky cliff, while hanging desperately to the burning bridge, flashed through his mind. This time, however, his hands were healthy, able to grasp tightly to the rope. The light source, tucked into his clothing, was instantly jarred loose. The object splashed into the acid, filling the chamber with a momentary bright flash. The sudden jerk also disturbed the rock pile, causing the rope to shift. Andy held his breath, hoping that the rope would catch itself on something, but it didn't. The rate of slippage increased, causing him to yell once again.

Joe and Steve where standing at the entrance to the tunnel, watching the events unfold. They resisted the instinct to duck into the tunnel for cover, as the flames from the light source jumped from the acid's surface.

A moment later, Andy's helpless body came tumbling down. In one swift motion, the two reached out, grabbing him as he slipped by. The trio came crashing to the floor of the tunnel, but all were safe.

"Are you all right?" Dave asked, rushing forward to make sure no one accidentally stumbled out into the fissure.

"Yes, I think so," Andy said, pushing his brother off his leg.

Ken tugged at the rope, which still had one end lying on the surface. The very gentlest of force caused the rope to fall free from its supposedly secure position under the rocks. The scientist was able to snatch the rope into the tunnel, before any of it could be damaged by the acid.

"I guess none of us are boy scouts," Steve said, watching Ken battle with the rope.

"Boy scouts?" Ken asked.

"Yeah, it's an organization that teaches kids things, like how to tie a knot."

"Oh," Ken answered, attempting to coil the rope.

"Just for the record, the knot didn't come loose," Joe said, lifting the end of the rope. The rock just slipped through the loop."

At that moment, Ronald and Bill emerged from the darkness of the newly discovered tunnel. They had gone to explore, while the rest of group made their way down from the ledge. The whining sound that had haunted the adventurers in the upper passages had stopped, or at least could no longer be heard. Silence was not something that the humans could revel in, however, as a splashing noise resembling running water echoed off the earth walls.

A brief examination of their clothing revealed that each traveler had suffered some degree of damage. The minor redness and pain was not enough to slow their progress, however.

"What did you find?" Joe asked.

"The tunnel goes on for a few hundred feet and then enters a set of stairs. The stairs spiral down, eventually turning into another passage, which heads back toward the fissure," Bill informed.

"I hope it goes through and is not another dead end," Ken added.

"Me too," Ronald agreed. He had been gingerly touching a quarter sized welt on the back of his right hand. The pain was nothing worse than the sunburn he received every year, while tending to his fields. "I hope we find a way out soon. I can't take much more of this air. It was bad enough when we started, but now with the fumes from the acid it's just over bearing."

Dave looked back toward the top of the chasm. "I doubt that we will be able to get back up this way, so we better hope this tunnel leads out."

"Maybe we should have explored down here first, before sending everyone down," Bill suggested.

"Probably," Dave replied. "Too late now."

Bill raised his gun and led the group through the passage. His mind wandered, wondering why he was trudging through this underground maze. Better yet, he asked himself, why had he come to this ancient land in the first place? The event that started this journey, the raid on his apartment was unexpected, but not entirely out of the realm of possibility. He knew that his work to overthrow the Protectors could lead to his being caught.

Bill also knew it to be a miracle that the untested time machine worked. Never in his wildest dreams did he expect the device to work on the first attempt. But it was that success, that moment in time, when he had lost control over the events in his life. He had chosen to fight against the Protectors, but he was not a warrior. He was fighting the war with his brain, leaving the physical activities to others. But somehow, he had been transformed from a brilliant scientist into an armed assassin. Now his battle was not even with the Protectors. In fact, he felt as if all his decision making power was lost. Instead of making the calls himself, fate was now dictating his course of action.

He was captured, so he had to escape. The time machine was stolen, so he had to find it. He escaped death and landed in a strange time, but he had to return to the past to save his friends. It was then that he actually felt as if he were regaining control of the recent hectic events. But when Dave wanted to return, control slipped through his grasp. The most powerful man in the revolution chose to forsake the cause and return to the historic past. Bill had no choice. He had to join the quest. It was not a matter he could have decided against. Through all that has happened, only one question rang through his mind. Why did the sword force Dave to seek revenge for an event that occurred hundreds of years earlier?

After seeing what this time offered. After seeing what Ronald's time offered. After being trapped underground for such a long time, his time didn't seem so bad. His position in the Protectors organization was a privileged one. He was entitled to many more freedoms than the population at large. But he knew it was all wrong. As he approached the spiral stairs, something in his mind snapped, a light switch turning back on. He knew what he was doing was right. It was the only thing to do.

The stairs, as with everything else the travelers had seen recently, was formed out of damp dirt. The group descended about twenty feet, before beginning a slow turn. A few moments later, the humans found themselves heading back toward the fissure in a relatively level corridor.

The earth floor slowly gave way to loose gravel, composed mainly of small blue rocks. The pebbles on the floor acted in the same manner as the walls in the original passage of the secret tunnel. As the travelers walked by, seven sets of glowing footprints were left behind. For a while the tunnel appeared to be promising, but they were soon faced with another obstacle.

A sheet of yellow liquid, which fell freely from a hole in the ceiling, blocked the corridor. The cascading liquid disappeared into a three inch slit in the floor. At times, through a break in the thin fluid wall, the other side of the passage could be seen.

"Another hang up," Joe said in disgust. "This trip is starting to get on my nerves."

"Why don't we just walk through it?" Steve asked, moving closer to the obstacle. "I bet it's only wat..."

"No," Bill yelled, gabbing hold of Steve's arm. "I'll bet any amount that liquid is acid from the chasm. The way I figure it, we are directly underneath it now."

Steve looked at the cascading liquid, quickly realizing the idiocy of his statement. Quietly he backed away, slipping to the rear of the group.

"You wouldn't think the Minomassa would slow us down with just an ordinary waterfall?" Andy asked sarcastically. "No, it has to use an acidfall."

Joe, his mind always searching for solutions using violence as a first option, raised his gun and fired several rounds into the liquid sheet. Upon contact, the bullets sizzled and ignited, before continuing their course down the corridor. As Bill suspected, the liquid was in fact acid.

"It looks as if we are trapped again," Ken said, leaning against the dirt wall. "An acidfall ahead of us and a chasm full of it behind."

"I doubt this tunnel even leads out of here. Those creatures are never going to let us out. We are going to walk through these tunnels, until we die of exhaustion," Ronald said with a sigh.

"Don't give up so easily, Ronald. I'm fairly sure this tunnel leads out," Dave said in a hopeful voice. "We just have to go about it the right way. The Minomassa wants to defeat us, but not here."

"Maybe we just have to wait until the chasm empties," Andy suggested. "It looks like the acid it draining at a good rate."

"It might take days," Bill said, shaking his head. He knew the provisions the group had brought would not last that long. "We don't know where the acid is going from here. They might be pumping it back into the chasm somehow. I don't think waiting will do us much good."

Steve began to fidget at the back of the group. He still felt embarrassed by his suggestion to walk through the acid. His embarrassment augmented his feelings of anger toward the five from the future. At first they seemed cordial, but ever since they landed in the ancient past he perceived that they were treating him and his father as less intelligent beings. His frustrations manifested themselves, as he picked up a large rock and hoisted it over his head. With a loud yell he rushed through the loitering time travelers toward the acidfall. He stopped five feet from the deadly sheet and hurled the rock at the liquid. Steve's surging adrenaline levels caused the boulder to stray, striking the ceiling several inches in front of the opening, before cascading into the acid with a brilliant flash of light.

The impact of the boulder was all that was needed to spoil the fragile integrity of the loosely packed earth ceiling. A large chunk of dirt immediately fell from the spot where the rock struck, crashing to the floor and scattering into the acid. The slit in the ceiling opened slightly, allowing more acid to fall through the hole. The increased volume of acid, in turn, tore down more chunks of dirt, opening the hole even larger.

"Let's get out of here," Bill yelled, pushing the others back up the tunnel.

The terrified humans did not need Bill's advice, as they had already turned to flee toward the stairs. Larger clumps of dirt fell and even more acid poured into the tunnel. The volume of acid entering the passage was so great that the drain in the floor could not accommodate the flow. As a result acid began to flood the corridor. The resulting explosions, from acid meeting rock and dirt shook the earth so violently that the humans thought the tunnel would collapse.

It took them less than a minute to ascend to the entrance of the chasm, just in time to see the level of acid in the fissure decrease rapidly. Several minutes later the once full chasm was empty, save for a few lingering puddles. In the center of the floor, a six foot hole sat where only a slit had existed just moments earlier.

"What did you do that for?" Andy yelled angrily at Steve.

"Yes, what *did* you do that for? You almost killed us. For the second time, I might add," Dave yelled, his face burning a bright red. "I think from now on you had better stay in the middle of us, so someone can keep an eye on you; before you succeed in doing away with us."

"Hey, why don't you guys just lay off. I was angry just like the rest of you. You told us we were going to make it through this place in a short time. Now look at us. We're trapped."

"I never said this trip was going to be easy. And I never said we were going to live through it," Dave yelled back. "But I'm not going to let you be the one that kills us. You came with me of your own free will, so don't go blaming me or anybody else if things aren't turning out the way you expected."

There followed a deep silence. Everyone just exchanged glances, while Bill looked hopelessly into the empty fissure. Except for the hole in the floor, there was no other exit from the fissure. The far wall was just as smooth as the wall they had climbed down, offering no way to reach the opposite ledge and the continuation of the original passage.

Ken finally broke the silence, "Do you think the passage below is flooded?"

"There's only one way to find out," Joe replied. He turned from the others and broke into a sprint for the stairs.

To his surprise, the passage had not flooded. A few large boulders littered the tunnel floor and several puddles of acid could be seen. Apparently all of the liquid had managed to drain through the original hole in the floor, which looked slightly larger than it did earlier. The travelers had no trouble avoiding the few lingering acid puddles and hurdling the drainage hole.

"It turned out that Steve did a good thing by throwing the rock," Ronald said, trying to defend his son. "He cleared the tunnel for us."

Dave turned, his face wearing no expression, as he stared into Steve's eyes. "Yes, it turned out for the best, but it just as easily could have turned into a disaster. Throwing the rock took us all by surprise. If he had warned us, so we would have been prepared, our lives wouldn't have been placed in so much danger." Dave shifted his focus toward the dark passage that lay ahead. His dislike for Steve grew with every passing minute, but he knew that keeping the group together mentally and physically was of the utmost importance. Silently he wished that the farmer's son had not come along on the journey, but nothing more would be said of Steve's blunders.

The gravel floor soon gave way to a thick mud. The traveler's feet sunk into the goo, causing a sucking sound as they tore their shoes from its grasp. The sloshing sound filled the tunnel, until several hundred feet later the composition of the floor turned into a fine white sand, dry as the desert dunes. Clear of the acid, but still without hope that the exit was near, the group trudged onward. The passage now followed many twists and turns, never offering the travelers any directional decisions. The slope of the floor also constantly changed, from an upward climb to a subtle descent, then back to another incline. Soon, even Bill had lost all sense of direction.

In the distance, their lights illuminated yet another barrier. The tunnel became clogged with numerous vines and plants. Dave approached the obstacle, hesitating before plucking a leaf from the tangle of vegetation.

"The leaves seem real enough," the rebel said, passing the leaf to Bill. "If the stems are real, and not metal like the trunks of the trees, the sword should have no problem cutting through."

He stepped back, waiting for the others to clear away, before slashing the blade of the sword into the foliage. The blade sliced easily through the thin green stems, scattering plant matter in all directions.

Several hacks later, the weary travelers were hit head on by a blast of fresh air. Sunlight greeted them, as Dave widened the hole with a renewed energy. The trip through the mountain had taken longer than expected. They had lost a few pieces of equipment along the way, but they were safely through.

The rising sun had just cleared the treetops, indicating that they had spent the entire time shortened night inside the mountain. A cold breeze blew down from the snow capped peaks, causing each to shiver, as the crisp air startled their tired bodies. The remaining three flood lights were switched off to conserve the batteries.

"How do we know that we are on the correct side of the mountain?" Ronald questioned. "We turned so many times, for all we know we are on the same side we started from."

The others quickly looked around to examine the surrounding area. They were standing at the bottom of a small valley measuring two hundred yards across. Towering cliffs, mostly featureless, enclosed the depression on both sides. Strangely, the landscape atop cliff on the right side of the valley was covered by countless charred trees and bushes.

"I know where we are," Joe shouted. "This is the chasm Andy and I crossed."

"Yes, now I recognize it. Those burnt trees are the remnants of the forest fire Joe started," Andy chided.

"You're lucky I started it. If I didn't you would have froze to death. Not to mention myself along with you."

"That answers Ronald's question," Bill said, shuffling over to a large rock. He let out a sigh, as he sat down. "We are on the correct side of the mountain. Now I think we are due for a well deserved rest."

"Take a few minutes, everyone," Dave said, finding a rock of his own. "We'll let our eyes adjust to the sun, then get moving again."

The valley had long been overgrown with wild plants, but the adventurers paid very little attention to the vegetation. Everyone, especially Ronald, was glad just to be free of the musty air and enclosed confines of the tunnel. Deep breaths were had by all, expelling any remnants of the acid's fumes into the atmosphere.

The rest period was brief, with Dave prodding everyone to rise and continue with the journey. Though no formal path could be seen, heavily trampled vegetation suggested that the valley had been used very recently, quite probably by the Ubeleutes. Andy and Joe kept glancing skyward toward the top of the cliff to the left. Not long into the hike, the object they were seeking became visible. A small portion of the burnt bridge hung over the edge, swaying lazily in the breeze. They secretly glanced at each other in recognition, neither wanting to bring up the horrible memory.

The walls of the valley ran straight, so straight that the humans thought they might not have been created naturally. But all conversation on the topic was purely recreational, simply a means to pass the time. The welcomed sound of birds and small animals put the group at ease. After the heightened stress levels brought on by Steve's potentially deadly actions, the serene setting gave them all a chance to relax.

The plentiful green vegetation suddenly reminded Joe of something he had seen many days before. "When we were up there," he said, pointing to the top of the chasm, trying to revisit his memory, "I saw a stream down here." His voice sounded hopeful, anticipating a cool drink of water. Eagerly he turned to looked up at the snow covered peaks, trying to remember which side of the valley housed the stream. A moment later, he pointed to the north. "We can top off our canteens there."

The travelers left the path. Dave led the way, cutting through the brush with the sword. It didn't take long for the group to stumble upon the waterway, but disappointment immediately set in. Only dry cracked mud sat between the banks of the stream. Without speaking, they knew it was the doings of the Minomassa. The creature had somehow stopped the water from flowing, just as it had stopped the falls in the hall. Dejectedly, the group headed back to the path.

Not long after, the once towering cliffs began to lose some of their height. To the traveler's discomfort, the temperature began to fall just as fast. Off in the distance, they could see where the cliffs joined the floor of the valley and disappeared.

A half hour of walking, sandwiched around another rest period brought on at Bill's request, brought the group to the end of the valley. Here the seven humans turned to face the mountain, only to be amazed at the enormity of the object. The peaks of the mountain range loomed so high and far away, that their features were distorted by a haze, yellow tinted of course. The size of the mountains were not fully comprehensible, however, since the ground still sloped downward, indicating that they had yet to reach the base.

"It is amazing," Ronald said. "I have seen several mountain ranges back home, but I doubt that anything in our time is as large as this."

"I assume that the natural course of events wore these magnificent structures down," Bill said, admiring the beauty of the scene.

Surveying the area, the group found that they were standing in the middle of a thickly grown forest. Fortunately, the inferno Joe had started burnt itself out, before reaching this location. Although several types of trees could be seen, the area was clearly dominated by towering pines. Fallen needles, accumulated over the years, formed a soft cushion-like surface to comfort the human's weary feet.

The air felt cool on their exposed skin, ironically offering relief to the burns left by the acid. A gentle breeze carried the fragrances of the surrounding vegetation, clearing all memories of the stagnant tunnel air from their minds. The seemingly calm environment, coupled with the openness of the forest, caused them to lower their guard.

But the serenity was shattered by the breaking of a branch. A loud snap filled the air, surprising humans, who spun around to see two Ubeleutes rushing toward them. The axe wielding beasts offered a battle cry, no more than a gurgled groan to the humans. Two more of the powerful creatures appeared on the path ahead of travelers, rushing ferociously toward the stunned group. A moment passed, before the humans reacted. Steve and Joe fired upon the original two, killing them instantly, but not before an axe sailed through the air, landing dangerously close between the two.

Bill once again maniacally fired his weapon, wasting far too many rounds for just two attackers, but effectively injuring the weapon bearing arm of one. The axe the wounded creature held fell to the ground with a loud thud. The beast looked stunned for a moment, as blood gushed from several wounds. Obviously guns were new to the creatures, as they were seemingly puzzled as to what had struck them. A second blast of bullets dropped the creature to the ground, where it remained motionless. The machine guns proved far more effective than the rifles, but between the aggregate fire power, the fourth Ubeleute had no chance. The overmatched creature suffered the full force of the human's arsenal.

Though all four Ubeleutes lie dead on the forest floor, the humans stood silent and ready for more. They scanned the surrounding forest, but no movement could be seen. When it became apparent that there would be no second wave, the group relaxed and examined the battle site. Dave walked up to the nearest corpse, poking at it with the sword. A cold chill instantly rose up his arm, spreading through his body. The rebel began to shake violently, before slowly calming down.

"What's the matter with you?" Andy asked in a serious tone.

Dave's eyes remained fixed on an unknown point in the distance. He blinked several times, before his consciousness returned to the present. "The sword just told me that it knows where we are. We are on the same path that Duzic traveled, before the Ubeleutes killed him. It is warning us that we are now in Totenplatz. This is the home of the enemy. It advises that we take extreme caution."

"It should have told us that a few minutes ago," Ken said, motioning to the four dead Ubeleutes.

"Well, the thing is a little rusty. After all, it has been immobile for the past few centuries," Joe joked, his eyes never leaving the shadows of the forest.

"You were right, Dave. The hard part is getting to the creatures. They are obviously no match for us," Steve said proudly. He jabbed the head of a dead Ubeleute with the barrel of his gun. "Now all we have to do is waste all these ugly animals."

"We still haven't found them," Dave said blankly.

"What?" Steve questioned. "You said this is where they live."

"I guess I haven't made everything clear to you. We still have to find the Ubeleutes. The Minomassa in particular. I was not expecting any resistance in the tunnel. As for these four, they were just meant to slow us down, nothing more. I had anticipated reaching this point, without seeing a single Ubeleute. That is why I say the hard part is still to come. So far we have faced unexpected dangers. Now we have to face the anticipated. We still have to pass through the dungeons of Mikokil. Only then will we have the opportunity to hunt down the Minomassa."

Queer stares focused on Dave, except for Joe, who would not allow a second group of Ubeleutes the chance at a surprise attack. The former Protector's policeman continuously scanned the forest for any potential danger.

"You see," Dave said, trying to satisfy the inquisitive stares, "as I told you before, the Ubeleutes have very strange beliefs. They have seven traps of death in their dungeons. One must pass through these labyrinths to reach the Ubeleute's city. It is said that any being who can penetrate and survive all seven traps, is a formidable opponent."

"If they don't know that we are formidable by now, then they must be as stupid as they look," Joe said, continuing to circle the group.

"In the beginning," Dave continued, "the human named Chaz successfully passed through the traps and conquered the Ubeleutes. He accomplished this feat single handed, because of the special powers he possessed; not to mention the fact that the Ubeleutes were taken completely off guard. No one had ever passed through the traps before. In fact, the Ubeleutes didn't even know that Chaz was in the labyrinth attempting to make it through.

"Unfortunately Chaz didn't kill all of the Ubeleutes, which in hind sight he should have done. The Minomassa organized the surviving Ubeleutes and swore to avenge Chaz and all humans. Chaz and his people lived in peace for many years, until the Minomassa had gained enough strength to mount an attack. After gaining control of several strategic pieces of land, the humans were attacked whenever they strayed too far from the halls. In an attempt to fight back, a group of humans reentered Mikokil. Unfortunately the traps had been rearranged. None of them survived." Dave paused for a moment to catch his breath. No one spoke, as they could tell he hadn't finished the story.

"Now you know why I was stunned when I found that the tunnel had been changed. For the most part, the Ubeleutes do not take the offensive. If someone wishes to challenge them, they have to fight on the Ubeleute's home turf. For some reason they are taking us to be more of a challenge than anyone who has challenged them in the past."

"Probably because we are more formidable than anyone they have ever run across," Bill added, as the group resumed walking.

From that point on the conversation was sparse. All members of the entourage were now focusing their attention on the surrounding characteristics of the forest. Strangely they did not find themselves in much of a hurry. Chaz's human population had been killed hundreds of years earlier and several more hours would not make a difference. Each had many questions about the ancient humans and the Ubeleutes, but none were asked.

A more pressing situation presented itself. The trees cleared and the dark form of two large metal doors appeared before them. The entrance to Mikokil. The doors were part of a fortress wall, which reached thirty feet into the sky. The stone walls were obviously too high to climb, drawing the travelers to focus on the massive doors.

"This is the spot where the Ubeleutes killed Duzic," Dave said, bowing his head out of respect to the fallen warrior. "He never made it into the dungeons. He was making one last attempt, before the final battle. Once again, the sword will be useless to us, as far as directions go. It is rumored that the Ubeleute city extends underground for miles in all directions."

"I think we should have our weapons ready at all times," Bill warned needlessly. "The enemy knows its way around here much better than we do."

Joe checked the ammunition in his gun, pointing the weapon at a tree. "I'm ready for them," he said in a half whisper.

The huge metal doors had long ago rusted through, a tribute to the weather of the past few centuries. A few blows with the blunt end of a rifle opened them enough for the humans to squeeze by and into the fort.

Inside the fort, the travelers from two different times were surrounded by an eerie darkness that each could attribute to some nightmarish dream of their past. The remaining three light sources were immediately turned on, revealing a massive fifty by seventy foot room. The empty chamber offered nothing, except for plain stone block walls.

A set of stairs, located at the far end of the room, disappeared into the underground darkness of the Ubeleute city. Old rotting tree trunks, pieces of which were falling into the adventurer's hair, comprised the ceiling. A cool breeze blew through the open doors, mixing with the musty stale air inside.

"I thought we were going to be rid of this foul air when we left the tunnel," gasped Ronald. He brushed at the rotting tree particles that fell onto his balding head, but refrained from prophesying that the ceiling was about to fall in.

"Me too," coughed Andy.

"It looks like we will have to put up with it a little while longer," Bill said, his feet crunching over a layer of dead insect shells.

"The entrance to Mikokil," Ken said, viewing the forbidden stairway. "I wonder if we shall ever leave this place? The sword says no one has, except for Chaz."

"Yes, but they were primitive people," Steve said, as they descended the old decaying rock stairs, not realizing the error in his statement.

"Look who's talking about primitive people," Joe said, referring to the time gap between the two of them.

"You know what I mean," Steve answered in self defense. Then he tapped his gun. "As long as we have these babies, we will be all right."

"Don't under estimate those humans," Dave added. "In many ways they were much more intelligent than we are. Just look at the halls. I doubt that primitive minds could have constructed them."

The three light sources amply lit the passage. The walls and ceiling were made of grey stone blocks, which were cracked and discolored due to their age. Every so often, the group would come across a section of the wall where one of the blocks was missing. Peering into the gaps, they could see a few inch hollow and then another stone wall.

"It looks like they don't bother to destroy old passageways when they build new ones," Bill said, observing that the second wall was built using a different type of rock than the walls they were traveling between.

"Maybe they reuse them," Andy suggested.

The stairs ended and the time travelers found themselves standing in the doorway of a twenty foot square chamber. A lone exit, located in the far left corner of the room, led into an unknown darkness. The air in the room felt cool and heavy.

"If the sword is right, there should be some sort of trap in there," Ronald said, peering into the room from the rear of the group.

"Keep your eyes open for anything that looks out of the ordinary," Bill warned.

"Everything in this time seems out of the ordinary to me," Andy remarked.

Dave stood just outside the room, scanning a beam of light across the floor of the chamber. Close examination revealed a dark discolored streak, varying from three to five feet wide, leading to the exit. The rest of the floor looked to be of a natural rock color.

"What do you make of that?" Ken asked. He crouched next to Dave in the doorway. "It looks as if they have left us a path to follow."

"It looks to me that the floor has been burnt by acid," Bill said, rustling his way to the front of the group. "And look at the walls near the opposite doorway. They have similar burn marks on them."

Dave swung his light up toward the ceiling. To his surprise, hundreds of small leathery bags were clinging to the rock. Strangely, the bags were located only over the burn marks on the floor. "I bet they caused the burns. Andy, fire a shot into the bags at the far end of the room."

The others retreated, giving the younger Marshall ample room. Andy aimed at an area ten feet from the opposite door. Due to the density of the bags, he did not need to shoot with accuracy, as even the worst marksman was sure to strike a random target. Andy's finger tightened around the trigger, sending the bullet zinging from the barrel of the gun. The loud popping sound that followed rattled off the human's eardrums. An unfortunate orange-sized bag was met by the speeding bullet, bursting upon impact. A liquid fell to the floor, where a small cloud of black smoke immediately formed.

"Acid?" Dave asked.

"Yes, just as I thought. The humans who passed into this room, walking under the sacks, never made it to the other side. They were fried before they knew what hit them," Bill stated flatly in his scientific voice.

"But what makes them break?" Andy asked. "Surely they weren't shot like that one."

"They probably burst when something passes underneath them," Bill surmised. "Possibly they are set off by the body heat of a living being."

"These creatures sure like to fool around with acid," Steve said. "They have already tried once to kill us with it."

"I bet it won't be the last time we come across it," Dave added, pushing his way past Andy to the doorway. "It looks like there are a couple feet of bags we have to pass beneath in order to reach the safe part of the room. I think we should take a running start down the hallway to reduce the time we are actually under the sacks."

"If we are quick enough, we will make it," Joe said, patting Bill on the shoulder, implying that the scientist was too heavy and slow.

"Don't patronize me," Bill replied with a smile. "I have lost so much weight since arriving in this time, that I shall be as slim as you before long."

The others stood aside, as Dave retreated up several stairs. Counting to three in his mind, he bolted down the stairway, across the short flat portion of the passage, diving into the room to the left of the burnt path. Several of the sacks exploded as he passed under them, but by the time the acid reached the floor Dave had safely cleared the area.

The others found equal success in entering the chamber, even Bill who performed an unexpected somersault, but was none the worse for the effort. The adventurers walked carefully along the edge of the burnt path, careful not to stray beneath any misplaced acid bags. They had to repeat the running and leaping sequence to leave the chamber, but the length of the jump to exit was not nearly as long the dive to enter.

The characteristics of the new passage where quite different from the passage that led to the acid bag room. The new corridor was wide enough for the humans to travel three abreast, but they decided it to be safer to walk in pairs. A thin layer of crushed rock, which sparkled in the dancing beams of light, covered the ground. Hard compressed dirt replaced the stone block walls and ceiling, reviving Ronald's fears of a cave-in.

"There doesn't appear to be any threats in here," Steve said, trying his best to impress the others. Even so, he walked a step behind Dave, not wanting to blindly walk into the next trap.

"Don't be too confident. You never can tell what type of traps the Ubeleutes have devised," Dave cautioned. He took the time to examine the walls, floor, and ceiling ahead, before taking each step. "If only one person has made it through this place, the Ubeleutes must be very good at hiding their traps."

"Keep an eye out for trip mechanisms on the floor," Joe warned, recalling several such devious devices the Protectors were fond of using. His eyes constantly surveyed the surrounding area, searching for any tell-tale signs of a trip device. He walked side-by-side with Steve, mostly so he could keep an eye on the farmer's son and prevent any trouble.

The other four followed several feet behind, taking great caution with every step. The passage, for the most part level and straight, stretched on for more than five hundred feet before turning. After making a ninety degree turn to the right, a second ninety degree turn followed a mere ten feet later. The corridor now facing the travelers looked just as straight and featureless as the passage they had just walked through. Unlike some of the previous underground passages they have encountered, the current one was deliberately formed. No rough cuts or spur of the moment additions could be seen.

"I'm amazed that these tunnels have been able to stay intact," Bill observed, scraping at the dirt wall with his fingernail. "They don't look very strong."

"Why did you have to bring that up?" Ronald complained.

"I don't mean to alarm you, Ronald," Bill replied. "I just find it curious."

"Actually, it looks like the walls are very old," Steve said, observing Bills actions. "The dirt appears to be all dried out. If they are really old, maybe some of the traps could be useless."

"I doubt it," Dave replied, his voice echoing slightly. "The Ubeleutes know we are coming. I doubt if they would leave any of the traps inoperable."

"For all we know they could have even added a few," Joe said.

"If they weren't such staunch believers in their faith, I would agree with you," Dave said, keeping his attention focused on the floor ahead. "But I don't think they would change just for us."

Seven hundred feet later, the passage turned off to the left. As with the previous turn, this ninety degree turn was followed by another ten feet later. The time travelers now found themselves heading in the same direction as the original tunnel, only displaced by some fifty feet.

"What is going on with this place?" Steve asked, as a disturbed look spread across his face. "Are we going to zig-zag forever?"

"Don't become impatient. That is how you will fall victim to their traps. Just take it easy. We must take each step of this journey slowly," Dave warned.

"I'm sure they know what they are doing," Ken added.

"I wish they would just show themselves and get this thing over with," Joe said angrily. "They are going to die sooner or later, so why put it off?"

The seven adventurers silently followed the thousand foot tunnel to its end. And to no surprise, the passage made two consecutive ninety degree turns to the right. By this time, the travelers had lost all sense of direction, not that it made much difference in the dark underground.

As they turned the second corner to enter the next long passage, a mesmerizing chiming sound found its way to their ears. The various high pitched frequencies echoed off the smooth walls, soon causing the sounds to blend together into an inharmonious jumble. The humans tried their best to ignore the obvious attempt at distraction, as they made their way to the end of the twelve hundred foot corridor. Once again, the tunnel made two consecutive ninety degree turns to the left.

"Maybe we should be mapping this place," Andy suggested.

"So far there has been no need," Bill replied. "Although we have been frequently changing direction, there have been no intersections. Without branches, it is impossible to get lost."

"I'm getting sick of this," Steve shouted over the chiming. "I want to get on with the fighting. You said we were going to fight, and all we are doing is exhausting ourselves walking through these stupid tunnels." Without looking back, he ran off down the passage with his gun raised.

"Stop!" Dave yelled. Steve either did not hear the order over the chiming or he decided to ignore it.

The farmer's son sped down the corridor, taking no time to search for traps. The rest of the group ran after him, yelling in futility for him to stop. Steve reached the end of the fifteen hundred foot tunnel, his breath heavy, before making two consecutive turns to the right. He stopped for moment, flashing his light down the tunnel, but nothing could be seen. Resting for a second, hands on his knees trying to catch his breath, he listened to the chiming. The irritating noise ground at his ears, aggravating him even more.

Feeling a bit revived, Steve started running again. In his haste, he became blind to his surroundings, failing to notice that larger rocks began to litter floor. He also failed to notice that the cycling frequencies of the chiming had quickened. It was no surprise then, that he stumbled over a large rock in the middle of the floor, stubbing his right foot and tumbling forward. Unfortunately, the rock was a triggering mechanism, releasing a large blade from the left wall. The blade sliced through the air with a blinding speed. Steve did not see the blade, nor did he feel any pain. The pendulum movement of the device easily sliced through the human flesh and bones.

The rest of the travelers turned the corner just in time to see the blade creak to a stop. The tremendous amount of blood splattered about, made it obvious that nothing could be done to save Steve.

"Oh my god!" Ronald cried, rushing forward in desperation. The shock of what lay before him drained the color from his face. "Look at him. Sliced to bits, and it's all my fault. Why did I ever come here?" The farmer fell to knees near the pool of blood, but he did not look at the remains of his son. His head was buried in his hands, tears filtering through his laborer's fingers.

The individual feelings of the group toward Steve were immaterial now. One of their own had been slain by the Ubeleutes. Bill approached Ronald and placed his hand on the farmer's shoulder, in a instinctive offer of support. The others stood back, staring silently into the darkness that lay beyond the murder site.

Ronald slowly tore his hands from his face. His eyes were swollen and red. The farmer rose to his feet, shaking off Bill's hand, and walked directly toward Dave. Ronald's chest rose and fell with heavy breathing, as he stared intently at Dave. The rebel could feel the hate radiate from the tear filled eyes, but did not divert his attention from them. Dave braced himself for the anticipated barrage of slurs and blame. He even expected that the farmer would try some sort of physical attack, but none came. Ronald's stern face slowly turned to stare at each member of the party for a second or two.

"I want to kill them," he shouted. "I want to kill all of the creatures that built this place. I'm going to make them pay for what they did to Steve." He turned and pushed the blood stained blade aside, rushing past it into the darkness.

Dave moved to chase after Ronald, but found himself blocked by a huge fissure, which had suddenly opened up in front of him. The portion of the floor, where the bloody remains lay, had fallen deep into the ground.

The earth began to rumble, as the walls on both sides of the fissure fell inward. The frightened onlookers backed away, panic spreading across their faces. A powerful blast of cool air rushed into the tunnel through the gap in the right wall, lifting ages worth of dust particles and scattering them into the air. The debris blocked Dave's view, causing him to lose sight of Ronald. The rumbling grew even louder, as a forceful gush of water filled the fissure, washing all of the remains into the void on the left.

The water rushed for what seemed like an eternity, but in reality only spanned a minute. The cleansing water abruptly stopped, allowing the walls to slowly return to their normal position. As the floor rose, the large blade now washed clean, swung back into its home inside the left wall. Soon, all was back to normal. A moment later the dust settled, allowing the group to see the dark figure of Ronald standing on the opposite side of the now concealed fissure.

"Be careful," Bill warned, pointing to the rock in the middle of the floor. "I bet that rock was the trigger for the..." his voice died off, not wanting to cause Ronald anymore pain. "Just stay clear of it."

The chiming sound had ceased, sensing that it had done its part in the murder, but the humans didn't even realize or remember that it had been sounding. Dave was the first to walk past the murder sight, the ground still wet. After seeing that he safely passed, the others quickly followed.

"That's two traps gone," Ken informed, trying to break the awkward silence. "There are still five left."

"At the rate we are going, we're not going to have too many of us left to fight the Minomassa," Joe said quietly to his brother.

"We must be careful from here on," Bill said, repeating a warning used many times by the group. "Both traps have had some sort of warning. We have to keep our attention focused on the task at hand and be patient."

"It is too bad he got killed," Joe said, still talking quietly with his brother. "An extra man can come in handy during a fight. Even if it was Steve."

"Yes, I'm sure he would have been a help, but I don't think Dave liked him that much," Andy replied in a whisper, making sure Ronald was out of earshot. "I think he is glad that he is dead."

"Maybe," Joe whispered, "but I doubt it. If anything, I think the sword is glad he is dead. He might have proved to be a liability on its quest for revenge."

The six travelers walked slowly to the end of the two thousand foot tunnel. The passage made a now familiar ninety degree turn to the left, but the expected second turn did not follow. To their relief, they had reached the end of the deadly zig-zagging passages. Besides losing Steve, they lost the use of his machine gun, which was washed away in the void.

Upon entering the new passage, the effectiveness of their light sources diminished considerably. The walls had suddenly turned into a dark empty blackness, absorbing most of the light. Apparently, the floor and ceiling also had the same light absorbing property. Without any reflection off these surfaces, the tunnel appeared to be pitch black, giving the impression that the group was falling though the emptiness of space.

"What's happened to the light?" Andy asked, checking his source to make sure it was still turned on.

"I think the walls are absorbing it," Bill said, flashing a beam of light off the wall. No trace of a reflection could be seen.

"I bet there's a trap ahead," Ken said, looking up the corridor nervously. He waited for someone else to resume walking, not wanting to stumble upon some deadly triggering device.

"We'll just take it slow," Dave said, resuming the journey with a determined agony.

But all of the cautionary effort was for not, as the group made it to the end of the black tunnel without incident. But they had little time to catch their breath. The black light absorbing material had been replaced with a colorful psychedelic design, while the shape of the tunnel turned circular.

"They are trying to confuse us," Bill warned, determined not to be distracted by the various designs and patterns. "Pay no attention to the art work. Keep you minds focused."

The advice was easier said than followed. The humans found walking in this new tube-like tunnel to be quite a challenge. With every step, the designs on the walls gave the impression that the tunnel was rotating, first one way then the other.

"I wish I could say, close your eyes," Bill said, "but with all the dangers down here, I don't think it would be advisable."

"I'm getting dizzy," Andy cried, stumbling forward several steps.

"Slow down," Ken replied, catching hold of Andy's arm.

"We are almost through," Dave informed, spying the end of the tunnel in the distance. Several stumbling minutes later, the group climbed from the raised floor of the tube tunnel to the floor of a small oblong room. Though distracting and nauseating, the circular passage did not house the third trap.

The six adventurers stood, sat, and leaned against the wall, trying to let the effects of the previous passage subside. Several moments passed, as each shook the dizziness from their heads. With their vision and sense of equilibrium returned to normal, the humans were able to study the room they had just entered. A jelly-like layer of orange slime grew on the walls and ceiling of the chamber, giving the room a grotesque feel. The floor, covered by the orange growth in only a few small patches, looked as if it were made out of a highly polished marble.

"I can't see anything but the slime," Dave noted.

"We know by now that seeing nothing is not necessarily cause for celebration," Bill added.

"I'd be careful of that stuff. It could be poisonous," Andy warned, not desiring to venture too close. He glanced nervously at the slime clinging to the ceiling overhead, but the growth seemed content to stay put, for the time being.

"Do you think it is safe to proceed?" Joe asked, standing guard against a rear attack. He would not allow himself to shift his attention from the tube tunnel entrance long enough to take a good look at the chamber.

"I don't know how safe it is, but we are going to have to pass through sooner or later. I guess now is as good a time as any," Dave replied. He paused for a second, taking a deep breath, before stepping out into the room.

He only took one step, then stopped. Something deep inside told him that something was wrong with this room, that the third trap was somehow triggered here. He turned back to the others, noting that the tube passage did not enter the room in the middle of a wall, but rather off near a corner. The exit stood some fifty feet away, in the middle if the opposite wall. His attention immediately shifted to the orange slime covered ceiling. Thoughts of the growth falling from its strategic position raced through his mind, but the slime had no movement. It seemed to be as inactive as mould.

With a heightened caution, Dave took another step, then another. Nothing happened. He walked within arms reach of the wall to his left, far enough away to avoid accidentally touching the slime, but close enough to offer some comfort. The sword was grasped tightly in his right hand, ready to defend. His eyes darted back and forth, but no movement could be seen. Thirty feet separated him from the wall to his right, but he had no intention of taking the time to examine it. His only thoughts were to reach the exit, while not stepping on any of the scattered orange patches in the process.

It was then he noticed a soft clicking sound. With all the thoughts racing through his mind, he could not be sure when the sound had started. The noise was so subtle, that for all he knew, it could have been present when he entered the chamber. The obviousness of the clicking grew with every metallic snap. Dave looked around nervously, not knowing what was causing the noise.

"Look out!" Ronald screamed, from his vantage point in the corner of the room. The movement was slight, and difficult to see in the dim light, but the movement of the right wall slowly slipping into the ground was cause for alarm. Disregarding the potential danger of the orange patches of slime, the farmer rushed into the room. In one fluid motion he tackled a still puzzled Dave to the ground, just as the wall disappeared into the floor. The missing wall revealed hundreds of spears, which were instantly jettisoned into the room.

Seeing what was happening, three of the four travelers remaining in the corner, instantly dropped to the ground. Joe heard the yells and had the presence of mind to jump back up into the psychedelic tunnel. The spears cut through the stagnant dungeon air, causing a high pitched whistling sound. Dave and Ronald flattened themselves against the floor, oblivious to the location of the orange slime patches. The spears crossed the width of the dark chamber in less that a second, shattering against the opposite wall. The dry wood exploded upon contact with the slime covered wall, showering the humans with an array of kindling and orange jelly-like particles.

Dave wasted no time lifting his head, seeing the wall slowly rise back into its original position. Without hesitating he jumped to his feet, pulling Ronald up with him. "Come on," he yelled to the others. "Hurry up." He motioned for the others to enter the room, not knowing if the mechanism that fired the spears was able to reload, or how long such an operation would take.

Upon reaching the exit, Dave placed his hand on Ronald's shoulder and looked him straight in the eye. "Thanks," the rebel said, with all sincerity. "I owe you one."

"No need for thanks," Ronald replied, smiling. "I figure that I'm going to need you, if I'm going to kill all these Ubeleutes."

A moment later, the remaining four adventurers reached the exit, each huffing slightly after the frantic sprint. The wall had returned to its original position and the soft clicking had stopped. The chamber was once again silent.

"That's three," Ken counted, holding up three fingers for all to see. He looked back into the room, unable to see the entrance to the tube tunnel in the darkness, but clearly seeing the pile of rubble scattered across the nearby floor.

"I'm sure glad Dave is up front," Andy said, picking through a pile of spear splinters, which he picked up during his sprint through the chamber. "I would have been killed three times already, if I were leading the way."

"That's because you don't think," Joe snapped back. He tapped his brother on the forehead with his index finger. "If you spent as much time thinking as you did in that laboratory, we wouldn't be here right now. We would be in our own time, not even knowing of the time machine."

"Well, if you weren't so nosy, you wouldn't have been following me around. You wouldn't have barged into the laboratory when you did and...

Dave cut him off. He had thought that the brothers had smoothed over their differences of opinion, but evidently he was wrong. "Calm down you two. We have enough fighting to do without wasting energy on each other."

Andy and Joe quickly separated and the travelers continued through the mysterious underground tunnels of the Ubeleute city. The ever changing scenery now offered an environment made up of large stone slabs. The slabs composing the floor reached from wall to wall, and appeared to be perfect squares. The seams in the walls were hard to find, considering that they were made out of a strange green rock, which gave the appearance of a frozen green waterfall. The air had also changed. The temperature had increased dramatically with a dryness only compared to that of an open oven door.

"These creatures sure believe in a changing atmosphere," Ken said. His breathing grew heavy as the temperature took its toll. "The floors and walls are constantly changing."

"My guess is that they do it to confuse us. Having things change this often can make a person act without thinking," Bill stated, immediately wishing he had used other words to prevent causing Ronald any more pain over the loss of his son.

"I think they are trying to dehydrate us," Ronald said, wiping a stream of sweat from his face. He grabbed for his canteen, but felt that it was more than half empty and decided to conserve what he had left.

"Carrying all this equipment is strenuous enough. Lord knows I'm not in the same shape I used to be."

If the beautiful effects of the shiny green walls weren't enough to keep the humans amused, the irregular sloping of the floor might turn the trick. The perfect grey squares were not aligned in a level fashion. One slab of rock would be slanted upwards at a twenty degree angle. The next square would level off. Immediately following, a slab would slant down at a twenty degree angle, while the next leveled off again. The pattern continued for some time, following every twist and turn. The humans did not let the redundant pattern annoy them, silently remembering the lesson learned from Steve's blind rampage. Instead, they methodically crossed each slab, searching as they walked for triggers that might set off the fourth trap.

The brother's tempers had calmed down, as neither could even remember what the most recent squabble was all about. The fact that Andy had no desire to fall victim to the next trap, put him in a reconciliatory mood. As the oscillating floor pattern ended, he quietly slipped back to the rear of the group, where his brother was keeping guard. He soon found himself interested in the patterns embedded in the green walls. Occasionally he would stop to study an image. On one such instance he found what appeared to be a tree branch protruding from the rushing waterfall. In another block of stone he saw the image of fish jumping through the cascading water.

His lax attention was a mistake he would quickly regret. After a brief pause, he found the group had progressed several yards ahead. He commenced an awkward jog to catch up, but a strange sensation of falling quickly spread through his body. A startled yell passed through his lips, as he fell through a previously unseen hole in the floor. The others turned, weapons ready, only to see two hands grasping at the edge of the floor by their fingertips. Joe and Ken instantly leapt forward, each grabbing an arm. As the two rescuers looked into the pit, lumps formed in their throats.

"Aghh!" Ken yelled turning away, momentarily loosening his grip on Andy, before regaining his composure.

"Help!" Andy screamed, still not fully comprehending what had happened.

"Pull him up," Bill yelled, trying in vain to find room near the edge of the pit to offer help.

Neither Joe nor Ken could focus their attention on pulling Andy to safety. Instead they stared in horror past Andy's dangling feet at what lie at the bottom of the pit. A mass of hungry larvae, to many to even give an estimate, were feasting on several oversized rats. The rats, still squirming with pain, had obviously just been sacrificed into the pit for the benefit of the humans. A few lone larvae, searching for some nonexistent flesh, were scouring a human skeleton in the corner.

"For heaven's sake, pull him out," Ronald yelled, jolting Ken and Joe back to the task at hand.

Deviating their vision from the grotesque feast, Joe and Ken lifted Andy to the surface with relative ease. As soon as the last of Andy's body left the pit, the image of a rock slab once again appeared over the swarming mass of larvae.

"What happened?" Andy asked, touching his nose and wincing with discomfort. Slamming face first into a vertical wall had become a recurring event for him in this ancient time.

"You fell into a pit," Joe replied, his eyes not moving from the area of the floor where the pit lay. "You should be more careful and watch where you are going."

"I was watching where I was going, but I didn't see any pit."

"You were just lucky that you didn't see what was at the bottom of the pit, or you would have lost your grip and fallen for sure," Ken stated, still trying to force down the lump in his throat.

Bill thrust the barrel of his gun into the area of the floor where the pit had been. Instantly, the slab disappeared, revealing a ten foot drop. He grimaced at the sight of the larvae.

"An illusionary floor," Dave said.

"Exactly," Bill replied. He withdrew his gun, concealing the pit. "He must have been the only one of us to step on that part of the floor. The rest of us passed with no problem."

"The Ubeleutes are more clever than I gave them credit for," Dave said, giving a curious glance at the floor. "Illusionary floors. That isn't something I would have thought they were capable of."

"At least we didn't lose another person," Ronald said, still recovering from the sudden loss of his son. Deep in his mind he was still in shock, denial in some instances. Occasionally he would think that he was in some sort of dream and that when he woke, everything would be back to normal.

"No, but we did lose a rifle. I dropped mine in the pit, when I fell," Andy said shamefully.

"Maybe we can get it out," Ronald suggested, "now that we know what to expect."

"I don't think that it is worth the risk," Joe said, feeling a queasy sensation in his stomach, as the image of the swarming larvae crossed his mind. "Those rats looked like they were in a lot of pain down there. Here, Andy, take my knife. I should let you continue barehanded. But the way you are going, you are going to need some protection."

"Thanks," Andy replied in a cynical tone.

"That's four traps. We are more than half way though," Ken noted.

"I doubt they will use another illusionary floor. Just to play it safe, we will probe the floor ahead," Dave said, resuming the lead position of the group.

The extra caution involved in probing the floor with every step slowed the group's progress considerably. But as Bill was quick to point out, they were not in any sort of race. After a few hundred feet, the passage changed again. The width of the ceiling slowly shrunk, as the walls angled inward to compensate. It did not take long for the tunnel to take the shape of a triangle. The base of the floor stretched over twenty feet, as did both walls. All three surfaces were made from the same blue rock the travelers found in the tunnel they used to pass through the mountain.

"I wonder what kind of trap could be in here?" Ronald mumbled to himself, purposefully staying several feet behind Dave.

The tunnel made several minor turns, before ending at a pair of wooden doors. The barrier, made out of six inch wooden planks, appeared to be in the shape of a triangle. The humans couldn't tell for sure, since they could not see a door frame or hinges. Unlike the aged appearance of the rest of the maze, the doors seemed to be made from freshly cut lumber.

"Whatever the next trap is, I bet it is behind those doors," Ken said, taking an instinctive backward step.

After a few moments Joe spoke, "Well, aren't you going to open them, Dave?"

"Why do you want him to open them? Why don't you open them yourself" Andy snapped, still smarting after Joe's comments regarding the pit. Joe gave a heated glance toward his brother and started to retort, when Dave broke him off.

"Don't you two start again. This is my quest. I'll open the doors."

Dave found opening the doors to be more complicated than anticipated. A brief search reveal no visible knobs or handles. The doors didn't even creak in response to him throwing all his weight against them.

"There must be a trick latch somewhere around here," Bill said. He felt around the edges of the door, finding nothing but a splinter in his right forefinger. Searching the blue stone walls near the door also proved fruitless. Before anyone could voice a suggestion as to what to do next, a loud moaning sound filled the ill shaped tunnel.

The six adventurers quickly turned to see a large jelly-like creature slowly creeping down the tunnel toward them. The creature's body filled the triangle shaped tunnel perfectly, not even the slightest opening could be seen between the two. A red substance, quickly assumed to be blood from past victims, was splattered randomly across the short yellow-gold fur of the monster. Six black eyes stared blankly at the bewildered time travelers. All told, the creature resembled a very large spider, minus the legs.

"You three try to open the doors, while we take care of this thing," Bill ordered. Assisted by Joe and Ronald, the three opened fire on the creature. Each gun bearer shot a few quick rounds, expecting the spider to drop, but to their surprise it didn't. The assault didn't even phase the beast.

As each bullet entered the tough skin of the spider, a fountain of yellow blood spilled out. Miraculously, the skin instantly closed around all of the bullet wounds. The spider didn't even act as if it felt any pain from lead pellets that entered its body, as it continued its slow but consistent crawl toward the trapped humans.

When it became apparent that the doors would not open in conventional fashion, Dave, Andy, and Ken quickly decided on a contingency plan. Each began to cut at the wooden planks. The wood slowly splintered at the force of their blades, but the planks were simply too hard for them to carve away major chunks. With every stroke, every splinter, the spider drew that much closer.

"Aren't you guys finished with that thing yet?" Ken yelled over the persistent moaning, which filled the shortening tunnel. The sound, originating somewhere deep within the creature, grew louder with every passing second.

"The bullets aren't killing it," Joe yelled back.

The three gun bearers opened up with a second attack. The barrage of bullets made plopping sounds as they penetrated the creature's skin. The plops were quickly followed by a sucking sound, as the jelly-like spider body closed around the wound. Thirty feet separated the spider from its prey, with the former giving no signs of stopping. Just then, a huge mouth appeared under the cluster of eyes. The opening seemed large enough to consume a human with one swallow.

"Ugh!" Ronald yelled, his eyes focusing on the yellow-green slop that filled the spider's mouth.

The three working on the door managed to break a hole through the wood, but at the moment it was only three inches wide. Dave, sensing that time was of the essence, ordered Ken and Andy back. He recalled the power of the sword, as it sliced effortlessly through the sapling near the shelter. Though the event had only happened days before, it seemed like a life time had passed. Gathering all his strength, he swung the blade at the door. Splinters flew in all directions with ever swing, but the wood was not breaking fast enough. The hole had opened to five inches, but the spider had closed to twenty-five feet. Dave took two more swings at the door, then looked up at the closing spider. Ronald, Bill, and Joe had stopped firing, since the bullets were having no effect.

"Get out of the way," Dave yelled, abandoning the door. Andy and Ken were quick to jump in and continue widening the hole.

A steady stream of sweat poured down Ronald's face, as he retreated back toward the doors. He began to kick at the wooden planks, but they would not budge. Nervously he looked back at the spider, realizing that if it could not be killed, he would probably die in this tunnel.

Dave held his sword up in front of the spider, hoping that the creature might somehow recognize the meaning of the powerful weapon. But the spider didn't even seem to recognize that there was someone standing in front of it. The beast had a task to complete, consume all that lie in the tunnel, and that was what it was about to do. The creature, propelled by some unknown mechanism, had closed the gap to only twenty feet. The sword pulsated in unison with the rebel's heart beat. With a new found strength, Dave plunged the blade into the beast.

A spurt of yellow liquid gushed out, but the wound instantly closed. Without delay, Dave slashed the sword at the group of eyes. Two of the organs popped open, spilling an orange liquid to the floor of the tunnel. The spider continued its slow march unabated. Dave popped the remaining four eyes, with two quick slashes, but the spider didn't even seem to mind.

Ken momentarily looked up from his work on the door. The spider's mouth, stretched wide open, silhouetted Dave's entire body. Andy finally managed to open the hole in the door wide enough for his slender body to squeeze through to the passage beyond, only to discover that the tunnel reached a dead end ten feet later. A quick look around the alcove revealed no obvious mechanisms that could possibly open the doors. Not wanting to waste precious time, he frantically resumed cutting at the hole in the wooden planks. If they couldn't escaped through the door, at least they could take shelter behind it.

In the mean time, Dave was running out of room. The creature had forced him and the others into a fifteen foot area. He raised his sword for another blow, slashing at the midsection of the spider. The blade glided effortlessly through the jelly-like insides of the spider. Buckets full of yellow liquid spilled onto the floor from the long gash. Once again the wound closed, but not quite as fast the earlier injuries.

Ronald watched in horror, as Dave hacked at the creature with nothing to show for the effort. He turned back to look at the hole in the door, which had been opened wide enough for Ken to squeeze through. Even so, he felt the situation to be hopeless. There was simply not going to be enough time for all of them to squeeze to safety.

But Dave had seen something that offered him some hope. The bullet wounds had healed almost instantaneously, as did the stab wounds from the sword. But there was an obvious delay in the healing of the long slash. Dave did not interpret this as the creature was weakening, but rather a flaw in its basic design. Dave turned to the door. The moaning intensified, making communication all but impossible. Andy and Ken had opened the hole wide enough for everyone to squeeze through. Bill, the largest of the group, almost became stuck, but a concentrated effort pushed and pulled him through, with only minor scratches on his stomach. Dave stopped slashing at the creature for a moment to cover his ears, as the pounding sound made him feel like his ear drums were going to explode.

"Dave, come on," Bill yelled through the opening in the door. Dave could see his friends mouth moving, but the words were simply drowned out by the perpetual pounding.

Dave, now confined to a ten foot space, realized that he would have to join the others in a moment. He didn't know, however, what lie beyond the doors, or if the doors would even offer protection from the massive creature. But he had to test his theory. Sensing that he only enough time to for one more attempt to kill the spider, he grasped the handle of sword tightly with both hands. He moved as far as possible toward the right wall and raised the sword over his head.

"What's he doing?" Joe asked, over the thunderous pounding, but no one heard his question.

Dave waited, frozen in place, as the spider creature inched its way forward. As the beast moved within two feet of his position, Dave saw what he was looking for. The front of the spider bulged out slightly, giving hope that his plan might work. The mouth of the beast opened wider. Even without its eyes, it could still sense that prey was immediately ahead. Taking a deep breath, Dave brought the blade of the sword down, slicing into the creature's face. The blade moved freely through the jelly-like substance, driven more by the force of sword rather than Dave's strength.

A slice of the spider fell to the ground. It wasn't a big slice, maybe two inches at its thickest, but that was all that was necessary. The yellow liquid inside the creature was instantly propelled into the passageway. The force of the bowel smelling innards whooshed Dave through the opening in the door and into the alcove beyond. He had no time to gain his footing, as the level of the liquid quickly rose. The trapped humans, who moments before were worrying about being eaten by a monster, were now struggling to stay afloat to prevent from drowning in the monster's guts.

The annoying pounding sound had stopped, only to be replaced the rushing sounds of water, actually created by the flood of spider innards filling the chamber. Surprisingly no one panicked, although they were busy yelling at each other. Still, nothing could be heard over the rumbling. The walls of the alcove were square, not triangular as the previous tunnel. This only mattered in the fact that the level of liquid rose at a slightly slower rate. But the extra volume the square room offered would buy the humans only an extra ten or twenty seconds of life, as the rising liquid buoyed the humans to within two feet of the ceiling.

Suddenly Ronald screamed, pointing upward. At first no one heard his cry, but miraculously the rushing water sounds retreated and he screamed again. Previously undetected, in the heat of battle, he spotted an opening in the ceiling. One by one, the time travelers swam to the opening and struggled into the chamber above.

"That was entirely too close," Bill gasped. His clothing, as well as the others, were thoroughly soaked by the gruesome yellow spider guts. The thick liquid had already begun to dry to his exposed skin.

"That's the understatement of the year," Joe said, gasping for fresh air. His heart was pounding so hard that his chest visibly moved with each beat. He tried in vain to wipe some of the spider innards away from his mouth, but the only thing he accomplished was to smear the yellow gunk even worse.

"Look on the bright side," Ken said in his optimistic way, this time lying flat on his back trying to regain his strength. "There are only two traps left. Then we meet the enemy face to face."

"I'm not sure a confrontation is what we should be wishing for at the moment," Dave quickly added. "The guns were useless against the spider. If there are any more obstacles like that, we might have some problems. We don't even know if this stuff has damaged the guns. They might be useless."

"We already have a problem," Ronald said, trying to wipe as much of the gunk off his clothes as possible. "We have one less gun and flood light. I dropped them while struggling to get up here." He stared dejectedly into the hole in the floor, where the yellow liquid appeared to have stopped rising only inches below the ceiling of the alcove.

"At the rate we are going, we aren't going to have any weapons left when we finally meet the Minomassa," Joe said. He began to remove a piece of his machine gun in an attempt to clean it. Taking a second look at the soiled weapon and at his equally soiled hands, he rejected the idea. "It's too bad we didn't bring the proper tools to clean these."

"Who would have thought that we would have run into a situation like this," Andy stated, gazing into the hole in the floor, where the yellow liquid calmly rippled.

The group found themselves standing in a small square depression in the center of a large circular room. The ceiling of the chamber loomed thirty feet above. Climbing out of the five foot depression proved to be a simple task. From their new vantage point, they could see only one exit.

To their delight, they found four large pools containing a clear liquid, equally spaced along the perimeter of the chamber. A small stairway led into each pool. The hot breeze, which blew in from the exit, further hardened the spider guts onto their clothing and skin. The two remaining light sources, a significant drop from the original five, cast eerie shadows on the dusty walls. The power of each lamp had been reduced, due to the thin film of gunk which could not be wiped clean from the lens. To make matters worse, the batteries appeared to be slowly dying.

Ken offered Ronald his knife, to compensate for the lost rifle. The weapon situation was as bad as the lights. The three guns they had remaining, cut their original fire power in half. Ammunition was also running low, as they had used a great deal in battling the spider.

"Maybe I should have tried to hold on to my gun a little longer," Ronald said in a low voice, "but I felt as if I was going to drown."

"Don't worry about it," Bill said in a comforting voice, but Ronald continued to mumble on dejectedly. "We can still win this battle. We just have to be meticulous."

"Bill's right. We can't worry about what has happened. The main thing is that we finish what we came here to do. We have no time to feel sorry for ourselves. There are only two traps left. If we are lucky, we will have no problem with them," Dave said, trying to encourage the group, even though he knew both of Ronald's losses were going to make the rest of the journey difficult.

Ken walked up to one of the pools and stared eagerly into its clear contents. "I sure could go for a swim right now and wash off all this spider gunk."

"That's sounds like a good idea to me," Andy agreed. He joined Ken at the edge of the pool. Sight of the clear liquid reminded him on the refreshing water they had found in the fissure at the halls. Thoughts of splashing freely in cool water caused him to smile. Forgetting where he was, he absentmindedly stepped down onto the first step. The soft light cast a dim reflection of himself off the calm surface of the liquid. He laughed, seeing his unrecognizable reflection. His features were totally covered with a fast hardening yellow film.

"What are you two, stupid or something? It's probably another trap," Joe yelled, stopping Andy, before he had a chance to take another step. "I think some of that spider stuff has leaked into your head."

"We can't trust that anything we find down here is safe. The pools were probably put here to tempt whoever made it past the spider," Dave added.

"Yes, I bet the Ubeleutes made the air in this room so hot that we would want to go for a quick swim," Bill said. He walked over to Ken, who still stood motionless by the pool, and pulled a sandwich out of his backpack. The foul yellow liquid had soaked it thoroughly. "Now our food supply is gone."

The scientist tossed the spoiled sandwich into the pool. Dave's surmise proved correct, the pool was a trap. Within a few seconds the sandwich, still wrapped in cellophane, turned black and shriveled up into a small charcoal lump.

"Acid," Ken said, backing away from the pool. "To think I could have jumped right in."

The sight of the black debris floating on the surface quickly wiped the memories of the refreshing swim at the fissure from Andy's mind. An ill feeling filled his stomach, as he realized that he had nearly committed suicide. The younger Marshall retreated up the stairs, thankful that he had not plunged in.

"Yes," Bill said, pulling the rest of the sandwiches out of Ken's backpack. He walked over to the next pool, tossing a sandwich into the liquid. Like the first, it shriveled up. To his surprise the third pool did not corrode the food. The yellowed bread floated calmly on the surface. The fourth pool acted as expected, dissolving the sandwich.

"Maybe this one is water," Andy said, standing by the third pool.

"It could be, but I wouldn't chance it," Dave replied. "Of course, if you want to take a swim and try it out."

Andy looked at the other three pools, then backed away. "No thanks, I think I'll pass. I can wait until we get out of here to take a bath. I can't smell any worse than the rest of you."

"I still don't like the idea of walking around with this gunk on me," Ken complained. He managed to pull a small strip of dried spider guts from his forearm, but the skin beneath still felt dirty.

"None of us do. It's just something we are going to have to live with, until we get out of here," Dave replied sourly. He was beginning to grow frustrated. The group was losing its equipment piece by piece. He hadn't planned on anyone getting killed, except for the Minomassa, but there was nothing he could do about Steve's death; or could have done. As he contemplated the actions that he had followed so far, a cold sensation ran up his right arm, snapping back to the present. The sword was urging him onward.

"I wonder if we can count the pools as trap number six?" Ronald asked. The adrenaline flowing through his body increased, as he realized that the final confrontation was near.

"I don't see why not," Bill replied.

"That would mean we only have one left," Joe added, with a trace of excitement in his voice. He could also sense that the fighting he had come here to do was not far off. "Time to check if the weapons still work."

He walked to the edge of the square depression and aimed his weapon into the yellow pool. As he pulled the trigger, a bullet exploded from the barrel, plopping into the remains of the spider. "Mine works."

The remaining gun bearers followed suit, relieved that all their weapons were still functional.

"Some good news for a change," Ken said, as the group walked to the exit.

Large stone blocks formed the passage leading from the circular room. To the dismay of the travelers, not only did the tunnel curve sharply off to the left, but it also began to descend at a very steep angle. The loose gravel covering the floor made the footing all the more treacherous.

"There is no way we can descend slow enough to check for traps," Bill stated, worried that trap number seven might be stumbled upon while descending the slope.

"If you are worried, then stay back several yards," Dave offered. "There's no turning back from here. I think I can slide down and maintain enough control to search for triggering devices."

"If you say so," Bill replied, gladly letting Dave test the route ahead.

The small rocks readily gave way underfoot, as Dave attempted to control his skid down the corridor. Leading with his left foot, he began to surf down the wave of gravel, kicking up a cloud of dust as he went. The rest of the group watched intently, as Dave disappeared from view around the bend.

"We can't let him get too far ahead," Ken said, jumping onto the slope to begin his slide down to the unseen bottom. One by one, the members of the group followed.

The temperature dropped in unison with their descent, reinforcing their belief that the pools were trap number six. With six pairs of feet kicking up dust, vision in the tunnel quickly became hampered. Those following Dave had to trust that the leader would spot any traps, because they were essentially blind.

After descending about a hundred feet, the tunnel turned to the right and leveled off. Dave briefly explored the barren passageway that stood before him, while waiting patiently for the remaining five to catch up. All survived the descent, with little more than a lungful of dust to complain about.

"I would hate to think how far underground we are now," Ronald said, glancing up the ceiling, relieved that it appeared to be structurally sound.

"Try no to think about it," Bill suggested, trying to shake the dust from his clothing. His actions were futile, seeing that the dirt had bonded to the sticky spider guts.

"Everyone ready?" Dave asked, not waiting for any responses, before moving off down the tunnel.

As soon as the group began walking, a low groan filled the tunnel, bouncing off the rock walls and ceiling. The groan lasted for only a second, before fading away. The humans stopped, looking at one another, hoping that one of their group was just playing a trick on the others. But this was not the case. Cautiously, the group raised their weapons, proceeding at an agonizingly slow pace. Approximately one minute after the first, a second groan filled the underground passage, this time a bit louder.

"Do you think that is the enemy?" Ronald asked nervously. A heavy sweat had formed on his brow.

"Whatever it is, it sure sounds awful," Andy noted. He slowed his pace, allowing Ken and Bill to pass. Even with all their differences, he still felt safest near his brother.

"There is only one way to find out," Joe said in an eager voice. He viewed this mission the same way that he viewed his missions for the Protectors. After all, he was a professional killer.

Dave cautioned the group with a raised hand, trying to slow their pace even further. He had no intention of falling victim to the trap that he was certain lay ahead. As they turned a corner, a dim light appeared at the end of the tunnel. The yellow light gradually grew in strength, as they approached. Soon, the light from the as yet unseen source illuminated the entire passage. Dave ordered the remaining light sources to be shut off, but warned the bearers to keep them handy just in case the yellow light terminated.

At the end of the passage, the time travelers found a large torch lit chamber. Stone tables and ornaments were scattered around in a haphazard manner. Lining the walls were human looking skeletons, bound at the ankles and wrists by metal binds. More bones littered the floor, but all of them were broken and crushed to various degrees.

An expected putrid odor of decay rose from all the remains in the room. The smell was so powerful that the humans actually forgot that they themselves reeked from the foul smelling spider guts. The group stood just outside the room, trying to absorb as much information as possible, before crossing the threshold.

"Do you think it is safe?" Ronald asked, eyeing the dangling skeletons.

"Has anything been safe down here?" Ken replied.

"Stay alert," Dave warned, stepping into the chamber.

Bone dust of the ancient beings rose from the floor with every footstep, casting an eerie mist into the air. With the six travelers walking all at once, the mist became so thick that their feet became lost in a white cloud. Once again, the sickly groan filled the air. This time they were certain that the origin was somewhere in the room.

Once again, Dave cautioned the others with a raised hand. The group scanned the room, but with the piles of rocks and debris blocking much of their line of sight, could not see the source of the groan. Per Joe's suggestion, the adventurers spaced themselves so that any attack would have minimal impact. The slow methodical march across the chamber revealed nothing, until they reached the far wall. There they saw a sight that none expected.

"A human," Andy shouted.

With mouths open in utter astonishment, the group closed in on the crumpled body of a small human. Like the numerous skeletons in the chamber, the man was manacled to the wall with metal bracelets and anklets. The shackles dug deep into his pale dry skin, almost revealing the fragile bone that lie beneath. The man's lips were obviously dry and swollen from thirst, while folds of skin hung loosely from his undernourished body. His eyes brightened at the sight of the time travelers. With a thin smile, all he could manage in his feeble state, he struggled to mumble something in an ancient tongue. Using the sword as translator, Dave listened to every word.

"He says that his name is Ploam and that he has been held prisoner here since the end of the war. The Ubeleutes have been constantly torturing him, keeping him alive with healing water. Only to torture him again."

"I wouldn't believe it, if I didn't see it," Andy said, staring at the human, but keeping his distance all the same. He felt genuine excitement at the thoughts of finding a human who had been alive during the days of Duzic. "There is still one of the humans alive."

"Imagine all the pain he must have gone through, being tortured everyday for all those years," Ken said, truly pitying the man.

"And knowing that he would go through the same pain everyday for eternity," Ronald added in a soft voice.

"I don't like it," Bill said warily. "Something doesn't seem right." He glanced around the room in a jerky motion, expecting a mass of Ubeleutes to come rushing in though previously unseen entrances. "Ask him where all the bones came from."

Dave contacted the sword. For the first time since finding the ancient weapon, a strange language came from his lips. The others were surprised at the language which Dave spoke. They listened intently, but the words were clearly foreign.

Ploam, on the other hand, understood every syllable. The human lifted his head, the smile growing larger with every word Dave spoke. It had been many years since he had heard his native tongue spoken by someone other than himself. With great difficulty, he mumbled a few sentences. Dave stood silent for several moments, waiting for the translation from the sword.

"He says the bones are the remains of all the humans who made it this far into the city. They, like him, were tortured. After the war the Ubeleutes let everyone die a painful death, except for him. Most died right in front of his eyes. He says that he felt totally helpless watching them squirm in pain, not being able to help."

"Right," Joe said sarcastically.

"Something doesn't add up," Bill persisted. He looked around the room, once again. "There are way too many bones in here to be from the humans. It doesn't make sense why they would keep him alive all this time."

"I agree with Bill," Joe added. "This is too far fetched to be true."

"Maybe the Ubeleutes are just torturous murderers," Andy said, staring into Ploam's pain riddled face.

"Why would they leave one of their foremost enemies alive?" Bill asked, suspiciously eyeing the prisoner. The man, dressed in rags that were close to decay. looked as old as the universe.

Silence followed, as Bill walked toward the center of the room, a cloud of bone dust following his movement. He kicked a skull, before looking back at Ploam. "This could be another trap. The last trap."

"He seems to be human to me," Andy said. "What do you think, Joe?"

"He looks human. But how can we tell? All I know is that I don't trust a word he says, especially with that sword translating."

"I have to agree with Bill," Ken stated, after pondering the situation for a moment. "Something isn't right with this guy. I can understand that the healing water would cure his wounds, but I doubt that it would prolong his life to this extent."

"I'm telling you this has to be a trap," Bill persisted. "If all the humans made it this far, then something killed them in this room. We have only seen one body before this room. Or was it two at the bottom of the pit Andy almost fell in? But no matter, I'll bet that the last trap is in this room."

"I'll give you one guess what that trap is," Joe added. Everyone looked at Ploam.

"I don't know why you are giving him such a hard time," Ronald said, in defense of the man. "Obviously he has been though so much already. Maybe these creatures have just brought all these bones in here from all the other traps."

Ploam let out another groan. Dave translated, "He senses that we don't trust him. So to prove that he is telling the truth, he will help us destroy the Ubeleutes."

"How is he going to do that?" Bill laughed. "If he could do that, why is he trapped here? I doubt that he has even killed a single Ubeleute in his entire life."

Dave looked at Ploam. The man struggle to form another sentence. "He says that there is a potion on the table across from him. The potion will give the drinker super strength. He says that the Ubeleutes left it there to make him suffer all the more."

Everyone in the group turned to look into the center of the room, except for Joe, who kept his weapon aimed at Ploam. Ronald moved to the table in question, studying its contents as he approached. Various shaped bones, many of which he doubted had human origins, covered the stone table. He found the bottle hidden in a decaying skull. "Here it is," he said, almost afraid to touch it.

Gathering his will, the farmer stuck his hand into the inverted skull. Slowly he pulled a clear glass bottle free, immediately finding solace in the rich purple liquid splashing against the inside wall of the container. He walked back to the group, holding the bottle for all to see. Upon seeing the bottle, Ploam mumbled several more sentences.

"Do you think we should give it to him?" Andy asked. "He looks as if he is going to die at any moment."

"No," Dave replied. A somewhat puzzled expression came over his face. "He says we should take it ourselves. It will give us strength that surpasses that of the Ubeleutes."

"I bet it will," Joe responded in a harsh voice. "We don't need that stuff. We already have all the fire power we need."

"What about him? Doesn't he want to free himself?" Bill asked, still very skeptical of Ploam. "We could give him a sip, just to keep him alive until we can get him out of here."

"He says that he just wants to die. He has been through so much already. He just wants to die and join all of his dead friends."

Ronald pulled the cork from the neck of the bottle, causing a soft popping sound to echo off the chamber walls. The liquid seemed to come to life, as small bubbles began to rise to the surface. A sweet odor gently rose from the bottle into Ronald's nostrils. In his semi-crazed state, and deep felt desire to annihilate the Ubeleutes, he slowly brought the mouth of the bottle up toward his own.

Just as the liquid was about to hit his lips, Bill rushed forward, knocking the bottle from the Ronald's hands. The container tumbled to the ground, but the glass did not break. Most of the purple liquid spilled onto the dust covered floor, before Ronald could retrieve the bottle.

"Are you crazy?" Bill yelled. "Can't you see that this is a trick?"

"How can you be sure?" Ronald replied, dusting off the mouth of the bottle and replacing the cork. A quick estimate revealed that only twenty percent of the liquid still remained in the bottle. "Maybe he really is one of the humans. Maybe he wants us to destroy the Ubeleutes."

"Offer the bottle to him," Bill said in a stern voice. "See if he drinks it."

Ronald eyed the bottle and the liquid. He then looked at Dave, who stood near Ploam with an expressionless face. Ronald slowly walked up to Ploam and uncorked the bottle. The cork popped free and the liquid began to bubble again. The farmer then offered the open bottle to the fragile little man. Ploam turned his head, refusing to take even a small sip. Ronald looked up at Bill, who stood silent. Once again the bottle was offered to Ploam. Once again the prisoner turned his head away.

"See, Bill was right. He is part of a trap," Joe said. Without hesitation he raised his gun, leveling the barrel at Ploam's chest. His trigger finger squeezed ever so slightly, firing a handful of bullets into the body of the helpless man.

"No," Ronald shouted, stepping forward. But he was too late to stop the attack.

Ploam turned to look at Joe, his face tensed with pain. A second later his body turned limp. Instantly the appearance of the corpse began to change. A strange metamorphism began, returning the human body to its original form; an Ubeleute. The weight of the creature snapped the rusted metal chains, allowing the carcass to slump to the floor.

"How did you know he wasn't human?" Ronald asked, throwing the bottle to the floor. This time the glass shattered, scattering the remaining liquid onto the ground.

"I didn't," Joe answered, with an emotionless stare. He had killed many people during his tenure with the Protectors and the deed did not bother him. "It didn't matter anyway. If he had been human, I was doing him a favor. After all, he did say that he wanted to die."

"The only thing left for us to do is seek out the Minomassa and make sure it never threatens humans again," Dave said, walking away from the dead Ubeleute.

The adventurers were now faced with their first decision regarding direction, since entering Mikokil. Three exits led from the horrible death chamber. All stood on one wall, spaced out ten feet apart. The first passage began with a steep incline. The second stayed level. The third began with a declining slope. All three were dark and featureless.

"Any suggestions?" Dave asked.

With no logical choice, the group decided on the middle passage. Just as they were about to leave the room, Ronald spotted something out of the corner of his eye. In an otherwise grey and dusty room, a golden shimmer caught his attention. The reflection, fueled by the many torches lining the walls, came from the bottom of a pile of decaying bones.

Ronald called for the others to wait, then rushed over to the pile of debris. Hurriedly he tossed the bones aside, many of them crumbling upon his touch. The his surprise, he had uncovered a small collection of gold and silver armor, chains, and jewelry. All remnants of the beings who were killed in this room.

"Look at all this stuff!" he exclaimed. "It must be worth a fortune. I'll never have to work another day in my life." He picked up a gold plated chest armor, savoring the gold finish.

"Don't get carried away," Dave said calmly. In his time these items weren't sought, since nothing could be done with them as long as the Protectors were running the government. "Just grab a few small pieces. We must hurry out of here. Our lights are dying. Once were are clear of this room we won't have the aid of the torches."

Everyone in the party pocketed several small pieces of jewelry. Reluctantly, Ronald left millions of dollars worth of precious metals behind. He tried to make a mental note of the treasure's location, hoping to return later and salvage it, but he could only make note of its location within this one room. In actuality he had no idea where he was.

"Okay, let's get on with the party," Joe said.

The passage they followed ran straight and smooth. Metal supports were placed periodically against the walls, lending structural support to the tunnel. Going on the assumption that all of the traps had been passed, the travelers quickened their pace. Ken and Joe lead the group, while the lesser protected Ronald and Andy stayed in the middle. The subtle odor of the enemy grew stronger with every step.

The corridor continued for some time without variation. A good five minutes had passed, since leaving Ploam, before the tunnel they were following entered onto a balcony of a large hall. The balcony ran along a wall for the entire length of the chamber, where it exited into darkness. Only two torches were visible in the hall below, but they were sure others were present, since ample light could be seen. From their hiding place in the shadows, they could see several Ubeleute scurrying about.

"This is a good place to drop a couple sticks of dynamite," Dave whispered softly, as he had no knowledge of how sensitive the Ubeleute's ears were. "They probably know that we have passed through all of the traps by now. If we're lucky, this might be a major spot in their city. We could cut off quite a few of them here."

The group quickly scurried the length of the balcony, making sure to stay below the solid rock wall, which protected the balcony's occupants from the drop to the floor below. Ken removed two sticks of dynamite from his backpack. The explosives had been tightly wrapped in plastic and seemed to have been untouched by the spider's innards. The former scientist for the Protectors lit the explosives, tossing one toward the far end of the chamber. The other he dropped straight down to the floor.

"Run!" he cried, as he bolted off the balcony into the safety of the tunnel.

A moment later two explosions rocked the ground. The balcony instantly collapsed, making any retreat by the humans impossible. Large boulders fell from the ceiling, crushing all that lie on the floor of hall. The walls of the tunnel shook violently, as billows of dust rose from the devastated chamber. With their vision hampered, the humans cautiously crept forward, not wanting to stay in one place for too long.

"That should stop any attack from the rear," Bill said, watching the dust begin to settle.

"Yes, but don't forget that we still have to find a way out of here," Andy said.

"I don't think we would want to go back the way we came," Dave said, remembering the traps that they had passed through.

"Still, he is right," Joe added, stopping in a crouched position. His weapon pointed forward, waiting for anything to cross his sights. Until now, they we only concerned with finding a route into the Ubeleute city. "We are going to have to plan on an escape route.

"We'll have to worry about finding a way out when the time comes," Dave said, trying not to let moral drop at this stage. "If we see anything promising, we will make note. Right now we have to keep moving and find the Minomassa."

The passage they were following soon ended in a small alcove. Two sets of stairs exited the small room. One led up, the other down. No sounds could be heard from either stairwell.

"Maybe we should go up," Andy suggested. "It will probably be easier for us to find a way out up there."

"Probably, but my guess is that the Minomassa would be deeper underground," Dave replied.

Without questioning the decision, the group embarked on a journey deeper into the earth. After thirty feet, the stairs began to spiral. Three complete circles later, the stairs stopped at an alcove similar in size to the previous. Three passages, all leading up at a gradual incline, where what the humans had to choose from.

"Let's go this way," Dave said, after a moments thought. He had no idea which passage, if any, led to the Minomassa, but he felt as if he had to make a quick decision. "Ken drop another stick here. We want to protect ourselves from the rear as much as possible."

Joe grabbed Dave by the arm. "Wait," he said, not trying to conceal his voice from any nearby Ubeleutes. "We can't continue to blow everything up. We have to keep these passages open in order to find a way out."

"We will find a way out," Dave replied. "Right now I'm only concerned about us staying alive long enough to make finding an exit a reality. Drop a stick here, Ken. I have a feeling we are going to need the extra protection."

Just as he finished speaking, three Ubeleutes came rushing down the passage to the right. The machine guns, however, proved too much for the beasts. The creatures dropped helplessly to the ground, unable to release their deadly axes. More Ubeleutes could be heard charging down the center tunnel. Ken quickly lit a stick of dynamite, while the group fled down the left hand passage.

Not ten seconds later the dynamite exploded. The explosion echoed off the walls, effectively drowning out the screams of pain from the unfortunate Ubeleutes who were buried in the subsequent cave-in. A blast of air carried with it clouds of dirt and dust, further hampering the vision of the adventurers. Joe reversed course back toward the alcove, returning a moment later, assuring the others that no one would be following. Feeling secure, the group slowed its pace.

"We could wander these tunnels forever and never find the Minomassa," Ronald complained, coughing in response to the floating debris.

"You did mention that this city is huge," Andy reminded.

"No, we'll find it," Dave said confidently. "The Minomassa is not far off. The sword can sense its presence."

"I'm getting tired of relying on that sword for my well being," Joe snapped.

"Too late to turn back now," Andy quipped.

The group soon came upon a four-way intersection. A beam of light down each new passage revealed nothing.

"Let's go straight," Dave ordered.

"Should I drop a stick here?" Ken asked.

"No," Dave replied, looking at Joe. "Joe had a good point earlier. Besides, I think we should be a little more conservative with our supplies."

Just then a strange whooshing sound came from the left hand corridor. Before any of the group could react, an axe sailed through the intersection striking Andy in the leg. The axe cut into his right calf, spilling blood onto the floor. Luckily, the blade missed the bone, but the resulting wound was large. Andy fell to the ground, a scream of pain rushing from his mouth. The gun bearers fired blindly into dark passage. Ubeleute cries of death followed.

"Come on," Joe said, lifting his brother up and helping him along. "We don't have time to cry over little scrapes."

The group struggled forward, scattering several rounds behind every few seconds. The corridor soon came to another four-way intersection. The sound of massive footsteps could be heard straight ahead, to the right, and behind. The intruders were forced to flee down the left hand tunnel.

"Good place for another stick, Ken," Dave said, as the war cries of the Ubeleute closed in. "They are getting too close for comfort."

Ken obeyed, hurling a stick of dynamite back toward the intersection. A moment later an explosion rang out, but not as forceful as the previous. The stick had been defective. Time could not be lost by checking on the damage. As Ken reached into his backpack for another stick, he heard a commotion up ahead.

Several Ubeleute had begun a frontal attack. Bill and Joe fired repeatedly into the rapidly closing group, dropping five before the others retreated. While fleeing, one of the attackers blindly hurled its axe. The poorly thrown weapon struck the wall, before the handle slammed into Ronald's chest, knocking him to the ground with the wind knocked out of him.

"This isn't good," Ken said, helping Dave drag Ronald into a side chamber.

The room was large and brilliantly lit with many torches. Colorful skins and tapestries lined the walls. The humans had no time to enjoy the decorations, however. Upon entering the room. a loud grinding sound began to echo off the low ceiling. The ground vibrated rhythmically, as a platform in the middle of the room slowly revolved. On the platform, actually a large throne, sat an oversized Ubeleute.

Without strain, the creature hurled an axe into the group of humans. The axe sliced into Ken's right shoulder, severing his arm. Ken dropped to the ground screaming in agonizing pain, as the axe continued its course, embedding itself into the stone wall behind.

Upon hearing Ken scream, Bill turned into the room. The scientist had no time to look for his friend, as the imposing figure of the Ubeleute immediately caught his attention. Bill instinctively fired at the creature. The axe the beast had just picked up, from a supply surrounding the throne, fell to the ground. Bill let loose with a second blast of bullets. The creature slumped from the throne, falling to the floor. This gave Bill a moment to tend to Ken, who lie bleeding on the floor.

"Take it easy, Ken, I'll get you patched up."

The sword vibrated violently in Dave's hand. The creature, now struggling to its feet, was the Minomassa. Dave ran forward, toward the injured Ubeleute, with the sword drawn in an attack position. The

Minomassa stirred to its knees, turning to pick up another axe. Dave kicked the weapon out the Minomassa's reach, simultaneously bringing the sword down on the beast's neck. As powerful as the sword was, able to slice through small trees like a knife through softened butter, it only made a wound an inch deep in the Minomassa's flesh. The Minomassa gave a sinister laugh, shaking off the wound as if it were a scratch. The beast lashed out with its huge right arm, knocking Dave to the ground. The rebel leader quickly scrambled to his feet, oblivious to the gash which had opened on his forehead. By now the Minomassa was also standing upright, dwarfing Dave with its huge size.

Ronald, who had recovered from the blow to his chest, had taken over tending to Ken, who was flirting with unconsciousness. Bill hastily returned to the hallway, where Joe was busy fighting off hoards of Ubeleute rushing to protect their master. Ronald had removed his shirt, tying the cloth around the stump of Ken's arm. Instantly, the blue shirt turned a rich red. After a few moments, Ronald felt a sense of relief, as the rate of blood loss appeared to have slowed.

The Minomassa turned away from Dave, apparently giving the human little thought. The creature moved back toward the throne, in an attempt to pick up another axe. Dave rushed the beast, plunging the sword into its back. The Minomassa let out an ear piercing yell, as it stumbled forward in surprise.

Dave remove the blade, releasing a fountain of bright purple blood. The Minomassa reeled around, again knocking Dave to the ground with its massive forearm. Evil laughter filtered through its grotesque feature, as the beast struggled to regain its footing. Just then several rifle shots filled the room.

Struggling against the massive pain in his wounded leg, Andy had grabbed Ken's gun and began firing at the Minomassa. The creature took two rounds to the head, forcing it to drop the axe it held. In an almost human way, the Minomassa reached for its new wounds, looking at its hand to verify that it was actually bleeding. Andy took the opportunity to fire several more rounds, dropping the beast to the ground for a second time.

"Stop!" Dave yelled, rising to his feet. "Let me finish it off."

Andy stopped firing, but kept the gun aimed at the stunned creature. Dave rushed to the Minomassa, which growled ferociously at the rebel. The beast's injuries had slowed it enough for Dave to attack unabated. The second slash opened the gash on the creature's neck even wider. The beast continued to squeal its evil laughter, making a futile attempt to lash out at Dave with its arm. Dave easily dodged the attack, swiping the sword at the head of his enemy, once again.

"Take Ken out into the hall. Leave his backpack. Try to find a safe place to hide. I'm going to blow this room," Dave ordered, as he prepared yet another attack on the badly injured beast.

The battle in the corridor had progressed favorably for the humans. The machine guns easily kept the Ubeleutes at bay. In fact, their massive stature actually helped the human's cause. The live beasts made for large targets, while the dead effectively clogged the passage to the point where the attackers had very little room to move or even throw their weapons.

"We have to find a safe place," Ronald yelled over the frequent machine gun bursts. "Dave's going to blow the room."

"We really don't have anywhere to go," Bill said, looking in both directions down the tunnel. Each way was littered with countless Ubeleute bodies. For the moment, the remaining Ubeleutes weren't attacking, giving the appearance that they were regrouping. "Let's just get away from the door. These walls seem thick enough to protect us from the explosion."

Bill slowly retreated down the corridor. Joe protected the rear, firing occasionally into the darkness. Ronald dragged Ken, obviously struggling with the semi-conscious scientist. Ken's entire shirt was now soaked with blood. The farmer knew that if Ken didn't receive medical treatment soon he would die.

Dave backed away from the Minomassa, who lay almost motionless on the floor. The beast continued to howl, but its strength had all but disappeared. Dave removed three sticks of dynamite from the backpack, before tossing the remaining explosives onto the large throne on the middle of the room. Keeping a watchful eye on his enemy, he lit the fuses on the explosives he held. The first stick was tossed toward the far end of the chamber. The second landed squarely on the seat of the throne. He held the last stick in his left hand, while holding the sword out in front with his right. He could actually feel excitement coming from the cold metal of Duzic's ancient weapon. Sensing that his quest was over, Dave tossed the stick at the injured Minomassa.

The beast watched, as the stick skidded across the floor, stopping only several feet from its leg. The wounded creature either didn't know what the sparkling fuse represented or it didn't have the strength to find out. Dave quickly darted from the room, desperately seeking the others in the darkened hallway. The explosions were quick and powerful. The ground shook, causing several segments of the ceiling to crash to the ground. Dave dove behind a fallen Ubeleute for cover, as debris shot wildly from the Minomassa's chamber, filling the tunnel with a deadly shower of shrapnel. Moments later all was quiet.

Dave opened his eyes, only seeing darkness. The burst of light from the explosion had caused his pupils to dilate. He remained motionless, trying to stay as invisible as possible, allowing the shadows around him to clarify. A spot of light became visible several yards away, obviously one of the light sources. Noticing that the light was moving, he pushed several clumps of muddy earth off his body and struggled to his feet. For the first time, he felt the blood streaming out of the gash in his forehead. The handle of the purple blood stained sword felt cold in his hand. He turned from the light, looking back down the corridor toward the Minomassa's chamber. The underground passage was unrecognizable. There were no walls or ceilings to speak of, just an indescribable assortment of rubble.

Dave felt relief, as a cool breeze blew through the ruins. He wiped the blood from his face, turning to look for the others. Slowly the outlines of his comrades appeared through the dusty mist. Ronald was still helping Ken, who just stared blankly out into space. Andy was hobbling along next to him, his wound dressed with his shirt. Bill and Joe followed, guarding the rear from attack, but none came.

"Do you think we killed them all?" Andy asked hopefully. Blood dripped from his lower lip, where he bit to compensate for the intense pain in his leg.

"I doubt it," Dave replied, wiping more of the blood away from his eyes. "But at least we killed the Minomassa. Without him, the rest of the Ubeleutes are virtually powerless."

"We have done it then. We have destroyed the enemy," Ronald said, smiling as he revenged his son's death. His face wore a thick layer of dirt, but other than that he had pulled through the battle unharmed.

Bill also shared in the excitement of the victory. Deep inside he wished it had been the Protectors who had been destroyed, not some strange creatures from his distant past. He kept his thoughts to himself though, not wanting to put a damper on the group's achievement.

The adventurers scrambled back to the Minomassa's chamber, the source of the fresh breeze. The room had been totally destroyed. Fragments of the decorative skins and tapestries were strewn about. Smoke rose from the rubble, but that was secondary to what lie before them.

The reason for the breeze was obvious. The explosion had caused part of the ceiling to collapse. A walkable path led up a forty foot pile of rocks to the outside.

The excited humans quickly scrambled, as fast as their injuries would allow, up the ruins. Thirty minutes later, they found themselves in the cool confines of a green forest. After all the time they had spent in the stagnant air of the tunnels, the yellow tint of the ancient atmosphere was indeed a pleasant sight.

Andy felt a burning sensation on his chest and quickly lifted the pendant. The globe was no longer black and cracked. A merry image of Chaz appeared. The man even offered a wink to the observers. The fist with the ring of lightning followed, soon to be replaced by an image of the Halls of Plebiscite. Water once again flowed through the fissure.

"I think it is telling us to go to the halls," Andy suggested.

"That's not a bad idea," Dave agreed. "We can heal our wounds there."

"Do you think Ken will be able to make it that far?" Ronald questioned. The incoherent scientist's wound seemed to have stopped bleeding, but his system was clearly in shock.

"I hope so," Bill said, helping his partner.

As the group scanned the area, looking for the best route back to the halls, a path seemed to open before them, leading directly to the mountain. The snow capped peaks no longer seemed evil or foreboding, but rather peaceful and inviting. The travelers followed the path to a cave entrance, which the sword immediately identified as the original entrance to the tunnel. It was the exit they were supposed to have walked through, before the Minomassa carried out its reconstruction. With the healthy taking turns helping the injured, the group made swift time through the tunnel.

Progress soon lead them to the spot where the Ubeleutes had blocked the original path. Miraculously, the two false passages, one of which lead to the acid chasm, were blocked.

The trip to the halls did seem slow though. Ken had to stop every so often, screaming in agonizing pain whenever he returned to the conscious world. After venting his pain, he would slip into a glassy-eyed stare. With the view of the waterfall still in the pendant, the group marched on.

Although they kept a keen eye for any unwanted guests, the jungle was void of all life. No birds, animals, or creatures could be detected. Upon reaching the halls, they found that the flow of water had indeed been restored. The water healed Ken's wound instantly, but the arm did not return, as silently hoped by several of the group. After a few drinks, and a refreshing swim, everyone felt revived.

"I don't know how I'm going to tell Mary about Steve," Ronald said. The reality of the situation had started to take hold. "She was against our coming here from the start." The others sat in silence, not knowing what, if anything, was appropriate to say.

The halls, like the humans, seemed to be refreshed. The wondrous structure continued to give off its own special glow, maybe a bit brighter than before. The air seemed to stir with life. Most surprisingly, the thick layer of dust that had covered everything, was gone. The marble and polished rock sparkled by some unseen hand. Even the stairway full of spider webs had been cleaned out.

"Do you think those little creatures cleaned this place up?" Andy asked. "You know the ones I saw rebuilding the tree."

"Possibly," Dave said, as he sat, feet dangling in the fissure. "There are a lot of things that are still unanswered about this place."

"Now we can resume our battle against the Protectors," Bill said suggestively.

"I have to talk to you about that," Dave replied. He looked into the clear stream of water that rushed past. "The sword has persuaded me to stay here and rule this land. It says, that since I am the one who led the attack against the enemy, I am the rightful ruler."

"Ruler of what?" Joe asked. "There is nobody here."

"You mean, you are going to give up the fight?" Bill asked.

"No," came the reply. "The sword is knowledgeable of our plight and sympathizes with us. It has suggested that we use this place as a base. We can keep our men here, until we are ready to attack," he paused. "You can't return to New York as a scientist, so you might as well join in formally with the underground. Since I am the leader of the underground, I am making Plebiscite our new base, as long as I have the time machine at my disposal."

"That's what we made it for," Bill replied.

"I will make one trip back to our time," Dave said. "I will stay long enough to inform the others of our discovery here. Then I will do my best to restore this place and bring the halls back to life. Just as they were when Chaz ruled."

"You found one citizen already," Andy interjected. "Provided, of course, that you give me an important position."

"That goes for me too," Joe said, realizing that his career working for the Protectors had ended several days ago.

"Perhaps we can form some sort of alliance with the people in the nineteen sixties," Dave suggested, trying to take Ronald's mind off the loss of his son. "We could sure use someone with the resources Ronald has."

Ronald looked up from his spot in the corner. "I have no problem with that," he said, fishing his hand into his pocket. "I do have some unfinished business here." With that said, he held up the gold chains he had taken from Mikokil.

Message from the author

I hope you enjoyed reading 'The Sword's Revenge'. It took over 15 years and countless revisions for me to complete this story. The first version was only 39 pages, typed out on a manual typewriter. In fact, I didn't even create Joe until I had Andy standing on top of the mountain after escaping from the Blieins. I figured that it would be more interesting for two people to be wandering around lost rather than one.

I've always felt that this story should be part of a trilogy. There are far too many unanswered questions to leave off at this point. In the second installment I hope to answer all the questions surrounding Chaz and his people, as well as the strange creatures in that time. It obvious that neither Chaz nor the creatures belong in that time period. Some other questions actually arose while proof reading the final copy. I never gave much thought as to the logical events that lead up to the Minomassa's spirit being entombed. But obviously some very interesting events must have happened from the time Duzic was killed at the gates of Mikokil (the extent of the sword's knowledge) and the Minomassa being captured.

I envision that the third book will follow through on the original premise of building the time machine, namely battling the Protectors. At this point, I don't know if Bill and Dave will actually continue the battle. I guess the events in the second book will help determine the outcome of the war against the Protectors.

If you have any comments on 'The Sword's Revenge', you may mail or e-mail them to Presage Publishing.

Presage Publishing
830 S. Boulder Highway
Box 136
Henderson, NV 89015

e-mail: presagepub@aol.com

Thanks,

Dutch D. Bird